Click

Gavin & Cora

A FRIENDS TO LOVERS, SECOND CHANCE
ROMANCE DUET

PERSEPHONE AUTUMN

BETWEEN WORDS PUBLISHING LLC

Books by Persephone Autumn

Lake Lavender Series

Depths Awakened

One Night Forsaken

Every Thought Taken

Devotion Series

Distorted Devotion

Undying Devotion

Beloved Devotion

Darkest Devotion

Sweetest Devotion

Bay Area Duet Series

Click Duet

Through the Lens

Time Exposure

Inked Duet

Fine Line

Love Buzz

Insomniac Duet

Restless Night

A Love So Bright

<u>Artist Duet</u>

Blank Canvas

Abstract Passion

<u>Novellas</u>

Reese

Penny

<u>Stone Bay Series</u>

Broken Sky—Prequel

Shattered Sun

Fractured Night

<u>Standalone Romance Novels</u>

Sweet Tooth

Transcendental

<u>Poetry Collections</u>

Ink Veins

Broken Metronome

Slipping From Existence

Poisonous Heart

Beneath Wildflowers

PUBLISHED UNDER P. AUTUMN

<u>Standalone Non-Romance Novels</u>

By Dawn

contents

THROUGH THE LENS

TIME EXPOSURE

Through the Lens

BOOK ONE

To every person who's had their heart ripped in two. Who thought they'd never find love again.

through the lens

Photography term.

Through-the-lens (TTL) metering refers to a feature of cameras whereby the intensity of light reflected from the scene is measured through the lens; as opposed to using a separate metering window or external hand-held light meter.

one

CORA

Is this real? This cannot be real.

I ball my fingers into loose fists, rub my eyes, and look ahead once more. Yep, still there. Still strutting around like a peacock fanning its tail feathers. How fortunate are we to bear witness to this monumental event? An event we could all live another day without seeing. An event I pray never repeats itself.

For the love of all that is good in this world, please make it end.

On the compact stage of our favorite bar and grill, a seventy-something grandpa wears an eighties rock band muscle tank top, ripped jeans, and faded black Converse high-tops that have seen better days. He holds the mic to his mouth, tips his head back, and belts out the words to Def Leppard's "Pour Some Sugar on Me." Some might say, *what's the big deal. Let the old man enjoy life.* And I would probably agree.

But singing is not all he is doing. Nope. Karaoke grandpa has added a little "show" to his rendition. Giving the crowd something to remember. For life.

Not ten seconds ago, he picked up his full glass of water,

tipped his head back, and poured it down his chest, driving us all down wet T-shirt contest lane. The crowd whistles and eggs him on, and he eats up every cheer given. Flaunts his man chest through the wet tank. But wait, it keeps getting better. Now… Some dumbass walked up to the stage and just handed him a soft-serve ice cream cone. Since when did the bar serve…

What the hell is he…

Oh. My. God!

No he isn't. Please tell me he did not just…

My hands fly up and mask my gaping mouth. My eyes unable to do anything except stare. I shake my head, barely noticeable to anyone not at my table.

How is this happening? How is it I am here right now? This will undoubtedly be scarred into my cerebral cortex for the rest of my life. Marked in my mental scrapbook for years of reference. A tale told to grandchildren to make them laugh at their grandfather.

Not only is grandpa up on the makeshift stage, singing to the world like he is fifty years younger. Not only has he ripped off his wet T-shirt and flashed his elderly man-boobs to the cat-calling natives. Now he has taken his soft-serve vanilla and is smearing it all over his now exposed nipples. But that is not the worst of it. Nope. Not even close. Because he just brought the dripping cone to his lips and is sucking on the dairy confection as if his life depends on it.

Gag!

Somehow, I manage to break my eyes away from the geriatric porn in front of me and glance over at Shelly and Jonas. When I see that both of their expressions are equally as awestruck as mine, all I do is laugh. I have yet to figure out if we are fortunate to have seen this. Or if we are being punished for something. It's a crapshoot.

"Are you two seeing what I'm seeing?" I ask, already knowing the answer. To be honest, I want to hear their interpretation of it all. There is no way I can be the only one thinking this is nutty as hell. Karaoke Grandpa has definitely fallen off his rocker.

"I think I need to go home and bleach my eyes. Some things cannot be unseen. Some things should never *be* seen," Shelly says on a chuckle.

"Mad props to the old-timer. One, such as myself, can only hope I'm that fucking cool when I'm his age," Jonas states, an echo of pride in his voice. I giggle as he sits taller on his stool.

And when he glances my way, his sweet smile lights up his face. The one that makes the dimple on his left cheek pop. The dimple that makes me question why we are only friends. Why does that damn dimple exist? Ugh.

But deep down, I know the answer. Or at least I believe I know the answer.

Jonas and I have been friends for most of my adult life. Close to ten years. He is sexy as hell and has a heart of gold. And I know he would be there for me in a heartbeat if I needed him. But I am not so sure if he is long-term relationship material. He has had girlfriends in the past, but most of his relationships only stick for a month or two. And I want more in life than a couple months of good times.

I wish I could be one of those women. The ones who have a couple months of great sex and move on. Just go with the wind. But I am not engineered that way. Never have been, never will be.

Sometimes, I wonder why his relationships have never

made it past the two-month mark. Is there an asshole side to Jonas I don't know about? Or is it the women who are assholes to him? Does the fun fizzle out at two months? Does he get bored with them? As badly as I want to ask him, I can't do that. It is none of my business, unless he wants to divulge. But still, I wonder. Often.

I laugh at Shelly and Jonas, slapping my hand on the table for good measure. "Tonight will not be forgotten anytime soon. I guarantee it."

"Word," Jonas adds.

His knee brushes mine under the table and I suddenly hear my pulse. Heat flushes my skin and dampens my palms. As much as I know I shouldn't be in a relationship with Jonas, I can't ignore the way he causes my heart to beat a little faster. The way my breathing turns a bit ragged. There is something about him. Something I have yet to pin down, but maybe one day I will figure it out. Maybe one day, my heart won't be overruled by my past.

A change of topic is needed, especially since sticky, sweet grandpa has now left the stage after his standing ovation. Bringing the brown bottle with the label peeling at the corners to my lips, I peer over at Shelly and ponder over the neutral things we can discuss. But I don't have to worry for long because she comes to my rescue.

"So, anything new or exciting happening with work?" she prompts.

Definite neutral ground. Bless you, my friend. Bless you.

"Yeah. I wrapped up a project for the parks department the other day. It was awesome to visit all the county parks and shoot pictures. I didn't realize how many parks we have in the area. Anyway, they're publishing a magazine next month and hoping to get people outdoors more."

"And why didn't you ask either of us to tag along while you were taking said photos?" Jonas shoots me with faux guilt. There is that damn dimple again.

Why am I choosing to not date him? The more I am near him, the more interaction we share, the more I ask this question. If only I had a legitimate answer before getting admitted to a psych ward.

"Next time," I mutter. "My next shoot is on Clearwater Beach, for the most part. It's an advertisement for beach attire—on the beach and off—including accessories. It will be the first time I've worked with Global Beach Magazine, which will be an amazing addition to my resume and portfolio. I'd invite you to watch, but that might be awkward. Not like visiting the park."

Jonas rests his hand over mine for the count of three, two, one. *Breathe, Cora. Breathe.*

"When does that start?" he asks as he lifts his hand and rests it beside mine.

"Next week. The first of April. The shoot is spread out over a week. Some indoors, but most on the beach. A few also taken in Dunedin. I'm excited and freaking out at the same time."

Shelly sets her fruity, pink drink on the table, but twirls the blue drink umbrella. "Why are you freaking out?"

"I have no idea. Every time I think of the shoot, I get this weird twinge in my gut. It's strange. I've never felt this way before a shoot. Maybe it's because my name will be plastered in a national magazine next to some pretty boy's face." I wince and shrug.

Snatching my beer from the table, I chug the rest and hold my bottle up, signaling to the waitress for another round. She catches my request and nods.

"But I thought you were hot for the pretty boys," Shelly teases.

I bat my eyelashes at her. "Damn! You got me."

And then we are all laughing. Yet another reason why I love hanging with Jonas and Shelly. We can say the stupidest shit and there is no judgment. We love each other for who we are and would never want anything different. That is how friendship should be—unconditional acceptance. Quirks and all.

The waitress drops off another round of drinks and I request an order of tortilla chips with salsa and guacamole. Might as well get comfortable, seeing as karaoke night started with a bang. One can only hope the next act is equally awesome. And by awesome, I mean not another rendition of geriatric porn.

"You guys want to hang tomorrow?" Shelly pipes up. "Maybe we can hit Putt-Putt and go-karts at Celebration Station. I'm feeling the need to speed past some prepubescent punks." She laughs then sips her fresh cocktail.

"I'm in," Jonas answers.

"Definitely," I say. "I'm always up for putting punks in their place."

Just as Shelly is about to screech with excitement, karaoke grandpa's competitor jumps onstage. Let's just say she is trying to up his show and is making a valiant effort. The unmistakable intro and beat of "Baby Got Back" by Sir Mix-A-Lot pours from the speaker. Every possible body part on her body is jiggling as she attempts to shake her ass.

Maybe I shouldn't have ordered food.

Dear Lord, someone save us from the hell we are being subjected to this evening. Shelly and Jonas simultaneously gape at the stage before turning to stare at me. All of us thinking the exact same thing.

"You guys want to head out?" I ask, praying one of them will relieve us all from this new form of torture.

"It's like you read my mind," Jonas states. "You want to hang somewhere else?"

It was still early in the evening and I had only had a couple drinks. I wasn't quite ready to say good night to my friends. "Yes. You want to go to another bar? Or we could hang at the house. Whichever you prefer."

Shelly pipes up. "Let's go to your place. We can stop and grab drinks on the way. Maybe watch a comedy on Netflix."

"Cool with me," I tell them both.

Bringing my beer to my lips, I swallow the remaining liquid and signal the server. When she steps up to the table, I ask her to pack my appetizer in a takeout box and bring us the check.

One more glance up at granny and I contemplate stopping at the grocery store across the street and raiding the cleaning products aisle. Is it a full moon? A new moon? Whatever celestial event is happening, it has definitely brought out the crazies tonight.

Will my eyes ever be wiped of this night? No. No they won't.

Three beers and two shots in me later, and the three of us are laughing our asses off to *Sausage Party* on Netflix. It is a toss-up between Shelly and me on who is drunker. I would suggest we flip a coin, but I don't think that will work out so well. We may have consumed equal amounts of alcohol, but her tolerance is higher than mine. Sometimes I envy her that. Either way, our inebriation is in full swing and life is good.

My eyes grow heavy and I lean more into Jonas's body with each passing second. The warmth of his skin on my bicep adds a new flush to my skin. Like the sensation of a fresh sunburn. Hot, but not unbearable.

It would be easy. Tipping my head, a little more to the right, I could kiss him. Just like that. And I want to. I really want to. But even in my tipsy/borderline drunken state, I still hesitate. I still resist the urge.

Why do I always keep us in the friend zone? What the hell is wrong with me?

Pressing more weight into his side, I inhale deeply and absorb the scent that is pure Jonas. A strange blend of sunscreen and gasoline and grease. His scent so familiar and somehow appealing. Pleasant and comforting and—

"Cora?" he cuts off my thoughts, my name spoken like a prayer on his lips.

Tipping my head back into the couch pillows, my eyes wobble to his as I half-ass smile. "Jonas?"

The air grows heavy between us. The room quieter than I remember from thirty seconds ago. It is one-hundred-percent possible Shelly fell asleep on the blankets near my feet. But I can't see her face, so there is no way to be certain.

"What are you doing?" His simple question comes out breathy.

My brows pinch together as I study his eyes. "What?"

He leans in closer, his lips inches from mine. "What are you doing?"

Was I doing something? I don't remember anything from a couple minutes ago. Having him this close, though, makes me dizzy. Dizzy with desire. Dizzy for more than his lips a breath away from mine. But I also think the alcohol is working some serious voodoo on my organs right now.

A light sheen of sweat breaks out over my skin as my stomach gurgles. I scoot forward on the couch and take a slow, measured breath. My gut groans at me again and I have a feeling everything is about to head south really quick. Or would it be north?

"I don't feel so good," I tell Jonas.

The back of his hand brushes over my forehead and I catch a blip of relief before he removes it. "Cora, you're kind of pale and clammy." He rises from the couch and extends his hand out to me. "Let me walk you to your bed. I'll grab you a cool cloth."

Slipping my hand into his, he walks me the short distance to my bedroom. As I go to sit on the bed, nausea rolls through my core and I bolt up and run for the bathroom. This will not be pretty.

Thank the angel watching over me for allowing me to make it to the porcelain throne in time. Besides the fact that I am expelling the contents of my stomach, the one takeaway from this moment… Jonas is by my side, rubbing my back and holding my hair. He really is a great guy.

two

GAVIN

Why can I not walk through this fucking airport without people smacking into me?

Flying is bad enough. Mix that in with LAX during the early morning and my life is a new version of hell. Some woman with a stroller smacks into my arm while the child who should be in said stroller hangs limp at her side. Literally hanging. Under normal circumstances, I might tell the woman her little girl is adorable. But circumstances aren't normal because the little girl is shrieking like a banshee. Limbs thrashing and kicking anything within reach. No doubt the entire terminal hears this girl.

Could the mom not just move out of the way and deal with her kid? Seriously. Why drag your kid around and make a show out of it? If it were my child, I would be embarrassed as hell.

"Gavin? Did you hear what I said?" Alyson asks through the phone pressed to my ear as I am about to knock some twenty-year-old prick out of the way. This whole situation is already shit. Is it everyone-get-in-Gavin's-way day?

"Can you repeat that, Alyson? There're more dicks than

normal in the airport today." I speak louder than necessary, hoping the dipshit hears me and gets out of my fucking way. He peers over his shoulder, catches my expression and hustles to get out of my way.

Thank fuck.

"You should be landing in Tampa around six fifteen p.m., eastern time. I emailed the hotel details to you. Please be on your best behavior. My flight leaves in the morning tomorrow, so I'll meet up with you for dinner and we can get caught up on your itinerary."

Of all the things that come along with this crazy job, I am glad it includes Alyson. I never realized how amazing it would be to have a personal assistant/agent. When I first started this gig, I thought it would be as easy as pose, click, done. Good looks should have made it simple. Boy, was I wrong.

Dead wrong.

It has taken years, but I have finally mastered the art of angles and lighting. Knowing which way to face in different lighting. How to dip or lift my chin. How to stand so the right muscles pop for the photo. Nothing is ever as easy as it seems. But with great mentors and years of practice, confidence is on my side.

After checking my luggage, I head to the terminal for my flight. I have about twenty minutes before they allow us to begin boarding. So, while I wait, I decide to hit one of the eateries and grab a quick bite and a drink.

The moment the airline calls for us to board, my palms break out in a cold sweat. I finish off the drink and the coolness calms me a fraction as I head for the gate.

Just breathe, dude.

I have flown enough times in the last eight years to be a

pro. Have racked up so many airline miles I can't redeem them quick enough. My job has taken me to some of the most amazing places, within the states and beyond. Not once have I been so nerve-wracked before boarding a plane.

So why now? What is so different about this trip?

The Bay Area is just another sunny oasis with hot chicks and tourists for days. Minus some of the landscape, it's not all that different from California. I honestly don't know why people prefer one oasis over the other. Guess it depends on if you prefer elevation or not.

I board the plane and locate my seat, throwing my carry-on in the overhead compartment. Staring out the window, my eyes zoom in on the wing of the plane, when the person I will sit beside for the next six hours bumps my elbow. I roll my eyes and shake my head.

Can people just stop knocking into me today? For the love of...

I turn to see who sits beside me and my breath catches a second. A sexy as sin blonde shifts, trying to wrangle her purse strap over her head, which seems to be caught on her necklace. What a perfect setup.

"May I?" I gesture toward her neck, offering to help separate the two.

"Please," she huffs, obviously frustrated and embarrassed with the state of what is happening.

Aiding her with the strand and strap, we free her from the entanglement. She tips her head back against the seat, inhales deeply and takes a moment to calm down. After a sigh, she turns in her seat to better face me.

"Thanks for that. As cute as this purse is, I think I'm going to get rid of it. That wasn't my first rodeo in the tangled department." She shakes her head and laughs.

"Sure thing. Glad I could help," I offer. I extend my hand to her. "I'm Gavin."

"Brandy. Nice to meet you," she says and shakes my hand. "Business or pleasure?"

"Sorry?" The way the word pleasure rolls off her tongue has me thinking of several ways I can give her exactly that. Blonde isn't generally my type, but when it's just for fun, does it really matter?

"Your trip. Is it for business or pleasure?"

Ah, yes. Generic question, generic conversation. I should be used to having meaningless conversations by now. Not like my job requires me to engage in deep, life-changing chats. Would be a nice change, though. Whatever. At least I get to sit next to someone who isn't painful on the eyes. Could be much worse.

"Business. You?"

"Pleasure. I'm meeting up with my boyfriend and a couple friends in Brandon. I was out here visiting family."

"Cool."

Nothing else comes to mind to say after learning she has a boyfriend. Automatic buzzkill. Sure, I could ask how her visit with her family went, but we don't know each other and it is none of my business. So, I don't dig.

At the mention of friends, I wonder if I will see anyone besides Micah from my teen years while I am on this trip. It will be nice to hang with Micah and catch up. I haven't been back to this part of Florida since my mom received a promotion thirteen years ago. A promotion that had us moving out of the Sunshine state and across the country to the Golden state. A move that changed my life in more ways than one.

Maybe that is what has me so on edge. The possibility.

Brandy retrieves her phone and plugs in her earbuds,

essentially talk-blocking me for the entire flight. So much for having a cute blonde to distract me. Generic conversation would have been better than nothing at all. This flight will last longer than the actual flight time.

I retrieve my phone from my back pocket, open up my Spotify app and hit play, looping the playlist. Leaning my head back against the seat, I gaze out the window and let my eyes lose focus on the skyline.

Ten days. I will only be there for ten days. A week and a half. It will fly by.

What is the likelihood I will run into anyone? Run into her? Slim. One in a million.

Majority of my time there will be wrapped up in photo shoots and dinners with Alyson and the photographer. There won't be any time to do anything else. And besides, I am sure everyone has moved away. I mean, who stays in the same place they grew up? As soon as they come of age, most people move away.

But a part of me begs the universe to let me see her again. Even from a distance. See how she is. If she is with someone. Happy. What she looks like. Has she changed from the girl I knew? God, I hope there is no animosity after all these years. After everything, I hope she doesn't hate me.

The plane taxis down the runway and we are off the ground seconds later. I pinch my eyes shut and focus on the music blaring in my ears. The music blankets the roar of the engine just barely, but does nothing to mask the vibration. Or the queasiness in my gut.

Just breathe, dude. The chances are slim.

three

CORA

"Where do you want me to put this?" Erin asks as she holds up the soft umbrella reflector.

I point over to the left of a small side table. "You can set it there. The stand should be ready, if you could put it on there for me."

"You got it, boss," she jokes.

The first day Erin and I worked together, she called me boss. I told her to never dub me with such a title again. Although she has worked as my assistant, we had known each other beforehand. Erin is my friend, who just so happens to help me with my job and I compensate her. We work well together and there is no sense in ruining a good thing.

But since that first day, when our friendship added business partners, she lives to mess with me. To keep our relationship light and fun and not so work-y. So, calling me boss is her work version of sarcasm. And I love all her witty and sarcastic tendencies.

Erin fumbles with setting up the lighting while I do some test shots with my camera. I point the camera off in the distance, catching sight of a few passersby and pressing the shutter release. Pulling the camera away from my eye, I glance down at the LCD screen and view the image. The lighting is sufficient, as is the image. Hopefully, we get all the shots in before the lighting from the windows shifts and adds unnecessary shadows. Not like I can't Photoshop them out, but the less I have to adjust, the better.

As I shoot a few more test shots, the door to the banquet room opens. I continue taking a few more test shots, not looking to see the model or his agent as they shuffle into the room. I don't know much about the shoot. Just that it's a male model and he is an up-and-comer in the fashion industry.

Snap. Shot of the framed art on the wall.

I make a couple adjustments and take the same shot again. Perfect.

Setting the camera down on the table loaded with my equipment, I school my expression and put on my professional face. Just as I prepare to turn and meet my clients, a familiar voice echoes in my ears and I freeze.

A voice I haven't heard since I was sixteen-years-old.

A voice that hasn't changed in the thirteen years since I last heard it.

A voice that tortured me in my dreams for almost a decade.

Sucking in a deep breath, I turn with a huge smile plastered across my face and greet my newest client. *Should I act as if I remember him? Or not?* I am baffled as to how I should respond. I haven't dealt with a similar situation yet.

I extend my hand to the agent first, seeing as she is the reason I work with her client in the first place. "Cora Davies. It's a pleasure to meet you." My smile as tight as a fresh facelift.

"Alyson Jameson." Her overly manicured hand slides into

mine, shaking it with no strength. "This is my client, Gavin Hunt."

When Alyson drops her hand from mine, I focus my attention on Gavin, offering my hand. His dark brows pinch together for half a second. Most people wouldn't catch the twitch, but I do. Not only because I am a photographer and part of my job depends on seeing beyond the superficial. But also, because I know Gavin. Intimately. And this shoot just became awkward with a capital A.

He shakes my hand, the rough contours of his skin tingle against my smooth palm. I study him a moment, our hands still connected. Not much has changed since I last saw him. Same height. Same brown-black hair, the style new—buzzed short from the base of his skull to a couple inches above his ear, the remaining hair seven or so inches long and swept to his right. His body, though… time and hard work show as evidence in the taut fabric pressed against his muscular frame. His shoulders seem broader than I remember. And his throat… I swallow just looking at it.

It is difficult to not speak with him like I knew him for years, but I do my best to maintain my businesslike persona. To present myself as the photographer the magazine chose. This is a job. Nothing more.

"Gavin, it's great to see you again. It has been far too long."

Too long didn't even begin to cover it. But no one else in the room needs to know the meaning behind my words. Or the hurt that pairs with them. I pray I have mastered my poker face by now. Because inside, I am seething. And weeping.

All of a sudden, a million questions run a marathon in my head. Except this marathon isn't on city streets, but on an old-school track. Circle after circle after circle. It makes me dizzy and breathless. My heart thumps erratically and beats against my ribcage harder than necessary. Of all the people I would be okay with not seeing again, Gavin ranked in the top three.

"Cora..." he drawls. My name, four simple letters, spills off his lips soft and wickedly. A smile kicks up the corners of his mouth, and it looks like something he flashes with frequency. It is not a personal smile and doesn't touch his eyes. Not the smile I was once overly familiar with. The smile I memorized for more than a year. Those must be reserved or nonexistent. This smile is forced and pretentious and ugly. I don't know this Gavin. Not really sure I want to, either. "Feels like it's been forever. A lifetime. I didn't know you were a photographer."

His words weren't meant to insult me, but they do. They literally feel like a slap to the cheek. *How would he know what I have been up to?* You would have to communicate with someone to know what is happening in their life. Am I right? I am tempted to say exactly that, but I somehow restrain myself. I need this shoot to go off without a hitch. The paycheck would be a great boost to my savings.

"And I didn't know you were a model. So many things have changed for us both, I'm sure." As much as I try to restrain my sarcasm, it pours out of me with ease. When it comes to Gavin, it is difficult to restrain my true feelings. With anyone else, I easily mask my emotions and go about my business. But with him, it just spills out of me. Always has.

The air around us is thick and heavy with our history. A history his agent and my assistant are unfamiliar with. A history I should put on the back burner while I am the photographer and he is the model. This is not the time or place to bring up the past. And if I am lucky, there won't be a time while he is here.

I can be the skilled photographer and focus on the task at hand. Can silence my emotions. And ignore the flutter circulating in my chest at the sight of him. Ignore the hunger building in my core at the resonance of his voice. Ignore the flashes of our past that float through my mind.

A glowing smirk lifts a corner of his lips, as if he knows he has gotten to me. As if he can read me like he did all those years ago. But he doesn't know me anymore. Doesn't know what I went through after he left. Doesn't know how much I have changed. And two can play his game.

"Mr. Hunt—" I cut the silence. "If you could please move over to the backdrop near the windows."

He cocks an eyebrow in challenge and his smirk deepens. "Sure thing, *Ms.* Davies." His emphasis on the prefix doesn't go unnoticed. Figures he would assume I am still single. Maybe I kept my name for my business. He doesn't know one way or the other. But it is irrelevant, because his assumption is correct. And that pisses me off further.

Prick.

He saunters to where I directed him and turns when his feet land on the fabric. "How do you want me?" he asks with a sultry rasp to his voice.

"Have a seat on the stool. We'll start with some headshots displaying the clothes and watch."

His smile bumps up a notch and the faint glimpse of his dimples appear. "You know, I always loved it when you bossed me around." This time, when he smiles wider, it touches his eyes. But it reeks of mischief versus genuineness.

If my eyes roll any farther back in my head, I will see the inside sutures of my skull. This is going to be a long week.

~

Three hours later, after endless banter and flirting from Gavin, I am ready to go home and drink away any thought ever including him. Drink away memories skirting on the edge of my mind. Drink myself into a stupor. Today was only three hours. But there are several days listed for the shoot, plus dinners.

Can I just request a drink from the hotel bar now?

There is no denying Gavin is gorgeous. Even more than the last time I saw him. Time has treated him kindly. Wish I could say the same for myself.

Seeing him today has stirred up so many festering emotions, bringing them to the surface. Pain and hurt I thought no longer existed or held me hostage. But the second I heard his voice; it was as if my prince returned and kissed his sleeping princess. My body stirred back to life and my heart resumed its rhythm. Hope flickered for the briefest moment for the first time in years.

But I shut that shit down. Reminding myself what he had done thirteen years earlier. Reminding myself how I felt after what he did thirteen years ago. And there is no way in hell I plan to relive that anytime soon.

Minutes ago, he and his agent strolled out and left Erin and me to clean up in awkward silence. But not before he managed to make things a little more confusing between us. He doesn't need to say or do much, just his presence put me on edge. Being close to him wasn't always like this. There wasn't always this looming tension hovering over us. But now, how can there not be?

I have this inkling to explain myself to Erin. To share fragments of my past to help her understand my behavior today.

The way I acted when he came in the room is out of character for me. On more than one occasion, Erin stared at me with shock in her eyes. I maintained my expert smile and kept my voice as neutral as possible. But the tension could be cut with a knife.

But I keep my cards close. If Erin broaches the subject, I will spill my heart out to her. Until she asks, though, I won't say a word. Until she asks, I will process it all and devise a plan on how to work with him for a week. Gavin is just one of those topics I hate bringing up.

As if she can hear my thoughts.

"So… what was up with all that?" She gestures to the doors, waving her hand aimlessly.

"What do you mean?" I play coy.

She freezes and glares at me as if to say *you're shitting me, right?* Silence stretches between the two of us for minutes —her glaring at me, me ignoring her penetrating gaze. A game of cat and mouse. But the longer we stand here, the more I come to realize she is not caving until I answer. *Damnit.*

"Ugh. Gavin and I knew each other in high school," I mutter.

"And…" She draws out the single syllable and leaves it hanging like bait on a hook. She is relentless and won't give in until I hand her more information. Only I don't know how much information I want to give up. Not that I am scared to share history with my close friends. More like I am scared of what will happen to *me* when I dredge everything up.

"And we dated for years."

There, I have said it. Got it out in the open. The sour taste on my tongue turns bitter.

I haven't discussed anything relating to Gavin in so long, I am not sure if I am being relieved of a burden or gaining a new one. Shelly, and her brother Micah, are the only two people in my current life, other than my parents, who know about me and Gavin. They also know not to mention him around me.

"You know I'm going to need more to go on. Spill," Erin coaxes.

But I am not surrendering everything I have worked so hard to forget in one sitting. I don't mind sharing with her, but will do so at my own pace. And now is definitely not the time.

"Maybe later. Right now, my head is pounding. I just want to gather up all the equipment, shove it in the car, and head home. Perhaps drink enough to pass out, but not so much I will have a hangover tomorrow. Since we'll be in the blinding sun for hours."

Erin nods and collects equipment from around the room, placing it in the appropriate storage crates. A few minutes pass as we break down the set in silence. Just as I think how great it is of her to stop playing twenty questions with me, she speaks up.

"I'll drop the subject for today. But tomorrow..." She pauses for a breath. "You're catching me up on this whole Gavin-Cora history. We can do it at your place or out somewhere. Either way, you're giving it up."

I stop and stare at her, realizing she is more than just an assistant. Erin is a bestie. One I am proud to have at my side. My team. All the years of not sharing this part of me, it was for selfish reasons. All because I didn't want to rehash old wounds. Or cut new ones when hope sparkled in my eyes at remembering him.

Wounds heal, right? Sure, some leave scars. But scars

don't define you; they mend you. Give you thicker skin. Show you different paths.

I am more than that small, worried, heartbroken girl. Now, I am a woman. A woman who takes no shit. Or allows anyone to trample over her heart. And gives no fucks to someone such as Gavin Hunt—a selfish asshole who didn't have the decency to try and keep his word and what we had.

He doesn't know it yet, but because of him… no one can ever knock me down. No one can take my heart captive.

No one. Not even him.

The last few hours of the shoot were a blur of confusion. I did my best to focus, but my head was all over the place. Every time Cora held the camera to her eye and peered through the lens, my skin flamed. Yes, she was doing her job, but it felt like so much more.

Thirteen years have passed since I last saw Cora. Thirteen years since I last spoke with her. And somehow, it feels like thirteen years is about to catch up with us in no time.

Just as Alyson and I prepare to leave, I ask Alyson to give me a moment. She checks her watch and nods with slight annoyance. Not sure if it is directed at me personally or the fact I am derailing her schedule. She lives and dies by schedules, but we have nothing planned after the shoot. Sure, she is just tired. It has definitely been a long day.

I walk over to Cora, her hands fidgeting with her equipment. As I step close to her, she stops but doesn't look up. Funny—or cruel—reality, we have always sensed each other's proximity. From the day I met Cora, her energy danced with mine. Her energy is my energy.

"It was good seeing you again," I mutter. For some

reason, I feel the need to keep this conversation quiet from the other sets of ears in the room. Alyson knows nothing about Cora, and I don't know if Cora's assistant knows of me.

She sets the camera on the table, takes a breath, then turns to face me. A softness hazes her green eyes. "You, too." Something resides beneath her exterior. Something she doesn't want me to see. And the notion bothers me.

"You want to grab dinner? We can catch up."

Her brow furrows a moment. Eyes twitch before working to right themselves. Lips pinch then loosen. Pain dances over her face for a breath and it stabs me straight in the heart. "Maybe another time. I'm tired and I think I'll just head home for the night."

Her rejection hits me harder than I care to admit. I blink away the sting behind my eyes. "Another time," I mumble, walking away and out of the room with Alyson on my heels.

I am so fucked.

Alyson drones on about today's shoot. Talking to me as if I had never stood in front of a camera before and had millions of photos taken. Telling me which shots she thinks will be the money makers and which I could have improved. I fucking hate it when she talks to me as if I am a goddamn child. How many years have I been doing this now? A decade, or close to it. I may not hold any *Man of the Year* awards, but people know me. People respect me.

When she gets like this, I zone out. Same conversation, new shoot.

While she carries on, we step into the elevator and ride up, away from the banquet room where Cora remains. Alyson gets props for hooking me up at a luxury hotel on Clearwater Beach. This place sits on the water and I have an unobstructed view of the beach and when the sun sets. Sunsets are the ideal end to my day. Hopefully not my life.

The elevator dings and the doors slide open. We step out and walk toward my room. Alyson yammers on beside me, saying how this shoot is somewhat of a new concept for me. How the majority of my work has been modeling for romance novel covers or risqué images. Personally, I enjoy the latter.

Today started a new journey for me. I stepped foot into the world of designer clothing modeling. Modeling clothing isn't foreign to me, but it has never been for an internationally known fashion designer. This contract could take me to the next level. This contract could open up so many future opportunities.

I hold my key card against the door lock and push through the door a second later. Alyson continues sharing what the company is looking for from the week-long shoot. At this point, I listen to her. This information I need to absorb. We talk back and forth as we sit on the couch in my suite. Strategizing how to maximize this shoot.

Click. Click. I recall the camera shutter sounds from hours ago when we stepped into the banquet room.

I shake my head in an attempt to dissolve the trickling memories of earlier and try to focus on what Alyson is saying. But it is no use. An impossibility.

The moment I was within twenty feet of Cora, a hum I haven't felt in years buzzed in my veins. A buzz only one woman created. When I glanced up to locate the source, I was rendered immobile. Confusion trickled through me as my chest tightened. All I kept thinking was *I know that black hair and slender frame.*

"Gavin, are you hearing a word I'm telling you?" Alyson asks as she grabs a bottled water from the mini-fridge.

"Yeah, I'm listening." Lie. I haven't heard a damn word she has said in the last ten minutes.

The second Alyson drones on about the contract, I zone out again.

Cora's forced, tight smile flashes in my head. The way it lit up her face, but wasn't exactly how I remembered it. And I never forgot her face. Never. It may not look the same as it did all those years ago—now a touch fuller and more woman than girl—but I would know it anywhere. Know *her* anywhere. Without question.

And her demeanor. Parts of her seemed so artificial now. From the fake smile to the handshake. I expected her to shake Alyson's hand, but mine… I don't know why, but part of me hoped to hug her. Begged to feel her petite frame pressed to mine. But we are here for business, so I suppose hugs would be inappropriate. With my career, I am not one to cross certain lines, but this is Cora. It is different. We are different.

Or so I thought…

But in front of my agent and her assistant, she put on a front that we were old friends, united once again. I know things between us ended in a shitty way, but let's get real. Once upon a time, we were way more than friends. We were… everything.

And suddenly, my wallet rests much heavier in my back pocket, knowing what I have kept under my license all these years. Something not another soul knows about. Something sacred.

Throughout the shoot, I messed with her. A little banter here. A dose of flirting there. Every chance I had to say her name, I swirled it over my tongue and plastered on a smile all women swoon over. At times, it amazes me what I have gotten out of using that smile. But that smile doesn't faze Cora. Not in the slightest.

Seeing as we haven't spoken in more than a decade, I'm sure I know very little about her anymore. Even when I chat with Micah from time to time, he hasn't said much about her.

Micah is one of my closest friends. We have known each other since I was eleven and him thirteen. He also happens to be the older brother of Cora's best friend, Shelly. Not sure how close Micah is with Cora, but seeing as he never spoke about her with me, I assume not close at all. Either that or he makes sure he doesn't broach a subject as sticky as me and Cora.

Even with the time and distance apart, Cora gave me a ration of shit as if we had seen each other days ago. A few times, it was easy to think she was flirting back. Her smirk. The way she peeked around the camera a little longer than typical. The occasional cock of her brow.

She is kind of feisty now. And the thought of provoking her further turns me on.

But each time she schooled her expression, flipping her photographer persona on, all I wanted to do is fuck with her more. And she made it way too easy. Like she was secretly enjoying it. Who knows, maybe she was.

As much as I feared the possibility of seeing her during my time here, feared her reaction and my own, a new burst of excitement courses through me. Every time our eyes met, I put on a snide, panty-dropping smile, and waited for her to direct me. It was better to be a distraction than own how I really felt. Because if I own my true feelings with her eyes on me, she will know. Without a doubt, she will read every wish and regret I own.

"Mr. Hunt, if you could please move over to the backdrop near the windows."

She was all business. But I was, and am, determined to challenge her.

I used her name like a weapon, shooting it off my tongue in slow motion.

"Earth to Gavin?" Alyson waves in front of my face.

"Huh?" *Shit.* It is blatantly obvious she has caught me ignoring her. Probably didn't miss anything noteworthy. "What did you say?"

She shakes her head at me. "I said you'd better not mess this up with whatever is going on with you and the photographer."

Alyson isn't being a bitch, but the way she said *the photographer* pisses me off. As if she doesn't know or remember her name. Makes me want to grab her shoulders and shake them. Get in her face and hiss Cora's name. But I don't.

"I won't," I promise. And I mean it.

As much fun as it is messing with Cora, I won't jeopardize my contract with the magazine. It has taken me years to get to this point in my career. No way I will ruin it overnight.

But I would be a liar if I said this shoot won't be a challenge. Without a doubt, it will be the most difficult shoot of my career. It will push me to the edge mentally. Have me second-guessing my every move. Have me wondering if I am being crazy. And I have done some crazy shit.

All the back and forth between us today, I had to have made a dent in her fortress. Chipped at her armor.

"Don't make me babysit you," Alyson threatens. "I don't like being that kind of agent."

"Yeah, yeah." I hold up three fingers. "Scout's honor."

Alyson rises from the couch, smoothing her skirt. "Also, I booked a shoot with you and Layla. It's a week after we fly back to Los Angeles. Okay? I'll leave you alone for the night. Be good." She points a finger at me. "And I'll see you in the morning."

I salute her. "Yes, ma'am."

She shakes her head at me and walks out the door, taking her cloud of tension with her.

As soon as she is gone, I collapse on the couch. This week will be tough, but I don't have a choice. I made a commitment. One I have no intention of backing out on. One that will take me to the next level. Cora is an unexpected surprise, but one I can handle. I just need to apply the techniques taught to us in school. Meditation. Shaking off self-doubt. Being my own cheerleader. Clearing my thoughts of everything not pertaining to the moment.

At times, it can be taxing to separate reality from the portrayal of who you are in an advertisement. Like an actor, I have to be whoever the people want me to be. Look the part. Play the role. Make the men want to mimic me. Make the women want to date me. And with Cora being around, I suspect I will be acting a lot.

And the most straining part of this shoot—not staring at her. *Fuck.* It is incomprehensible how much I have missed her. Beyond wrong to sit there and have absolute silence between us. A lot can be said in silence, but we were not those people years ago.

But isn't that how most shoots go? The only talking occurs when the photographer gives direction or I give feedback. With her, though, it is different. The silence a heavy burden crushing my windpipe.

Click. Click.

The shutter snap will repeat in my sleep tonight. The click sounded so many times today. More than I recall from other shoots. She must have taken enough photos to fill a terabyte of memory. And if honest, I hope she keeps the photos somewhere sacred after I leave.

I wish I had current photos of her. Maybe I will snag one —or a few—before I leave. There has to be a way to sneak in a photo with my phone.

Tomorrow, we will be on the pristine sands of Clearwater Beach. The beach is one of the best parts of this trip. The sand, the sunsets, the salty air. And after everything today, I don't want to be holed up in my hotel room. I need to get out of here. As enticing as the beach is, I need some other form of release.

Reaching for my cell, I type out a new message.

Hey bro, want to grab a bite?

MICAH

I'm down. Where?

We pick a bar between the beach and his place and agree to meet in an hour. I riffle through my suitcase, toss the designer's pieces in the box they came out of, and head for the shower.

As the hot spray rains between my shoulder blades, I hang my head and wonder how I am going to survive after my time here. Leaving the first time was hard enough. Leaving again will be hell.

five
CORA

My purse hits the floor with a loud thump, startling Luna as she weaves between my legs. "Sorry, pretty girl."

I bend down and run a hand over her soft, black fur and she purrs in return. Scooping both hands under her belly, I lift and flip her belly-side up, doting kisses on her. She is the sweetest cat I have owned, never wanting to leave my side. She also serves as the world's best cuddle buddy.

As I land on the couch with her snuggled in my arms, my phone rings from my abandoned purse. *Ugh.* I just want to unwind and get some sleep before tomorrow. No rest for the weary.

I set Luna down and kiss her head before I snag my phone from my purse. Shelly.

"Hey, girl," I answer.

"You sound beat. Want me to let you go?"

"Long day, and no. What's up?"

"You'll never guess who's in town," she says in a rush. If we were on FaceTime right now, I would see her jumping up and down, hands flailing. That's just Shelly. A big ball of unending enthusiasm.

"Bet I can." I burst her bubble of excitement.

"Wait, wha—?" she stumbles. "How did you know?" She actually sounds bummed to not break the news to me.

I huff into the phone, wishing to escape all things related to Gavin Hunt. But as usual, everything cycles back to him. "Because he's the model I'm currently shooting."

A shriek tears through the line and I hold the phone away from my face until she stops. "Shut the fuck up. Are you serious? How weird. Or maybe not. Is it weird?"

What is she talking about? "Huh?" It is all I can say.

"You know it's not his fault he moved to California years ago. Maybe fate has found a way to bring you back together," she says, words all dreamy.

Although she has been single for some time, Shelly is adamant about the topic of love and fate and how everything happens for a reason. I have lost count of how many times she has told me I will find my Prince Charming one day soon.

While she can't see me, I roll my eyes. Fate. *What a load of bullshit.* If fate existed, things between Gavin and I wouldn't have ended how they did. He would have done more. Would have at least tried.

"I know it wasn't his fault, but he didn't even try for long. It's like he gave up or caved or moved on. Like I no longer mattered. It…" I will not fucking cry. Nope, I refuse to shed another tear over Gavin Hunt. I tip my head back and blink in rapid succession. I inhale deep and continue. "It hurt seeing him today. He acted as if nothing existed between us before. He's not the same Gavin I once knew."

"Yeah, I get that. I'm sorry if him being here is digging up old memories. But you know something?" Shelly's voice escalates in pitch the more she talks.

"What?"

"I love you," she croons, wrapping me in a virtual hug. "And we should go out and grab dinner and a couple drinks. You should be celebrating your new contract. Not worrying over Gavin or the past."

As much as I would love to lay in bed, watch reruns of *Supernatural* and eat leftover Chinese food with Luna at my side, how can I say no to Shelly. Still somewhat early, it would be nice to chat with her about how I am in emotional overload right now. Shelly's the only person who knows everything there is to know about me. She is the one person I can pour my heart out to and she won't judge me.

"I can never say no to you. Where should we go? No karaoke. I'm still having strange dreams from the last one."

Her laughter pierces the air, one I would recognize in a room full of strangers. "We can hit that Thai and sushi restaurant on Patricia. I've been craving green curry for days."

Now it is my turn to laugh. Not only does my best friend know me well, she also caters to my hankering for Asian food. I also believe I have made her as equally addicted, which warms my heart.

"Sounds good. I'll meet you there in thirty."

"Thirty," she agrees and disconnects the call.

The server sets down a plate of Pad See-Ew with tofu in front of me and I lean over and breathe deep. My mouth waters at the sweet and savory aroma and I can't wait to dive in. What is it about Asian food that makes me so damn happy? No one knows the answer—not even me—and I will die happily oblivious. Years ago, Shelly joked I must have been Asian in a former life. When she suggested it, I shrugged and continued shoveling udon noodles in my mouth.

After the server walks off, I finish my last spring roll while Shelly begins attacking her rice and chicken with green curry. A moan rips from her throat and I laugh at her lack of shame. It is one of her many qualities that makes me love her. Shelly is just one of those humans who is one-hundred-percent herself. Her candid nature refreshing.

"Good?" I inquire with a layer of sarcasm.

"Mmm. You have no idea," she mumbles around the food in her mouth.

All I can do is shake my head and laugh again. It is at the exact moment when I am shoving my noodle-packed chopsticks between my teeth that Shelly decides to ask me a question. Is that a secret rule at the dinner table? To ask people questions when it is most inconvenient? Seems the case.

"So, what was it like seeing him again?" Her question is innocent, but I almost choke on my noodles when she asks.

What was it like?

Like thirteen years vanished and I saw the first guy I fell in love with standing in front of me. My heart beat behind my rib cage as if I had locked it in a coffin and tossed the key. My heart has never thumped and thrashed so hard, so loud, so uncontrollably in my chest. I broke out in a sweat, nervous to be near him. Nervous to know if he missed me in all the ways I missed him. Nervous to know if he ever thought about me as often as I did—do—him. It was—is—terrifying.

"It was strange," I lull. I want to own my truths, but I don't know what they all are yet. How can I express emotions I don't quite understand right now? How can I express the cacophony of feelings when they're a cyclone in my skull?

Was I ecstatic? Without a doubt. Did I freak out? Definitely. I still am. Did every memory of him come sprinting to the forefront? Most of them. My favorite memories, anyway.

But it has been several years since we have seen or spoken to each other. He may look the same—with the exception of some added muscles and a semi-different hairstyle—but we are poles apart from who we once were. I can't speak for Gavin, but our breakup broke me. The loss of him made me view relationships differently.

Shelly regards me a minute, looking in my eyes and trying to read the deeper meaning I avoid speaking aloud. "No doubt. How many days is he here?"

"Not sure," I tell her. Because it is true. I have no idea how long he will stay. Part of me wants and doesn't want to know when he leaves. "But the shoot ends in seven days. Each shoot is a different location in the area. There's also a rest day scheduled. How long he's here after... I'm not asking."

She shovels a forkful of meat and rice into her mouth, nodding. When she finishes chewing, her eyes meet mine and she has her protective mask on. "Do you need me to hang around more? While you're doing the shoot, that is. Kind of like reinforcement, in case he's being an ass or you need a minute."

My heart melts at her sentiment. I have no idea what I did to garner such an amazing friend, but I love Shelly hard. No one comes to my rescue as much as she does. She protects my heart as if it were her own. And she knows I would recipro-cate in a heartbeat, if need be.

"Nah. I'll be alright. I just need to keep my focus and not let my mind drift to the *what ifs* like it has before." Too often, I have thought over every possible what if. And it does nothing but give me anxiety.

"Fine. But the first time he fucks shit up, I'm kicking his ass."

Her face is dead serious, but all I respond with is a laugh. One that starts in my belly and rises quickly in my throat. The hearty laugh cathartic and exactly what I need after today. There is my Shelly. The best sidekick a friend could ask for.

"I know you will." I reach over the table and pat her shoulder. "I know you will."

six
GAVIN

People. Are. Everywhere. Surrounding and trapping me. Bodies rub against mine. Music blares so loud, hearing will be a challenge in the morning. Micah picked some bar and restaurant on North Indian Rocks Beach. I don't remember the name, nor do I care. All that matters is being out of that hotel.

What I *do* care about is personal space. And these fucking people don't seem to understand the concept. Claustrophobia has never come up as an issue, but in the last couple of days it has consumed me. I just like personal boundaries. And it seems as if everyone has forgotten what they are. Seems as if everyone is in on some massive joke to crowd me.

"You alright, man?" Micah asks when he notices me tense on my stool.

"Just a little crowded in here."

"Sorry about that. You know how it is this time of year. Spring break seems to go on till the end of April. You want to head somewhere else?"

Dragging in a breath, I answer, "No. Crowds tend to freak me out more now. You think I'd be used to crowds with my job and people doing whatever they can to catch my attention. But nope. Still don't want people in my perimeter." I draw an imaginary bubble around my body for emphasis.

Micah slaps me on the back and adds a laugh for good measure. "Some things never change." He pauses to take a swig from his beer. "How've you been, man? It's been a while since I've heard from you."

Guilt rushes through me. It had been close to six months since I last spoke with Micah. Time escaped me as life got busier. But I had known for a few months I was returning to the area. So why hadn't I messaged or called him to let him know? The answer hits me like a bulldozer and I know exactly why I didn't tell him.

Cora.

Although Micah's connection to Cora is weak at best, his sister *is* best friends with her. So, if I had told Micah, he might have shared with his sister without thinking and so on. Things would have been much worse than they were today. And the potential for Cora backing out of the magazine shoot early on was higher. Although neither of us knew we would be working together, she would have put two and two together if Micah started talking.

"Yeah, I apologize. Things have been mad busy with work. Every time I thought to reach out to you, I was in the middle of something. By the time I was free, I'd forgotten. Time got away from me." I give him a sheepish shrug.

"It's all good. Just don't do it again," he teases.

For the next two hours, we sit on stools and drink beers and share chicken wings. We catch up on what has been happening outside our work lives. At all costs, we both do a damn fine job of avoiding the topic of Cora. And although it is still early, we both agree to leave. In the time since we have come in, the bar has gone from packed to overflowing and I am at my whit's end.

Micah offers to drive me back to my hotel, rather than let me wait for an Uber. No doubt they are probably bombarded this time of year on the beach. On the short drive, we discuss getting together another few times before I leave. When he drops me at the hotel, we agree to go out night after tomorrow. And as Micah drives off, I vow to be a better friend to my best friend. Thousands of miles may divide our houses, but calls and texts and airplanes can solve those problems and I need to put in more effort.

The elevator ride is brief. Although I took a shower earlier, the sea of sweaty bodies from the bar has me jumping in the shower again.

The hot water hits my back and I brace my hands on the white tile wall in front of me and hang my head. My breath comes heavy and fast. My mind running overtime as it scans its memory bank for images of Cora. It doesn't take long. Never has. One of my favorites pops up. An image I have plucked from my memory bank numerous times when shit has gotten bad.

Her onyx black hair hugged her face like an embrace. A smile lit up her lips and curved the corners of her pale green eyes. Eyes that stole my breath every time she looked at me. Every time she got serious and told me she loved me. That she would love me forever, no matter what.

That blip in time was the week before my mom received a promotion and was transferred from Florida to California. I had only been given two weeks before my life would become something polar opposite. And like an asshole, I waited until a week before we had to leave to tell Cora. It was selfish of me, but I didn't want to ruin the last bit of time with her. I didn't want to spend our last weeks together like one of us was on our death bed and trying to complete some bucket list.

Does that still hold true? Does she still love me? After the separation—the rift—is it possible there is still a part of her that loves me? Even if the tiniest of slivers, a micro-blip in the cosmos, I will accept whatever she offers.

Does that make me a fool? Desperate? Probably. Fuck if I care.

Her face flashes across the backs of my eyelids like a movie. The way she used to smile at me and press her lips to mine. Heat radiates in my chest and I press a hand against my breastbone, suppressing the ache that slowly builds every time I allow myself to fantasize about her. And after thirteen years, the ache burns fresh.

I remember the first time she laid beneath me, her bare flesh warm and trembling against mine. I had asked her why she was shaking and she had said *because I love you so much.* I clutch my chest harder as the backs of my eyes sting.

We were so many firsts for each other. Relationship. Kiss. Love. Sexual partner. And heartbreak.

And even though I broke her heart, even though I broke every promise I made her, I will kill any man who does the same.

Shoving back the curtains and sliding the balcony door open, I stare out at the beach and notice how quiet it is this time of the morning. The waves break at the shoreline. Salt and a hint of shea butter linger in the air, sticking to my skin. The horizon still somewhat dark with a tinge of peach skirting between the water and sky.

Silent. Peaceful. And the perfect start to my day.

Couples holding hands. Single people with their dog. Majority of the people walking through the sand at this hour are probably residents, enjoying the beach before it is littered with tourists.

I plan to do the same.

Slipping on a pair of board shorts and a plain T-shirt, I step into my flip-flops and head for the beach. The moment my feet hit the sand, I take off my shoes and wiggle the fine grains between my toes. Beaches in California are different than those in Florida. People flock to the beach in California, but not like they do in Florida. Out west, the sand is course and damp. The water cold, even during the hottest part of the year.

But not in West Florida. Here, the sand is fine like fairy dust and as warm as a lasting hug. I rake my toes in the grains before walking to the edge of the surf. Stare at the horizon and soak in the view. *God, I have missed this place.* The warmth and smells and sounds and vibrance.

I walk along the shoreline, lost in my own head for an hour, before heading back to my room and dressing in the beach gear for today's shoot. Basically, I trade one pair of board shorts for another. The same with my shirt and shoes. Stupid, but it pays the bills.

As I walk out of my room, my phone chimes and I check to see a text from Alyson.

> Good morning. I won't be at the shoot today. Think I caught something on the plane. In bed & not doing so well.

> Sorry you feel like shit. Need me to get you anything?

No. I called room service and they're bringing me the works. Thanks.

Okay. Let me know if you need me to get you anything later.

All I need is for you to take awesome photos & be on your best behavior.

Aren't I always?

Our texts end when she sends me an eye-rolling emoji. She knows me too well. But Alyson also knows I won't ruin this for any of us. Personally, there is no doubt she loves messing with me as much as I do her. Probably the reason we work so well together.

And although Alyson lies in bed sick, an over-stretched smile tightens my cheeks. Knowing I will see Cora in less than ten minutes has my synapsis firing double time. We are scheduled to meet on the beach by the gate for the hotel patrons. If lucky, maybe today I can convince her to have dinner with me. Just me and her. Some good food and conversation. No promises. Just two people with history catching up with each other.

At least that is what I try to convince myself.

seven

CORA

It might be completely out of my way, but I leave my house early and drive to my favorite juice place in Dunedin. When I step inside, the owner is busy making an açai bowl for the only other person. I walk over to the cooler across from the bar top seating and grab my favorite juice from the shelf.

The owner promises she will be with me in a minute and I nod. I sit at the long dining table and look at the cute bohemian décor along the walls and tables. There is a small couch, chairs, and coffee table opposite the dining table. A couple times, I have come in and sat at this very table and done photo edits while enjoying one of their bowls. It can be noisy at times, but it doesn't bother me when I get in the zone.

The woman before me pays and leaves. I head for the register and am surprised when I spot my favorite bowl packed into a container and waiting for me. Setting my juice down, she bags everything and I pay.

"Thanks for remembering," I tell her. Perhaps I visit more than I realize. Guess there are worse addictions to have.

"You're welcome. Have a great one," she says and waves as I go.

I decide to drive along Edgewater and am glad I do. The sun is barely in the sky, so the hues are soft and muted and it makes for a beautiful morning and backdrop to wake up to. For me, to love photography is to love getting lost in everything. Landscape and architecture and strangers. Everything and everyone has its own beauty. My job is to locate that one angle or profile or perfect lighting and accentuate it. The job is equal parts challenging and artistic. Keeps my blood pumping and my mind churning.

I glimpse the skyline as I drive over the Memorial Causeway. If it remains a little cloudy, it will be perfect for taking photos. One less piece of equipment to lug on the beach.

Arriving at the hotel thirty minutes earlier than necessary, I park and take my breakfast to a bench by the sand. I sit and watch the surf, enjoying the quiet before all the bodies fill in the empty sand. I am two bites away from finishing when I see a familiar silhouette walking toward the hotel's guest gate on and off the beach.

Gavin.

For the love of all that is holy in this world. Some divine intervention needs to swoop down and rescue me from this man. As hard as I work to keep him at arm's length, failure takes residence in my veins. Gavin has been —and probably will always be—my one weakness. The boy who captured my heart, held it prisoner, and took it with him when he left.

Last night, for the first time in years, my sleep was shit. My mind cycled through every moment we were together. Remembering the way my skin heated when his fingers painted over my flesh. How he always found a way to touch me, even if it was only him tucking my hair behind my ear. The way his eyes held mine. As if nothing else mattered or ever would. And his smell… an odd mix of beach and pine. Nothing compared to Gavin's hypnotic scent.

All night, memories of him and us flickered through my head like an old black and white movie. And no matter how hard I tried, no matter what I did, the flashbacks wouldn't shut off. Eventually, exhaustion overtook me and I fell asleep. This was four hours ago.

Seeing him now, when he is himself and oblivious to my voyeurism, has my stomach doing somersaults. How much of Gavin is real and how much is for show? Working in an industry where you're in the limelight hardens you. Changes fragments and splinters of who you are. But in the end, how much of Gavin is still inside?

The Gavin I knew, those two perfect years, is not the same as the man walking inside the hotel. Yes, they are spitting images—time has been kind to him—but when it comes to personality… current Gavin is a douchebag. He has got an ego bigger than the state of Florida. And his general attitude could use a little love.

Parts of me want to believe it is forced; all for show. Yes, he was a bit confident when we were together, but he never displayed it in front of others like a badge of honor. Is he like this with his family? The day he acts like a dick in front of his parents is the day lightning strikes me down.

I finish the last of my bowl and toss my container and utensil in the recycling bin. Walking back to the car, I spot Erin pulling in and give her a wave. She parks near me and we start hauling equipment from our cars and into a collapsible buggy. We lock up and start walking to where we told Gavin to meet us.

Erin glances at me from the corner of her eye and her inspection weighs heavy. It is way too early for this. Too early for inquisitions and judgment. *Please don't let this be how my entire day goes.*

"Yes?"

"Nothing." She is quick to respond. "You look a little tired is all."

"Your assessment would be accurate. I had trouble sleeping last night."

If possible, she studies me harder. Her eyes narrow and her head tilts as she assesses me like a mother. "Any particular reason why?"

And seeing as I am fueled on three hours of sleep and the breakfast I just consumed, I fire off, "Oh, you know. Just another asshole I have to take pictures of." *Damn, I am feisty already.*

She stops walking and gasps, her hand flying over her mouth. "Did you just say that? Or am I hearing things?"

"Depends," I say. "What did you hear?"

She repeats my words and I hear the surprise in her tone. Yeah, today will suck. Challenging enough to be near the man who swore we would be together forever, let alone doing so on zero sleep. And zero sleep means my brain to mouth functionality does its own thing.

Fuck my life.

We approach the gate and spot Gavin. Erin waves his way and I give him a half-hearted smile. The action brief and cold and says *don't fuck with me today*. If he is able to still read me like he used to, I hope he reads me loud and clear. I don't have the time or patience for games or bullshit today.

He rises from the chair and offers to help us wheel the equipment to the beach. I happily forfeit my cart and follow in his wake as we go through the gate. After a minute of trudging through the sand, reality catches up to me.

"Hey." I tap his shoulder. "Where's your agent? Alyson, right?"

"Alyson," he confirms. "She said she's not feeling good. Thinks she caught a bug on the plane or something. She locked herself in her room and will only open the door for room service."

"That sucks. Is she okay with us still doing the shoot today?" I don't need to step on any toes. Or not follow a specific itinerary she set. In a single day, I learned the type of woman Alyson is—regimented. Organization isn't a bad quality. Just one I don't want to fuck with. Not with this shoot.

He peeks at me over his shoulder, a small, sweet smile touching his lips. A different smile than those he gave me yesterday. A smile that wakes me up further and quickens my pulse. *Fuck.*

"Yeah, it's fine. Most of the time, she stands there and hovers, checking emails and text messages. She feels obligated to be present in case something happens."

In case something happens? What does that mean?

"Like what?" I ask, my curiosity getting the best of me. If I had gotten better sleep, I probably wouldn't have asked. Maybe. Who really knows at this point.

He laughs, his body shaking from the extent of it. "One of her previous clients got a little too *involved* with things during the shoot. So now she's always on set with her clients. Either that or someone within the company."

I am still confused. I should have bought an espresso with my breakfast. "A little too involved?"

His smile glows brighter than the rising sun. "Yes. As in, unprofessional things occurred during the shoot. They were mutual, but it later caused issues."

Light bulb moment. One of her clients slept with a

photographer. While they were supposed to be doing the shoot. Woah. Seriously unethical.

"Well, she doesn't have to worry about that with us," I blurt out, mentally slapping the side of my head when I realize I had spoken the words aloud and not in my head. Foot meet mouth.

When I meet his eyes, an odd sadness lingers. I don't think the solemnity shadows him because I said we won't have sex while in the middle of working. No, I assume the actual reason digs deeper. The expansive roots wrapped tightly around one another. I shake off the thought and try to focus on where to take photos.

"Here," I belt out, then apologize for my volume. "Let's work from here."

Gavin nods and walks off for a minute, his hands resting on top of his head, fingers laced together. He walks ten, twenty, thirty feet down the beach before he stops and stares out at the vacant water. His eyes don't avert. His body a sand sculpture. And for a moment, I see the Gavin I knew all those years ago. Without armor or ego. Just the man.

Erin softly touches my shoulder and startles me. "Sorry," she says. "You okay?"

I meet her eyes a second, nod and return to watching Gavin. "I'll be okay." *I hope I will be okay. Please let me be okay.*

"If you need anything at all, say the word. Even if it's a breather."

My eyes fall back on her. Erin is such a great friend and I am beyond lucky to be surrounded by so many wonderful people. I place my hand over hers. "Thanks for always being here for me. I don't say thank you often enough."

She swats the air between us. "Some things don't have to be said, but I appreciate it nonetheless."

After Gavin walks back, we discuss the various images the brand is seeking and the photos we will shoot today. I recognize the moment when Gavin slips into model-mode—the shift in his expression, his body language more exposed, the wall he erects to protect the deeper parts of himself. The way he carries himself in model-mode, it is obvious he is not a model only for the attention or the paycheck. He enjoys the end result as well as what comes along with it.

He may have been a cocky prick yesterday. He may have pressed every button under my skin. But today, Gavin flaunts an unexpected side of himself. One rawer and more appealing. One he should show more frequently when working. A side most photographers would drool over.

Is it because of Alyson's absence? Does she smother this side of him?

We take numerous shots with him in the board shorts, shirt, and flip-flops. We scroll through several of the images, hemming and hawing. After he and I are satisfied with what has been taken, we move to the next feature. Gavin in board shorts only.

Yes, I have seen Gavin naked. Yes, I understand Gavin will not be naked for the shoot. But does that halt the rapid flutter of butterflies beneath my breastbone? Nope, not one bit. Does the idea cause my breath to hitch? One-hundred-percent. Like a damn teenager again.

He kicks the shoes off, flinging them toward the cart. A small laugh erupts from his chest as he catches me ogling him, my eyes averting and coming back faster than a ping-pong ball. In my semi-awake state, there is no point in resisting what I want. Like alcohol, sleeplessness drops your inhibitions. Makes you do things your rational mind would lecture you on.

Erin giggles under her breath and I give her a *shut up* look. But as I turn to face Gavin again, he peels his shirt overhead with his back to me. As the cotton rises further up his back, I gasp and am certain he can hear it plain as day.

A tattoo inked into the flesh rests between his shoulder blades. Guessing, I would estimate it is six or seven inches wide and a foot tall. My shock isn't over the fact that Gavin has a tattoo. Not by a longshot. Really isn't too surprising, to be honest. What has me sucking in a breath is the art he selected to permanently etch into his skin.

When we were together, one of the things he always picked on me for was my love for *Lord of the Rings*. He would joke with me and tell me I couldn't watch it anymore because I knew every line and scene. I would rebut and tell him he was just jealous and wished he could be as cool as me. A nonstop banterfest over my adoration of the movies.

Now… I stare at the back of his torso, my jaw slack, tongue tasting the salty air. I rub my eyes for good measure, to check if what I am seeing is real. To make sure I'm not still sleeping. I drag my hands away and stare at his back. Yep, still there.

There it rests, in all its glory. A tattoo of the tree of Gondor, seven stars hovering above the limbs, a word in elvish above and below the tree.

As for me, I have no words.

Before I turn to see her reaction, I hear her gasp. An obvious reaction because she sees my tattoo. But I am also curious if her elvish is as good as it once was. When I peek over my shoulder and see she works to decipher the words, a smirk kicks up my lips. *She doesn't remember. Good.* It will give her something to work on while I am here.

She catches me studying her and stutters. "Wha… are you… y-you had…"

This moment will definitely get stored in my memory bank. Her lack of speech and wide-eyed ogle is absolutely adorable. "Use your words, Cora," I tease as I turn to face her.

"Shut up," she retorts. "Since when do *you* love the *Lord of the Rings* that much?" Her eyes dance obsessively over my skin and I love the fire it stirs inside of me. A flickering flame swelling to an inferno. Will she stare at me longer if I don't answer her immediately?

I shrug. "Someone I know watches it a lot. Guess it kind of stuck with me."

Like you did. I long to say the words, but resist the temptation. Not speaking my mind with her is the hardest challenge I have faced in years. Almost all of my life-challenging moments revolve around Cora. But I won't tell her that. For starters, she probably wouldn't believe me.

Her eyes dance back and forth between mine like she is reading between the lines of my soul, seeking clues to hundreds of unanswered questions. I would love nothing more than to profess my feelings to her. Tell her I never stopped loving her. Share with her the reason I didn't call or write after her last letter. A million words rest on the tip of my tongue, but I won't say them. Not now.

Because now is not the time.

When the timing is right, I will know. And when the time arrives, I will tell her everything. Confess all the fractured pieces of my soul. Spill my heart on the pavement.

As for now, I watch her and wait. Wait for her eyes to unlock from mine. For her to look down my body and absorb me. The temptation is there. Just below the surface. But her actions remain guarded and unsure. She wants to scan me head to toe, but doesn't want me to watch her observation in action.

Too fucking bad, tu es les étoiles de ma lune. We aren't kids anymore. And I enjoy as each second passes and her eyes linger. As they fight against the tide.

We are at a standoff. Pure, undiluted energy spills off her in waves. Anxious and molten and a touch of exasperation. As much as I hate making her this way, frustrating her more than turns me on.

The waves crash along the shore. Children scream in delight, ordering their parents to join them in the water. A dog barks nearby, excited for its owner to play with them.

Meanwhile, clouds pass, dimming and brightening the sky around us. Cora refuses to cave, but she forgets how well

I know her. Forgets, regardless of the amount of time we have spent apart, that I can read her body like Braille. I know her tells. Know what each arch and bow and breath and flush means. Know her stubbornness and passion and strength. But I also know her weakness. A commonality we share.

When you are acquainted with another person like I am Cora, you don't forget those little snippets. They are rare gems and get tucked away for safekeeping. She may not be the woman from thirteen years ago, but some traits never vanish. They adjust with the journey.

She tries to disguise it, but I know she sighs. Know she is throwing in the towel.

Her eyes fall to my lips, lingering for a moment. Her tongue sweeps out and brushes across her lower lip. The sight sends a pang to my groin, but I control my actions and don't let her see how it affects me. How it makes me want her more.

When she leaves my lips, her eyes trace my throat in no hurry. Skirting from one shoulder, across my collarbones, and landing on the other. Her eyes drop and her body jerks in shock as a brief smirk pops on my lips.

"Like what you see?" I rasp, my voice thick with the desire my body masks.

Her eyes shoot back to mine as her mouth opens and closes and opens again. "When did you…" She points to my chest, unable to finish the question.

"Get my nipples pierced?" I finish what I assume she was going to ask.

"Yes," she sputters. "When did you do that?"

How cute is it that she flushes a scarlet resembling her cherry lips? How cute is it that she is embarrassed to ask about my nipple piercings? "A few years back."

"Oh. Huh. Well, I'm not sure how to compliment them," she mumbles.

"The same way you compliment anything else." I put on my best impression of her voice. "*Hey, Gavin. Those nipple piercings are hot.*" I bite my lip to resist laughing.

She smacks my chest, hard. "Shut up, asshole."

"Ow. I think that's going to leave a mark," I tease.

"Shit! I'm sorry. Damnit. Now we'll have to wait. Can't have red handprints on your chest in the photos." She places a finger over her lips. "Although, I could just Photoshop it out." She shrugs, noncommittal.

"You're the one running the show. If you want to take handprint photos, then that's what we'll do."

She cocks her head to the side, a curious look about her. I may be able to still read her, but she has lost that finesse with me. I have had years to learn how to plaster on a different face. To pretend to be someone I am not. That is the thing with actors and models, we are taught how to be someone else. To be whoever the camera or customer is supposed to see. We live different lives and portray different personalities daily.

We are a façade.

"Since the light has shifted, let's move over there." She points over to a patch of seagrass. "Different light, different background, different reach."

"You're the boss." In more ways than one.

Time becomes this nonexistent entity when I am near Cora. Hours pass as if time is a delusion. Tons of pictures get taken in various places along this stretch of the beach. As nervous as I originally was for this campaign, posing for the camera while Cora looks through the lens gives me an ease I haven't felt in a long time. Being in her presence has never felt more right.

Like coming home. *My home.*

I help her and Erin put everything in their carts, hauling Cora's to her car after. Everything gets unloaded into the cars and we wave goodbye to Erin as she drives away. Erin is a sweet girl—timid but a devoted friend to Cora. And for a time today, I forgot she was on the beach with us. Obviously, she assists Cora with her shoots, but most of the time she hangs on the sidelines, quiet.

After she drives out of the lot, I face Cora and my fingers brush against hers. Flickers spark from our minor touch and I feel compelled to touch her again. More. Trace my fingers along her forearm, her bicep, her collarbone. My eyes flit to her throat as she swallows hard. I finish the ascent, her eyes riveted to mine.

Our eyes have a silent standoff. Questions appear as quickly as they disappear.

"Have dinner with me," I state.

Last time I asked, she said no. Now I want it more like a command, but not in a *you must do this* way. More of a *just agree with me* way. I want her to want to say yes.

The motion is subtle, but she shakes her head as she drops her chin and breaks eye contact. "I can't. You know I can't. It goes against the contract we've both signed."

I stare down at my feet and hers, shaking my head. "Bullshit," I mutter.

My irritation isn't directed at her, more the situation. But I bet she takes it as the former. The last thing I am is upset with her. She has to know this. Right?

"You know we can't," she whispers, refusing to look at me.

But I need to see her eyes. Need to know what she is really thinking. Her eyes will tell me all the words her mouth refuses to speak.

Tucking a finger under her chin, I lift and bring her eyes back to mine. She has told me no twice, but her eyes tell another story. They speak of her hesitation and fear. Worried if she says yes that I will hurt her again. And I want to reassure her that will never happen again, but how can I? Words are useless. Especially with our past. Only my actions will supersede my words.

Plus, the evidence is stacked against us.

She lives here. I live thousands of miles across the country. Her life is here. My life is out west.

With reluctance, I lean in close to her ear and whisper, "True, but you don't know how much I want to."

And with that, I step back, drop my hand, and walk back to the hotel. To my empty hotel room. My soundless existence. My life without her.

Sleeplessness has become a plague since Gavin walked through those banquet doors two days ago. When my head hit the pillow last night, my body melted against the sheets as exhaustion radiated in my bones. Luna curled up beside me, her purr fading as she drifted to sleep.

With heavy eyes, my lids closed. Just as my body began hitting solid sleep, my phone wailed on my dresser. I shot up as worry flooded me. My *Do Not Disturb* mode set and only select people could break through the function.

When I answered the phone in a groggy voice, Shelly instantly apologized. She had called on a whim, wanting to hang out but not knowing I had gone to bed early. I asked her why she really called and she told me we could talk about it in the morning.

But I was exhausted and angry and allowed my frustrations to sneak out and snap at her. Two minutes of apology later—and zero information as to why she called—and we agreed to talk tomorrow. Several times, she had done this to me and the conversation consisted of nothing significant. But I was a good friend and I let it slide.

Unfortunate for me, sleep didn't creep up as easily after as it did before her disruption.

I laid in my bed until two-thirty in the morning, thinking about the rough texture of Gavin's hands when they were on me earlier. And the words he whispered to me, I listened to them on a loop in my head, trying to decipher what exactly he was saying.

Were his words genuine? Did he just say those things to get into my pants? Or is it all a load of bullshit?

I felt clueless, and the lack of sleep didn't help the situation. There had to be some hidden meaning behind it. There just had to be. In the wee hours of the morning, I convinced myself Gavin had an ulterior motive.

After hours of watching the ceiling fan spin circles above me, my body relaxed enough and I fell asleep.

My alarm startles me awake at six forty-five and I slap the beast, groaning and cursing the universe. A little more than four hours of sleep won't get me far today. Not after having five and a half the night before.

I cannot live like this. Anyone glancing my way today will surely do a double take—because my resemblance to a zombie will be uncanny—and whisper behind my back. Honestly, I give no fucks.

Luna paws at my face, meowing and purring. "At least one of us gets sleep," I grumble as I run a hand over her soft fur.

She rubs her face along my cheek, silently asking me to get up and give her breakfast. Shoving the comforter to my waist, I huff and scoot up to a sitting position. Luna meows her excitement, jumps off the bed, and trots out of the bedroom. I follow behind her, walking half alert to the kitchen. Thankfully, this part of the morning routine requires no brainpower.

One scoop of food and a few pets later, Luna purrs like a champ while she eats. I wish my morning could be so simple. Wake up whenever, disturb my parental, make them feed me, then go about my day. If only…

I head for the bathroom and jerk back when I see myself in the mirror.

Hot. Fucking. Mess.

A hot shower and a smear of makeup can only do so much. By the looks of it, I need a couple bottles of concealer. Fingers crossed I can perform miracles and mask the dark half-moons under my eyes. *Lord, help me.*

After my shower, I dress and do my makeup, adding more concealer than normal. Not two bottles worth, but enough to feel like I now have three additional layers of skin. I snag my phone from the charger and sift through my notifications while I eat a quick breakfast.

One of the first alerts I see… an email from Alyson Jameson, Gavin's agent. Emails in the middle of a shoot gives me hives. Especially after the comment Gavin made yesterday about one of Alyson's prior clients.

My finger taps on the notification and my email opens. Eyes scanning the email, I read the message twice, making sure I read and decipher it accurately.

Ms. Davies,

I would like to extend a personal thank you for your time. Sorry I missed yesterday's photo shoot due to circumstances I couldn't prevent. Today is a new day.

Tonight, we would like to sit down with you and talk

about the remaining days. Please join us for dinner at the Island Way Grill at six thirty p.m.

Cordially,
Alyson Jameson

Why is she calling a dinner meeting to discuss the photo shoot? Seems odd. The itinerary is written and has been reviewed countless times before this week. By myself, the agent, and the company.

Shit.

Did she see me and Gavin last night in the parking lot? Not that there was anything noteworthy. Nothing inappropriate or unprofessional occurred. But that is the only possible reason I can think of as to why she is requesting I meet with them for dinner.

Taking my remaining breakfast to the garbage can, I scrape the last few bites into the bag. At least I had eaten the majority of the food before the taste turned bitter on my tongue. As long as it stays down, everything will be alright.

I do a few last-minute checks in the house before grabbing my purse and heading to my car. My head in a fog, a list of scenarios running rampant in my head as to why we are having a dinner meeting. The distraction gets the best of me and before I realize what is happening, I trip over an uneven paver and fall face-first into the grass. I turn my head and grimace at the paver I have been meaning to fix for months but have ignored.

"Shit," I curse into the wind.

It is my fault, I recognize this. But it doesn't make it hurt less.

What I need to do is focus. Quit worrying over *what if* and pay attention to *what is*. And right now, my sole focus is this photo shoot. Not the man whose picture I take this week. This is my job, my livelihood. The only thing that will remain constant when he leaves again. Because he will leave again.

Thirty minutes later, I wind through the two-lane road inside Sand Key Park. The sun hasn't been up long, which is why the park remains quiet. None of the locals, or spring breakers, have arrived yet. But within an hour or two, this place will be inundated with exposed flesh and sunscreen.

Driving past a few covered shelters, I glimpse the birds and squirrels as they peck at the semi-scraped BBQ grills in hopes they will find a morsel. Half a minute later, the road winds left and I near more shelters, restrooms, and the beach access parking. This park is the perfect mix of park-life and beach-life. And makes an excellent backdrop for any outdoor photo shoot in the area.

I park the car and feed the meter station. Leaving my equipment in the car, I walk down the path leading to the beach and look for potential places to work today. Sitting on a boulder-sized rock, I stare out at the water and get lost for a moment.

Although my job takes me to various locations, I never have the time to stop and enjoy where I am. The beach is great at times—in the early morning or late evening. But I love wandering in the parks and nature preserves. There is something magical about being in the thick of nature. Disconnecting from life and reconnecting with yourself. Forgetting about social media or texts or all the distractions and simply focusing on you.

And in my zoned-out mindset, I recall the occasions when Gavin and I would play-bicker over the beach versus the park. How he stated the beach was superior because of sunsets (on our coast) and sunrises (the east coast). My rebuttal consisted of how the sunlight filtered through the trees and the connection with the earth. We debated over it for hours before deciding it didn't matter.

Spotting a few places, I head back to the car and wait for Erin to arrive. As I take out the last few things I will need, I hear a car and look up. Erin waves at me as she parks in the space beside me.

"Morning," she hollers as she gets out of the car. "Present!"

I am momentarily confused until I see her retrieve and then hand me an oversized iced coconut milk matcha latte and a chocolate croissant from a local bakery.

Swooning at the treats, I kiss her cheek and snatch them from her. "Have I told you how much I love you?" I ask as I bite into the sweet pastry and moan.

Two seconds later, I regret that moan. Because that is the exact moment Gavin walks up behind me, rests his hands on my hips, and scares the shit out of me.

"That's a sound I haven't heard in years," he says then smirks.

Almost dropping my drink, I whip around and glare at him. "JFC, Gavin. You scared the bejesus out of me."

He laughs before asking, "JFC?"

Erin shakes her head and answers his question, noticing how I am hunched over and still trying to catch my breath. "It stands for Jesus fucking Christ. She uses the acronym in public, so she doesn't offend anyone."

"Ah," he lilts. "Still so considerate of everyone else. Good to see the good qualities haven't changed."

Briefly, I want to ask what other qualities he remembers. Or consider good? But I opt not to. The last thing I need after a second night of shitty sleep is a trip down memory lane. Because memory lane when you're not altogether there is a dangerous setup.

Once I locate my voice, I scold him. "Don't do that again! You know how much I don't like people sneaking up on me."

His smile is subtle, falling away as quickly as it appears. His actions were intentional and got the result he was hoping for, that much I read from his smirk. "I can't make any promises, but I'll try." Great, now Gavin plans to use my quirks against me.

I look around the lot, expecting to see Alyson. Although she spends a great deal of time on her phone, she seems the type to be involved. Especially after receiving her email earlier. But she is nowhere in sight. "Where's your agent?"

Gavin gazes out toward the beach, his sunglasses shielding his eyes from mine. "She'll be here soon. After yesterday, she's taking her time waking up today. Says she may have had a twenty-four-hour bug or food poisoning. She's not sure, but doesn't want to run full force this morning."

I let Erin know the three places I want to be sure we shoot today. We take a few minutes to prioritize the order, guaranteeing the best shots with the least amount of beachgoers, and how to use the natural lighting to our advantage in each spot.

When we finish talking strategy, I glance around the lot again and something dawns on me. "Gavin, how did you get here?"

"I walked," he replies flatly. As if it should be obvious.

But for all I know, he could have gotten an Uber and let them drop him off at the entrance of the park.

"*Over the bridge?* The walk is long enough, but that incline is ridiculous." Walking the distance probably wasn't too bad. It was maybe three miles. But with the traffic, the tourists, and the bridge incline, I would have fallen over by now. Not to mention the mix of humidity and sweat.

As if he can hear my thoughts, a smile perches on his lips. "I've hiked worse trails in Cali. I didn't even break a sweat. Should give it a try sometime."

Shrugging him off, I face Erin as we toss everything in one cart today. Today's shoot should be easier and less obstructed than yesterday.

As I reach for the cart handle, Gavin does also. Our fingers touch for two breaths, and that old familiar current buzzes up my arms and slithers directly to my chest. Warm and comforting and libidinous. I yank mine away and try not to think about why my body is reacting to his. After everything that happened and how much time has passed, no part of me should be thrilled or eager or accepting. If anything, his touch should garner loss and heartbreak and depression.

He laughs at me, gestures with his other hand in front of him. "Lead the way, boss."

"Shouldn't we wait for Alyson?" I ask. Definitely don't need his agent pissed because we didn't wait for her arrival.

"When we get to wherever, I'll text her. Don't worry about it," Gavin says breezily.

But therein lies the problem… I am worried about it.

ten

GAVIN

Being near Cora intoxicates me. After so many years apart, and seeing her for hours each day since I arrived, it has been a challenge to feign my feelings. If I thought leaving her the first time was difficult, this time will be a hundred times worse. If not more.

But what if it didn't have to be that way? What if we didn't have to go our separate ways after the photo shoot?

Both our careers allow flexibility. And I am sure she travels for work as much as I do. So why couldn't things be different now? Our circumstances are not what they were thirteen years ago. We are no longer children, forced to go where our family takes us. We are adults, and we decide how to run our lives.

So why can we not make this work? Why can we not give *us* another shot?

I want to tell her this. Tell her I would like—after this shoot is over—to try and get back to where we were. Although we are no longer the same people we once were, my feelings for her have never waned. If anything, they have only amplified over time, not revealing themselves until I prepared to board that plane in Los Angeles.

We stand near a jetty of rocks. Cora and Erin mess with cameras and equipment as they prep for the shoot. Knowing they don't need assistance from me, I wander toward the water. Silent and deep in thought.

"You okay?" Cora asks before I step out of earshot.

I peek over my shoulder at her, subtly smile, and nod. "Yeah, I'm good."

After about fifteen feet, I stop and stare out at the Gulf. The water crashes against the rocks and sand in choppy, small waves. Salt absorbs the humidity and dampens my skin. Seaweed and the earthy scent of sand permeate my nose. The rising sun warms my exposed arms and legs. And I am thankful this time of year isn't scorching, but the heat will be here soon enough. That is one thing I don't miss—the heat. Sure, California gets hot, but it's not equivalent to Florida and neither is the humidity.

I get lost in my thoughts, working to clear my head, when flip-flops smack in the sand behind me. But I don't turn toward the sound. Instead, I close my eyes and imagine what it would be like to be here with her without our jobs in the mix. To slip my fingers between hers and walk hand in hand down the beach. To watch the sunset together and talk about everything we have missed about each other. And kiss her lips for the first time in forever. To simply just exist with her at my side.

Absolute perfection.

Warm, delicate fingers brush down my bicep, stopping at my elbow. I stop breathing.

"Gavin," she whispers. "We're ready when you are. Take your time."

I glance over my shoulder at her and give a small smile. "I'll be just a second," I rasp, my voice rattled with emotion. I swallow, aiming to moisten my suddenly dry throat. As much moisture as there is in the air, you would think there is no possible way to be parched.

She nods and I watch as she walks back over to where Erin stands. They talk quietly and I am unable to hear them over the waves hitting the rocks. When I start walking their way, I catch how Cora peeks up at me then looks away. A step later, Erin mimics her. Interesting.

I conclude with this minor detail they're talking about me. And as soon as I reach them, they both fall silent. Yep, they were most definitely gossiping about me. The idea does strange things to me. Twists my stomach in heart-shaped knots. Alters my breathing pattern into an odd staccato. Adds a new layer of sweat beneath my salty, humid skin. Makes my fingers fidget enough that I want to shove them in my pockets. Pockets I don't have today.

Cora's eyes refuse to meet mine. If honest with myself, I would venture to guess she is avoiding eye contact on purpose. But her avoidance isn't cold. It's as if she donned a new suit of armor, the type designed for the sole purpose of protecting one's heart. Her heart. The same heart I shattered into a million shards. And another blade stabs me for what I did to her. What I could have fixed if I had the balls to do it.

My heart beats so violently, as if it's trying to rip its way out of my chest. But the pericardium encasing my heart holds it back, restrains me, as hers does the same. I have to keep reminding myself, I am the reason for her walls. I am the reason she keeps telling me no. But I also hope to be the reason those walls come down.

We are ten minutes into the shoot when Alyson

approaches. For someone who said she was on death's door yesterday, she looks a few shades tanner. Maybe it's the white summer apparel she wears, making her skin pop against the stark color. Or maybe she wanted to enjoy a little downtime while here, knowing she could trust me to do the right thing.

No matter. Neither scenario bothers me. Just glad she is okay. Alyson may be the bridezilla version of a talent agent, but I have known her years and still care about her as a person.

We finish up shooting near the rocks, then spend an hour snapping photos by seagrasses. The shoot wraps after we take numerous photos on a path resembling a pier in the sand. Cora takes photos from several different angles and I honestly cannot wait to see the end results.

Erin packs a few things into the cart when I approach Cora. "So, I'll see you at six-thirty?"

She checks her watch, noting our dinner is a little more than three hours from now. "Yes, I'll be there. I let Alyson know earlier."

Right, Alyson. I ignore the idea of Alyson disrupting dinner and change the topic.

"Do you need help?" I point to the cart.

"No, I'm good. Thanks, though."

We all shuffle back to the cars. And although I walked here this morning, the temperature is much warmer now and I don't want to spend over an hour with the heat beating down on me. I ask Alyson for a ride back. She concedes and we hop in the rental after saying goodbye to Cora and Erin.

We are out of the park and turning off the bridge when Alyson turns down the radio, muting the local rock station. "So, what's the plan for tonight?"

I peer over at her, her eyes glued to the road as she

watches for pedestrians. "Not sure I understand the question," I answer. I have an idea of where this is headed, but I won't put words in her mouth or give her fuel for the fire.

Stopped at a red light for Hamden Drive, she faces me a second and then returns her eyes to the street. "The dinner *meeting*." I don't miss the way she emphasizes the word meeting. Her tone mirroring a bad taste on her tongue. Yep. Just as I suspected.

"I thought we already discussed this. I really don't feel like repeating myself," I clip.

She turns onto Hamden and we wade through traffic for the next twenty minutes. Not another word passes between us and the silence leans more toward uncomfortable than not.

Once she parks the car, we head into the hotel. I press the call button for the elevator and notice her slight fidget as we wait.

Is she nervous? Why the hell would she be nervous?

"You okay?" I ask as the elevator car arrives and we step in.

We press the buttons for our respective floors and the doors close. Once we are in the confines of the elevator, she answers, "I'm fine. Just…"

I hold up a hand, stopping her from continuing. Already aware of what she is going to say. She is warning me. Telling me to *be on my best behavior*. As if I am a fucking child. As if I am her former client who liked to stick his dick in anything with a hole. I understand her role in our business relationship, but she needs to give me some slack. She needs to trust me.

The elevator pings for her floor and she hesitates a moment. A second later, she steps out and faces me. "Enjoy your dinner, Gavin."

I nod, a snide smile on my face. *Thanks, I will.*

~

Searching through my memory, I cannot recall a time I remember being as nervous as I am right now. It has been ten minutes since the host seated me. Eight minutes since the server came to the table, pouring two glasses of ice water and asking if I would prefer something else to drink. Five minutes since I picked up the menu, scanned the options but didn't read a single word of it.

But none of that matters. None of it.

As I twist and untwist the cloth napkin in my lap, the only thing that matters is standing at the host podium. She is utter perfection. And I am second-guessing this whole situation I masterminded.

While she waits for the host to return and direct her to the table, I sit in silence and watch her. Her silky, straight hair grazes the tops of her shoulders. The inky black strands parted off-center, the side with less hair tucked behind her ear. The other side hangs straight and blankets half of her cheek.

God, I miss running my fingers through her hair.

She bounces from one leg to the other as she waits, her bare calves accentuated by the black chunky-heeled Mary Jane's she wears. My eyes stroll up the length of her body, pausing and relishing on the dress that stops just above her knees. It hugs her body like a glove. Matching her hair and shoes, it's black in color but embellished with large rivets.

This is my Cora. The girl I knew all those years ago. The girl I fell in love with. The woman I still love.

Regardless of how much time has passed, she still manages to keep the root of who she is alive. And although she dresses as expected for her career, she hasn't abandoned who she is at heart.

The host returns to the podium and they exchange words, her smile lighting up the room before he turns to walk her to the table. Should I keep my eyes on her? Or should I avert my gaze and play it cool? As if I wait for her arrival disinterested.

The napkin rubs against my palms as I wring the cloth tighter. When she sees me—and only me—her brows scrunch in question. She stands ten feet from the table when a bead of sweat rolls down the side of my neck. Five feet when I swallow the boulder in my throat.

I can do this.

"Hey," I stammer as she sits, the host unfolding her napkin and offering to place it in her lap.

Once the host walks away, she looks around the room before circling back to me. "Hi," she says. "Where's Alyson?"

I don't want to lie to her, but I fear what she will do when I tell her the truth. If I ever want anything more with her again, I can't lie. Honesty is essential. No matter the consequences.

"Not sure. She's doing her own thing. Exploring the area and whatnot."

I mentally prepare for the backlash. The anger. For her to get up and stomp off and not talk to me again. Because she has to be upset at the fact that I coordinated a dinner with her and made her believe it was a meeting.

My eyes dart between hers, watching her expression and waiting for the fire that is bound to blaze at any moment. But I don't see anger. Confusion still paints lines on her forehead, her eyes pinching at the corners.

"So, there's no meeting?"

"Sorry to disappoint," I tell her.

Her shoulders drop as she exhales a deep breath. *Was the idea of having a meeting a concern for her?* I hadn't read the email Alyson sent Cora, but I told her to make certain it was vague. Had it been so vague she was concerned for her job? *Shit.*

"You okay?" I ask.

"Yeah. I've just been pondering over why we were having a meeting. Everything has been laid out since the beginning, so I wasn't sure if something had changed. I'm relieved everything's good." She takes a sip of her water, sets the glass down, and then points her finger at me. "You, on the other hand, I'm a little peeved at."

I knew I wouldn't be let off the hook so easily, but I feign innocence for shiggles. "Me? What did I do?" I press a hand against my chest and pop my mouth open in mock horror.

"Please," she drawls out the word, lacing it with sarcasm and making me smile. "You've asked me to have dinner with you twice. Both times I've told you no. So instead of hearing a third rejection, you tell your *I'll-kiss-your-ass-every-day-of-the-week* agent to orchestrate a phony dinner meeting and not be at said meeting. Am I missing anything?"

Her spunk and tenacity spark a thrill in my chest, a fire I haven't felt in years. If anything, her spunk seems to have grown. I would give up everything to keep our fire burning. To keep her.

"You kept saying no. How else am I supposed to get you to have dinner with me?" I joke.

She rolls her eyes. "I don't know, maybe ask another time or two. I would've caved."

That's an admission I wasn't expecting. *She would have given in? She would have said yes?* This adds a whole new layer to our already complicated situation. I open my mouth to respond, but have absolutely no idea what to say. So, I close my mouth and simply stare at her awestruck.

"Yes. Eventually I would have said yes," she admits.

Wait… what? "Did I just say that out loud?"

"If you mean, *she would have said yes?* Then yes, you said it out loud."

Fuck my head for not operating at full capacity.

"Well, I'm humiliated," I tell her, heat crawling up my neck and scorching my face. I pick up my water and down half the glass.

"Gavin…" she says my name like it's her favorite, and not, at the same time. "I need this contract. This is huge for me." Her words are a plea for understanding. "I can't risk messing it up. This shoot will be the most valuable item on my future resume. When future clients see that I've done a shoot for Global Beach Magazine, it'll push me to the next level. Open doors I've dreamed about for years."

I stare at the empty white plate in front of me, nodding in realization. Me asking her to dinner could royally screw her career. The contract we each signed explicitly stated no fraternization between the model and photographer. And my selfishness could fuck that up for her. "Sorry," I whisper.

She reaches over and places her hand on mine. The heat from her skin penetrates mine, sending a ripple of emotions from my fingertips to my core. I have no idea how I survived the last thirteen years without her. Without her touch, without her embrace, without her lips on mine.

"Don't apologize. I just need you to understand. This career is my life and I have to be careful not to jeopardize it," Cora states as her forehead scrunches.

"I get it. Things are somewhat the same for me. Sure, I could justify us having dinner together as being old friends, but I know it's more than that. At least it is for me."

Cora opens her mouth to respond, but is cut off when the

server sidles up beside the table and asks for our drink orders. We order drinks, telling the server we need a few more minutes before ordering our meals.

The moment he walks away, I catch her watching me. Her green eyes soft and caring. She doesn't say a word. Doesn't have to. We lock eyes for twenty rapid beats of my heart before my eyes break away first.

I am so fucked.

"We should probably decide what we're eating before the server returns," I tell her.

With a nod, she removes her hand from mine and picks up her menu. The heat she ignited minutes ago… it evaporates the second her skin leaves mine.

And now, I will do whatever necessary to have it again.

eleven

CORA

After the server takes our dinner order, Gavin and I fall into comfortable conversation. Although we had once known everything about each other, there is so much we don't know now. We spend the time, before our dinner arrives, playing twenty questions.

I ask him about California. What he likes and dislikes. His favorite places there. Where else he has traveled for work. What he does when he isn't working.

As challenging as it is, I do my best to steer clear of the topic of him leaving. The first time as well as the next time. It's inevitable he will leave again. And as much as I hate the idea of him leaving, I remind myself of this regularly. His home is thousands of miles from here. Everything he has is there—family, career, friends—waiting for him to return.

Another topic I dare not mention… relationship status. His or my own.

The way he has acted around me, I am unsure how to digest it all. Is it just old feelings coming to the surface because he is here again? Does he act like this with other women photographers? Or women of interest in general? Is he a player? Is he playing me?

But the biggest of them all… does he have someone waiting in California for his return?

After all these years, there is no way Gavin is single. It isn't possible. Yes, he is busy with his career. But a busy career doesn't equal single status. Not with his good looks.

My endless mental list of questions is disrupted when the server sets a plate of coconut shrimp and coconut almond rice in front of me. I lean over the plate and inhale the delicious aroma, moaning my delight.

Gavin laughs, "Now that's a sound I haven't heard in a long time. Not quite the same as your breakfast today." He gazes at me with a tenderness I haven't seen in a long time. A tenderness I am all too familiar with. Hummingbirds take flight in my chest, flapping their wings beneath my sternum and causing palpitations.

I play it off and swat him with my napkin. "Shut up," I say with a giggle.

We eat and laugh and share great conversation over dinner. Being here with Gavin feels normal. Natural. When we finish eating, he asks if I will meet him at an ice cream shop across from his hotel. Without hesitation, I tell him yes.

Tonight has been fun. It has been a long time since I have been this relaxed and more myself. As if a part of me has returned with Gavin here. I miss that part of myself. The carefree, jubilant, and eccentric girl. He has been the only person who loved every side of me. And the only person I have exposed so much of myself to.

When he moved away, a slice of me went with him. The piece of me reserved only for him. The piece that feels as if it has returned home.

We stroll down Mandalay Avenue, hands clasped while he eats a cone topped with cookie dough ice cream and mine topped with mint avalanche. Our hands swing between us, our lips silent as we consume our confections.

Simple moments like this are ones I will never forget. Memories stashed away for the days when he is gone. Memories of all the wonderful times we have shared.

We don't need to say anything. We don't have to do anything. As long as it is just us, everything in life is perfect. Our time apart resides in some nether region of the universe.

At a crosswalk, we wait for the traffic to stop and move to the beachside of the street. He leads us down one of the small side streets and toward a public access point for the beach. As he pops the last of his cone in his mouth, he bends and begins removing his shoes.

"Will you walk with me?" he asks as he stands upright. His love for the beach hasn't vanished over the years. He was lucky his mom's promotion led them to another coastal state. If Gavin didn't have the beach, I don't think he would be whole. Not sure if it's the sand or the water or the salty air, but Gavin was born to be near a beach.

Part of me wants to give him a hard time and say *isn't that what we've been doing?* But I stop myself. It's one thing to weave in and out of people on a busy, pedestrian-loaded street. It is completely different to step onto the fine-grained beach, barefoot, and walk in the dark along the surf holding someone's hand. Though the beach may not be pitch black, it's dark enough to make the level of intimacy go from zero to one hundred in seconds.

He studies my face, waiting for me to answer. I take the last bite of my cone, buying myself a few more seconds. I reach forward and take his hand again, squeeze it gently and nod. Before I bend down to remove my shoes, I catch a glimpse of the smile I remember. The smile that flashes in my memories. The smile that lured me in when I was fourteen.

~

I park in my driveway and grab my purse and shoes from the passenger seat before getting out. My thoughts swim and swirl and blend together. Old memories of Gavin and me. Happy memories. Memories I will never forget.

Once inside, I add food to Luna's bowl and pet her a few times before heading for my bedroom. I toss my shoes in the closet and strip off my dress, heading for the shower. The walk on the beach with Gavin was wonderful, but I need to wash the sticky beach air and sand off my skin.

With a towel wrapped around my torso, I dig through my dresser and grab a pair of boy shorts and a tank top. Clad in my nightwear, I plop down on my bed and flick on the television, scanning Netflix for something to watch. I pick a random movie, which ends up becoming background noise to my racing mind.

A pair of warm hands cover my eyes, too large to belong to any girl I know. His hot breath on my ear sends a chill down my spine. My breath hitches and my heart beats as if it will never have the chance after today.

"Guess who..." his whisper like sun and thunder and a bolt of lightning to my heart.

"Hmm..." I toy with him. "I can't be sure. Jake?" I tease.

His hands rip from my eyes, the bright light instantly returns and makes me squint. "Who?" He spins me around and hugs me so tight I can't speak.

"Nope, not Jake," I joke again.

"Who the hell is Jake?" he asks, defensive.

I love it when he becomes possessive. "I don't know. Just made up the name to mess with you. Of course I knew it was you." Pushing up onto my tiptoes, I press a kiss on the corner of his mouth. "Don't be mad."

"I'm not mad," he mumbles, but the grumpy doesn't leave his face. We are about to turn the corner in the hallway when he lifts me up and hoists me over his shoulder, fireman-style. Everyone at their lockers starts laughing at the spectacle. And it is most definitely a spectacle.

Because as he is walking down the hall with me over his shoulder, I am smacking his ass and kicking my feet in the air, begging for him to put me down. It wouldn't shock me if this scene floods the internet once it ends.

As we walk out the double doors, his stride grows faster and more urgent. He stops next to a big oak—our tree—and sets me on the ground, smacking my ass for good measure.

"Gavin! Why did you do that? That was so embarrassing." It was beyond embarrassing, yet I loved every second of it. Loved that he didn't care who was watching.

He takes a step closer to me, eliminating the empty space between us. I suck in a breath, my body straightening and my breasts brushing against his chest. His hands dance along my jawline before his fingers lace in my hair and he brings his mouth to mine.

He kisses me with such intensity, I forget how to breathe. His tongue traces over my lower lip and I open for him. Our tongues begin this wild dance, fevered and needy. Wolf whis-

tles erupt around us, but we ignore every one of them. It is just me and Gavin as the world disappears. And as quickly as the kiss began, it ends.

I grab hold of his biceps, dragging in ragged breaths while trying to calm my heart.

"You are forgiven," I tell him when my lungs settle.

He presses a sweet kiss to the center of my lips. "Thanks."

When he pulls away from our embrace, he looks over at the tree beside us. My eyes shift to see what he is looking at, and my jaw falls to the ground.

"When? How? Did you?" I fumble over what I am trying to ask him.

"This morning. With the pocket knife I snuck into school. And yes, I did."

My fingers brush over the chipped away bark. On the trunk of the tree, he has carved "C+G tu es les étoiles de ma lune." He had been taking French for the last three years, but I'd chosen Spanish and had no idea what this said.

"What does it mean?" I ask, my fingers still caressing each of the indentations he had made. Must have taken him a while.

He brushes the back of his index finger along my jawline to my chin. "It says 'the stars to my moon,'" he whispers, although I'm the only person close enough to hear.

My face hurts from the smile he has given me. "I love you, too."

A tear rolls down my cheek and I wonder if that tree—inside the confines of our high school—still displays our initials. Or if the bark has grown and covered it over the years. The younger, lovestruck part of me wants to visit the tree again. The tree where it all began. Our tree.

Luna curls up beside me, purring with vigor as I stroke her soft fur. And after a few minutes pass, I drift off to a deep sleep where I dream about trees and love and the starry skies above.

Today is the fourth day of the shoot and I am nervous as to how it will go.

Last night was one of the best times I have had in a while. We didn't do anything extravagant—a nice dinner, an ice cream cone, and a walk on the beach. Breezy conversation and a comfort that only comes with familiarity. It was better than any other night I have shared with a woman. And there is only one reason.

Cora.

Being near her again is like learning how to breathe for the first time in years. Sure, breathing happened while we were apart, but it was merely to exist until I found my way back to her. And it feels as if I have finally rediscovered her. I only hope she has managed to do the same.

During today's shoot, we are supposed to be strolling through parts of downtown Dunedin. Me in some hoity-toity outfit while Cora walks five to ten paces behind me, snapping photos of me "looking casual" on the street. Looking casual in my world translates into walking along the sidewalk and turning to look at something with your profile or whole face toward the camera. But don't look at the camera. Because looking at the camera is not natural, or so they say. Whatever.

It's all ridiculous if you ask me. But that's what the companies and consumers love. At least for this particular brand. The shoots for romance novels and risqué, they want your hungry eyes straight on. They want the consumer to feel as if you're reaching out and luring them in.

So, after my morning walk on the beach and a shower, I dress in a linen short-sleeve, white button-up, a pair of khaki cargo shorts with more pockets than I'd ever fill and a pair of boat-style shoes. And don't forget the chunky watch and dark-tint sunglasses. Each shoot's ensemble hangs in plastic wardrobe bags in my closet, labeled, courtesy of my wonderful agent.

The only part of this whole ensemble I would use again is probably the sunglasses. They mask the sun better than any pair I have owned in recent years. Lucky for me, I get to keep everything from the shoot.

Alyson and I meet in the lobby and walk to her rental car, sliding in and driving off the beach. The shoot doesn't start for a little more than an hour, so we agreed to grab breakfast nearby.

Once we are seated and place our breakfast orders, Alyson chimes in and starts asking about last night. I expect nothing less from her.

"So, how was dinner? Anything I need to be concerned over?" A look of genuine worry pinches her brow line.

"Dinner was good. She was worried at first, because she didn't see you. But after we talked for a few, everything went well."

"And I'll ask again. Anything I need to be concerned over?" Alyson persists.

"Nope. Just two old friends, eating together and sharing good conversation." Maybe if I say it enough times, I will start believing it myself. Because Cora and I will always be more than "old friends."

"And there were no flashes going off anywhere? From your phone or anyone else's?"

"I didn't catch any. No one around here knows me as a model. The only people who know me are the few friends I have still living here." If anyone recognizes me as a model while I'm here, shocked wouldn't begin to cover it. Yes, celebrities live in the area. But this isn't Los Angeles, and people aren't stalking celebrities. Not that I consider myself one. For the most part, when people spot celebrities here, they just whisper and go on with life.

She spins her fork in a circle on her napkin. "I hope you're right."

We finish breakfast in silence, and I take the time to do a self-evaluation of how I feel.

Being around Cora stirs up loads of memories and emotions I suppressed for years. But I can't ignore how I feel when near her. The way my heart rattles my ribcage. Or how my stomach quivers with excitement. Of course, I plan to follow etiquette and maintain a professional appearance while working, but once "off the clock" I cannot speak for my actions. I also won't resist what is right in front of me.

Because each moment I have with Cora, I intend to take full advantage. This shoot could be complete happenstance. Or maybe it is kismet. Personally, I believe in the latter.

After Alyson and I leave the restaurant, we stop at the juice place up the street. Cora had one of their juices the other day, so I Googled the business. Once I buy something for each of us, even grabbing a duplicate of Cora's drink for Erin, we jump back in the car and drive up the street to the main hub of downtown.

It is eight-thirty in the morning on a Thursday, and the streets already have people walking and bicycling everywhere. Downtown Dunedin is a quaint place. I hadn't come here much when I lived in the area, but I can see I missed out.

Restaurants and boutiques and eclectic shops line the streets. People bustle along the sidewalk, going from one shop to the next. Some people just sit on benches under trees and chat about what a nice day it is outside. And as busy as it is, it's not busy at the same time. Everyone is friendly as smiles are shared amongst complete strangers.

It's pieces of home like this that make me want to return.

Don't get me wrong. There are many stretches of California I love. Forests and mountains and waterfalls. Many I would love to show to Cora, knowing her love for the wilderness. But I haven't been anywhere resembling this. The happy town with ever happier residents. Everyone shares warm greetings and pleasant words and exchanges hugs. It makes me homesick for a place I haven't called home in a long time.

Alyson parks the car in a small lot near the epicenter of downtown and we walk over to the outdoor trail, standing in the shade. Cyclists whip past us, waving and smiling. Dogs sniff the grass as they walk alongside their owner. People window shop the storefronts nearby.

"She emailed me early this morning and said for us to meet her here," Alyson tells me.

A moment later, Cora and Erin pull into the parking lot at the same time and park beside Alyson's rental car. My eyes remain fixed on Cora behind my sunglasses as she gets out of the car and strolls to the back hatch, opening it and taking out her camera bag.

"Check yourself, Hunt," Alyson chirps behind me.

"Did I do something, *Miss Jameson*?" I curl my lip at her. She is really starting to piss me off.

"First, remember that you hired me to do exactly what it is I am doing. Second, don't take that tone with me. You will respect me." Alyson stares at me like a mother scolding a child. In some respects, she is correct. I did hire her to keep me "in line."

But she also needs to remember her place in the grand scheme of things.

"I know what I hired you to do. And since I'm the one signing your paycheck, I suggest *you* check yourself. I'm fully aware of my boundaries. And if I want to cross them, it'll be when the shoot is done. Which, by the way, is only a few days from now." I pause and lower my voice since Cora and Erin are walking our way. "I'll be here a few days after the shoot ends, I intend on enjoying that time however I see fit."

Alyson purses her lips. "You're the boss."

Damn right I am. Best you remember.

Cora and Erin step up and I hand them the juices I bought them. "Good morning, ladies. Just something to help keep you going today."

Cora's lips curve up at the corners while Erin blushes at the gift. It's just juice, not a bundle of flowers. Maybe Erin is naturally timid and the rosiness comes easily. Or there is the possibility she knows about the "meeting" last night. Whatever, it doesn't bother me either way.

I glance down at the chunky watch on my wrist to see it is just after one when we wrap up for the day. This shoot dragged out longer due to the amount of pedestrian traffic we had to avoid for photos. It's challenging to capture someone's face, and their attire, when people walk all around you.

Erin heads to her car, and Alyson to the rental. I tug on Cora's hand and keep the two of us by the trail for a minute, giving us a fraction of privacy while we talk.

"What's up?" she asks, her tone casual and light.

"Just wanted to say thanks again. For not walking away from me last night. And for hanging out. Was nice to see you outside of all this." I wave my hand around us.

"It was nice," she says as a smile softens her features. "Do you want to go out with everyone tomorrow? We're going bowling."

"I'd love to. Who's everyone?"

"Me, Erin, Shelly, and Jonas. We can ask Micah, too. If you want."

All but one of those names is familiar. "I'll text Micah and see if he wants to go. Who's Jonas?" Because I really want to know. Jonas is not the name of any female I have ever met. Micah would have told me if Shelly has a boyfriend. And Erin seems too innocent to be dating—although, I could be way off base with her.

"Jonas is a friend. He helped me try to fix my old car years ago. It had so many problems and I was a frequent shopper at the mechanic shop he works at and we just became friends. He's a nice guy. I think you'll like him."

A furnace boils in my veins as I try tapering my emotions before I say something harsh. It is not my place to play the jealous anything. I lost that privilege years before she met this Jonas person. And I know absolutely nothing about him.

But that doesn't stop my truths from surfacing.

Am I still in love with Cora? Absolutely. There is not a day of my future I foresee not loving her.

Does that give me the right to dictate who she hangs around? Nope, not one bit. If she tells me she and this Jonas character are just friends, I believe her.

So, I suck it up like a trooper and put on the smile I have been trained to use. "If you think so, I'm sure it's true." I relax my forced expression, only because she is looking at me as if she can see right through it. "Will you give me your number?"

She shakes her head for a few beats. "Why? Don't misunderstand me," she says as she jerks her head toward Alyson. Her teeth tug on her lip as she regards Alyson's eyes on us. But I don't give a fuck. Alyson can take her sinister stares and fly them back to California.

"So I can text you after I talk with Micah." That's a perfectly sufficient reason to need her number, seeing as she asked me to join them.

"Okay." She nods and I pull out my phone.

I open up a new text and she prattles off her cell to me. When she finishes, I type a message and send it to her. Her phone chimes in her back pocket and a smile dons my face as my heart beats a little faster.

I glance up and see Alyson drilling holes through me with her eyes. Her irritation is raking my nerves. "I should head out," I tell Cora, although it's the last thing I want to do. If anything, I would love to spend the rest of the day wandering downtown, holding her hand and chatting more.

"Me, too. I'll see you tomorrow."

"See you tomorrow." I lean into her, wrap my arms around her midsection and inhale her scent. She smells so much better than I remember. The perfect blend of frankincense and gardenia. Against every fibrous desire in my body, I release her and head to the car, giving her a small wave after I get in.

Once we are out of the lot and driving back toward the hotel, Alyson decides it is time to give me her two cents. "I get that you think you know what you're doing, but please be careful. There are only two days left for the shoot. All I'm saying is to be mindful."

I opt to not respond, and the drive back to Clearwater Beach takes twice as long. But during the entire ride, Alyson's words repeat in my head.

Be mindful.

The fifth day of the shoot comes and goes and remains uneventful. Which boggles my mind.

The shoot was on the beachside of the hotel, this time in the water. Normally, a shoot like this would be classified as simple, easy. The model is out in the water, playing amongst the waves, posing on occasion and I snap the shot. Easy peasy lemon squeezy.

But, of course, with Gavin it is the complete opposite.

The shots weren't difficult to capture. My breath, on the other hand, seemed to get lost in the breeze. My racing heart chasing on its heels.

Sitting cross-legged on my bed, I pick up my camera and remove the SD card. After inserting it in the card reader, I plug it into my laptop and download the photos. A few minutes later, my eyes are inundated with thousands of photos of Gavin in the surf. I scroll through the tiled photos, clicking on this one and that one. Some appear the same with maybe a slight angle change with his chin or eyes. Others are notice-ably different.

My finger taps the trackpad and the next photo fills the

screen, corner to corner. I suck in a breath at the sight before me, my eyes glued to the screen and glazing over. I can't look away. Can't stop the category five hurricane wreaking havoc on my insides.

Today's shoot started earlier than the previous days. We needed to have Gavin in the water with no one nearby. In order to do that, he was in the water as soon as the sun started rising behind us in the east. The lighting was just enough to see him and the shorts hanging low on his hips.

The photo in front of me left me speechless.

Gavin stood in the water, the surface a few inches below the waistband of the shorts. His torso slightly twisted, palms resting on top of the water outstretched, his profile staring south into the distance. The dim morning light just enough to outline his silhouette. The length of his hair hiding parts of his profile. His contours defined with glimpses of curves and valleys and sinew, and droplets of water beaded on his skin. And the sharp edge of his stubble-covered jawline.

"Wow," I whisper-gasp to myself.

This photo… consider me stunned.

Stunned by his gorgeous features, the relaxed muscles peaking and dipping and contouring in all the right places. Breathless by his form and posture in the light. Shocked by the way my chest heats and thumps vigorously at the sight of him like this. In his element and one-hundred-percent himself.

Flashes of his love for the beach wake from my memory. Not for the fine, white sands or the warm, salty water. But for the serenity it provides him. The occasional stillness mixing with absolute chaos. How the sun dips below the horizon and lights the sky in breathtaking pinks and oranges. We watched so many sunsets together before he left. No two the same.

And each time, I watched him from the corner of my eye, captivated by his tranquility.

This is him. Pure and uninhibited.

And this photo may not be what the brand is looking for, but it is something I will never let go of. A piece of him. The real him. The Gavin I fell in love with all those years ago.

My finger strokes over the photo, the outline of his triceps and forearm. I sigh and drop my hand from the screen.

I am fucking hopeless. And screwed.

I save the photos to my external drive and shut down the computer. My head still in the clouds as I dream of Gavin in my life in ways he never has been. Jumping up from the bed, I startle Luna in the process.

"Sorry, Luna. Momma's head is somewhere in la-la-land right now."

I head for the bathroom and crank the hot water in the shower, praying the spray will snap me out of my thoughts. Thoughts which will more than likely lead down a fresh path of sadness and heartache. I should be trying to erase the daydreams running circles in my head, right? Erase them and replace them with Gavin's inevitable departure. The more days that pass, the closer it gets to the end of the shoot. And the sooner this dream will fade away. Because that is all this is. A dream.

The parking lot of the bowling alley is packed. I wind up and down the rows in search of a vacant space, finally parking after I hit the fourth row. Jogging up to the entrance, I spot Shelly and Micah and slow when I notice they are in a heated conversation.

As I approach, Micah notices me and stops speaking, an artificial smile marking his face.

Great. I must have been the topic they were arguing politely about.

"Hey, Micah," I say, laying the sweetness on a little thick. "Long time no see."

Shelly bounds over to me and squeezes me as if I'm her lifeblood. Micah watches us, a smirk pulling at the corner of his mouth as he mumbles something unintelligible.

What the hell is his problem?

"Just ignore him. He's pissed because he thinks you and Gavin will ruin his night of fun," Shelly tells me before sticking her tongue out at her brother.

Not quite sure how he thinks us bowling together is going to disrupt his good time. And if I'm honest, I don't really care about his feelings. I have seen Micah a couple times over the last year. About the same number of times I see him every year. And usually that is because I attend gatherings with Shelly where he happens to be also.

Whatever. He can suck it up like the thirty-one-year-old big boy he is.

"Micah," I say, snagging his attention from the parking lot. "The only person that can ruin your night is you. So…"

In all his my-best-friends-big-brother glory, he salutes me with his middle finger. Asshole. And so immature. An outsider would peg him as the youngest out of all of us.

I loop my arm in Shelly's and we skip into the bowling alley, ignoring the dipshit standing outside. We head over to the check-in counter, pay for shoes and receive our lane number. I shoot a text to Erin and Jonas, letting them know Shelly and I are inside and which lane number we are at.

Shoes laced up, Shelly and I go in search of the perfect

bowling ball. When we return to the lane, Jonas is there and swapping his steel-toe boots for the snappy red and blue bowling shoes. He notices us step into the bowling circle and lifts his head up, a megawatt smile spreading his lips. I have missed his face this week.

"Hey, ladies. What time does galactic bowling begin?"

I wrap my arms around him, hugging him as hard as I normally do. "In about fifteen minutes."

Just as I release him of the hug, I hear footsteps thunder behind me. I turn to see Micah and Gavin, and before I can greet Gavin, I stop myself. The relaxed and soothing demeanor Gavin has displayed toward me all week is nowhere to be seen. Instead, it has been replaced with ego and rage and maybe a hint of jealousy.

He needs to chill the fuck out.

"Gavin," I sing, "this is Jonas. Jonas, this is Gavin."

I wait for one of them to be the bigger man and offer their hand to shake. An eternity passes before Jonas rises from the plastic bucket-style seat and offers his hand. How did I know he would be the one to extend the olive branch? Maybe because he and I don't share the same sort of history Gavin and I do.

"Hey, man. Nice to meet you. Cora's told me a little about you."

Gavin shakes his hand, his eyes sizing up Jonas in the process. "Has she now? And what, pray tell, has she told you about me?" His voice laden with sarcasm and authority and ownership.

For fuck's sake. Put your dick away, Gavin. This is not the time or place.

"Just that you guys dated in high school and she hasn't seen you in years. Until this week, of course. She said the shoot has been great, though." Jonas's tone is calm and collected. But his choice of words is meant to inflict guilt and envy.

Seriously? I do not want to be the center of some stupid pissing match. Why is it so difficult to be friends with men?

Gavin's eyes narrow and I almost see the witty comeback he works hard to deliver. Everything inside me just wants this to stop, so we can have a few drinks, eat some greasy pizza, and play hours of black light bowling.

And just when I think Gavin might keep his mouth shut, he proves me wrong.

"It has been great. Nothing like spending several hours of the day with a beautiful woman. And an evening too."

That's it. I have had it. I shove against Gavin's chest. Hard. "Okay, okay. We all get it. You both have dicks. Could you stop being one so we can have a good time? I don't plan to spend my evening defending myself against testosterone."

I watch as he stares at Jonas, jaw clenched, before he softens his features and shifts to look at me. "Sure thing. Let's have some fun."

And before I realize what is happening, he bends down and kisses the corner of my mouth. I don't respond. No flinch. No kiss in return. Nothing.

Instead, fire ignites in my chest and radiates through every molecule in my body. Fire from feeling his lips on me again. But also because he did it to use me as a pawn. And I am no one's pawn. How can desire and anger be so in unison? I don't have the answer, but they both flood my veins like the Nile. Fuel my indignation. And slowly steal every bit of happiness I had about having a night out with friends.

I stare up into his eyes, his face a look of victory. But I am ready to slap it right off his pretty little lips.

Pressing up on my toes and leaning toward his ear, I whisper-hiss, "If you ever try to use me like I'm some sort of prize again, you'll wish you'd never returned here."

I step back and set my expression to a level so frigid he shivers. We stare at each other a minute. His eyes never leave mine. They ask me a million questions regarding me and Jonas and him. But I hold my ground. Jonas is my friend and I made that abundantly clear to him when I invited him. If he can't handle me having other men in my life, then this second chance at whatever will end faster than it began.

He nods and his lips move without sound, *I'm sorry.*

I give him a tight smile and return to my friends. Erin joined us sometime during that whole showdown. Sitting between Jonas and Erin, I watch as Shelly types names on the screen—giving each of us an alternate identity.

I have been dubbed "The Raven." Shelly "The Queen." Jonas landed "The Machine." Erin bows at "The Peacekeeper." Micah gets "The Asshole." Because that is what happens when your sister picks your name. And Gavin receives "The Dreamer."

Everyone except me questions their names and tells her to change them. The raven suits me on many levels, and the temporary nickname perks my lips. First and foremost, black is life. Second, intelligence. No doubt there are plenty more sufficient reasons, but I will just stick with those two.

Once everyone stops antagonizing Shelly about name changes, bowling balls are chosen and the game begins. Five minutes into the first game, the bright fluorescent bulbs go out and are replaced with black lights and flashing party lights. A DJ belts out of the speakers and prattles on about people coming to the booth for music requests.

The first of many remixed or electronic songs comes on

and I start bopping in my seat. Erin currently rolls her ball down the lane, a sad puppy expression on her face when she turns after only knocking one pin down. My hand comes up in a *rock on* gesture and I smile at her in encouragement. Her next ball yields seven more pins and she walks away with a smile.

"That's my girl," I holler. Her beaming smile is the best response and I put my hand up for a high five.

Frames are played and pitchers of beer and greasy pizza get ordered as laughter and goofiness ensue. For the next two hours, everything goes well. No testosterone battles. No bitching. It almost feels like old times.

Until one minor touch.

I grab my ball from the return, shift into the approach area and line my feet where I typically set them. Lifting the ball, I hold it steady and study the pins in front of me. When ready, I take a left-right-left, followed by a swing back and release as I swing forward. Normally, the ball would glide off my fingers and spin down the lane, the marble pattern hypnotizing on its path to the pins.

But that is not what happens.

What actually occurs is left-right-left, swing back, a smack to the leg and a twist of the ankle as the ball flies backward. It hurts like a son of a bitch and I cry out as I crumple to the floor.

Within seconds, Jonas is at my side, asking if I am okay. When I let him know I will be fine and I just need to sit a minute, he offers to help me up. Up to this point, everything is okay and I realize this because Gavin and Micah had walked off to get more beer.

The moment I stand upright, Jonas steadies me with both

his hands resting on my shoulders, his eyes scrutinizing my face. "You sure you're good?"

"Yeah. Thanks for helping me up."

And that is when it happens. When the shit hits the fan.

Jonas brings his hand to my cheek, brushing his thumb along my cheekbone and down to my jaw. He tugs lightly on strands of my hair before swiping them behind my ear. The gesture is tender and sweet and is taken away the second Gavin is within eyeshot.

"What the fuck do you think you're doing?" Gavin rages, his hands balled into fists at his sides.

"What's your deal, man? She just hurt herself and I was helping," Jonas charges back.

Gavin takes two steps closer. "I can see you helping. Keep your fucking hands to yourself, asshole."

What the actual fuck?

"Gavin," I soothe. "Jonas was helping me. I hit my leg with the ball and fell. He was making sure I was okay and helped me stand back up. You'd know that if you were here." My voice transitions from soothing to bold to anger in a flash.

Who does he think he is? He has no hold over me. He has no right to step in and assume the role he is taking right now. That role was extinguished when he stopped calling and writing. That role was extinguished the day he abandoned me.

He steps up to me, looks me square in the eyes, ignoring the fact that Jonas is less than two feet away. His eyes bounce back and forth between mine as he searches my face for answers. Answers to questions he has been dying to ask me, but is scared to know the truth. If he wants the truth, he will need to man up and ask what he is so desperate to know.

"Please," I beg then close my eyes. As much as I would like to continue staring into his mesmerizing eyes, I can't focus when I do. I continue speaking with my vision shielded. My voice just above a whisper. "Please stop doing this. You can't do this. You can't come back after thirteen years and act as if nothing has changed. *Everything has changed.*"

"Look at me," he whispers.

I pinch my eyes tighter a moment before opening them and refocusing on his face. His face is inches from mine, and it is both exhilarating and unnerving. In my periphery, I notice everyone has moved away from us. Even Jonas.

The music morphs to one song then another, and we stand in silence. His eyes hypnotize me more with each passing beat and I swear he is figuring out a way to imprint his soul onto mine. Little does he know, he already has.

And when his finger traces the line of my jaw, I stop breathing. My eyes close and I wish on every star I have ever seen in the night sky that he will kiss me. But he doesn't.

He leans forward, his stubbled cheek lightly scrapes against mine, and whispers in my ear. "Not everything has changed. At least not for me."

He doesn't pull away from me. His warm, cotton-covered chest presses against mine and I feel the acceleration of his breathing—on my chest and at my ear. Calloused fingers traipse, with the slightest pressure, from my upper bicep down to my elbow and follow the lines of my forearm until he reaches the tips of my fingers. His fingers leave a trail of sparks everywhere he touches me and I can't ignore the swirl of energy erupting in my body.

"Gavin…" *Fuck*, I can't breathe. Can't think.

His breath is hot on my ear. "I won't come out and say it, but my feelings for you… if anything, they've only gotten stronger."

No. No, no, no, no. He can't do this. Not now. Not after all this time.

My brain jumbles into a fog of confusion. How can this be happening? It took me years to get over him. Years. To accept that he was never coming back. To accept I would never have the same connection with another person like I did him. Accept that I would exist among my friends and become some old cat lady.

And then he waltzes back into town—although it was his job that brought him and no other reason—and acts as if it is okay to resume his role beside me. It is *not* so simple.

It sounds strange, but I mourned his loss. Literally mourned him. Laid in my bed for weeks, aside from school, and cried until the tears would no longer fall. I lost sleep over him, far too many hours to track. This went on for months. So many months it was almost a year before I stopped crying for him. But the crying wasn't the end of it. It got replaced with well-disguised depression. Depression that still lingers to this day.

I won't let myself be that girl again. He can't do this. Make me fall in love with him again and then hop on a plane and fly back to the other coast. I won't survive. Not again.

Coolness replaces the heat of his breath at my ear, but I know he hasn't shifted far because his chest still rises and falls against mine. Not knowing what I will see, I take a chance and open my eyes and am met with the softest gaze. His grays spill into me. Plead with me. Implore me. Their silky silence calls to my heart and begs me to be something more. Begs me to be vulnerable for him again. And it hurts that I want to. So much.

"You can't say that. Not to me." The harsh scrape of my own words is an unfamiliar sound to my ears.

His eyes hold mine as he weaves his fingers between my own. "Why?"

"Because you can't say things like that and then leave me," I blurt, my body trembling. "The last time you left." My voice breaks. "It took me a really long time to find myself again. And even after I did, there were still days I lapsed. If it happens again…"

His eyes darken as he studies me. If he moves two inches closer, his lips will be on mine. And as much as I long to know how it would feel again, I fear the consequences my heart will endure.

"I'm sorry how things happened last time. You *know* I had no control in that scenario. But now…" He takes my chin between his thumb and first finger. "You and I have all the control."

"Do we?" I counter. "We live almost three thousand miles apart. How do we have control?"

The pad of his thumb brushes over my lower lip, causing me to close my eyes and suck in a breath. Blood whooshes loudly in my ear. My fingers tighten around his. Adrenaline parades throughout my body as flutters swarm beneath my sternum.

"What if we didn't live so far apart?"

Red and yellow lights spin circles around us when my eyes bolt open. Hundreds of people hurl globes of plastic-resin along oil-slicked hardwood in the hopes of knocking over wooden pins. Music wails from speakers and I have zero clue as to what is playing. Our friends resumed bowling without us, presumably playing our turns when they came around.

"What?" I stumble. The question is twofold. One—did I

hear him correctly? Two—is he suggesting what I think he is suggesting? That one of us moves?

"It's something I've thought about for a while now. The only reason I moved away was because I *had* to. That's not a sufficient enough reason for me to be there anymore."

My mind dizzies with his confession. Part of me is ecstatic at the possibility of him moving back to Florida. Another part of me is wary. Wary things can never go back to how they were, regardless of how either of us feels.

"But how? Your job. Friends. Life," I ramble.

His thumb strokes my lip again and he moves a breath closer. "I can do my job from anywhere. As it is, I'm almost never home. I fly somewhere new every week or two. But I've stockpiled and I can lessen how much I work. As well as be pickier about the shoots I do. The few friends I have there will understand. Believe me. And my life? It has never been in Cali. I may live there, but my life is here. Always has been."

This is too much information all at once. My free hand comes up to his bicep and I brace myself against his weight. *I can't get my hopes up. Not again. Not after last time.*

"I need to sit down," I tell him.

He helps me to a seat and squats down in front of me. The look in his eyes says three words I haven't said to another soul since he left. And right now, it is way too much.

"Tell me what you're thinking," he stammers.

I memorize his expression and then drop my head in my hands. "I'm thinking this is going to slay me in the end. That I'll wither and crumble."

His fingers play with the strands of my hair that cover my hands. It is a balm to the conflicting emotions that spiral around my heart. And I temporarily relish in the feel of such an intimate gesture.

"I won't let that happen," he promises.

My head jerks up. "How can you be certain? How can you make such a colossal vow?"

His eyes lock on mine, assurance backing his words. "Because it's the only thing I've wanted since I was forced to leave you. Cora…" he says as he strokes a hand down the side of my face. "You are everything to me. You are the reason I breathe."

I drop my head back into my hands, hiding my face from the world and convincing myself not to cry. After a few minutes, I inhale deeply and force myself upright. When I check the time, I realize an hour has passed and guilt washes over me at how I have abandoned my friends.

"We need to continue this conversation, but not now. Right now, I need to drink more and throw a ten-pound ball. I need to hang out with my friends. Okay?"

He nods and stands up in front of me. "Okay," he whispers as he kisses the top of my head.

We turn back to the group and talk with everyone. The night has morphed into an awkward ball of tension. No one is sure how they should act or what to say. But I do my best to ignore the weirdness and continue bowling and drinking.

But when the night ends, everyone is quick to leave. Too quick. And, unfortunate for me, I am too inebriated to drive and Gavin is the only person standing beside me.

Fuck. My. Life.

Since I took an Uber to the bowling alley, I assumed I would leave with Micah. Assumed he and I would hang after. But that is not how things happened. Instead, Micah changed his shoes and headed out without a word. When I shot him a text to check on him, his response was lackluster.

We'll catch up another time bro.

Lame. But after the whole debacle in the bowling alley, I don't blame him. And I am a shitty friend for ignoring him most of the night. Something I need to correct. But not now.

Because now I am driving Cora's car and following her slurred directions. Toward her house. Just me and her. Alone. And my nerves zap like live wires.

Not so sure this is the best idea. But there was no way in hell I would let her get behind the wheel when she consumed close to a pitcher of beer after our talk. Erin or Shelly could have driven her home, but then she would have had to worry about her car tomorrow.

It is easier for me to drop her home and catch an Uber back to the hotel. To make sure she gets home safely. To make sure she gets inside and locks the door. At least that is what I keep telling myself.

She slurs from the passenger seat as she points like a madwoman at the exit sign. "Take exit Drew. Snot so much traffic," she snorts. "I said snot."

I shake my head and laugh at her. The last time I saw her, we were too young to drink. Not that age stops people from drinking alcohol, but we didn't back then. Seeing her like this, I'm not quite sure how I feel about it.

Is this a normal thing for her? Going out with her friends and getting hammered. Does she drink heavily and drive after? Does she get wasted with that Jonas prick around? My blood boils at the idea. Has he tried to make a move on her while she was tipsy or drunk?

Fuck.

Just the thought of her with another guy pisses me off. Not like I expected her to not move on or see other people after everything. Hell, I did my best to soothe my crippled heart. Had meaningless sex with countless women. Tried to date. None of it stuck, though.

But seeing another man near Cora—his interest in her far beyond friendship—was a smack in the face. My blood turned molten and I was pumped and ready to kick his ass. If she hadn't been there to stop me, I probably would have and regretted it later.

What intrigues me most is how Cora thinks this Jonas prick only wants to be friends with her. Is she blind to the way he looks at her? Or how eager he is to touch her? Their hug earlier… the way he stroked her cheek and hair after she fell… *Fuck.* Either she is oblivious or doesn't want to believe.

I can't let these thoughts fester inside me. I need to know what sort of relationship exists between Cora and this Jonas guy. She doesn't owe me anything, and I would be shocked if she answers me, but I have to ask.

"Hey," I start, and she looks over at me. "What's up with you and this Jonas guy?"

She tilts her head to the side and remains silent in the passenger seat. After a minute, she starts laughing. At first, it is her typical laugh, but then it morphs into hysterics and snort-laughing. And then she laughs at her own snort-laughing. It's kind of cute.

This goes on for another minute until she tells me to turn left at the next light. We take a left and another left a couple blocks later. Less than a quarter mile later and we are parked in her driveway.

She still hasn't answered my question and I wonder if she even remembers I asked it. We sit in silence after I cut the engine and neither of us moves to get out.

"He's just a friend," she whispers into the quiet, her voice somber. "I know he wants to be more than friends, and it's crossed my mind on occasion, but we've been friends too long to ruin it. At least that's my opinion."

She sounds more sober than she did fifteen minutes ago and I wonder if it is the topic at hand or if she wasn't that drunk to begin with. I don't plan on asking her. But if she will keep talking, I will probe for more.

"If he asked you," I hesitate, unsure if I want to know her truth. I search her eyes, wondering if she can read me in the darkness of the car. Her eyes used to read me like a book. She knew all my answers before I did. Knew all my tells. "If he asked you, would you guys be together?"

Her silhouette is all I see in the car as a light on the back of her house casts an aura around her. I am unable to see what she thinks, but I *feel* her eyes scan over every part of my face. Look into the windows of my soul. Wonder what would provoke me to ask her. Memorize the curves along my cheekbones in search for a twitch or indication of doubt. She studies the line of my jaw and waits for me to speak more. I may not be able to see her face, but with the angle of the light I know she sees mine.

She reaches toward me, finds my hand in the dark and wraps it in hers. "I… I don't think so," she whispers, her words clear. "He's a great guy and has been a good friend. It's just…" She shakes her head. "Relationships and me haven't had the best of luck in my adult life. So, I just do the friend thing with sporadic dating. But never the same guy for more than one date."

Shit. Did I do this to her? Did I ruin love for her? God, I hope she is not like this because of me. The selfish part of me jumps up and down in victory. But the selfless part of me, he stands in the corner with a baseball bat, beating the shit out of himself.

"I'm sorry," I say the words before I stop myself.

"For what? Ruining me for every other man in the world. Don't be sorry. I don't want or need your pity. If I wanted to, I could have dated more and been in a solid relationship. But I get to decide. Is it such a bad thing to be picky? Especially after your soul has been crushed by the one person who was supposed to protect it."

Slap. Fuck, that stings. But I sure as shit deserve it.

"Can I walk you in?" I ask, wanting to steer us away from talking about this now. Not when I know she's not sober. Not when we can't discuss what happened rationally.

"What? That's it? You're done talking about it, so conversation over?"

She shoves her door open and gets out, slamming the door behind her. I rush to get out, to catch up to her before she gets inside. Halfway to her back door, I catch her wrist in my grip.

"No. That's not it at all. I just don't think we should be having this discussion when you're not one-hundred-percent coherent."

She huffs, trying to yank her arm from my hand. "You're ridiculous. You bring up the topic of discussion, but when it gets too thick… conversation done. It makes me dizzy."

She sways and I want to tell her it's not the conversation making her dizzy. But I don't because she is already pissed at me. Yanking her arm, I release her wrist and she wobbles to the door, me on her heels.

I hand her the key ring with three keys and she unlocks the door. As she steps through the door, I go to follow her and she stops.

"What are you doing?"

"It's late. Can I sleep on your couch? I won't bother you and I'll leave in the morning. If not, I'll find a ride."

Her eyes wobble a little as she studies my face. After a few breaths, she nods. "Couch." It's all she says as she walks toward a door I can only assume is her bedroom.

"Thanks," I whisper into the darkness.

Walking slowly through her quaint house, I locate the couch and kick off my shoes. I check my watch and realize it is really fucking late. Or is it really fucking early at this point? Whatever. Thank God tomorrow is an off day for the shoot. Because both of us would be fucked if it wasn't.

I stretch out on the couch, situating pillows and a blanket around me. Shifting my hips and my neck until I get comfortable. Am I really in her house? Or is this all just some bizarre dream? It all seems so surreal. Seeing her again. Touching her again. Smelling her again. Fuck, how I have missed everything about her. Even the way she says my name.

Her adorable smile. The subtle fragrance she wears. How she peers up at me. The way her body reacts to mine. As if no time has passed.

But it has. And I fucked up. Big time.

Staring up at the ceiling, my eyes lose focus as the moonlight casts shadows from the tree outside the window. Shadows of limbs and leaves dance and entertain me. Tonight, so many things have happened and changed. It's overwhelming to think of how life and our relationship could possibly shift in the future. Shift in a positive way.

The future… something I always dreamed I would have with Cora, but wasn't sure would happen. I wasn't sure I would ever see her again, but wished for it often. Wished on every star in the night sky. Wished with every penny I threw in a fountain. And wished every time I blew out a birthday candle.

When I boarded the plane in Los Angeles, the possibility of seeing her seemed minuscule. So outlandish. So impossible.

But fate intervened. Slapping us together and giving us the opportunity to discover each other again. To learn about all the years we missed out on. Learn how much we have changed yet remained the same. And now that things are lining up for both of us in our respective careers, the possibility of a future with her has greater potential. If a future with me is what she wants.

Please let it be what she wants.

If she would be willing to try with me again—if she

gave me a chance to explain—I would move my life back here again. Back home. To her. For her. In a heartbeat. Regardless of my life and family and friends back in California, I would leave it all behind if I knew we stood a chance.

The day I was forced to tell her my mom received a promotion and we were moving out of state was the day my life started falling apart. One speck at a time. When my mom told me the news, I hesitated to tell Cora. Not because I didn't want to, but because when I did tell her, reality would hit hard. And when I shared the news with her, expressing the pain and anguish I felt at leaving, she held me and soothed me. She was the strong one, telling me we would be apart for less than two years. That we would see each other during breaks and summer. Less than two years and we could be by each other's side again.

We had it all mapped out.

Unfortunately for us, it didn't work that way. Within ten days of being in California, my life was utter chaos. Upset and angry, I lashed out. Got in fights and provoked anyone near me. I think a part of me thought if I acted out, I would be able to return to where I wanted to be most. Where I belonged. With Cora.

But it didn't work that way and I shut down. To my family and Cora. I allowed my anger and frustration and sadness to consume me until numbness took over. A numbness that pushed me forward, but I lost every real part of who I had been. Including Cora.

It may have taken thirteen years for me to return—by complete accident—but I am here. And I plan to do whatever it takes to regain all I have lost. I will make up for every tear she cried. Every sadness she suffered. I will make up for every pain and absence of love she has endured since I left. She deserves nothing less from me.

I surveil the shadows as they continue to sway and, within minutes, I drift off and hope I dream about the most incredible woman I have ever loved. The woman who sleeps less than twenty feet from me. The woman I hope will forgive me in the end. And somehow, love me again.

Fifteen years ago

I jump out of the bus and land on the concrete sidewalk of my new school. *High school. I am in the big leagues now.* No stopping me.

Freshman year holds so much promise. Making new friends. Meeting new people. Hot new females. Life couldn't possibly get any better.

I toss my backpack over one shoulder and head for the class where my homeroom is said to be. The first day is usually full of chaos, and today is no exception. Even though it is corny as hell, I am glad my mom forced me to come to orientation so I at least got a lay of the land. The last thing I need is to look like a dope wandering the halls while staring at a map.

Navigating the hall, I locate the correct room and find a desk in the back row. There is still another six minutes until the bell, so I pull out my notebook and begin doodling while I wait. Stomps and thuds and soft pitter-patters echo off the sterile white walls as everyone files into the room. I ignore all their steps and continue my artwork, the buzzing of the bell causing me to stop.

When I peer up at the front of the room, a raven-haired girl walks through the door, huffing and bending at the waist as she tries to catch her breath. Her skin is pale as cream, her onyx hair as bold of a contrast as her bloodred lips. She reminds me of a modern-day, punk rock version of Snow White, except with shorter hair. And I immediately like everything about her.

When her breath catches enough, she stands and wanders through the rows of desks, picking an available seat two over from me. I try not to stare at her, but can't help how she has caught my eye. Surely, she has caught the eye of many others as well. And not just because of her entrance. Everything about her is bewitching.

I avert my gaze when the teacher introduces himself and begins going over some of the basic school rules and hands out paperwork for our parents, the code of conduct, and our class schedules. Typical first day of school stuff. I scan over my class schedule, check I was assigned all the appropriate classes, and then wonder what classes the raven-haired girl has. Hopeful we will have at least one or more classes together.

The bell sounds and I sidle up beside her, trying to spark a conversation.

"Hey," I say with a wave. "I'm Gavin. Crazy morning?"

She glances over at me, confused. "Hi," she mumbles. "Cora. And yes."

Maybe she isn't a morning person? Or maybe she is not having the best morning. Whatever.

"Sorry to hear. Anything I can do to help?" Why not offer, right? No harm, no foul.

"Gavin, is it?" I nod. "Thanks, but I'm good," she says with a brush-off.

But I don't back down so easily. Something about her begs me to keep trying. "Well, let me know," I offer with a smile.

When she walks away, I check to see which class I head to first and make my way to the science wing. Honestly, who thinks it is a good idea for people to learn science this early in the morning?

~

Slap.

My geometry book closes too loud in the room and several sets of eyes stare at me like I am their next meal. *Sorry*. Why does everyone seem so touchy today? *Just brush it off, man*. No one likes the first day of school. Actually, no one cares for school on any day. But no one needs to bite my head off.

I shoulder my backpack and head to the cafeteria. After I load up a tray of random crap food, I head out to the tables in the sun. The summer heat still blazes, but I would rather be outside than in the dank cafeteria. The cafeteria feels claustrophobic and I question the cleanliness.

When I step out and search for a good place to sit, I spot her. The raven-haired girl with bright red lips. Cora. She sits under a tree, eating a sandwich and reading a book. Before I realize what I am doing, I trudge over and stop in front of her. She ignores me for a few seconds, bookmarks her page, and finally looks up.

Shielding her eyes with her hands, she squints and tilts her head to the side. "Can I help you with something?"

"Mind if I sit with you?"

"Gavin… right?" I nod at her. "Well, Gavin, I'm kind of a loner."

It is not a denial, only a statement meant to scare me away. But it won't work on me. If anything, the attempt at a brush-off has me wanting to sit with her more. Cora… what a fascinating creature.

"We don't have to talk. I'm just here for the tree," I joke.

She shakes her head in disbelief, a subtle laugh under her breath as she gestures to the landscape beside her. "It's not my tree."

I squat down and manage to sit cross-legged without dropping anything from my tray. *Thanks to whoever is looking out for me so I don't embarrass myself in front of this girl.*

We sit in companionable silence—me munching on the cafeteria's mystery casserole and her eating a banana while reading *Wuthering Heights*. The book tattered and well-loved —cover curling and faded, multiple pages dog-eared.

Part of me wonders if she is reading the book for school or pleasure. My bet is on the latter considering the appearance of the novel. Can't say I have ever read the book. I'm sure it is good, but reading isn't much of a priority for me. Haven't heard of anything noteworthy.

After finishing the semi-decent casserole, I finish off my bottled water. Although our silence under the tree has been enjoyable, I itch to talk with this girl. Spark some form of conversation. Get to know the girl with the bright red lips. But she doesn't seem like the type of person who fills space with meaningless conversation. Part of me is intimidated by this. Another part of me enchanted. What do I say to someone like her?

So, I aim for obvious.

"Good book?" I ask, smacking myself upside the head internally.

Of course it is a good book, dumbass! Otherwise, it wouldn't look like she has read it a hundred times. Idiot.

She finishes the sentence or paragraph she is reading and faces me, a slight hint of annoyance on her face. It both frightens and intrigues me. "Yes." It is all she says before turning back to the book and ignoring me again.

Okay...

I stay under the tree with her for a few more minutes before rising to take my tray back to the cafeteria. After I dump the trash and deposit the tray in the bin, I turn to catch one more glimpse of her before heading to my next class. But the moment I look, she is no longer there. A strange sadness takes hold, but I brush it off.

"I'll try again tomorrow," I mumble to myself.

The art quad is located at the back of campus, on the farthest outskirts. As if sketching and paints and clays need their own world away from the books and projectors and regimented studies. As odd as it is to be isolated at the back of the school, I enjoy the fact I won't hear anything else on campus while in this class.

Walking into the large and open classroom, I scan all the various projects the teacher has kept throughout the years. Oils and watercolors, charcoals and pencil. Each unique on their own. The air rich with canvas and pencil shavings and earth. As my eyes follow around the room, they stop when they spot a head of black-as-night hair.

Cora sits at one of a dozen long, rectangular tables. Her head down as her fingers draw vigorously on a sketch pad. Almost like the artist version of a mad scientist. No one sits beside her, so I gather myself and head for the table. Of all the classes I could share with her, art feels beyond perfect. A way to express yourself without speaking.

When I sit down beside her, my wooden stool squeaking against the linoleum floor, she doesn't move. Doesn't lift her head or greet me. She is so focused on what is in front of her, it's as if the rest of the world isn't really here. And a part of me kind of digs her level of concentration.

Seconds pass and her head remains down, hovering six inches above the table. I peer around her hunched body and sneak a peek at what she sketches, my eyes widening and breath falling short as I see it come to life.

The trunk of a tree. Shade and foliage hovering above. A raven-haired girl, her face hidden by an open book. And a boy. Taller than her, lean in stature. He watches her from the corner of his eye, a timid smile on his face.

It's her. *And me.*

A strange contentment washes over me. Although the image is nowhere near done—no shading or fine lines and details—the outlines are all in black and white. She abandoned the tree early to come draw the two of us beneath it. My stomach is sort of queasy, and I don't think it is from the mystery casserole.

How has she put this on paper so quickly?

And it occurs to me. Maybe she had previously drawn herself alone under a tree. She did say she was a loner. Five minutes was definitely not enough time to have this much detail on paper. Not even by the best.

The bell rings and I inspect another twenty bodies in the room, all seated at the other tables. Footsteps tick on the tile and the teacher walks to the front of the room. But I don't look at the five foot, four inch red-haired woman at the head of the room introducing herself as the art teacher.

Because just as the teacher begins speaking, Cora lifts her head and realizes I'm sitting beside her. And that I have seen her drawing. Her face is stoic and as unreadable as a professional poker player.

A smile breaches my lips and I face the teacher at the head of the room. Beside me, I hear the sketchbook close and a soft sigh. A sigh I will remember for the rest of my days.

sixteen

GAVIN

Present

The sun wakes me up just before seven, although sections of the house remain somewhat dark. Cora still sleeps and the house is quiet. Too quiet. As if no noise exists here. Seems odd to have no noise. No cars driving by. No people talking outside. Not even the chirp of birds in the early morning light.

I should leave. The last thing I need is for Cora to wake up, find me in her house and not remember why I am here in the first place. All it would do is freak her out and set us back. When it comes to Cora, I need all the forward momentum possible.

Rising from the couch, I stretch out my limbs then fold the blanket and drape it over the couch. I tiptoe through the house in search of the bathroom. After I relieve myself, I wash up and tiptoe back out.

Finding a piece of paper and pen on the desk nestled between the living and dining area, I write a quick note. As I set the pen back in its place, I bump the corner of her open laptop and the screen lights up.

Shit.

Snagging the note, I go to close the lid of the laptop and hide its bright light. But just as I begin to push the top down, I see a photo from one of our shoots this week. A photo she left open. A photo of me.

Confusion flickers in my veins. Rapid-fire questions pop up left and right. Was the photo left open because of work and editing? Or was it left open for other reasons?

A strange, woozy sensation floats in my chest at the possibility of her ogling a photo of me. Of her sitting in this very spot and gawking at my images. But I shut down the idea, not wanting my hopes to get the best of me.

I ignore the laptop and leave it open since it will return to sleep mode within minutes.

Walking over to her bedroom door, I stand in front of it and close my eyes. Do I go in and leave the note where I know she will find it? Or should I slip it under the door? This isn't my house. And technically, Cora isn't my girl.

My internal battle continues a minute before I choose the obvious path.

I slowly twist the knob and am thankful the door stays silent as it opens. Padding through the room darkened by black-out curtains, I walk toward her bed and set the note on top of her phone. A place I know she will find it.

Before turning to leave, I stare down at her a moment. Although I should leave now, the selfish part of me stays to observe Cora without distraction. To take in the woman who has held my heart captive most of my life.

And for a moment, I study the lines of her face as she sleeps. How her brows arch up, not in the middle but closer to a lateral point. The way her long lashes fan across the purple half-moons beneath her eyes. How her black strands splay across the dark gray cotton pillowcase.

A red tank covers her chest, but rises up her midriff to unintentionally display her navel. A small locket rests atop her shirt, and I remember it as the one her mom gave her. The sheet bunches near the thick band of her underwear. Her body askew on the mattress, taking up half of the queen-size space like a giant starfish.

A contented sigh leaves my lips as I pivot to leave the room. As much as I would like to stay, now is not the day. After closing the door behind me, I retrieve my phone from the living room and head for the door. I lock the handle as I step out the back. Scanning the street, I try to orient myself and figure out where I am.

Across the street from Cora's house is a large, open park. Honestly, doesn't surprise me she purchased a home within fifty-feet of a park. I cross the street, land on a small paved path and wander through the greenery in the faint morning light.

It is peaceful here. Most of this side of the park is filled with lush oak trees and a pathway for leisurely strolls. No wonder it was so quiet in her house.

I stand near the edge of a pond in the center of the park and watch a raft of ducks as they splash and quack and say good morning to each other. Squirrels dig at the earth in search of hidden food. A gentle breeze blows off the water, cuts the morning heat and rustles the leaves. A few people pass by with dogs and wave as if I live in the neighborhood. Everything about this place is quaint and chill and absolutely perfect.

After fifteen minutes of wandering the park and collecting my thoughts, I locate a bench on the outskirts and request an

Uber. I pluck a twig from the ground, twirl it between my fingers and zone out while I wait.

Thank God I have today to myself. After everything last night, I need the time. To think and map out what happens next. Because after last night, I won't deny myself or Cora. Not again.

seventeen

CORA

Something wet scrapes over my nose. My cheek. My eye. It stops after a minute, but starts up again. My eyebrow. The corner of my mouth. Then my ear. Argh! *What the hell is that?* I swat at the air and come in contact with a bulky body of fur.

Luna.

She paws my face, a sweet and pleading meow only inches from my ear. When I don't respond, she paws me again and meows louder. It is a scratchy-whiny meow. One that tells me it is past time to wake up. One that tells me I need to pay her attention.

Grr… I shove her to the side and scoot to sit up. Luna rubs the side of her body against my arm, doing a figure eight and coming back for more, a noticeable purr echoing in the darkness. Giving her a light pat and a few pets, I creep out from under the sheet.

"Come on pretty girl. Let's get you some breakfast." As soon as the word breakfast is said, her cries morph into a frenzy as if I never feed her. Ridiculous, but adorable.

When she hops off the bed, I reach for my phone and pick

up a piece of paper resting atop it. I pinch my eyes together in the darkness and see it is a note from Gavin.

> *C,*
>
> *I didn't want to wake you. Or disturb your morn-ing. Or make things awkward when you woke up and I was still here.*
>
> *See you tomorrow. Enjoy your day off.*
>
> *G*

I flip the paper over as if looking for more. Or him. But find neither. No more words. No Gavin.

After drinking far too much last night, things are a bit foggy. I walk to the kitchen and pour some food into Luna's bowl before grabbing a glass of water. His note still in my hand, I walk over to the couch and plop down, a waft of his beachy pine scent hits my nose and I close my eyes as I inhale deeply.

I am so very fucked.

I reread the note a few times, trying to find some hidden meaning in his words. But nothing stands out. There is no hidden agenda. No secret meaning. It is just Gavin being Gavin.

I tip my head back and stare at the ceiling. Stare at the minor imperfections and connect them like constellations. Which makes me think of stars and night skies and sunsets. *Ugh.*

No way I can sit in this house all day. If I stare at the walls, my mind will keep venturing off into uncharted waters. Waters that always circle back to Gavin. I need to get out and do something. Anything. Maybe have a girl's day with Shelly.

Watch some memorable karaoke and eat fried foods with her and Jonas. Like we always do.

Rising from the couch, I go snag my phone from the charger and shoot a text to Shelly.

Got plans today?

Not sure what her work schedule is since it fluctuates week to week, but fingers crossed we can hang today. I just need to get out of my head. And in order to do that, I need distractions and meaningless conversation.

Off work soon. What's up?

Hang out when you're done?

I'm down. 2:00ish good?

I'll be ready. See you soon.

Happy to have a planned distraction, I eat a yogurt with granola before heading to the shower. As I wash away every-thing that happened last night—professed feelings back out in the open and slapped across my friends' faces—I make a vow to myself.

I will not fall in love with Gavin Hunt. *Again.* I will not. Or at least that is what I keep telling myself.

"How's it look?" Shelly asks through the fitting room door.

I stare at myself in the wide, full-length mirror and wonder what the hell I am doing. *Being a goddamn idiot is what I'm doing.*

My fingers toy with the black lacy boy short underwear, my eyes glued to the bra—also lacy, but resembling that of a leather cage. If I really want to, I can snap a few clips and the two undergarments connect and resemble a vixen-like leotard.

"Uh… I like it. I think."

Actually, I love it. Shelly doesn't need to know that, though. But why the hell would I need to buy lingerie like this? Not as if I have someone to wear it for. And I haven't stepped foot in a club in years—the only other place I might wear something like this.

I stare at myself in the mirror as I fiddle with the lace under my fingertips.

Not as if I need clarity to strike, but let's be honest. I know why I want to buy this. Want to wear it. The exact reason. The one person who has infiltrated my thoughts since the beginning of the week is said reason. Gavin. I picked up this sexy-as-hell lingerie set because I was thinking about him when we walked past the table. Part of me snatched it because it is black and punk and risqué. Another part of me is optimistic I will have a reason to wear it.

Many women wear sexy lingerie because it provides an air of power. Even if no one else sees it, they come alive with the provocative attire on their skin.

"You think? How can you not know? Let me see," Shelly insists. And before I realize what is happening, the fitting room door opens and she steps in.

"What are you doing?" I whisper-yell.

"If you didn't want me coming in, you should've locked the door."

"Lesson learned," I mumble.

Shelly's eyes sweep over the racy ensemble before a low whistle leaves her lips.

Her scrutiny isn't uncomfortable or awkward. Neither is the fact that she stands in a five-by-five dressing room with me while I wear next to nothing and she ogles my semi-naked body. We have been friends long enough to have more of a sister bond than anything else. That is not to say we didn't share the curiosity phase in our younger years. But that was all it was for both of us, curiosity.

"He'll love it." She claps her hands together, a wicked gleam dancing on her face.

"Who?" Confusion laces my tone as I cock my head and stare at my best friend.

"Gavin," she says, looking at me as if I have two heads for questioning her comment. "He *is* the reason you're trying this on. Right? I mean, I know you're unique in many ways, but no woman tries on lingerie like this unless she has a reason."

Of course she is right, but I will not admit it. Not to her and not aloud. Geez. When did I become such a hot mess of confusion? Oh, I know. Since the moment I heard his voice drift into that banquet room. The logical side of me gets up in my face and screams. She tells me to finish this shoot and act as if he never stepped foot back in Florida.

But the rest of me... she is off traipsing along the beach, holding hands with the only person she has ever loved. The only person who stripped her bare and shattered her to pieces.

No, I refuse to be that lost, melancholy girl again. Downright refuse.

"Get out," I mutter. "I need to change."

Shelly registers the shift in my demeanor and steps out of the fitting room. When the door clicks shut, I take one last look at the siren lingerie on my body before stripping it off and tossing it to the side. After I redress, I leave the room and hand the lingerie to the attendant, thanking her.

"Not buying it?" Shelly asks, a sorrowful look aimed my way.

"No. I have no reason to."

And that sad, lonely truth hits me harder with each step as we exit the store.

eighteen
CORA

Fifteen years ago

Three weeks have passed since the first time Gavin sat next to me under the oak tree at school. Three weeks and we had become friends. Good friends. So good, we spend time together outside of school.

Gavin has even become a close runner up in the best friend department. Shelly will always take the lead. But after the first day, after he saw me adding his frame to my loner girl drawing, it had been nothing except uphill.

Besides hanging at lunch, we saw each other in art and English. Our conversations started off basic, discussing our family life and what we liked doing outside of school. Gavin seems to love art as much as I do, but swears his talents are nowhere as amazing as mine. Only time will tell that truth. We also like similar genres of movies.

By the end of the first week of school, I learned about his love for fish tacos, the beach, music, and sunsets. He told me a great day involved all four and the thought makes me smile at how easily they could be done together.

I lean against the wide trunk of the oak tree. *Our tree.* Retrieving the baby carrots and hummus from my bag, I start snacking as I flip through my book and wait for Gavin to join me. A page and a half later, he sits beside me and grumbles under his breath.

"You okay?" I ask and pause reading my book when I notice the firm pout on his face. His pouty face is kind of cute.

"Yeah. Just a little turned off by this tuna noodle casserole they're serving today. It's gnarly looking." His pouty face resumes and I bite my lip to stop myself from laughing.

"News flash, Gavin. All the cafeteria food is gnarly looking. Why do you think I bring my own food?"

He pokes his fork at the pale, goopy casserole and pushes it to all corners of the tray. As if spreading it out will magically make it more appealing.

"I might have to start waking up ten minutes earlier, so I can make something. Or…" He peeks over at me with a shit-eating grin. "You could always make lunch for both of us. I'll pay you instead of the school."

I toss a carrot at him. "I'm not your mama, boy," I tease.

He catches the carrot, sets his tray on the ground, and pops the snack in his mouth. But what I don't expect is when he starts reaching for more of my food, play fighting with me as I try to push him away. This happens for a couple minutes—him trying to steal my food, me defending my territory. We both laugh and taunt each other.

But then something shifts.

His playfulness stops when he knocks me to the ground and hovers inches above me. Carrots forgotten. Steely-gray eyes pierce mine and my breath hitches. If he lowers himself a few more inches, his lips would touch mine. And this fact heats parts of me I didn't know existed. Like I have a new organ named Gavin.

I want him to kiss me.

Only two boys have kissed me before. Greg Barton and Jeremy Ashford. Greg, two years ago. And Jeremy last school year.

Greg Barton is a year older than me and I thought kissing him would be life-altering. And it was, just not in the way I had hoped. It actually grossed me out. He had kissed me sloppily, his saliva-coated lips and tongue painting my mouth like they had no idea *where* my mouth was. I never kissed him back because the thought terrified me.

Jeremy Ashford went to middle school with me and was the most popular boy in the school. I was so nervous just before we kissed. Probably because we were at a friend's party playing truth or dare. He was dared to kiss me. Poor guy. I still feel bad for him and the bite I'd given his tongue when he pushed it between my lips.

Needless to say, after my most recent experience, rumors spread about how I didn't know how to kiss or make out. And everyone consoled Jeremy and his marred tongue. Whatever. He was a douche. Besides, I always did better on my own. Loner girl and all.

But looking into Gavin's eyes above mine, his lips separated just enough for him to draw in breath, I know kissing him would be different. Not another awkward kiss to add to the list of strange life experiences. But maybe on another list. One where you write down all the things you never want to forget because nothing else will compare.

We may have only met three weeks ago, but Gavin is not like every other guy. And I don't know how that makes me feel.

His body presses heavier into my belly and chest, his lips a breath from mine. I close my eyes, sending a message to the gods above and thanking them for whatever is happening. My breath hitches again in anticipation and then he is gone. His weight removed from my body and the warm breeze blowing my hair in my face.

My eyes fly open and glance over to where he sits up, a gleam of pure joy smeared across his face as he pops a carrot in his mouth.

Did he only want the stupid carrot? Or did he want to kiss me too?

Rising up from the ground, I tackle him and reach for my stolen lunch. It's not long before we share my food and his tray of scary casserole is long forgotten. We munch on veggies and hummus, and I share half of my cashew butter and banana sandwich with him. We share jokes and laugh. And I promise to make him lunch every day, as long as he foots the cost.

But when we walk away from our tree today, a new sensation flutters inside me. A new wish to be fulfilled. A desire to be kissed by the boy walking beside me.

nineteen

CORA

Present

"Another round?" the server asks as she deposits loaded fries, onion rings, and our specified burgers on the table.

"Please," I tell her as I stuff the veggie burger between my lips.

I glance over at the stage and wish karaoke grandpa was doing his number up there. Could really use the laugh. Instead, I am forced to watch some fifty-something guy going through a midlife crisis. He practically makes out with the microphone—*I hope someone sanitizes that thing before anyone else uses it*—while he sings "Every Rose Has Its Thorns" by Poison.

...and I think his tongue just grazed the mic. Ew!

Our table is momentarily quiet as the four of us scarf down our burgers, occasionally snatching an onion ring or fry. When I come up for air, I notice I have three sets of eyes on me. Erin, Shelly, and Jonas each drill their own hole into my skull, mining for details of why I am acting off. Their weighted stares like an unannounced party in my head. Shelly and I spent the afternoon together, so her matched stares can take a pill.

Personally, I always think I'm strange. So, I don't know what their deal is.

"I wish you would've invited me shopping earlier," Erin speaks up, bringing conversation back to the table.

"Sorry," I confess. "I didn't purposely exclude you. Just wasn't thinking straight. Guess my brain was still a little foggy from drinking too much last night." Amongst other things. But I am not announcing that to the table.

To be honest, my day out with Shelly didn't clear any of the fog either. Not like I hoped it would. Every store we passed, something caught my eye and sent my thought train Gavin's direction. It's only been a matter of days, yet he consumes every part of my day. Even now, while I sit with three of my friends and try to have a night of fun.

"It's okay. Next time," she indicates.

"Next time," I promise.

Another round of silence ensues as the woe-is-me guy leaves the karaoke stage. I cross my fingers under the table, hoping the next person is better and more upbeat. And as I watch a pair of ladies walk up to the stage, each grabbing a mic and whispering to each other before the music kicks in, I hope my prayers will be answered.

Seconds later, "Bootylicious" by Destiny's Child crackles in the air and the two begin singing. They aren't horrible, but also not great. But at least the way they are shaking their asses onstage is entertaining. I laugh lightly and keep my eyes on the stage.

"You make it home okay last night?" Jonas's voice breaks my trance on the singing duo. And when I peer over at him to speak, guilt riddles me at the concern stretched over his face.

Normal me would have let him know I made it home safely. Normal me was absent last night.

Since the day Jonas and I met, there has always been an easy way about us. Jonas is a great guy. Genuine and thoughtful and kindhearted. He knows how to have fun and make people laugh. And there is no denying I like him. But nothing more could ever happen between us. It wouldn't be fair to him if I couldn't be all in. That and his former relationship statuses.

"Yeah," I mumble. "Gavin drove me home in my car."

He nods, slow and steady, as his eyes stay fixed on his plate. Although his head is down, I notice the twitches in his expression. The flickers of emotion he doesn't want on display. And it's a stab to the heart that he doesn't want me to know what he feels or thinks.

Please look at me. Don't shut me out. That is what I *want* to say to him, but I stop myself. I don't want to send him mixed messages. Say words that mean one thing but could be interpreted in some misconstrued way.

Jonas and I have been friends for years now. I don't have many male friends or acquaintances—not on purpose—and I can't imagine having a better guy friend than him. Things with Jonas… nothing is complicated or artificial. What you see is what you get. And that is not a bad thing. I never have to question our friendship or who he is or what his motives are.

He is sweet and funny and would go out of his way to help a stranger. Having him in my company has never been weird. And although I know things have shifted a little between us, he would do anything for me. As I would for him. Like a true friend.

"Can I ask you something?" Jonas asks. Erin and Shelly sit across from us, chatting separately.

"You know you can," I tell him. Because it's true. I don't hide who I am from people I trust.

"What's going on with you and Gavin?" His face serious. More serious than I have seen it over the years.

"Not sure what you mean. He's the model I'm shooting right now."

In actuality, I know exactly what he means. Where his question is directed. He wants to know the history between us, and how that affects things now. I have no intention of lying to Jonas, but I don't want to spew word vomit and overshare information he doesn't want to hear. There is no need to dredge up things better left behind.

He cocks his head and studies my face a moment. "You know that's not what I mean. There's something else going on between the two of you. Am I right?"

I have no clue. God, I wish I knew the answer. The seesaw of emotions makes me nauseous. "Maybe. But I don't know," I say with a shrug.

His bluish-hazel eyes bore into mine as he tries to read the words left unsaid. Under the table, his knee brushes against my leg and I close my eyes as the contact sends a rush of jitters through my chest. There is no use in denying my attraction to Jonas. After all, he is easy on the eyes and looks at me as if no other woman walks the earth.

What woman doesn't want a man like that? Someone who only sees her.

The music fades into the background as his knee stays pressed against me. My eyes remain closed and my food forgotten. His weight shifts against me, his knee sliding higher up the outside of my thigh as I feel him lean into me. My breathing picks up as his rough stubble grazes against my cheek. *What is he doing?* I might just have a heart attack in the middle of the bar.

His breath is hot on my ear and I stop breathing altogether. "I hope not," he whispers. "Because that wouldn't bode well for me." And then he kisses me below the ear, trailing two more below it before pulling away.

Damnit. I am so royally fucked.

My heart hammers against my rib cage while my lungs try to remember how to work. His knee slides back to where it was moments earlier, but still touches me. The three spots where his lips touched my skin singe and sting, as if branding me with his essence.

The idea of opening my eyes scares the hell out of me. I'm scared of what I will see and feel and possibly realize. The overwhelming sensation has crept into my veins many times, but I purposely shove it down. Emotions and thoughts that tell me it is okay to like Jonas more than a friend. That it's okay to want someone other than the boy—now man—who holds my heart prisoner.

God, what do Shelly and Erin think of me right now? As I sit on this stool and fight the urge to kiss a man I have thought about kissing countless times, but stopped myself because my heart steps up to the plate.

I take a deep breath and harness every ounce of bravery inside me as I open my eyes. Jonas's link to mine immediately. Something different resides within them, though. Fire. Passion. Desires he has kept smoldering for years. Has all this come to life because Gavin is here? Is he finally acting on how he feels for me because he fears his chances are fading?

Or has jealousy brought them to the forefront? I don't want jealousy to be the reason he chooses to make a move.

Jealousy isn't the right reason to tell someone you care for them.

Looking across the table, I realize Erin and Shelly are absent. "Where are…" I trail off.

"They went to the bathroom before stepping outside to make a call," he informs me.

"Together?" I ask, the absurdity of it layering my tone.

"I guess so. They got up at the same time and went the same way." His eyes never leave me. "Does that bother you? That they left us alone."

My eyes dart between his and I suddenly see him a little different than I did ten minutes ago. "No. Don't be silly. Of course it doesn't bother me." I snatch an onion ring to occupy my mouth before I ramble any further.

"Good." His arm inches closer to me and his warm hand rests atop my bopping knee. "Because I'd hate to think you're nervous to be around me now."

It is not that I'm nervous per se to be around Jonas. More like I don't want history repeating itself. The last guy I loved —who had also been my best friend beforehand—moved across the country. Granted, it wasn't his choice to do so, but he made zero effort to return. I put in all the effort and he just didn't. The only reason Gavin is here now is because his work brought him here. Not me.

If this shoot hadn't come up, would he have returned?

I have asked myself this question too many times this week. Have questioned if he ever had intentions of returning. Even if I ask Gavin, would he tell me the truth? Or only what I want to hear? Would he sugarcoat the reason it took him more than a decade to come back here? To me. If he is doing so well in his career, if he still loves me the way he claims, why didn't he return sooner? This whole situation frustrates me on so many levels. I don't know which way is up anymore.

God, it feels as if I'm in the middle of an epic battle. The battle for my affection. And somehow, I became the prize. Against my own volition. What if I want things to stay how they are? What if I don't want a relationship—other than friendship—with either one of them? Do I get a say in the matter? Of all the people in this situation, I should get the biggest say in the outcome. My heart is the one on the line, after all.

"I'm not nervous to be around you," I say after a long stretch of silence. "More worried, I guess."

"Worried?" He is quick to ask.

"Yes. I don't want things to change. And whether intentional or not, relationships change the dynamic between people and friendships. This" —I point between the two of us — "is perfect right now. What if us being more than what we are changes that? I can't lose you as a friend, Jonas. It would crush me."

Jonas's fingers trace small circles above my knee, the gentle motion is soothing and worrisome. I have always enjoyed Jonas's company. Always smiled and laughed and had a good time when we were together. A time here and there, I thought maybe he wanted more than friendship, but he never made a move or asked me on a date. So I brushed it off and assumed I read him wrong.

Ninety-nine percent of our outings include Shelly and/or Erin. It isn't me not wanting to spend individual time with him. More like the thought never occurred to me for us to hang out alone. Jonas is my friend, and I usually do friend stuff in group settings. Things have always been that way. And only occasionally veer off.

"Believe me, I know exactly where you're coming from. That's the reason I've never said anything. Never put myself out there to you. Because I'd be broken without you," he confesses then pauses, taking a breath before locking eyes with me. "But now… it seems like if I wait to tell you how I feel, I'll miss the opportunity. Or I could lose you. He's had your heart once before. If he's lucky enough to have it again, I…"

He doesn't finish his thought as he drops his chin, but I know what he would have said. *I wouldn't stand a chance.* Is he right? If Gavin somehow won my heart again, would I cave and be with him? Part of me instantly says yes—the part that has longed for him for years. Another part of me says no—that being the logical, rational side. The side that reminds me of the painful days, the loneliness and the heartache from before. All the tears and cold nights and nightmares.

I lay my hand over Jonas's and his eyes jerk up to meet mine. "I know," I tell him. "But no matter what, you'll always be a part of me."

Seconds later, Shelly and Erin plop back on their stools and look over at the woman singing karaoke. My thoughts run on high speed, and I have no clue what song is playing, nor do I care. All I know is, below the wooden grain of this tall tabletop, Jonas hasn't removed his hand, and neither have I.

Fifteen years ago

One more hour and Thanksgiving break starts. Nine glorious days of not getting up before the sun. Of sleeping in and zero required reading or assignments. But those aren't the best parts of time off school. Not by a long shot.

What I'm really over the moon about is having uninterrupted time with Cora.

Sure, I see her throughout the week at school. And sporadically we see each other on the weekend to "study." But we are never really alone. When we are "studying," it is in her living room or mine, our parents not far away. One of us on the couch, the other between their legs on the floor.

On occasion, I catch myself playing with a strand of her hair while she sits in front of me, arms warm against the inside of my calves. Or I lean into her legs when I'm cross-legged on the floor. She never brushes me off or acts as if the gesture makes her uncomfortable. And every once in a while, the light brushing of her fingertips draws on the skin of my neck. When she does this, I have to remember how to breathe. How to think.

We have preplanned a couple days of Thanksgiving break. Meeting with friends, hanging out and playing Putt-Putt or bowling. But I hope she will want to spend more time together, just the pair of us. Within a week of school starting, she easily slipped into friend—if not best friend—territory. A week after that, I craved to see her as much as possible and had an inkling she would always be more. At least to me. And I hope she reciprocates.

The bell rings and cheers can be heard throughout the school. Cheers of a week of freedom and sleep and no schedule. Cheers to less supervision and good times with friends. Closing my textbook, I stuff it and my notebook into my backpack. I slide out of my seat with a smile plastered on my face and head out the door. This week will be perfect.

Through the dark lenses on my sunglasses, I stare out at the water and watch Cora as she splashes Shelly in the shallows. Although it is late November, the sun beats down mild temperatures ranging from the low eighties to the high seventies in this part of Florida. The Gulf is still warm, but will cool in the next couple of weeks.

Micah, Shelly's older brother and my best friend for the last few years, sits next to me and doesn't hide the fact he ogles women ten-plus years his senior. But I'm cool with him being distracted. It disguises the fact I can't seem to remove my eyes from Cora's creamy white skin. The pallor similar to the snow I saw last winter when my parents took us on a road trip during winter break.

Hair black as coal, skin white as cotton, lips red as fresh cherries. Her smile bright as the sun on a summer day and her laugh a sound that sings to my heartstrings the moment I hear it.

Everything about her stunning. Spellbinding. Hypnotizing.

It's not until Micah backhands my bicep that I realize he has been talking to me and I have no clue what he said. "Sorry, man. What?" And I will my eyes to leave Cora to look over at Micah.

"I said we picked the perfect day to come out here. Lots of oil-slicked beauties out today," he states, brows waggling. Today is one of those days when Micah behaves like the typical horny teenage boy. Both annoying and not. But he is my best friend and I tolerate his ways.

There is only one person I have an interest in looking at, but for the sake of not being razzed, I nod and add, "Definitely a perfect day." I leave my response generic, hoping he won't press further.

But Micah isn't the type of guy to leave things unsaid. I have only known him a short time, but it hasn't taken long to learn how outgoing he is. "Anyone catching your eye? You've been a little zoned out."

Only one person has caught my eye, but I have no intention of divulging this tidbit. Not now. "No one in particular. You?"

"There's a trio of blondes at three o'clock I've been watching for a few. Think I might go say hello. You want to go with?"

"Nah. Think I'll cool off in the water for a bit."

I would rather be inches away from the magnetic girl sporting a black two-piece with curves in all the right places.

Micah rises from the blanket, brushes sand off his legs and

board shorts, and straightens his spine. I'm half tempted to tell him it doesn't matter if you have sand on you, dipshit, you're at the beach. We are surrounded by sand. But I opt to refrain from jabbing him.

In a few quick strides, he walks away from me and makes a beeline for the females who I hope will occupy his time a while. After I'm certain he is not turning back, I scoot to the edge of the blanket and stare out at the water a moment. Cora and Shelly tread water just deep enough to reach the edge of their shoulders. They talk about something, Shelly's hand animating above the water every five seconds. Cora watches her studiously behind the dark tint of her sunglasses and smiles here and there.

Deep breath in, I stand from our reserved spot on the beach and trek fifty feet toward the water's edge. The small waves break over my shins as I shuffle into the water. Once I stand waist deep in the salty surf, I sink in the water, and wet my hair before swimming to Cora and Shelly.

As I approach them, I hear them talking about seeing a movie later. Intrigued, I wonder if I will be invited to said movie. Who cares what plays on the screen, I would love to just sit beside Cora for two hours in the dim-lit theater. Would I even be able to focus on the movie? Probably not.

"Hey," Cora says, breathless. I tread water on her right until I realize I can reach the sand below, planting my feet but keeping my body the same height as the two of them. "Tired of tanning yourself." A teasing smile lights her face.

"Ha-ha. Micah walked off to hit on some chicks and I was getting toasty on the blanket. Thought I'd see what you two were up to."

"We were just talking about seeing a movie later," Shelly chimes in. "Not sure what's playing, but we could pick whatever. Usually, there's always something good at the theater around the holidays."

"I'm in, if that's okay with you guys," I tell them both.

"Cool," Shelly pants, her body winded from treading water so long. "I'm gonna head back to the blanket, tan for a little, and see if anyone else wants to join us."

Before either of us says another word, Shelly swims to shore and leaves me alone with Cora. Exactly what I was hoping for.

In the anonymity of the water, my hands itch to reach forward and grab hold of her waist. I stare at her dark lenses through mine, neither of us uttering a word. We have never needed to fill time with meaningless conversation. By some unknown universal connection, we can read each other without ever speaking a word.

As if she hears my thoughts, as if she knows the urge building inside me, she swims closer and stops inches from my frame. The water surrounding me ebbs and flows with her arm and leg movements as she continues to tread. I stop fighting my instinct. Stop resisting what is in front of me.

The moment my hands grasp the curves of her waist, her arms and legs still. To anyone looking from the shore, nothing has changed except for her lack of distance. Our bodies hidden in the wide open. It is exhilarating. Not that I care if anyone sees us together. If anything, it would be heaven to tell the world my feelings for Cora. Feelings that have been growing stronger by the minute.

One hand holds her steady while the other begins to trace lines along the side of her torso. Up and down. Bikini top to bikini bottom. Her lips part just enough to see past the bold red rouge.

Under the water, her chest expands and contracts under

my touch. She doesn't stop me, but I have to know if she is okay with me touching her like this. As much as it would devastate me to hear her say no, I would never press her for something she had no desire to pursue. I don't want to ruin what we have.

Leaning forward, my face an inch or two from hers, I whisper, "Is this okay?"

Her breath hitches, and I wonder if her eyes are closed behind her heavy-tinted lenses. She nods, her voice breathy when she speaks. "Yes."

Her fingertips brush over my chest, startling me. "Sorry," I mutter. "Just unexpected."

She doesn't say anything in response, her fingers exploring my chest as we bob in the water. Minutes pass, the sounds of other beachgoers fade away. All that exists is her and me and our bodies growing closer and closer as we explore each other's skin.

My eyes drop from her frames, focusing on her lips and wondering what it would be like to kiss her. I have dreamed of kissing a few girls before, but that is all. Just dreams. But I think if I kiss Cora, I will never want to kiss another person in my life. My eyes pop back up to hers, wishing I could see her bold green irises. See what she is thinking. What she is feeling. If they hold the same questions or possibility mine do.

Without thinking, I close the last inches between us. My head tilting, lips hovering breathless above hers, waiting to see if she backs away. When she doesn't draw back, I take the gesture as invitation and seal my lips to hers.

Warm, soft lips press against mine, her hands breaching the water's surface and wrapping around my neck. I pull her impossibly closer to me, swiping the tip of my tongue over her lips and relishing in the sensation when she parts them and lets me in.

Her mouth is sweet and hungry on mine. And when a small whimper echoes in her chest, I am a goner. My hands roam her body under the security blanket of the water, kneading and caressing her hips. We stay like this, the measure of time nonexistent.

But when I feel her legs wrap around my waist, her strength locking us together at the hips, I break my mouth from hers, gasping. At this rate, things will progress much quicker than either of us is prepared to handle. In public, no less.

"Why'd you stop?" she asks, confusion lacing her voice.

"Because we have forever. And I don't want to rush anything with you."

She leans into me, pressing a sweet, brief kiss to my lips. "I like the sound of that."

Present

"I don't understand the issue, man," Micah harps from the driver's seat. "I may not grasp what's going on between the two of you. Honestly, I never have. But you got to do what's best for you."

Why is it so hard to talk about women and relationships with guy friends? Unless they are in a relationship, everything comes out piggish.

Over the years, I've had several female friends. One of my best friends in Cali is female. We could talk about anything. Have in-depth conversations, no matter the topic, and come out feeling resolute. None of that is happening right now. Maybe because Micah has never been in my position. Never felt torn or anguished or helpless because of someone else.

"That's the problem. I'm not sure I know what's best for me anymore," I groan. "Before my mom took the promotion and moved us across the country, I had everything mapped out. Things changed days after we landed in California. Not only was my life turned upside down, everything I thought I'd have was ripped away from me." I pause, taking a swig of water before continuing. "Over the last decade-plus, she's always been the one thing I held on to. Even if I was the only one who knew. And now…"

Music blares from the speakers, masking the silence between us. Micah has no comprehension of what I am going through. My inner turmoil. A waging war roaring inside me. One side says I should head back to California when this shoot ends, leave her behind and allow her to resume the life she has built without me. The other side screams at me to return to California, sell my shit, strategize my future gigs and return to Cora's side. Sensible versus senseless.

The decision is one only I can make, but I was hoping for some form of support. Maybe some strong words of advice. Or just some *if I were in your shoes* talk. And unfortunately for me, Micah is no help whatsoever.

"And now, someone else is trying to step up to the plate," Micah states over the music. He states the obvious and my blood runs cold. I shiver at the thought of Cora being with someone. Someone who isn't me. Yes, I am a selfish ass for even thinking that way. But I left my heart with her all those years ago. I refuse to let an outsider stomp his steel-toes on it and whisk away my girl.

He steers the car into a parking lot, finding a spot amongst the crowd. We step out of the car and head for the entrance. Music blares loud and obnoxious every time the doors swing open. As we climb the few steps, I slap the back of his shoulder. "Thanks for bringing me out tonight. And thanks for listening."

"I'd be a dick if I didn't."

The whole situation with me and Cora is the furthest thing from what Micah wants to discuss, but he has always been a good friend. If anything, he probably just wants us to get things figured out—whichever way it turns out—and be done with all this back and forth shit.

We walk through the doors and the music hits me like a wall. Micah gestures to the bar when he steps up to the hostess stand and she signals us to head over. Both of us park on a stool and order a beer when the bartender comes over. After she deposits them in front of us, we each take a sip before sparking more conversation.

Micah and I catch up on life, avoiding all subject matter that could lead to Cora. He relays how the nightclub he manages is going. I suggest he brings me out there before I leave. He talks about an older woman, Rochelle, he dated for a little over a year. How serious his and Rochelle's relationship was until he found her fucking another guy. A guy ten years younger than Micah, and twenty-three years younger than Rochelle. Many heated words were exchanged between the two of them, but Micah said he would never be able to trust her again.

Since the relationship with Rochelle, Micah hasn't committed to anyone. He no longer sees the value in devoting yourself to one person. In his words, "setting yourself up for pain and heartbreak." Now, over the last year since they broke up, he is a proud manwhore. And when he tells me this, a pang of guilt hits me over the manwhore moments I have had myself.

Because over the last thirteen years, I have never wanted a relationship with anyone other than Cora. Although, I have gone on dates. Fucked a sea of women. Never once feeling guilt over suppressing the loneliness inside me. But now that I am back here. Now that I am within proximity of her. Everything is changing.

Micah prattles on about themed nights they do at the club, and I zone out while my eyes wander around the bar. The place is packed, which isn't abnormal for a Friday night anywhere. Bodies dancing on a makeshift dance floor. Tall tabletops littered with brown bottles, fried foods, and pint glassware. Horrible, screechy voices up on an eight-by-eight stage attempting to sing lyrics on a prompter. No matter where you are in the States, bars are bars. The only thing different is the accents and clothing.

As I make a final visual circuit of the bar, I freeze when I hit a tabletop close to the corner of the room.

Rage gushes in my bloodstream. My heart bashing against my ribcage like a boxer to a punching bag. Everything inside me molten lava and I am ready to beat the shit out of someone. Specifically, the brown-haired motherfucker touching my girl.

I kick back the stool, hitting the person behind me and causing Micah's head to swing my way. "Dude, you okay?" he asks.

My eyes fix across the room, hands balled into fists at my sides, breath heaving in my chest. Micah touches my arm and I flinch at the contact. When I don't answer him, he follows my line of sight and mutters *fuck me* under his breath.

"Let's just go, man. They're friends."

I hear his words, but can't take my eyes off *his* hand on *her* thigh. *Friends, my ass.* They may be *friends*, but he definitely wants to be more than her friend. And I am not having it.

Yanking my wallet out, I drop a twenty on the bar and storm off, half my beer forgotten. As I weave my way through the crowded bar, I hear Micah yelling for me, telling me to just leave it alone. But there is no chance in hell I am walking out of here and ignoring the two of them together. No fucking way.

I am ten feet and three bodies away from them when Cora looks up, her eyes going wide and her body scooting off the stool. She reaches me before I can get close enough to the table. Close enough to beat the shit out of this guy.

"Gavin!" she yells at me over the music. My eyes lock on his, and the self-assured smile he throws at me has me trying to push Cora aside. But her hand comes to my face and instantly stops me. "Gavin!" she yells again. This time I look down at her, noticing the fear in her soft green eyes.

We stare at each other a minute, her eyes trying to tell me that everything is not as it appears. I want to believe her. God, how I want to believe her. I have no reason to doubt her or her truths. But my insecurities sit on my shoulder, mocking me and whispering falsehoods into my ear. Telling me I will never have her again. Reminding me how I lost her once and how I will lose her again.

"It's not what you think," she whispers, and I have to read her lips over the noise.

"And what was I thinking?" I prompt.

"That we're on a date. That we're more than friends." Her voice grows loud enough to break the volume barrier, but not loud enough for others to hear us.

"His hand looked quite cozy on your thigh. For someone who's *just a friend*," I sneer.

Her hand runs down my chest and squeezes my hand. "Come outside with me." And then she pushes past me, towing me out of the bar and away from *him*.

We weave through the crowd, exit the front and continue walking until she stops us beside her car in the back of the lot.

When she spins around, she drops my hand and hits me with years of anger and frustration.

"What the hell, Gavin!"

"Sorry I interrupted your date with mister auto shop," I jab, laying the sarcasm on thick. "I thought you two were just friends. Looks like he seems to think otherwise. Maybe I should go back inside and reiterate the definition for him."

"First of all" —she points her finger in my face— "you have no say in regards to who I date and who I don't. Second, why do you suddenly think you're all high and mighty? What… you stroll back into town and think the whole place stopped existing when you left. That everything is exactly as it was when you left. Newsflash, asshole. Nothing is how you left it. Nothing."

"I can see that," I seethe, stepping closer into her space. "If it was how I left it, this conversation wouldn't ever happen. We'd be…" I bite my tongue.

"What? What exactly would we be doing, Gavin?"

God, she is gorgeous when she gets angry. Dangerously so. And before I can form a rational response in my head, I reach for her face and drag her into me, crushing my lips to hers. Her hands shove and beat against my chest, her lips trying to pull away. But I strengthen my grip and get lost in the feel of her. The warmth. Her taste.

In two breaths, her will caves and she melts into me. Her hands fist my shirt as she kisses me with a fervor I have never known. I wrap one arm around her waist while the other hand skims up her back and gets lost in the length of her strands.

The kiss is packed with anger and frustration, fear and worry, happiness and pain. But most of all, it shares the depth of our deprivation. How neither of us has been complete since the day my mother put me on a plane and flew me thousands of miles away. How we have gone about life, but had forgotten what it was like to live.

She breaks the kiss, gasping for air as she tries to come back down to earth. When both of our bodies have calmed, she peeks up at me. "Gavin…" My name a blessing and a curse on her tongue. "Please. Please don't hurt me again. I can't…" she pleads. Begs me not to put her through the heartache she suffered thirteen years ago.

I yank her impossibly close to my chest, my arms cocooning her frail frame. "Shh. I know, baby. I know." The ease with which the term of endearment slips out isn't lost on me. It also doesn't appear to bother Cora. We stand like this—her clutching me and me pressing her to my chest, rocking her—for minutes, maybe hours. Letting her go isn't an option I am comfortable with, so I hold her and wait for her to break the connection. Praying she never will.

"Can we go somewhere to talk? I really don't want to stand in this parking lot all night," she whispers.

"Yeah. Wherever you want to go, baby."

Somehow, we land on the beach. Of all the places we could have gone, not quite sure why she picked the beach. The park across the street from her house is more her style. But maybe she chose the beach because it is mine. Or maybe she chose the beach because that is where everything evolved for us. Where everything went from friends to something words can't describe.

Either way, she is with me now and it is the only thing I focus on.

When we arrive at the beach, she pays a meter and we

stroll north. After separating from the busier section of the beach, everything around us grows quieter and calmer. The only sounds are the crunch of sand under our shoes and the choppy water breaking on the shore. The air thick with humidity and salty on our skin. This part of the beach darker with the lack of businesses to illuminate it. A few residents out for a late-night walk.

Her hand presses softly against mine as she stops us from walking any further in the soft sand. Plopping down, our fingers still woven together, we sit on the beach and face the darkness of the Gulf. Neither of us says a word. We simply sit in silence and lean into each other for a while. Her ink-black hair whips across her face and mine.

The ease I have with Cora has never been replicated with any other person. Over the years, I tried dating. Tried putting myself out there and moving on, certain Cora was doing the same. And over time, I learned I would never find someone else who I'd want to be in a long-term relationship with. So, I shifted my ways. Became the polar opposite of how everyone knew me. Morphed into a slut. Because slutting around was easier than finding someone else and losing the one person you really wanted all along.

Because regardless of how things go between us now, Cora is it for me. The one soul on this planet, packed with eight billion others, meant for me. I have known it since the first day I saw her in high school, when she bolted into home-room out of breath, making me out of breath. Confirmed it when we kissed for the first time, a beach not many miles from this one, and my soul sighed while my heart soared. I will never experience that with another person.

Nor do I want to.

"Gavin," she whispers into the darkness, breaking me

from my introspection.

I turn and kiss her temple. "What, baby?"

She rests her chin on my shoulder, the waning moonlight illuminating her enough to where I can make out the soft lines and strong features of her face. Eyes a muted green in the shadows. Skin seemingly paler. Lips red and full and inviting. "How can this possibly work?" Her question weighs heavy and is full of doubt.

How can I reassure her everything will work out? That I have the capability to move closer to her. How I don't have to be located on the other side of the country to work. I know she should know this, with what she does for work. But there is only one way she will believe it all. Proof. And I have to give it to her.

My eyes hone in on hers. "I want to move back. The sooner, the better," I admit.

She straightens her back, stiffening at my admission. A thick strand of her ebony hair whips across her face, hiding her eyes from me. She doesn't move to swipe the hairs aside, and I force myself to keep my hands rooted in place, as challenging as it is. Minutes pass, the wind shifts and brushes the hair away. As desperate as she is to school her expressions, I read her like a book. Always have.

Curiosity. Speculation. Doubt. Fear. Elation. It is all written there in an ink only my eyes see.

I grab hold of the elation and press it close to my chest. Of all the emotions swirling in her eyes, it is the one that raises my hope for us. That we can find our way back to each other.

"But how?" Her question as wispy as the wind.

Cupping her left cheek, I brush my thumb over her plump lower lip. *God, I want to kiss her again.* But I must wait. Wait until she is certain that I am still what she wants. As much as it guts me to think of her with another guy, it isn't right of me to assume she will come back to me as easily. I hurt her.

"Baby, I can live anywhere and do my job. With what you do, you have to know this."

"But what about your life out there? Your parents? How can I ask you to leave everything you've built out there? It isn't fair for me to do that."

Her question about my parents strikes a chord in my chest. I'm not ready to update her on what has happened in that part of my life. Not until I know she is open to exploring *us* again. "You don't need to worry about that. Since the day we set foot in California, my mom has heard nothing except my orchestrated plans to leave. And you may believe it isn't fair for you to ask me to come back here. Back to you." I reach forward and press my palm against her sternum. "But this is where I belong. This is where I have always belonged. You are all that matters. All that has ever mattered."

She sucks in a breath as her eyes pool with unshed tears. In the shadowed night of the beach, everything is heightened and intensified. As if being in the darkness provides a blanket of security and you feel safe enough to expose your heart. There is something to be said about the darkness and its allure. Not just the darkness of night, but the yin in all things. That is what she is… my yin. The strong, feminine cosmic force who took hold of my heart and molded it with hers. Without her, I am a pointless yang. No balance, no life, no love.

Soft, thin fingers rest atop mine, encompassing my hand in the warmth of her skin. Below my palm, her heart beats wildly. Irrationally. While her heart tells me tales of excitement and joy, her eyes shed tears of insecurity and apprehension. Both of which I understand.

But a glint of something else resides there. Hope. A belief there is truth behind my words. That I am not just saying these things to taunt or mislead her. That there is an actual chance for us to rekindle something that never should have been diffused in the first place. A new opportunity to share the undeniable magnetism we have always had for each other. Hope for a new version of us. A better version.

"How?" The single word a question that rests heavy on her lips.

"I've been talking about moving back home for years. And now that my career has a better base, I can live anywhere. I don't have to be in the thick of Hollywood for people to find me. It was different in the beginning. Being out there helped get my foot in the door. Got me in front of the right people. But now… now I can be wherever. Alyson deals with all the contractual and legal aspects. She lets me know when someone is interested in hiring me. Sure, me living out there makes life easier for her. But she can still be my agent no matter where I am. Technology allows people to be on opposite sides of the world and still work together."

Beside me, Cora's body softens and relaxes into my side once more. And it feels so fucking good to have her body pressed against mine. Her warmth and energy radiating into me. Soothing me. Revitalizing me. Like being home again. She rests her head on my shoulder and I rest mine on hers, closing my eyes and breathing in this moment.

Waves crash along the shoreline, cars rev and honk in the distance, wind whips our hair and I can't tell where hers stops and mine begins. But neither of us moves. Both of us in a strange limbo of emotions and confessions. Our hearts thrown on the line, praying to not suffer the same pain as before.

Promises exposed and hanging on the line as we breathe the same air for the first time in years.

But one truth holds absolute. I could sit with her on this beach for hours, not a soul around us, and feel nothing except bliss for the rest of my days. Everything about this moment is perfect. Everything about this moment is us.

Time evades us and I get lost in thoughts of what could be, causing me to almost miss when she speaks again.

"When?"

I am half tempted to tease her regarding the singular worded questions, but I bite my tongue. Now isn't the time to tease and play.

"When the shoot ends, I'll obviously need to go back. Alyson set up another shoot for me, but it should only be a day or two. And even though I don't have to do it in person, I need to go talk with my mom. Tell her I plan to move back as soon as possible. She is the only person, besides Alyson, who needs to know."

She lifts her head, stopping me. "What about your dad?" she asks, confused at why I only mentioned my mom.

I didn't want tonight to be when I brought this to light, but it looks as though I will have to tell her now. I take a deep breath and hold her gaze. The only set of eyes to ever provide me solace. "My dad passed away a couple years ago. Heart attack."

Instantly, her arms pull me into an embrace, lips at my ears softly whispering through light sobs. "Gavin, I'm so sorry. I didn't know."

Instinctively, my arms curl around her frame and I bring her closer to me. Within seconds, her legs straddle my lap and lock together at my backside. Yin and Yang. She weeps for me and my family. And I allow myself this moment to be raw, shedding tears for a man who was my role model for so many years. A man I have grieved for and thought I would eventually find peace after his passing. Until now. Sharing this with Cora makes the loss of him more potent and noteworthy. More real and closer to my heart.

Part of me forgot my mom and I weren't the only people to lose him. When Cora and I started dating, my parents became hers too. After so many years apart, it never dawned on me to let her know sooner of his passing. Especially since we hadn't spoken for more than a decade.

When the tears quiet, she doesn't remove herself from our embrace. As if she knows the power it holds. As if she isn't ready to let it float off with the tide.

"Thank you," I whisper into her hair, my hands stroking lazy trails up and down her back.

"For what?" she asks, head tucked in the crook of my neck.

"For saying the right words. And just being you. Everyone I've told says or shows me pity. Or walks on eggshells when we're in the same room. As if I'm this fragile creature who will crumple. So, thank you. You've always known how to say just enough to convey the right thing."

I press a kiss to her temple and her arms and legs squeeze me tighter. We sit like this a little while longer before I make a suggestion to check the time. She pulls her phone from her back pocket, lighting the screen and mutters *shit*.

"Must be late," I assume. We have been here a while. Felt like hours. But when emotions are heightened, time has a tendency to not measure the same way clocks do.

"Almost two. We should go. We have to be at Honeymoon Island by ten. Somewhere in there, both of us need to sleep and eat and whatever else."

I laugh at her slight state of panic. "It'll be fine." I stand us up, her legs tightening around my waist, arms circling my neck. "Let me walk you back to your car."

After a few strides, she unhooks her ankles and drops her feet to the sand. Once she is upright, I weave my fingers with hers and we trudge through the powdery sand and back to her car. Every six or seven steps, I glance down at her and happiness floods my heart. Warmth and love and everything right in the world.

Fuck, I have missed her.

We reach her car ten minutes later. She offers to drive me the quarter mile back to my hotel, but I decline, wanting to walk back and reminisce over tonight. She slips into the driver's seat, starts the car and rolls down the front windows. Her hair whips across her face and steals my view of her perfect, soft green irises.

Bending down, I tuck the strands behind her ear and relish the way she leans into my touch. "I'll see you in the morning." *Fuck, I want to kiss her again.* My thumb brushes over her lower lip and she shudders, eyes slipping shut. How easy would it be to kiss her right now? But I don't. I won't. From now on, she needs to lead me. She needs to let me know she wants this as much as I do. I cannot be the only one putting myself out there. The only one pressing for this. For us.

When her eyes open, they smolder and I feel it deep in my groin. "See you soon," she mumbles, releasing a deep breath.

I step back from the window, internally cursing myself for not taking what I want. But I know I am doing the right thing. All good things come to those who wait. Right? She pulls out of the parking space, gives me a brief wave and drives down the road. Taking a chunk of me with her into the night.

Fourteen years ago

Thank God it is the last day of school. I have never really been one to not like school, in fact I have always been eager to be there. But I am counting down the minutes, psyched to have the summer off and spending more time with Gavin. This school year is one to go down as a year worth remembering. So much has happened, and it is unimaginable that I am dating my best friend.

Weekdays seem to snail along, with the exception of when Gavin and I are together. Most weeknights we study together. And by study, I mean finish homework between make-out sessions. Not that I have another person to compare it to, but Gavin really knows how to kiss a girl senseless. It is ironic we are both each other's firsts. First real relationship. First kiss. Those two kisses before Gavin don't count since neither guy knew what they were doing either.

Oftentimes, I wonder what other firsts we will share. Perhaps we will be the first people, besides our family, we say *I love you* to. Just thinking about him makes me want to scream it to the world. Let everyone know he belongs to me. And I belong to him. But I want to wait for the perfect time. To say the words to him when everything feels perfect.

Another first that has crossed my mind is sex. I know neither of us is quite ready yet.

We have been friends since the beginning of the school year, which turned into best friends within weeks. But we have only been girlfriend and boyfriend for six and a half months. Plus, we are only fifteen. Isn't sex something you wait to do when you are closer to adulthood? At least that is what all the adults tell you. But who knows when it's actually okay.

Any day now, it wouldn't surprise me if Mom and Dad have "the talk" with me. The talk is just a load of crap they tell you so you will stay focused on whatever it is they want you to focus on. Parents think having sex equals not doing anything else in life. I wonder if my parents dreaded the infamous talk. By now, everyone the same age as me has had at least one or two sex-ed classes—we aren't stupid. And we all have access to the internet.

But now… as I sit here in my English honors class, I'm not focused on the teacher—who yammers on about what books we should be reading over summer break. Nope. Instead, my mind swims with thoughts of me and Gavin and summer break and making out and sex. Anyone glancing my way would certainly notice the flush spreading along my face and neck.

From head to toe, I am hot. And it has nothing to do with the stifling outdoor temperatures.

Sex isn't a topic either of us has broached while together. But the thought has probably crossed his mind if it has crossed mine. How could it not? Don't guys think about sex more often than girls? That is what everyone says. Is he sitting in class right now thinking about it? Probably not. Geometry and sex aren't two subjects that pair well. Then again, I'm ignoring everything my teacher says and thinking about it. What's to say Gavin isn't doing the same. If I think about sex every other minute of the day, is Gavin constantly thinking about it?

Sex, sex, sex.

I shake my head, trying to clear my thoughts and catch Ms. Winters' final thoughts on summer reading. "Everyone, be sure to pick up a copy of the summer reading list from my desk before you go," she says a minute before the bell rings. "The sheet also has a few minor assignments you can earn extra credit on from your sophomore English teacher when school resumes." Thank God everything she just told us is on paper.

The bell buzzes for the final time of my freshman year and cheers erupt from every classroom in the quad. Twenty-three of us rise from our desks, gather our belongings and head for the door. I grab a copy of the printout and wish Ms. Winters a happy summer break. She gives me a brief smile on my way to the door and returns the sentiment.

When I step out into the summer sun, I take a deep breath and tilt my chin to the sky, closing my eyes. I stand there a moment, hundreds of bodies moving around me like the running of the bulls. Summer fever is in the air and everyone is excited to not be here for months. Me included.

Strong, warm arms circle around my waist, tugging me back until I make contact with the body behind me. *Gavin.* I would know him anywhere. Even if I couldn't see him, I would know he was there. That is just the connection we have with each other. An inexplicable bond fusing us together. Like a form of symbiosis.

I twist in his arms and turn enough to see his radiant smile in the sunlight. "Hey," I say.

He kisses me sweetly on the lips before responding. "Hey. You ready to get out of here?"

"Definitely. Want to grab something to eat? I think a bunch of people are headed to the sub shop."

"Yeah. Micah and Shelly are going. He said he'd give us a ride after if we went," Gavin states.

"Cool. Anything you want to do after?"

"I thought maybe we could hang and watch your favorite movies on repeat."

Like a five-year-old, I start jumping up and down like a fool. "Seriously?!" I plant a quick kiss on his lips. "You really are the best boyfriend ever."

His returning smile and hug tells me he knows.

We are curled up on the couch, my back to Gavin's front, as *Lord of the Rings* plays on the television. We have just reached the part where Arwen is trying to help save Frodo's life because he had the ring on too long. Gavin stretches behind me, adjusting his arm as we spoon in the dim living room of my house.

His finger slowly skims up and down the side of my torso, repeating the circuit over and over. Since we started dating, he has touched me like this countless times. The soft strokes are sweet and soothing and stir flutters in my chest. But today, his touch feels different. My skin hotter. My body needier. Breath heavier. Heart more anxious. Only I'm not sure if it is just me feeling it.

God, I hope it isn't just me feeling it.

My parents won't be home from work for at least another two hours. And the realization of this tidbit causes perspiration to break free across my skin. My heart thump, thump, thumps louder in my chest. A tight pinch in my lungs as I try to breathe normal and not start panting. His fingers light a frenzy under my skin everywhere he touches.

When his fingers graze over the curve of my hip, my eyes roll back and I close my lids. A deep breath later and I roll over to face him. Once I resituate, his fingers continue their slow, sensual tease of my opposite side. I study his face, the light from the screen dimming and brightening with the scene and hiding his face every few seconds.

"You don't want to watch the movie?" he asks, confused.

I swallow hard and want to laugh at his question. Want to ask if he is joking. He knows I have seen this a hundred plus times. I have most of the lines memorized. Have backup DVDs in case one gets scratched. But he knows how much I love it, so I don't laugh. He watches them over and over with me because of how he feels for me. If that isn't some form of love, I don't know what is.

Reaching up, I thread my fingers through his hair and lean forward, bringing my lips to his. My top leg wiggles between his as he throws his over my hip, pulling me closer. We have made out on the couch before—at my house and his—but today feels different. More heated. More intense. A desire to go further. To take the next step.

His hand dips under my shirt and he grazes my navel with the tops of his short nails. The stroke has me drawing back and gasping. A second later, I bring my lips back to his in a frenzy. My hands roam his face, his neck, his chest through the cotton rock band tee. When I reach his waist, my fingertips tickle along the skin there, eliciting a hiss from his lips.

The urge to take it further lingers in the gravity surrounding us. Weighs us down. Both of us greedy. The fire. The hunger. The raw intensity of lust and desire. It drives us forward. As much as I have thought about waiting until we are a little older, I can't deny how much I want him in this moment. And if I want him like this, I can only imagine what he must be feeling.

But he breaks the kiss. Our breaths panting, hearts hammering. And neither one of us can shift our eyes from the other.

"Do you not want to…" I leave the question unfinished, unsure if this is something he wants. He has as much of a choice to make as I do.

He catches the worry on my face and his answer is immediate. "I do. Believe me, I do. It's just… what if your parents come home? That'd be a moment no one would ever forget. Plus" —he sweeps a few straggler hairs aside— "I'd like our first time to be more special than the couch while watching a movie. Not that we have to plan it, but it's a big deal. For both of us."

He makes a valid point. But I can't help the rapid-fire pulse banging in my chest right now. Or the intense craving that grows low in my belly. "I guess you're right. But can we keep making out? I was enjoying myself immensely."

His laugh is loud and throaty and vibrates against my chest as he brings me closer to him. "Sorry I cut you off, baby."

And then he leans down, brings my mouth back to his and we get lost in each other for the remainder of the movie. Arms and legs, hands and fingers, feet in tangles, skin touching skin. It's hot and needy and all-consuming. When the credits scroll up the screen, we have to tear ourselves away from each other. Gasping and overheated.

Everything is perfect. Everything is wonderful. And I pray it will be like this forever.

twenty-three

CORA

Present

Can exhaustion and jubilation go hand in hand? Most days I would answer with a resolute no. Absolutely not.

But today, after only five hours of sleep, I haven't stopped smiling since my eyes opened. It was the first reaction I had when my alarm sounded. Made brushing my teeth a bit more challenging. Even Luna noticed the difference in my demeanor when I poured kibble into her bowl, her furry little body weaving between my legs and purring loudly. If her mama is happy, she is happy.

The young woman behind the counter at the juice bar hands me my coffee and a small brown bag containing my coconut bowl. I sip the delicious brew before exiting and hopping back in my car. Before starting up the engine, I steal a quick bite of my bowl and relish in the creaminess.

The drive from Main Street to Causeway Boulevard is brief, loaded with sights and people. Runners and cyclists and families. Parks and playgrounds and golfers. One of my favorite parts of Dunedin is the small-town vibe. Everyone here is friendly. The town bursts with energy. Events pop up every weekend, if not more frequently. Not every city has the same community atmosphere. It is invigorating and refreshing to know places like this still exist.

The line to get into the state park is long, as is typical on a beautiful day like today. I pay the attendant and drive into the park, heading for the agreed-upon meeting location. Blue skies with sparse clouds make up the view as a gentle breeze blows through my rolled down windows. The trees lining the road inside the park sway and glow under the beaming sunlight. This time of year is when my slice of Florida is perfect. A slight coolness with a ghost of the summer to come.

Parking under a small, rare patch of shade with my car backed in, I scan the lot for Alyson's rental. When I don't see it, I retrieve my bowl and enjoy my breakfast while waiting for her and Gavin to arrive. Rock music vibrates through the speakers around me. Five bites from finishing and three songs later, Alyson and Gavin drive through the lot in search of a space.

Dark sunglasses mask Gavin's eyes from the world, his head pressed against the headrest. I imagine he is as tired as I am. No doubt his eyes are closed behind the lenses. We have exhausted each other, but are taking things in stride this week. I wouldn't change any of it. More than happy to have exhaustion bleeding through my veins if things between us will shift for the better. Head back down the path we once traveled.

"God, I missed him," I whisper to myself.

Although I haven't dreamed it for two or three years, envisioning Gavin in my arms again has been something I never let go of. How could I let him go completely? How could I wipe away what we had? Our history… we didn't just share the best two years of my teenage life. Two years that tattooed every perfect moment and emotion on my heart. Every important exchange between two people in a relationship, we had every single of those experiences together. First legitimate relationship. First real kiss. And sex… no one ever forgets their first. He was mine and I his. And no one can change any of that. No one can rewrite our firsts.

When he left, I was certain he would come back as soon as he could. We had it all planned out. Down to the very last detail. Or so we thought. But when you're young, and can't pay to travel across the country, plans change. Promises slip through the cracks. People fade into the background.

Alyson parks three spaces down and across from me. I sit in my car a minute longer, watching from the driver's seat as Gavin gets out of the car and scans the parking lot, a hand hovering above his sunglasses. The moment he spots my car, his shaded eyes landing on mine, a monumental smile stretches across his face.

"Damn," I whisper on a sigh.

I have only seen this smile a few times from him, including the one he gifts me now. It echoes off him, bounces through the atmosphere, and hits me with a force that knocks me breathless. My lips part as I suck in a breath, his eyes not missing the effect he has on me—even fifty feet away—causing his smile to brighten further.

Walking with a bounce in his stride, he sidles up to my door and pokes his head through the open window. "Good morning, baby." His lips warm against my neck as he imprints his lips on the skin below my ear.

An audible sigh exhales from my chest as my eyes roll back before my lids shut out the world around us. Heat fires in my chest; surging, rising, spreading to every nerve ending in my body. His lips and tongue travel a path along the curve of my neck. All coherent thoughts vanish and I melt into a puddle in my car.

A cough from behind him interrupts the moment and snaps us both back to the reason why we are here. My eyes flick to Gavin's, his happiness reflecting my beaming smile. "Good morning," I say, breathless.

"Shouldn't we get started?" Alyson gripes, a hint of irritation in her voice.

"Yes. Sorry," I apologize, rolling up my windows and stepping out of the car. "Let me grab my equipment from the back and then we can start."

She nods, then asks, "Where's your assistant? Do we need to wait for her too?" Her tone transitions from irritation to annoyance in point-five seconds.

What crawled up her ass and died?

"Erin won't be here today. Minimal equipment is necessary for today's shoot. Plus, she had a prior engagement." My tone is courteous, when all I want is to give her the same level of shit she dishes out to me. But, as always, I take the higher ground.

She starts walking toward her car, speaking over her shoulder at us. "I'm grabbing my bag from the car. Be ready when I walk back over."

As soon as she is out of earshot, I glance up at Gavin, silently asking why the hell Alyson is being a top-notch bitch to me today. Lifting the hatch on the back, I grab the cameras I plan to use today, hooking the straps over my head.

Seconds pass before he speaks up, his voice raspy and low. "She's upset with me. This morning, I broke the news to her that I plan to move back to Florida. She knows I still want her as my agent, but isn't thrilled with the idea of doing the job from the other side of the country."

Hanging my head, I mumble, "So, this is also about me. Her frustration isn't just with you, but also with me. Am I right?" I hate that us being together will cause a rift in his career.

He brushes my hair behind my ear and follows the gesture with his eyes. "I didn't mention you when I spoke with her earlier. But I'm sure she put two and two together with my greeting you. None of that matters, though. I'll talk with her. Explain things she knows nothing about."

My chest tightens as guilt riddles me. I don't want animosity—between him and his agent or me, by proxy. "Okay. But, Gavin…" I pause and he locks his gaze on mine. "Please don't make me the sole reason you return."

He cocks his head and studies me a minute. His eyes narrow then relax behind his sunglasses as he starts to shake his head. "You don't get it, do you?"

"Get what?" I furrow my brows, obviously unaware. A small piece of my heart tells me I know the answer. Whispers it softly in my ear. But the gut-wrenching memories step out of the shadows and remind me to never assume. Assumptions kill dreams and crush hearts.

"It has always been about you. It always will be."

"Gavin…" He can't say things like that. Not unless he is prepared to back every sentiment. And not with more words or promises, but with actions. Actions are what I need.

His fingers brush along my jawline, from my temple to my chin. "You don't get it, baby. I have missed you every day since the moment my mom packed our life up and moved us away. It's been four thousand six hundred and ninety-eight days, Cora. And until I'm back here, with you beside me again, I won't stop counting. Because it's the only thing that gives me hope."

My throat squeezes at his words, making it hard to swallow the lump building from emotional overload. Making it difficult to breathe. How do I follow up after he confesses facts so heavy? Anything I say after seems minuscule. But not responding makes me an asshole. Just as I am about to formulate a response, about to use my words, Alyson steps up to us and huffs.

"You two ready? The day won't last forever," Alyson snaps.

"Yep," I snap in return. "Just discussing things while we waited for you." I am over her shit already. It is too damn early to be bitter, but my lack of sleep is making me grouchier than usual. "Follow me," I command, turning and walking away, not looking to see if either of them follows.

I understand her pissy state—I do. But being a bitch because someone chooses their happiness over yours is just plain shitty. Yeah, her job won't be as easy going forward, but it's manageable. Several professions nowadays don't require people to reside in the same city, let alone state.

We walk a while, maybe thirty minutes. None of us mutters a word. The silence between the three of us borders on awkward. But the quiet gives me time to replay Gavin's earlier confession. To come to the realization that he has missed me more than I previously suspected. But if he has pined for me all these years, why has he not done anything to remedy it? Why didn't he reach out to me? He should have at least tried to explain what changed. It makes no sense. In the beginning, sure. Neither of us had the means to visit each other. But if he has wanted to return so badly, what has stopped him? His job? His mom? Maybe someone else?

The thought of another woman being the reason has my stomach churning. No doubt Gavin spent time with or dated other women over the last thirteen years. I'd be shocked if he hadn't. But the idea of him being in a relationship *now* has bile coating my throat. So, I shove it aside and file it in the *ask Gavin later* part of my mind.

A quarter mile down the trail, I stop in my tracks, and Gavin runs into my backside.

"Sorry," I mutter. "I should've said something to let you know we were here."

"It's okay, baby." He kisses my temple before correcting his stance.

Behind us, I hear Alyson huff and mumble something under her breath. Honestly, if she doesn't chill the hell out, I am going to open my mouth and bark out things I cannot take back. I won't regret a single word, but they will reflect poorly on my professionalism. And today is not the day to test my sanity.

Alyson slides a collapsible chair from a bag, opens it and plops down. After a minute, her focus shifts from me and Gavin to her incessantly dinging cell phone. Whatever keeps her attention focused elsewhere is good with me. Because every ounce of my rational side prays she remains silent the entire shoot. For her sake and mine.

This section of the trail is near the water, so we have the ability to get photos in the greenery, near the water, and a combination of both. The location is absolutely perfect. Not only for the scenery, but also because today's shoot entails more skin. More skin than I typically shoot. More skin than I have probably seen on another guy in years. And not just any skin, but Gavin's skin.

Please, powers that be, let me make it through today without doing or saying something stupid. Please.

Hence the need for partial seclusion. Alyson is nearby, but not close enough to see us in clear view. Let alone, hear us.

Don't get me wrong, I have taken intimate pictures before. Couples who wanted to capture special moments such as pregnancy. Women—and men—who wanted to do something special for their significant other such as boudoir sessions. Boudoir sessions are the extent of the raciness in my portfolio. And they were saucy, steamy, and intimate as hell, but very different from this.

Because this is Gavin. The only guy I have loved. The only person I have imagined having a future with. And the one guy who ran away with my heart thirteen years ago and held it hostage.

The first shots are simplistic. Him in board shorts against the foliage backdrop. Some with the waterfront at his backside. All reflecting the strength of his chest and arms without flaunting it. The shorts rest low on his hips, the definition of his lower abdominals peeking at the front of the waistband. I swallow and do my best to maintain composure. After I'm satisfied with the number of shots taken with all backdrops, we prep for the next set of photos.

When he drops his shorts, and I glimpse the thick-banded boxer briefs hugging his toned gluts and upper quads, I swallow. Hard. My insides swirl with a new thread of desire. My thighs clench together as I gawk at the outline of him in the branded underwear. And for a moment, I forget I am here to do a job.

I am so fucked.

When my eyes come back to his, a teasing smile occupies his face. Not only was I checking out the lines and definitions of his body, but I was caught doing so. And he is eating it up.

Should I be embarrassed? Normally, the answer would be

one-hundred-percent yes. If it were any other client, I would be apologizing endlessly. But with Gavin, I wear my ogling with pride. It's difficult not to smile back at him. And let's get real, Gavin is hot as hell.

Bringing the camera to my eye, I flush as I stare through the lens. He is enjoying this way too much. It is written all over him—how he flexes his muscles and contorts his body, how he eats me alive with his eyes, and how the prideful smirk refuses to leave his lips. I inhale deep, realizing I have had the camera pressed to my face for more than a minute without taking a single photo.

And he knows it.

"See something you like, baby?" His smugness penetrates the air and drifts my way.

Don't answer him. Stay strong. Keep your mouth shut. Don't…

"Maybe," I tease. "Still up for debate."

His laugh pierces the silence of the pathway and echoes through the trees and out to the water. While not posing, I hold down the shutter and capture Gavin in his natural state. Candid photos have always been my favorite, although most of them are kept in my own private collection. The shots just taken will more than likely never leave my laptop. And I will enjoy them for years to come.

After we capture enough shots along the path, we walk to the small section of beach. Some poses on the sand before he enters the water. Several poses while he is in the water, the waistband and a couple inches of the cotton below it visible. And then he strolls out of the water, prepared for the shots of him lying wet in the sand near the surf.

In this moment, three things hit me with complete clarity.

1. Gavin is wearing white underwear.
2. The fabric isn't as thick as I originally thought.
3. Gavin is hard as steel as he walks toward me with
   a shit-eating grin on his face.

I can't breathe. Can't speak. Am rendered immobile. My face is hot, and not from the sun beaming down on us for hours. My limbs have forgotten how to function and my jaw is stuck in the open position.

Breathe, Cora. Inhale… Exhale… You can do this.

I can't do this.

Shit. Fuck. Damn.

The camera hangs suspended in my hand, just below my rosy face, as my sole focus is on his body. Yes, my eyes are zeroed in on the girth below the now see-through cotton. But my periphery catches the ripples of his lower abdomen, his V more visible and pointing directly at his pot of gold at the end of the rainbow.

It's not as if this is the first time I have seen Gavin in all his glory. But the last time I saw him anywhere remotely close to naked, we were sixteen and his body looked nothing like the one before me. The Gavin from my memories is good-looking and desirable and made my heart sing.

But this older version of Gavin…

Heat rises in my chest, trickling throughout my torso and seeping into my limbs. It isn't as simple as me being turned on by his appearance—I have seen numerous attractive men over the years that never sparked this incendiary feeling inside me. Part of it is visual, but another part is the knowledge that he only has eyes for me. That he only wants me. That every part of him is reserved for me.

"You okay, baby? You look a little heated," he teases then adds a soft chuckle. "We can take a break. Grab some water."

I stick my tongue out at him as if we are kids again, following it up with a goofy face. Bringing the camera to my eye, I drag in a deep breath.

This is work, Cora. Focus on the work aspect.

"Nope. I'm good," I tell him, coughing to clear my throat. "Although, I'm not sure how many of these shots will be usable."

Through the lens, I see his head cock to the side as his brows pinch together. The shutter closes at a rapid-fire pace, photo after photo taken and stored on the SD card. He steps closer and closer as I try to focus the lens higher and higher.

A hundred or so frames later, Gavin speaks up. "Why?"

For a moment, I am confused by his question. Not sure what he is asking about. "Why what?"

"Why won't some of the shots be usable?"

I continue shooting as I speak, not taking my eye away from the viewfinder. "Well, from what I've been told, this shoot is for magazines everywhere. An ad campaign for the clothing and accessories."

He nods. "Yeah. So?"

"And I think it's meant to reach a wide age range, starting with teens."

"Okay…"

He is not picking up on this. Not one bit. And damnit, I am going to have to come right out and say it. Internally, my hand slaps my forehead. *Just say it. We are both adults, for fuck's sake.*

"Gavin, parents won't want their teenage kids looking at an ad where the model has an erection, which is one-hundred-percent visible through the wet material. Many of the older female population may enjoy it, maybe some men too, but that won't be the only eyes on the ad."

His laugh is throaty, his abs contracting in ways that coil my insides tight. I continue taking photo after photo, capturing more candid shots. When he finishes laughing, he walks the small distance to me. My camera still glued to my face as he approaches, snapping as many photos as possible. He slowly pushes the camera aside and tips my chin up so we are eye to eye.

"Do you know how *hard* it is to stand practically naked in front of you? Knowing your job is to look at me. To take photos of me. Your visual assessment has me hungrier for you with each press of the shutter release."

I swallow hard, the sound from the action echoes loud in my head and I wonder if he hears it too. His pupils dilate more, his steely-gray irises darkening with each passing second. If he believes it is challenging to be in front of the camera, he has no idea how difficult it is to be on the other side. To view him through the lens and attempt to keep every thought I have as practiced as possible. To remind myself I am working and to be on my best behavior.

"It's not so easy from where I'm standing either. Having to maintain complete photographer-client idiosyncrasies while I snap photos of the one person who incinerates my insides. When—right now—the only thing I want to do is trace my fingers over every line of your body."

Neither of us looks away. His chest rises and falls faster with each breath he takes. The friction of his chest brushing against my nipples builds a delicious, insatiable heat between my legs. Right here, on the white sands of the small beachfront, I want him to kiss me. Want to feel the heat of his lips brush against mine. Against my skin, down my throat and…

A cough rings out behind me, and I snap out of my fantasy. Gavin peeks over my head, his smile faltering when he sees who stands there. Only one possible person could be there. Alyson. And from the scene she walked in on, I would not be shocked if she policed the rest of the shoot.

Gavin's eyes come back to mine before he bends to press a soft kiss on my lips. "I'll try to think about something else so we can wrap this up."

I nod, blurting, "shitty diapers."

He tips his head in question. "Shitty diapers…" he says, dragging out the words.

"Yeah. Think about that and it'll solve the current *setback*."

He walks backward, a hearty laugh bellowing from his chest. "You always know the right thing to say."

We hike back to the cars, Alyson leading the way twenty feet ahead of us and griping over how bloodthirsty the insects are in Florida. Gavin falls in step beside me, his fingers wrapped around mine and clutching me as if I might slip away. Not a single word is spoken for ten minutes as we follow the trail.

When we reach the opening, I hear Alyson mutter *thank God* under her breath. Gavin laughs loud enough for only me to hear, shaking his head at her bitching. Obviously, the mosquito population isn't as predominant in California. Seeing as summer exists the majority of the year in Florida, I would not be shocked if mosquitos were dubbed the state insect one day.

Once we are back in the lot, Alyson walks over to her rental, but not before sending a knowing look to Gavin. A look that says she understands, but also not to push her boundaries. What those boundaries are, I am not privy to.

I press the unlock button on my key fob, lifting the hatch and tucking my cameras into the bags under the cover. Gavin stands inches away as his gaze sears me. After everything is in its rightful place, I step back and close the hatch. When I turn to face Gavin, my eyes roam his body. Starting at the waistband of his board shorts—which barely hang on his hips—trailing up the grooves and curves of his abdomen, falling on his pecs—where my mouth waters at the sight of the barbells through his nipples—rising up his throat. I watch his Adam's apple bob as my eyes scrape over his stubble and lips, and eventually land on eyes that want to devour me.

Fuck me.

His expression says everything his mouth is not. The way his tongue jets out and swipes along his bottom lip before he clamps it between his teeth. The slight smirk that follows. How his irises shift from steel to pewter. A slight rise and fall of his shoulders as his breath comes faster. How his pulse noticeably pumps harder in that spot just below his ear.

Not only does he want to kiss me. He wants to peel away my shorts and tank. But he also aches to run his fingers through my hair, ball them into fists and yank the strands taught against my scalp. To see my body bow and plead for his touch, his mouth, his tongue. Along every inch of my skin, rebranding and rememorizing all the places he has been once before.

Both of us stand stock-still. Not touching. Not speaking. Sharing a bond our bodies and hearts have never forgotten. The void between us grows less dark and vacant with each passing second.

He flings the shirt he's been holding over his shoulder,

sliding his sunglasses down and shielding his eyes from the sun. "Have dinner with me tonight," he states. It is not a question, but also not a command.

Every coherent thought in my mind screams at me to tell him no. That we shouldn't be doing things together as if we are a couple. At least not until this shoot is over and I know I'm not throwing my heart on the line. My brain fights with my heart—battles with my soul—and tells me to be rational, to think this through and understand the repercussions if something goes amiss.

But I ignore my brain. Tell it to shut the hell up and let me live in the moment. Because it has been so long since I have lived in the moment. Or lived life to its fullest. And I am tired of hiding—who I am and what I want. Tired of missing out on life and love.

"Yes." It's all I say. Because I don't trust myself to say anything else right now. If I open my mouth, I may say words I said once before but should wait to say again.

His body comes alive and his expression mirrors a jubilance I have not seen in ages. It rolls off him in waves, piercing my aura and infecting me with a dose. I cannot help but smile at his behavior, his energy, his life force.

"Any requests? I'm open to whatever," he says.

Feigning indecision, I tap a finger against my lips. If Gavin remembers anything about me at all, he would know my answer. But for good measure, I drag out my supposed thinking. When I feel I have sufficiently tortured him enough, I answer.

"Maybe we could grab some Asian," I suggest, biting my lower lip.

A laugh rips from his throat as he shakes from head to toe.

"I should have known that would be your answer," he chuckles out. "Anywhere in particular you'd like to go?"

"How about I figure that part out, seeing as I'm more familiar with the area. Want me to pick you up?"

"It wouldn't be a proper date if you're the one picking me up. How about I meet you at your place and we drive from there?"

"Seriously? We're almost thirty and it's the twenty-first century. Women can pick up men for a date."

He nods, his laugh sparking back to life. "I realize what era we live in, baby. Doesn't mean I can't try to be somewhat of a gentleman. Even if I don't have my car with me. But I'll find a way to get there, then you can take the helm."

I walk to the driver's side door, Gavin a step behind me with his hand on my hip. Opening the door, I toss my phone on the seat before turning to face him and say goodbye. When I turn, his face is a breath from mine. His lips hovering dangerously close and his eyes locked with determination. As he leans closer, my eyes close, my body ready and waiting to feel his lips on mine. Just as warmth paints my lips, Alyson honks the rental's horn.

"Let's go!" she hollers.

And just like that, she has plucked my last nerve today. I swallow it down and don't let it ruin the moment.

Reluctantly, we pull apart. Our bodies now separated by feet rather than inches. But the vibrating energy between us remains. Almost like when we were teens and our parents walked in the room.

His hand squeezes my hip. "I'll see you later, baby. Is five thirty okay?"

"That's fine. See you then," I say as he releases my hip and walks away.

Immobile, I watch as he gets into the car and Alyson backs out. He gives me a sweet half smile as they drive past me. The car leaves the lot, drives on the paved two-lane road and heads for the exit. It's not until the car is out of sight that I slide into my car, start the engine and roll down the windows. And as I drive out of the park, my mind drifts over all the possibilities of what tonight means. For us. For our future.

This is really happening. The only person I have ever truly loved is back in my life. And he has promised to return to me. To stay with me. To keep me forever.

twenty-four

GAVIN

Fuck if I am not excited about tonight. About the possibility of a future with the one person who has been tattooed on my heart for more than a decade. The one person I never want to be apart from again. The one person I cannot wait to spend every day of forever with.

The entire way back to the hotel, Alyson chews me a new asshole. Bitching and moaning about how I need to be more mindful in regards to my actions. Scolding me worse than any occasion my parents did. And how I better not forget I am under contract—with her, the clothing designer and the magazine. As if I need reminding. As if this is my first shoot.

I let her have her moment. Allow her to complain and reiterate the same shit on repeat. Spew the same garbage she has since the first day of the shoot. But when she finishes, I take it as a sign that I finally get a chance to speak. To tell her what is on my mind. To shut down her tirade.

"Alyson, you know how much I value your opinion and expertise. But there are a few parts of my life that are *not* what *I* pay *you* to handle. My love life is not part of your job and most definitely will never be a part of your pay grade. Do you understand?"

There is no plainer way to express this to her. I only hope she gets where I am coming from. That I am not trying to be a dick and just laying the basics out there. She needs to understand me being with Cora is permanent. She needs to get used to us being together and me living my life how I want.

We drive south on Edgewater, not far from the Dunedin-Clearwater border. "Of course, I understand. But you pay me to make decisions that will impact the future of your career. And this" —she gestures behind us— "her, will impact your future. In more ways than one."

That is what I am hoping.

"I realize she'll change my future. It's what I'm hoping for. The one thing I've wanted for years. And now I have the ability of returning to her." I pause a moment and ponder over my next words. "This will make things different with our relationship, but you can either represent me from afar or I can find someone else. The choice is yours."

I hate to throw ultimatums on the table, but I will not have her or anyone else hindering my return. Not Alyson. Not my mother. No one. Although, a small part of me thinks my mom may be happy for me. After our move to Cali, I witnessed how sad she was for me. How guilty she felt for removing me from my friends and girlfriend. It hurt me, and her by proxy.

"Well, aside from your plan to move—" she says hesitantly, then continues. "—don't forget about the shoot you have booked with Layla. And speaking of Layla, how will all of that work out if you move across the country?"

I shoot her a pointed look, but she doesn't catch it with her eyes on the road. "I'll talk with her. She'll understand. Besides, she's good now."

"I hope you're right."

"What's that supposed to mean?" I question, fire building in my chest. I am so over Alyson, her selfishness and her annoyance with me living my life how I choose.

"Nothing. All it means is I hope it doesn't ruin you or her."

"It won't," I snap. Alyson is grasping at straws. Trying to make something of nothing. Trying to rile me up. But I won't feed into her line of bullshit.

The remainder of our drive is quiet. Alyson churning my words in her head, realizing she has an important decision to make. She is either on board or she isn't. And trying to throw bullshit about Layla in the mix—it is a low blow, even for Alyson. I have been working for years to get to this point. To return to Cora. And now that I am able, nothing will stop me. Nothing will take this away from me. From us.

The Uber driver dropped me off in front of Cora's house five minutes ago. So why am I standing out front? My feet locked in place on the rustic paver pathway leading to her front stoop. I stare at the gray siding, black shutters, and black-framed glass door, taking my first, true assessment of her home.

A large oak tree shadows most of the yard with lush ferns growing around the base of the trunk. Two ducks waddle away from the ferns and cross the street to head for the park's pond. A brick chimney painted dark gray crawls up the eastern wall of the house—and although fireplaces aren't used often in Florida, I bet she uses it every chance she gets. Small flowered plants encompass the border of the house—pops of yellow and red and purple in the foliage—white rocks at their base. Large windows take up the majority of the exterior walls and allow for hours of natural light. Strands of starry lights dangle from the roof over the stoop. Everything about this house screams her style. Simple. Clean-cut. Monochromatic. With the exception of the colorful plants.

I remain rooted another minute before dragging in a deep breath. The reality of us coming back together hits me like a lead weight. A burning tightness takes residence in my chest, building and expanding with every breath. It consumes every molecule of oxygen, every drop of blood, every fiber and jolts me back to life.

This is my future. She is my future.

God, I have dreamed about this moment for so long. Dreamed of her in my arms again. Imagined what life would be like waking up in the same bed every day. Moving around each other in the kitchen while making breakfast. Spooning on the couch as we watch movies in the dark. Discussing our day over dinner. Laughing together with friends. Creating a family and growing old together.

She is it for me. Always has been. Always will be. Not a single day has passed where I haven't thought of Cora. Wondered what she was doing. How she fit into the world now. If she still thought of me. If she would be able to love me again.

Fuck, I love her so much.

The front door opens and Cora stands in the doorway looking at me with questions in her eyes. "You okay?" she asks, doubt in her voice. No doubt she has seen me standing out here. Hopefully not for too long.

"Yeah. Sorry." I stride up the path and stop in front of her. I plant a kiss on her forehead and inhale deeply, filling my nose with the scent that is one-hundred-percent her. "Was just admiring your house. You've done so well for yourself. And it suits you so much."

"Thank you," she says, a timid smile pushing up her cheeks. "You coming in? Or do you plan to stand out here until we leave?"

I step past her, seeing the inside of her house in a new light. The interior isn't overly spacious, but it is enough for her. *For us.* I love how easily I picture our future. Our road may have had major detours, but we are finally coming back to the path we belong on. *Together.*

To the right, the living room—maybe twelve square-feet—showcases the fireplace from the eastern wall with a charcoal and gray fabric couch opposite. A resin-coated wood slice coffee table rests between the two, decorated with a wide bowl of succulents. To the left is the kitchen and dining area. The kitchen is small yet vast. A large fridge at one end, the range near the other end. On the small island sitting between the kitchen and dining is a farmhouse sink and enough space for a few people to sit on stools and eat at the bar. Planked wood and riveted steel make up the dining table with four seats attached that swing underneath. Along the far wall of the dining area is her desk—a restored piece with distressed black paint and two shallow drawers. Simplistic art decorates the walls while minimal pieces adorn the furniture. With a tall vaulted ceiling, the cozy house is more spacious than it would appear from the outside.

I smile as I take it all in. There is not one part of this house that doesn't have a piece of her in its grain or plaster or beams. Without a doubt, I would recognize this place as hers in a heartbeat. Her style screams from every nook and cranny.

Her predilection for minimalism and simplicity shine from every corner, wall, and piece of décor.

"I was almost finished getting ready when I saw you outside. Give me a minute and then we can go."

"Take all the time you need, baby. I'll be out here waiting," I say as I sit on the couch.

Seconds after I sit, an all-black cat jumps up beside me, purring and rubbing its head on my arm. I scratch and pet the cat as it takes a liking to me. *Glad you like me because I will be around quite often.*

"And that would be Luna," Cora shares. "She's a lover and will probably coat you in her fur before we leave. Good thing I own several lint rollers."

I laugh as I pet Luna and she loves on me further. As I stroke her soft fur, the thought of her one day being *my* Luna brings a smile to my face. Since becoming a model, I have never owned a pet. As much as I wanted one, the thought of leaving a dog or cat behind for weeks on end doesn't sit well with me. It would be unfair to them, and me, to have someone pet sit and me not spend time with them. They may not be human, but they are your children all the same.

Cora breaks my introspection when she walks back into the room. "Ready when you are. Unless you'd rather spend date night with Luna," she says and giggles, a sound I haven't heard in so long. I almost forgot how musical her laugh is. Almost.

Patting Luna's backside, I whisper my apologies to her before rising from the couch. "Lead the way, baby."

We head out the back door, get in her car and drive to dinner. A little over thirty minutes later, we pull into a small parking lot beside an Asian vegan restaurant. She leads us inside and I love it immediately. The restaurant is small and simple, low-key. Absolutely perfect.

Once we are seated, we look over the menu and choose a few appetizers as well as our meals. We talk about life and key things that have happened to us over the last thirteen years. And as awkward as it is, we discuss relationships we have had. Funny enough, neither of us has had a relationship that lasted more than a few months. Neither of us finding someone who fulfilled us in the same way we do each other. And to me, that speaks volumes.

I share with her my plan to move back after the shoot in Cali and how I will still be able to work being out here. She points out why she is skeptical it will work—not us, but me working. That I won't have the same connections as I do now. But I beg to differ. Since I have been working in the industry for the last ten years, I have developed several contacts and am able to find work whenever and wherever I choose. And moving to Florida, I will end up discovering a whole new array of connections. Ones I would never have in California. Tampa, Orlando, and Miami are major cities picking up steam in the modeling industry.

The rest of dinner goes by seamlessly. Conversations about both of our work lives cease. We pack up our leftovers and I pay the bill. Soon thereafter, we are on our way back to her house. The drive back absent of conversation as we listen to music and enjoy the feel of our fingers laced together. And when we park in her driveway, the atmosphere between us grows heavy. With questions. With uncertainty. And most of all... desire.

Thirteen and a half years ago

As dorky as it sounds, I can't wait to celebrate our one-year anniversary together. Although we have been best friends for the last year and a half, we weren't dubbed "official" until this time last year. Most people assume it is only the girl who gets excited about these moments. But I am buzzing with the thrill and ready to celebrate with the one person who means the world to me.

Brakes squeak as Cora parks in the driveway, the new-to-her Toyota a little rumbly. Her parents bought her the used car a couple weeks ago after she officially got her license. It has been great to be able to do our own thing, within reason, and not be subjected to our parents taking us places or annoying older friends with cars.

I run out the front door, yelling to my parents that I will be home by curfew. Swinging open the passenger door with a bit more oomph than expected, I slip into the seat, lean over the center console and kiss my girl breathless. When we come up for air, I stare at the hazy expression on her face. It is a dash of euphoria mixed with the soft lines of her angelic face. And I never tire of seeing her this way. Happy.

"You can't do that," she whispers, her eyes hidden behind her lids.

Leaning back into her space, my lips hover a breath from hers. "Can't do what, baby?"

"Kiss me like that and expect me to be able to function afterward."

I press a soft, chaste kiss to her lips. "How can I not kiss you like you hold the other half of my soul?"

Her eyes flick open, her green irises shimmering in the fading light of the day. Darting back and forth between mine, her eyes expressive in their desire to know how we could both feel the way we do. We idle in the driveway another minute, the car vibrating beneath us, as so many things are said without a single word spoken. How is it I know everything she is thinking without her even telling me?

The answer is simple really. Cora is my home. She is the one place where I feel most at ease. The one person I can be myself around and never feel a sense of shame or reservation or judgment. She makes my breathing spike and my heart soar. And her fingers on me… her touch is lightning in my veins.

There is no other person I could imagine spending my life with. I may be only fifteen—almost sixteen—and less experienced with life, but this fact is etched in my bones. Carved since the day I was born. Not just for me, but for her as well.

After a moment, she drags in a breath and faces the steering wheel. "You ready?" she asks, her voice unsteady.

"As ready as I'll ever be."

Rock music spills out of the speakers as we drive toward Indian Rocks Beach. For our one-year anniversary, we decided to go to a small Italian restaurant between the beach and intercoastal. Asian food is Cora's version of crack, but she wanted to do something different tonight. And as many times as I told her we could go to our favorite Thai or Japanese restaurant, she gracefully suggested we go somewhere new.

To create a new memory for this milestone moment. A memory we will never forget. I wanted to tell her there is no way I would ever forget any minute involving her.

Pulling into the parking lot, she finds a space and parks. We get out of the car and it is the first time tonight I get the opportunity to see what she wears. Part of me is shocked, while another part of me is turned on.

For the first time ever, Cora is in a dress. Her usual denim bottoms and cotton graphic tee are nowhere to be found. But this dress suits her. In more ways than one. The fabric clings to her like a second skin, accentuating all the curves lying beneath. Curves I have touched, but not really seen altogether. Nestled in the black material are small shapes I can't make out from where I stand. As I inch closer to her, looping her arm in mine, I see the shapes are cat faces. From afar, anyone could misconstrue them as polka dots. Her dress is the perfect mix of black, rock and Cora.

"You look beautiful," I tell her, planting a kiss at her temple.

"Thank you. You're looking pretty good yourself."

To be honest, I feel underdressed next to her. In a pair of black jeans and a navy button-down with the cuffs rolled to my elbows, this is the most dressed up I have been since I was little and my mom dressed me for special occasions. It isn't that I don't look nice, but Cora is stunning.

The hostess walks us to our table, a flickering votive

candle and a small vase holding two red roses rest in the center. Our server greets and informs us of the specials for the evening, then takes our drink orders and disappears. We are both silent as we look over the menu, my mouth watering at all the delicious options. In my periphery, I catch Cora setting her menu down.

"Do you know what you're having?" I inquire.

"Yeah. I was tossed up between the spaghetti carbonara and the gnocchi a la Villa Gallace. They both sound amazing, but I think I'll get the carbonara. You want to share the Caesar salad for two?"

"Caesar sounds good. I'm still on the fence. Lasagna or rigatoni Bolognese?" I look to her for guidance.

"Ooh, that's a tough call," she says, tapping a finger against her pushed out lips. "Layers or tubes, layers or tubes." She bobs her head side to side as she tries to help me decide. "Tubes," she exclaims. "That's what I would choose."

"Tubes for the win!" I belt out a little too loud, mouthing my apologies to the other patrons when they look at me. "Oops," I whisper, both of us laughing with hands over our mouths.

Our server returns, setting our drinks and a basket of bread with garlic and herb oil on the table, then takes our order. When he walks away, we simply gaze at one another. In the time since Cora and I first met, we have learned we don't need to fill time by talking about things that don't hold value to us. We have a bond, a language all our own. Words don't need to be spoken. *We just know.* I stretch my hand across the table and she places hers in mine. Connected. Everything is always better when we are connected.

Our dinner arrives and we dive right in. On the small bread plates, we each portion our dish and pass it to the other.

As we eat, we talk about school and friends and our plans during the summer. When we finish, I pay the bill and we leave the restaurant.

Cora drives the car to a beach access parking lot on the other side of the two-lane street. This time of day is generally busy and it can be challenging to find a space, but we land one and make our way to the sand. Just before we step onto the beach, both of us slip our shoes off and carry them as we stroll onto the warmed, soft grains.

After walking for five minutes, we locate a spot where no one obstructs the view in front of us. Plopping down on the sand, Cora leans into me as we watch the sunset. We had timed dinner perfectly so we wouldn't miss this moment. If you have never watched the sunset along the water's horizon, you have been deprived.

The sunset was a favorite of mine. Sharing it with my girl made it more special.

Right now, the sun radiates a hot orange glow like the sphere of fire it is. The sky surrounding it shifts from a soft blue to a light yellow. And the lower the sun drops on the horizon, the more brilliant the colors. Yellow morphs into faint and then bold oranges. A mixture of orange and pink spark next, filtering between the clouds. Shadows and hints of purple edge the stratocumulus clouds floating above as the sun slowly descends.

When the sun dips below the horizon, the sky still dances with colors and clouds. The visual is magical and I am so lucky I get to share it with someone I love.

I shift and turn to face Cora more, her head lifting from my shoulder. One arm still wrapped around her waist, I bring the other to her face and cup her jaw, brushing my thumb over her lips. "I love you," I whisper.

Just now, it is the first time those words have been said in our relationship, but I mean them with every fiber in my soul. Whether or not she reciprocates doesn't matter. Something inside me yearned to release the sentiment. Like a ticking timebomb would detonate inside me if I held it in any longer.

Her eyes hold mine—unmoving, welling. She kisses my thumb that continues to stroke her lips. "I love you, too." The second those words leave her lips, every single molecule inside me radiates warmth. My soul is complete, whole.

Under the brilliance of the setting sun, I lean in and kiss the hell out of the only person in this world that matters to me. The only girl I will ever say those three miraculous words to. My Cora. My love.

~

We stumble into Cora's house, giddy as school girls. After our proclamations, we left the beach and headed back to her house to watch a movie since I have a few hours until curfew. No doubt it would be *Lord of the Rings* again. But I don't care, as long as she is beside me. In my arms.

When I notice all the lights are off, I prompt, "Where are your parents?"

"At some charity function in Tampa. They probably won't be home till close to midnight, if it's anything like last year."

A sudden rush of anxiety trickles up my spine, spreads through my limbs, and explodes beneath my sternum. Today is our anniversary. We are alone. After professing our love for each other. And she is looking at me like she has no desire to watch a movie, but perhaps do something else. Something more.

She stalks closer, locks eyes with me and stops when her

chest brushes mine. Her fingers reach out and draw lines down my bicep, my forearm, interlocking our fingers. Heat expands and contracts like a breathing organism in my chest. My breath comes in quick, short bursts as she inches closer and closer. And when she pushes up on her toes and kisses me, I forget how to breathe altogether.

The kiss starts off tender and gentle. She slides her hands back up my arms and laces them behind my neck, toying with the edges of my hair. Her tongue darts out and swipes a slow and sinful line over my lower lip, and I moan at the sensation as I part my lips and invite her in. My arms snake around her waist and draw her impossibly closer. Within seconds, the kiss elevates into more. More heated. More passionate. And I can't get enough of her. Her lips, her warmth, her taste.

We start moving, but I don't open my eyes as she slowly guides us. It seems as if we have been walking for hours when her body weight shifts and we settle in place. Our lips break for a moment, which is exactly when I realize we are in her bedroom. Next to her bed. Dim moonlight illuminates the space between the slats of her blinds. And the sudden proximity to her—in the darkness, in her bedroom—amplifies everything I feel for her.

Standing tall, I gaze down at her as she lies back on the bed, elbows propping her up. I want this—want her—but I need to know she feels the same. That she doesn't feel a sense of obligation to take us to the next level. That she wants to do this of her own volition. I would never pressure her into doing something she isn't ready for. Never.

"Cora..." I rasp, my voice thick with emotion as I draw out her name.

She reaches out her hand, her eyes telling me to take it. Wrapping her fingers with mine, she drags me closer. My knees bump the edge of the bed and sweat breaks out across my skin. "Yes, Gavin."

Yes? As in she is responding to me. Or yes, she wants to do this? Wants to take the next step. Sex. What exactly is she saying yes to?

"Are you sure?" I ask, reluctance in my tone. I don't want her saying yes because she thinks it's what I want her to say. "Because we don't have to if you're not ready."

Her brilliant green eyes pierce mine, her voice steady and firm when she speaks. "I am sure. I don't think I've ever felt more ready in my life." She gives my hand a gentle tug, signaling me to join her on the bed.

This exact moment has infiltrated my dreams for months. I never knew when it would happen, but the fantasy of it was a regular occurrence. Now that it is happening, I am not sure what to do. My feet remain rooted to the floor as I look down at her on the bed. She wants me as much as I want her, although it may be a bit lopsided in my favor. Am I ready for this? To share this once-in-a-lifetime moment with her? Yes, I have never been more ready. So, why am I not moving? Why can I not put my knee on the bed and crawl my way up her body?

"Gavin?" She peers up at me, confusion furrowing her brow. "Are you okay?"

"Yeah, I'm okay. Just give me a second."

"If you're not—"

I cut her off. "I am. It's just… you don't know how long I've waited for this moment. And now that it's here…" I trail off, not knowing how to explain how overwhelmed and buoyant and in love with her I feel right now.

She rises on the bed, perching up on her knees on the

mattress edge. "We can go slow. Maybe just fool around with clothes on. Go from there."

I nod, inhale deeply and focus on her eyes. The way they glimmer in the dim light in her room. Her lips. And how soft they feel when I press mine against them. The warmth of her hands as she frames my face and leans forward, her breath teasing my lips. Her frankincense and gardenia scent wafts around me and entices me further. Makes my pulse throb in my ears and my heart pound in my chest. Has my breaths coming faster, dizzyingly. And when I lean in to kiss her, we melt together.

Our kiss starts off slow, two sets of soft lips brushing together. Her hands slide down my neck and onto my chest as her delicate fingers separate buttons from fabric. I break out in goose bumps when she spreads the cotton, pushes it down my arms, leaves it to dangle from my waist and exposes my skin. A new form of hunger surges beneath my ribcage and in my groin. The kiss morphs, growing in intensity and becoming more animalistic when her nails scratch light lines down the backside of my torso. I tip my head back and gasp.

She takes hold of my hips and starts to crawl backward on her knees, pulling me on the bed. And this time, I don't stop her. Every part of me is desperate for her. Lips, mouth, tongue, hands… more.

Our kiss never falters as she lies back on the mattress and brings me with her. A frenzy erupts between us, and the urge to taste more of her grows stronger with each passing second.

Breaking the kiss, I paint my lips along her jaw, her ear, down the curve of her neck. Her breath ragged beneath me as her chest rises and falls faster with each taste as I consume every inch of her. Running my hands down the sides of her dress, I slide down her body and begin kissing her ankles, her calves, her thighs. When I reach her dress, I slip my fingers under the hem—warranting a gasp from her—and scoot the material up her body. Cora sits up, helping me lift the tight, stretchy fabric and yanking it off her body.

As her body lands on the mattress again, my dick jolts at the sight of her. Matching black lace covers her breasts and the junction of her thighs, the material sheer enough to see her pert nipples and a thin patch of curls. *Holy shit.*

She wrenches me down, and we are all mouths and tongues and roaming hands. Minutes later, she tosses my shirt away as she unbuttons my jeans and shoves them down my legs. The second my pants hit the floor, my lips move down her chest and explore. My tongue lavishes her nipples before licking its way down her navel and hovering above her panties.

My eyes lock with hers, asking permission. She nods, running her fingers through my hair and tugging. Slipping my thumbs under the elastic, I slide the lacy triangle down her thighs and to the floor. When I come back to her body, I taste her for the first time. Her addictive flavor a blend of salty and sweetness on my tongue. A moan rips from her throat as I melt into her, my dick throbbing between my legs.

"Oh, god..." she garbles.

She is sweeter than any confection I have ever tasted or imagined. But when I kiss my way up her body, and our tongues collide again, I become even hungrier for her. Her hips grind against me, begging for me to give her more.

Rising from the bed, I reach for my pants and remove my wallet, taking the condom out of the hidden pocket. Holding it between my teeth, I shove down my underwear, tear the package open and roll the condom in place.

Hovering above her on the mattress, I hold her gaze.

Neither of us moves. Neither of us says a word. We stay like this a minute, letting the reality of what we are about to do settle in. Then, I press a soft kiss to her lips. I kiss her slow. I kiss her as if no one else exists.

"I love you, baby."

"I love you, too."

And then I learn about heaven.

Present

Why does it feel like this is our first date? The passion and heat and uncertainty. Will he kiss me? Will he stay the night? What will happen once we exit the car? Should I invite him inside?

Why the hell am I so nervous? This is Gavin.

I find it funny that I feel all these things because we have done this once before. Every. Single. Part. Of course, the experience is different when you are sixteen and your hormones are on a one-way track to Sex Town. The excitement and lust are tenfold because the experience is new. But as an adult, it all just feels… different.

My heart and mind no longer ruled by my hormones. Not that I discount them because I know they lurk in the shadows. But as a woman… if Gavin and I go there. If we do this again —us—and it doesn't work out, I won't recover. Us trying to reignite what we once were, our history has been magnified times a thousand. Every memory is amplified and with more definition. Each new touch is layered with a newer meaning, a promise of forever. Something we thought we understood all those years ago, but couldn't quite grasp the magnitude.

But now... we comprehend it all. And spending forever with someone you love resonates in a whole new light.

We get out of the car and walk to the back door off of the driveway. He walks me inside and goes to the couch, Luna jumping on his lap the second he sits down. *Traitor.* But in the same breath, it melts my heart that my faithful companion has taken such an easy liking to him.

"Do you want to watch a movie?" I ask, hoping to break the pressure mounting between us. No doubt he feels it too.

"Sure. Whatever you'd like."

I kick off my shoes and settle in on the couch beside him, Luna looking at me as if I am invisible. *Double traitor.* Grabbing the remotes, I turn on the soundbar and Apple TV. After scrolling through my movie library, I click on *Hunger Games.*

Gavin wraps his arm around me and I lean into his chest, my head resting just below his shoulder. When the weight of his head rests atop mine, I sigh at the closeness we share. It has been a long time since I have had this connection. A bond that never goes away, never breaks. Something I have longed to have again, but came up empty-handed in every search.

For a brief time, I had thought maybe Jonas and I shared such a bond. But the more I tried with him, the more it felt forced and inappropriate. An imitation in a nice package. The only feelings I have for Jonas are strictly platonic. All I can hope is for his understanding. As my relationship with Gavin progresses, my relationship with Jonas will taper. Yes, I will always be his friend and he mine. But the boundary lines must be firmly drawn.

Luna purrs in Gavin's lap as the three of us cuddle on the couch. This is the closest I have felt to home in thirteen years.

Warm and comfortable. As if the stars have realigned and everything is as it should be. And I pray I get to feel it every day going forward. The day Gavin left; a void took over the part of my heart reserved for him. A black hole. Life no longer functioned quite the same. The only thing that kept me going was knowing we would see each other again.

I secluded myself from friends and family. Found comfort in nothing as I sat thoughtlessly in my room, day after day. Went to school as required, but lost all sense of focus or determination. I ate less and slept more. Never left the house unless mandatory. Was forced to bathe and put on something other than pajamas or pieces of Gavin's clothes. Clothes which I refused to wash.

When minutes became hours and hours became days, days turning into weeks and months, a light inside me died. A light I thought would never burn bright again. Sure, the world wasn't quite as dim as the years became a decade and more. But now… now there is a flicker.

I wake wrapped in Gavin's arms, my body curled and pressing against his chest. Snuggling into him further, I inhale his beachy pine scent before he lays me on my bed and pulls the comforter over me. Beneath the covers, I undo my jeans, sliding them off and tossing them to the floor. He plants a kiss on my forehead and starts for the door.

"Stay." It is all I tell him. All I croak out in the darkness.

He spins around and his eyes search mine. Indecision highlights his face. So, I fold back the comforter on the other side of the bed and pat the sheet. I have no idea what the time is, but it is late and he has to be tired. No need for him to request an Uber at this late/early hour when he can just stay here.

"Are you sure?" His voice is riddled with insecurity.

"I'm tired. You're tired. We both need to sleep. So, just come lay down and get some sleep."

My words sound simple enough, but is the notion of sleeping in bed with Gavin really so simple? Sex is the furthest thing from my mind. His arms around me, though…

He hesitates a minute, watching me with an unreadable expression. Soon, his will caves and a thump hits the floor as he toes off his shoes. A second later, he tugs his shirt over his head and drops his jeans to the floor. The bed dips under his weight, the comforter shifting as he gets situated. When he stills, I roll to my side and snuggle close to him. Into him.

Oh god, how I have missed this.

For a solid minute, I swear he stops breathing. I lay my hand to the left of his sternum and feel his heart beating a vicious rhythm beneath my palm. *Is he nervous? Why on earth would he be nervous?*

"Gavin, is this okay? Me being this close," I whisper against his skin.

As his breath returns, his hand covers mine and holds it in place. His other arm snakes around my shoulders and hauls me closer. "Yes, better than okay. It's just been a long time."

I press my lips to his chest and settle against him, cocooned in his embrace. "Good night, Gavin."

"Night, baby."

My body is hot. Like I have been tanning in the sun for countless hours during mid-August slathered in tanning oil. Every inch consumed by heat and sweat. The sweltering heat inescapable and becoming far beyond unbearable. I may suffer heatstroke any second.

On the cusp of sleep and awake, I shift between the sheets and kick a leg out, hoping to cool my body. As I scoot closer to the edge, pushing the comforter down to my waist, the bed shifts beside me as a hand crawls across my belly.

In a matter of seconds, I go from foggy and semi-alert to eyes wide open and body hyper-aware.

A groan rumbles next to me, a weighted thigh draping over my waist, the calf falling down my leg. The black-out curtains in my room make it close to impossible to see anything in my room. Under normal circumstances, I would be ecstatic not to see a single thing in my room. But that doesn't apply in the current situation.

Moving as slow as humanly possible, I turn my head and look to my side. Next to me, Gavin lies asleep. His face relaxed and flaunting the soft yet masculine lines of his face. I take this quiet moment, the one where he isn't studying my every observation or movement, and absorb all the parts of him I have missed over the years.

With my eyes, I trace the thick curves of his brow. Drift down and get lost in the feather of his long, dark lashes. Follow the line and curve of his nose to the philtrum above his upper lip, the small indentation masked by a day's worth of dark stubble. Stubble I want against my soft skin. And then resting on his full pink lips.

Seconds become minutes and I can't seem to locate the strength to look away from his mouth. My own mouth waters at the sight, the temptation to lean forward and wake him with my lips pressed against his grows with every beat of my heart. But as much as I want this man—this beautiful and enigmatic man—part of me screams to keep my heart protected. Memories flash in my head like old photographs, providing me with glimpses of the past and how I crumbled when he left. How impossible it was to breathe without him here.

With every cell inside my body, I want to believe what he tells me. That he is moving back. That he has never stopped thinking of me or us or the future we always wanted. And that his only desire is to be with me again. Believing those words, those sentiments, is all I have longed for with him. All I need. I want to breathe again.

But listening to your heart and protecting it don't always go hand in hand. They are two different plates on the scale and weighed separately. And I need to make a choice on which matters most. Giving in to what my heart desires or shielding my heart from future pain.

"Good morning, baby," Gavin rasps, my body jumping at the sound.

My eyes bolt to his as if I have been caught doing something forbidden. The top length of his dark hair sits partially on the pillow and his forehead. I gaze into his steely-gray eyes, the irises a thin outline of his dilated pupils—which are immersed in me. His fixation on me is possessive and powerful. And as captivated as I am, I am also fearful and nervous.

What if we do this and we find out we are not who we used to be?

What if the affection is one-sided? Or too lopsided to make things work?

What if he moves back and it negatively impacts his career—or both of ours—and he resents me? Can we continue a happy and healthy relationship in that instance?

What if we get back together and everything is perfect?

I allow the last question to tumble through my thought processes for a moment. Allow myself to believe that us coming back together is nothing short of amazing and perfect.

Allow myself to believe this is our chance at a happily ever after. One can only hope we are fortunate enough for life to ebb and flow with ease and bliss.

"I can practically hear the cogs in your head cranking. What could require so much thought this early in the morning?" Gavin's eyes bore into mine, a lighthearted act meant to bring my thoughts to life.

"It is early." Closing the gap between us, I give him a chaste kiss before continuing. "And way too early for in-depth conversations. Maybe after we have some coffee and breakfast."

His fingertips trail along my cheekbone, tracing to my ear and leaving a current in its wake as he tucks my hair behind my ear. "Breakfast sounds fantastic. Here or out?"

"I think I have everything needed here, so let's stay in. Plus, I think Luna is upset with me and the lack of attention I've been giving her over the last week. She needs a little mom time and affection."

Gavin groans as he closes his eyes, his arm drawing me in closer to his warm body. He caresses the tip of his nose over the flesh of my collarbone, skimming up the front of my throat and inhaling deep below my ear. When he speaks, his words reverberate from his chest to mine and dampen my panties.

"Mmm, I can understand the need for time and affection. If I purr and rub on your leg, will I get something in exchange?"

My breath hitches as intensity and hunger bloom between my legs. As much as I want to play-shove him, I ache to bring him impossibly closer. To tear off the remaining clothes on our bodies and rememorize every freckle and scar and curvature that has changed over the years.

But I am not ready for us to take that step yet. At least that is what I keep telling myself. Maybe if I repeat it enough times, I will believe it.

"You know you're making it really difficult to leave this bed," I whine.

"Maybe we can have a different form of breakfast," he coaxes.

"As tempting as that is, I'm going to vote we do the real food thing. I'm not sure I'm ready…" I trail off.

His thumb brushes over my cheek, eyes sweet and conveying his agreement. "Baby, I will wait forever for you. It feels as if I already have. When you're ready" —he kisses me tenderly— "that's when I'll be ready."

Although I am not ready to voice the words aloud again, all I can think about is how much I love this man. How I have always loved him, even when I had found a way to shove every memory of him and us into some desolate corner of my mind. He is my foundation, cracked or whole.

"Thank you." The words barely audible.

"For you—" he says. "Anything."

And without a care in the world, our lips and tongues do a dance as old as time.

twenty-seven

GAVIN

This view will never get old.

After a half hour of lips sucking and tongues tasting and hands groping, we finally decided it was best for us to get out of the bed. Not that a bed is required for the many things I want to do with her. Although we have already had sex, that time of our lives was different. Back then, everything was awkward and new and questionable.

But now…

Our time apart is not something I relish, but it does give both of us a different vantage point. For me, I respect people and life on a whole new level. Everything has a fresher perspective, is more eye-opening. That is not to say I don't do stupid shit from time to time—because don't we all. Just that I now know, understand, and am willing to deal with the consequences of my actions. Whatever they may be.

Right now, I refuse to disguise my ogling of Cora's body. She moves around the kitchen—her back facing me—in a black cotton ribbed tank top. The hem clings to her hips while the bust line accentuates the curvature of her tits and shows a hint of natural cleavage. I know she isn't wearing a bra beneath the tank as evidenced by the occasional visual of her firm nipples against the fabric. Below the tank, cherry red low-cut boy short panties cover most of her round ass cheeks.

Watching her—I groan internally—has my dick hardening and my mouth watering. Her body is not the only part of her I love, but it is a nice bonus. The last time I got such an intimate view of her body, we were teenagers and our bodies still had a year or two of developing to go. Cora's body is as curvaceous now as it was then, but not quite the same. She has taken care of herself—diet, exercise, enjoying life as best she can—and it shows.

Cora moves around the kitchen—slicing strawberries and apples, adding them to a bowl with blueberries and squeezing a lemon over top. Stirring a large frying pan loaded with shredded potatoes, chopped onions, oil, herbs and spices. Flipping a few "sausage" links—I learned this morning Cora is slowly eliminating meat from her diet. And occasionally checking the time on her Instant Pot, where she cooks a batch of cinnamon steel-cut oatmeal.

When she told me she was removing meat from her diet, I rattled off twenty questions asking why. I also questioned whether or not the food she was making would be any good. But the savory aroma of garlic and the sweetness of maple and cinnamon flitting through the air has me hungrier than ever. The true test will be when I taste it all. Honestly, the links are the only thing I am questioning. Everything else is somewhat normal.

The Instant Pot signals it is done cooking the oatmeal as she flips the potatoes one last time. One thing I remember from our breakfast excursions years ago, Cora likes her hash browns dark with a crispy crust and tends to pile them high on her plate. And it looks as if nothing has changed in that department.

She heads to the cabinet holding the dishware, grabbing two plates and mugs. Setting the plates beside the stovetop, she pops a K-Cup in the Keurig and presses the large brew button after her mug is under the drip. When it finishes, she repeats the process for me.

Everything about this blip in time is perfect. This is how my life should be. Our life. We ebb and flow in synchronization. Natural. Comfortable. Synergistically.

As much as I tried, I never found another person who made me feel more myself than Cora. Being with her... everything just fits in place. Nothing is forced. It just... is.

"Would you like anything in your coffee? Sugar? Creamer?" she asks, breaking me from my endless one-sided staring contest.

"Creamer. Dare I ask what my options are?" I give her my best goofy-scary face.

"I only have one and it's coconut milk-based. It's good. You'll like it," she states with confidence.

I nod. "Then that's what I'll have," I tease.

Cora adds creamer to both cups and a small spoonful of sugar to hers. She sets my cup in front of me, then turns back to the stove and begins plating the food. Before I can offer to help, she sets a plate and bowl in front of me. Within seconds, she adds maple syrup, a jar of cinnamon and a jar of garlic between our place settings. A smile perks up the corners of my mouth at the sight.

My love for maple and cinnamon.

Her indescribable love and obsession for garlic.

When we were younger, Waffle House was a regular occurrence—as it is with most teens and partiers. But she always ordered a triple portion of hash browns—scattered and smothered—and brought her own container of garlic powder. The small jar an additional accessory in her purse. I had gotten used to seeing it for the almost two years we were together. It was second nature. But seeing it today has me laughing at the fact she still has the habit.

"What are you laughing at?"

Rather than saying it, I simply point to the jar before spearing a sliced strawberry with my fork.

"There is no shame in loving garlic. If I knew you loved it, I would have added it to the hash browns. Normally, when I make my own, I add at least three or four cloves of garlic. The more, the merrier."

Shock registers in my expression. "Three or four? In a single serving? That's a lot of damn garlic, baby. You worried about vampire attacks?" I joke.

"Ha-ha," she deadpans. "No, goofball. With anything else, you build a tolerance level over time. What would be a potent level of garlic to some, I barely taste. What can I say—it's not just my favorite food, but it is also good for you." She shrugs off her response as if it should be public knowledge.

"Next time, just add the garlic in with the potatoes. I'm a big boy. I can handle it."

"Alright, big shot. As long as you promise not to bitch about it," she prompts me.

I hold up my right hand. "I swear I won't complain—" I hesitate, but continue. "Much."

She sticks her tongue out at me, crossing her eyes and cocking her head to the side. And I fall a little harder.

～

We spend the work-free day driving all over. She takes me to downtown St. Petersburg, where we stroll along Beach Drive, check out some of the storefronts and visit the Dali Museum. So much of downtown has changed and it is as if I am in a whole new version of an old city.

The St. Petersburg Pier is no longer there. Cora tells me it was torn down about five or six years ago. Now, a large outdoor area has taken its place. A restaurant sits closer inland and the pier is more outdoor activity focused. It is kind of weird to wander around here and not see the old inverted pyramid building. I had so much fun there as a kid. Hopefully the city builds something that adds more flare to the current structure, which seems blah in comparison.

The Dali has also been relocated and looks nothing like the original. Now it resembles a piece of art and is amazing without even stepping foot inside. But we do walk through the exhibit. Dali's work has always fascinated me, with all the droopy clocks and ants or distorted images of his wife. One of my favorites is the *Geopoliticus Child*. It just reaches me on some strange level; intrigues me.

When we leave the Dali, we opt to leave Cora's car in the garage we parked in earlier. Hand in hand, we stroll along the waterfront near the marina and eventually walk toward the shops and restaurants. After about ten minutes, we are trekking down First Avenue North.

As we head for the entrance of a restaurant to grab lunch, I push out a quiet laugh at her choice of location. No matter how much time has passed, some things about her will always be predictable. And I love that those parts of her remain. That time hasn't changed her completely. She is still the same girl I fell in love with. Only now, she is one-hundred-percent woman.

"Are you laughing at me?" she insinuates.

I squeeze her fingers with mine. "You're joking, right? I mean, I should have guessed we'd be having Asian for lunch," I tease.

"Why mess with a good thing." It is all she says, her shoulders shrugging as if eating what you love should be a given. I suppose she is right.

The hostess seats us at a table, handing us menus and letting us know our server will be with us soon. As my eyes dance over the options—sushi and non-sushi alike—I am a bit overwhelmed at the options available.

"Do you know what you're getting?" I ask Cora, praying her order will guide me in some direction.

She taps a finger to her lip. "We're about to see what you really think about me," she states, her words cryptic and confusing the hell out of me.

"Huh?"

Laughter bursts from her lips, dying quickly before she rambles off her intended order. "Here we go… I'm getting an order of spring rolls, seaweed salad, the vegetable ramen—which comes with a salad—and a yam yam sushi roll minus the eel sauce."

My gaze locks in place, the sight of her blurring. *Is she going to actually eat all of that?*

"Um. Is there something you're not telling me? That's a lot of food for just one person."

Cora just shakes her head at me. "Nope. I like ordering a lot so I have leftovers to take home. I won't eat it all while we're here. Swear," she states with a giggle.

Thank fuck. I was seriously worried some other reason had her ordering enough food for two.

"Maybe I won't need to order anything if you're getting so much," I taunt.

"Makes no difference to me. But you should get whatever you want to eat." Then she smiles and I forget what to do. I snap out of my Cora-fog and shake my head, internally laughing at myself and how easily she sidetracks me.

I scan the menu one last time as the server approaches. Gesturing for her to order first, she prattles off her mile-long lunch order. When the server looks to me, I feel like a pussy for only ordering a shrimp tempura appetizer and a Tampa roll. As if we reversed roles in the food consumption department and my masculinity has been knocked down a couple notches.

We chat while we wait for our food. And once everything is spread out on the table before us, to say I am overwhelmed would be an understatement. Everything has its own dish and there are currently seven dishes on our tiny two-person table. Seven. But I'm intrigued to see how much she actually does eat.

Bite after bite, the food begins to vanish. Needless to say, I am done eating before Cora, and all I can do is sit back and enjoy the entertainment before me. She pops a piece of her sushi in her mouth, moaning around the tempura fried sweet potato and rice. The sound stirs me up. Has me dying to hear that moan —and all other delicious sounds—with me hovering above her.

When we were younger, we'd had sex a number of times before my mother shipped us off to California. In the beginning, things were awkward and uncoordinated—as it is for anyone having sex for the first time. But the six months that followed our first time, we learned and explored many things with each other. One thing I never remember Cora doing was groaning in pleasure. It's not that she didn't enjoy sex or that she wasn't orgasming—she was just a quiet lover.

And so many parts of me want to know if that little fact still holds true.

Today has been one of the best days I have experienced in a long time.

Gavin and I walked around downtown St. Petersburg for hours and had a great lunch, although he teased me endlessly about the amount of food I ordered and ate. What can I say? I love my Asian food and I love it more when I can enjoy it a second go-around.

After eating lunch, we strolled a few blocks before turning around and heading back to the parking garage. We blared music from my Spotify playlist through the speakers and drove with the windows down, the wind whipping our hair everywhere on the short stretch of interstate and highway driving. Close to an hour later, I drove over the backed up Memorial Causeway and on to popular Clearwater Beach.

As I pulled into the parking lot, Gavin spoke up for the first time since we had gotten in the car. "Come up with me."

Once I found a place to park, I looked over at Gavin, unsure of what to say.

"Come up with me," he repeats, soft-spoken.

Should I? Everything about us is molding back into place.

Him asking me to come up to his room could be completely innocent. After all, he did say he would wait until I was ready before we took things further. And I believe him.

"Okay," I stammer. "Yes, I'll come up."

We hold hands from the parking lot to the bank of elevators, my bag of leftovers in his other hand. No words or sentiments are exchanged, not that they need to be. His body language and expressions tell me everything I need to know.

How much he cares for me.

How excited he is for us to be together again.

How nervous he is, his palm clammy against mine.

But most of all, how much he loves me.

Neither of us has broached the infamous *L* word, but it is there, dangling in front of us both. A few times I have almost let it slip from my lips. But I caught myself and battened down the hatches.

It's not that I don't want to tell him I love him. The complete opposite, actually. But if I allow myself to say the word, to convey the enormous level of emotion that partners up with confessing such a sentiment, it may change everything. And right now, I have no idea if the change would be for the better or worse. The way he has been around me— calling me *baby* like he did years ago—leads me to believe it would be the former.

And if I muster up the courage to profess my love for him —again—will he do the same? I can't put my heart on the line, not if I am unsure he will do the same. Not enough time has passed since his return. Not enough to know whether or not he will run off again.

The elevator pings when we reach his floor and we step out. Retrieving his wallet from his back pocket, he unlocks the door and ushers me in. With a loud thump, the door closes and he wanders over to the kitchenette, placing my food in the refrigerator. I stand in the entryway, staring at the room and how messy it looks. It is obvious he has told the maid service to ignore his room, which makes me want to laugh.

Thirty minutes later, we sit cuddled on a small loveseat, laughing at an episode of *Lucifer* on Netflix. We munch on chips and candy he had purchased on his first night here. The episode is almost over when a knock sounds at the door.

We both look at each other, confused. Before we started watching the show, we talked about grabbing dinner after, but not from room service. Maybe the maid was upset over not being able to clean his room for more than a week.

Gavin rises from the couch, kissing me on the crown of my head. "Probably someone knocking on the wrong door. I'll be back in a sec."

His bare feet pad across the floor as he disappears from my direct line of sight. The loud clunk of the deadbolt disengaging echoes in the room, followed by a slight creak of hinges. When he got up to leave the couch, he had paused the show and created a vacant silence in the room. Right now, that silence is deafening.

Mumbled voices come from where Gavin went to open the door. A door which has yet to be closed. Which means whoever is at the door is either lost or is someone Gavin knows. My stomach suddenly constricts, a heavy sickness settling in my core.

Is it Alyson? Is she giving him more shit regarding us?

Curious as to what is taking Gavin so long to return, I rise from the couch and walk toward the door, my stride quiet and slow. The closer I get, the clearer I hear the conversation. A woman's voice chirps from the hall, her words sweet and her tone casual. And I determine by their exchange she is someone Gavin knows. And knows well. And it isn't Alyson.

When I take a few more steps, I hear Gavin muttering under his breath, anger seeping into his voice. A couple more steps and I can see the door. Can see Gavin's back and the slightest bit of wavy, blonde locks. His words to her are venomous as he tries to make her leave. But when he shifts to his left an inch or so, she catches sight of me and a devilish smile takes over her features.

Who the hell is this woman?

twenty-nine

Thirteen years ago

"What do you mean you're moving?" I ask, tears welling in my eyes and threatening to spill at any second.

He runs his fingers through his hair, grabbing hold at the roots and yanking as he bows his head. "My mom. She got transferred; promoted. Whatever. But her new position is in California. So, we have to move." He tugs his hair harder before releasing it from his grip and looking at me with blood-shot eyes.

I have no clue what to say. Or what to do. How to react. In this situation, is there really anything I can do? There is no way I can stop his mom from accepting the promotion she rightfully deserves. Nor can I stop her from taking the only person I care about to the other side of the country, almost three thousand miles away. If we were older, maybe we would have a say.

Covering my face with my hands, I mumble, "When?" Although, I am terrified to know the answer.

"She said we're leaving next week," he says, his voice cracking at the end.

"Next week?" I whisper. "But what about school? And us?" My voice shrinking the more I speak.

A vignette darkens the edges of my vision. My world slowly closing in on itself. Nausea roils in my belly and crawls up my throat.

He wraps his arms around me, enveloping me in a tight embrace. His warmth is pure comfort, and I close my eyes and allow myself a moment to get lost in the feel of him. Breathe in his scent, the earthy beach smell that only Gavin has. Hear the sound of his erratic heartbeat beneath my ear on his chest. My head shifting with the rise and fall of his lungs.

He can't leave. He just can't. Gavin is home. Where I belong. And I am where he belongs.

One of his hands caresses the back of my head as his lips pepper small kisses on the crown while he shushes me. Our bodies rock back and forth, the movement subtle. And I squeeze him as tight as humanly possible, my body trembling as I am wracked with sobs. Maybe if I hold him tight enough, he won't leave.

"We'll figure something out, baby. This is just as painful for me as it is you. I don't want to leave," he confesses. "Not you. Not here. You are my home, Cora." He echoes my internal sentiment.

"You're my home, too," I reply as tears flood my cheeks. "If you're not here, I'll be so lost."

He wraps me more securely in his arms as if he is trying to prevent the eventual departure we both know we have no control over. I wish it were that simple. I wish we had a say in the matter. A voice. But we don't and that hurts even more.

He withdraws from me, bringing his fingers to my chin

and tipping my head back. Our tear-stained, puffy red eyes hold each other's. The pain in my chest swells more with each passing second. My lungs burn as I refuse to breathe in this form of reality. This cannot be happening. This cannot be real. If I don't believe it, maybe it won't happen. Maybe he won't leave.

"I will find a way back to you, baby. It may not be right away. But never doubt that I will return. The only place I want to be is beside you. Forever."

A heavy sigh escapes my lips. *Why could this have not waited another two years? When he could stay behind.*

"I love you, Gavin," I tell him, and it reaches deeper than the hundreds of times I have told him before.

He brushes a cluster of stray hairs from my face, tucking them behind my ear. "And I love you, Cora. More than anything else in existence."

I sniffle back my tears and congested nasal phlegm, the sound and motion very unladylike. We both laugh at me. But when we stop, both our faces locked in serious expressions, I whisper-rasp, "Happy Birthday, Gavin."

And seconds later he has me wrapped in his arms again.

I help Gavin put the last of his things in a cardboard box, closing the flaps and sealing it with tape. Grabbing the Sharpie on the floor, I write *Gavin's room* on the box and proceed to doodle a quick image of a beach beside it. If having a small drawing by my hand on cardboard is the only piece of me he can take with him, I will draw on every box possible.

"Thanks," he mutters, his mood growing infinitely more

sour as we packed up his life here. I don't blame him. If our roles were reversed, I would behave the same.

"You're welcome."

Looking around his room, I take in the bare blue walls. Before he was required to pack everything he owned, the walls had been littered with rock band posters and concert flyers. Images of surfers and the beach and us as well as our friends. Now, all those pieces rest in boxes or tubes, waiting to be added to new walls. In a new house. Thousands of miles from here.

The built-in bookshelf is now coated in a layer of dust after his collection of magazines and books got tucked away and packed inside the large moving truck outside. All the furniture had been taken out of his room a few hours ago. The carpet depressed from the feet of the bed and dresser, and outlined with the faded color where the sunlight couldn't reach.

His room now a skeleton of a space I once deemed comforting and warm. His room as hollow as the hole growing in my chest.

He lifts the box from the floor and heads for the door. The last box. And the last time we would be in his room. I carry the packing tape and marker, trudging down the hall and blindly following his footsteps.

With each step we take, the world as I know it slips further and further away. No more lunches at school or meetups before or after. No more laughter or teasing. And no more movie nights or walks on the beach or sunsets. Or holding hands, embraces, or lips against mine. No more Gavin. And no more us.

By the time we reach the moving truck, tears flow like

rivers down my cheeks. I do my best to make no sounds, but the restraint it requires is fading fast. It feels as if I am intentionally giving the love of my life away. Shoving everything he owns into this truck and saying goodbye forever. Packing him up and shipping him off to who knows where.

Over the last week, we spent every possible moment together. Not a moment wasted. Yes, he had to pack up his life. But he tried to do that after curfew so we could have as much us time as possible. Yet it feels as if we had no time at all. It feels as if every moment we have shared for the last two years is being ripped away and shredded into a million pieces.

As soon as he gets to California, I bet I won't hear from him often. He will be busy unpacking and adjusting to a new school just before the year ends. It isn't only a major adjustment for me, but more so for him. Not only is he losing me—losing us—he is also being thrown into a foreign place with zero friends. The only people there to comfort him are his parents. The people upending his life.

He sets the box in the truck, taking the tape and marker from my hands and placing them beside it.

Before I can think of a single word to say, he yanks me close and holds me as if his life depends on it. On me. My sobs come faster and harder. His chest shakes around me with his own turmoil. Anguish and heartache leak from both of us and there isn't a damn thing we can do about it.

Minutes later, his dad taps on his shoulder and tells him it is time for them to leave.

After a few labored breaths, he pulls back with hesitancy. His eyes swollen and red as he looks into mine. "I love you, baby. Hopefully, I can come back during the summer." He kisses me and steals my breath, my pulse soaring in my veins.

"I love you, too, Gavin. Call me when you land."

We exchange one last kiss and embrace, and then he is whisked away. My legs giving out as I collapse to the ground, where I cry for the next three hours. Alone. In the front yard of the boy I love. The boy who just left.

Present

When I open the door, I am beyond shocked to see Layla in the hall.

"Hey," she singsongs, waving a hand at me.

"What are you *doing* here?" I whisper-yell. "And how did you know where my room is?"

Her bright smile fades as her brows furrow in confusion. "I had a shoot in Miami. Just thought I'd surprise you on my way home. Alyson adjusted my flight for me, so I'm here till tomorrow morning. She told me which room you were in and suggested you might want to grab dinner."

What. The. Actual. Fuck. Alyson?

She knows Cora and I have been working on mending our relationship. And she also knows I have every intention of moving back to Florida as soon as I can sort out the details. Is this her play on keeping me in California? Sending Layla to my door and having her attempt to swoon me over dinner.

Not that Layla could ever hold my attention in that way.

Now I have got some choice words for Alyson the next

time we talk. And they won't be pleasant. In fact, they will be downright ugly.

"That was nice of her, but I already have plans for the evening," I tell her as I start closing the door.

Her hand comes up, preventing the door from moving any farther into the frame. "What the hell, Gavin? So, *you have plans* and now I'm no longer good enough to be around?"

I really wish she would lower her fucking voice. Not only do I not want Cora hearing her, but I also don't need the people staying in the other rooms to hear her flipping her shit. I give her a pointed look, telling her to quiet down. She huffs and rolls her eyes like she gives two shits what anyone else thinks. After all, Layla is quite the attention whore.

"It's not that. I have plans with someone else. Plain and simple. Please don't try to peg me as the bad guy here. If you would've called or texted me and told me you were coming, I could have made different plans," I press, my body heating and becoming more anxious with each passing second I am away from Cora. As it is, I have been at the door far too long for it to be a wrong room situation.

"Why are you being such a dick?"

"Me? You randomly show up and expect me to drop whatever it is I am doing because you're here. Sorry. Doesn't work that way."

She needs to fucking leave. Now.

"You're different," she accuses. "Alyson was right."

"What the fuck does *that* mean?" Now Alyson is talking shit behind my back. I groan as I picture Alyson calling Layla in for interference. And at this point, pissed doesn't even begin to cover how I feel.

"Don't worry, she didn't go into any specific details with

me. But she told me you've changed since being out here. That you plan to make bigger changes, too."

Tomorrow, Alyson and I are going to sit down and have a very detailed conversation about keeping her mouth shut and her nose out of other people's business. One—I pay her. Two—her job is to do what's best for me, not her. And in no way is this benefiting me. This is all about her. I cannot believe she brought Layla here, purposely changed her flight and gave her my room number. What sort of game does she think she is playing? Does she seriously think this will sway my decision? My privacy is more invaded than ever now and a newfound rage builds inside me. A rage neither Alyson nor Layla will enjoy.

"Not that it is any of your business, but yes. I plan on moving back to Florida after I get a few things situated in California."

"You cannot be serious. How will you work from here? What is so goddamn alluring about this place?"

I shift my weight, her questions irritating me. This conversation is done. And I'm done. With her and Alyson.

Just as I am about to shut the door again, a wicked grin lights up Layla's face. A grin I know all too well. One that tells me she is about to do something spiteful and vindictive. Her eyes look past me, over my shoulder and into the room.

The hair on the back of my neck stands at attention. A boulder sinks in my gut. Before I even turn around, I know Cora is standing behind me. I *feel* her. More than likely, she was curious as to what was taking me so long to return. She has no idea who Layla is, but Layla knows about her. Not her name, but that the one person I cared about most lives here. Right now, I am one-hundred-percent certain she knows this is her. And I know her well enough to know she is about to fuck everything up.

Before I turn to face Cora, I give Layla a glare of warning. Wordlessly telling her to keep her mouth shut and leave. But her smile grows wider and I know nothing good will come of this.

"Gavin—" Cora calls out behind me. "Is everything okay?"

I school my expression and turn to face her. "Everything is fine." I want to add more, but I am at a loss for what to say.

"Hi," Layla speaks up, my body going rigid at the sound. "I'm Layla. And you are?"

Layla extends her hand in Cora's direction, but I step in front of her and block their possible connection. I don't want her touching Cora, let alone getting within arm's length.

"And you need to leave," I tell her over my shoulder, trying once more to close the door.

"Why are you being so rude, Gavin?" Layla says, her pitch an octave higher and she reaches out and touches my bicep. I cringe away from her and start pushing the door closed, only to be met with Layla's boot.

"Gavin, what's going on?" Cora asks, hundreds of questions skittering across her face.

"Yeah, Gavin, what's going on?" Layla's tone becomes venomous and shrill.

I stand between the two of them, hoping this nightmare will end. Praying I fell asleep while Cora and I were watching television and this is all one huge, fucked-up dream. But somewhere in the back of my mind, I know it isn't. And Layla is really standing here. And I am about to lose Cora all over again. Because what other plausible reason would Alyson have for bringing Layla here? None. Not a single one. And I don't know which emotion holds more power over me in this moment—fear or fury.

The silence in the room has every nerve in my body on edge. My heart slams against my ribcage, grabbing the bones and rattling like a madman. I can't breathe. Can't speak. The light at the end of a very long tunnel slowly dims and fades. I have no idea what to do. Where to be. How to function. But just as I am about to spew out something, Layla shatters the silence in the room. Along with everything that matters in my life.

"Well, since no one else is speaking, I guess I'll take the stage." Layla steps closer to me, her hands clasping around my arm. "Like I said, I'm Layla. Gavin's fiancée."

Fuuuuck...

Time Exposure

BOOK TWO

To those who looked challenge in the face and said, "You don't choose my fate. I do."

exposure

Photography term.

Exposure is the total amount of light that hits the sensor for one frame or shot. It is determined by the exposure triangle settings (ISO, aperture and shutter speed).

How much light is captured depends on three things: aperture size in the lens, ISO sensitivity on your camera's sensor, and the length of *time* you leave the shutter open.

one

GAVIN

"Like I said, I'm Layla. Gavin's fiancée."

Fuck, fuck, fuck...

Why the hell is she doing this? What does Layla stand to gain by doing this? By ruining the one chance I have at getting Cora back. What did Alyson offer her in return?

Cora's eyes grow impossibly wide as her soft green irises darken and tears pool in the corners. Her jaw drops as she stands stoic, eyes bouncing between me and Layla. For a moment, she doesn't move a muscle or utter a single word. And her stillness scares the shit out of me.

When her synapsis fire again, Cora takes a few cautious steps forward, bends over and picks her shoes up from the floor. I stand helpless, less than five feet away, and observe her as she squats down to sit on the floor and slides the sneakers on. Her movements are slow and measured. She makes it a point to make zero eye contact with me as she ties her laces with precision. The longer she keeps her head down, focusing on the task, the less I breathe.

Every moment we shared over the last week just nosedived off my balcony. Every word I said, every promise I made, she will now perceive as a lie. After all this time, after everything we have endured, our second chance at forever will be ruined at the hands of two petty, jealous, greedy bitches.

But not if I get a say in the matter.

I rip my arm from Layla's grip and jerk away from her. Heat and anger boil my blood and explode from my pores as I turn to face Layla. "Fucking leave. Now!" My voice is venomous and louder than she expects and she startles. Her momentary wide eyes twitch before she yanks on her bitter bitch mask.

"What the fuck, Gavin?" Layla bites back. "You don't want your *soul mate* to know about us?" The way she rolls soul mate over her tongue is dangerous. Poisonous. Vile.

What the fuck is Layla's deal? She has never been like this. Never stepped up and blocked me from what I want. Acting like a jealous girlfriend. Or a straight-up bitch. This is a whole new side and it disgusts me.

"There is no *us*," I snap. "Your need for attention has no bounds, does it? Get the fuck away from me. Your little arrangement… done. I'm done."

I shove Layla out the door and her eyes widen once more before I slam the door in her face. Not sure what provoked her to act vindictively, but as soon as I fix things with Cora, I will settle things with Layla.

Bitch.

I walk over to where Cora sits on the floor and hesitantly kneel in front of her. Lowering my head, I try to get her to look up at me. Her head hangs low as her eyes hone in on her shoes. Slowly, she loops and ties them, but doesn't peek up. I desperately want to reach forward, slip my fingers under her chin and tip her head back so she will look at me. But I don't. Because it scares the shit out of me to see what is in her eyes right now.

"Cora? Baby? Look at me," I whisper. My voice is gruff and dry, and I don't recognize the pitch with my own ears.

Her chin pops up and her eyes snap to mine. "Don't you dare," she seethes as she scoots away from me with a finger pointed at my face.

"What?" I ask, confused. "Don't what, baby?" This won't be good, but I need her to tell me what she is thinking. What she is feeling. Because fuck, I am scared shitless.

Cora unsteadily rises to her feet and locks eyes with me as I stand. I take a step in her direction and she steps back before lifting her hands to stop me. Tears well in her eyes. Her exposed skin painted in red blotchy patterns. Eyes narrow and straighten over and over as she assesses me. Pain etches the lines of her forehead as her chin starts to quiver.

And fuck if I am not losing my goddamn mind because she won't let me get any closer to her. Won't let me touch her. Won't let me connect with and soothe her. The once-old stab wound in my heart slices wide open and the pain of this whole situation lances me.

I cannot lose her. Not again.

"Don't call me *baby*." My term of endearment for her spits out like acid on her tongue. "Not after some woman you've never mentioned tells me she's your fiancée. What the actual fuck, Gavin?" With each word Cora speaks, her volume goes from soft to livid in a matter of seconds.

Cora isn't just angry with me or this situation, she is fucking furious. Can't say I blame her, but I wish there was an abbreviated way to explain it. One where she would understand. One where the nightmare we are currently stuck in will transition into your average dream.

Unfortunately, this nightmare is very real. And it won't go away with the blink of an eye.

Just out of arm's reach, her frame shakes as she clenches her fists so tight her knuckles whiten. Her jaw tightens as she stares at me and subtly shakes her head. Eyes glassy, but the tears have yet to spill down her cheeks.

I take another step forward and she steps back again. Each step she takes away from me is a knife twisting my heart. Raw and painful and a reminder of the suffering we both endured thirteen years ago. A pain neither of us will survive again.

Holding my hands up in surrender, I gaze into her wet, red eyes. "Baby," I say, cringing when she grinds her teeth. "Please, let me explain. It's not what you think. Layla is just a friend. We aren't actually engaged."

Cora cocks her head and glares at me, unbelieving. Her eyes lock on mine and study them as if I just asked her to read my palm. She scrutinizes them a moment before eyeing the lines of my face and finally dropping to stare at my lips. I know what she is doing. Because Cora and I don't have to speak for reality to be stated. So, instead of asking me more questions, she tries to read the truth through my expressions and body language.

And god I hope she sees the truth in my words. Because they are nothing but real.

Layla has never been anything other than a friend. Our relationship has never skirted any line other than friendship. And Layla stating she is my fiancée… there is more to the story than meets the eye. A story privy to me, Layla, and Alyson. A story I hope Cora gives me a chance to explain.

Just when I spot a glimmer of hope, Cora speaks. And her words are far from what I expect to come out of her mouth.

"This can't happen, Gavin." She gestures between us. "This is too much. Even if you are telling me the truth now, I can't deal with bullshit drama like this. Women claiming ownership over you. Women saying vicious things to steal you from me. Why would you hide something like this from me? Because you thought it would never be an issue between us?" She pauses to catch her breath. "I knew this was a mistake. I need to leave."

No. No, no, no. This cannot be happening. This cannot be fucking happening. I cannot lose her. Not again. And not over this.

She swipes her purse from the table and starts for the door. I freeze momentarily, not wanting to believe this is my reality. That I am losing her again after finally getting her back. It's like I am sixteen all over again. Like I don't have a say in the matter. Like what I want doesn't count and won't be taken into consideration.

I refuse to let this be how we end. Downright refuse.

The heavy hotel room door slams shut and snaps me back to reality. *No!*

I bolt to the door and yank it open. Stepping out into the hall, I look left then right before spotting Cora. She isn't running, but her feet trek along the carpet faster than a steady walk. I sprint after her, giving no fucks that I have just locked myself out of my room.

"Cora," I yell. "Wait. Please, let me fix this."

She stands in front of the elevator banks and religiously mashes the down button like her life depends on it. Her teary eyes glance my way and it rips open every suture in my stitched-up heart.

I did this to her. I hurt her. Again.

The elevator car arrives and she steps in, the doors closing just as I approach. *Damnit.* I smash the down button, hopeful the elevator car she stepped in reopens. Seconds later, the other set of doors opens and I jump in and hit the button for the bottom floor. The car pings as it passes each floor, my heart wrenching tighter and tighter with each second I spend away from her. Not knowing if she has already reached the lobby and is darting out the doors to her car.

When the doors slide open, I dash out and scan the lobby for Cora. My eyes land on her as she weaves between people in the full reception area and I race toward her. As long as she remains in my line of sight, I will catch her. I will not let her go this easily. Not after the strides we have made this week. Not after I got back the only person who matters.

"Cora," I yell. Instantly, every set of eyes on the ground floor whips my way. "Please wait."

She peers over her shoulder, tears trailing down her cheeks, and makes a beeline for the exit. Just as she makes it to the door, I catch up to her and grab hold of her arm. As badly as I want to haul her into me, to wrap my arms around her and pin her to my chest, I stop myself. Now is not the time. Although I won't let her leave without a fight, I won't be the man who doesn't give her a choice. After everything we have endured, she deserves to choose what happens next.

"Let me go, Gavin," she spits out as she tries to yank her arm from my grasp.

"No, baby. Please, let's talk about this," I beg. "Please let me explain everything. I wasn't intentionally keeping this from you. And, like I said, it's not real."

Her soft, sad bloodshot eyes stare up at me, pleading with me to let her go as nonstop tears spill down her cheeks.

This pain, her pain… what she is experiencing in this very moment. If it is even remotely close to what she felt when I left thirteen years ago, I hate myself. I hate myself for doing this to her. For letting her experience such heartbreaking emotions. Again. No one should have to undergo this form of torture—once, let alone twice.

"Please, Gavin," she mumbles, her eyes darting around the room. Embarrassment creases her brow as she squeezes her eyes shut. "Please just let me go." When she opens her eyes, a new emotion paints her expression. Disparity and numbness. An emptiness that has me stumbling back, physically and mentally. "Can't you see?"

See what? That I have inflicted the worst pain on the sole person I live and breathe for. Yes, I see it. I hate that I see it. But something twists in my gut and stabs at my heart. And I have a feeling her words have an ulterior meaning. Definition unbeknownst to me.

"See what, baby?" I ask, terrified to know the answer. Terrified of what she will say next.

I ache to touch her. Yearn to embrace her and pepper kisses on her hair, her temples, her forehead. But I fear the worst. That she will pull away. Reject me. And her rejection would sting worse than any words. So, I keep my hands at my sides and imagine all the ways I wish to right my wrongs.

"Isn't it obvious?" she asks, not waiting for me to answer before she continues. "It's like the universe is trying to tell us something."

Cocking my head, I narrow my eyes in confusion. Is she suggesting what I think she is? That we don't belong together. That as much as we love each other, we aren't meant to have each other.

How could something so perfect not be meant to exist?

The universe isn't trying to tell us shit. And if for some nonsensical reason she believes fate is telling us we don't belong together; I will grab fate by the balls until it comprehends the truth. That Cora and I belong together. Always have and always will.

And until I fix this, nothing else matters.

"Baby, I have no idea what you're thinking, but it better not be anything along the lines that we aren't meant to be together. Because that's bullshit and you know it."

Cora turns away from me and walks out the exit with me hot on her heels. Her pace picks up and I jog to keep up with her. She darts past the valet and heads for the lot where she parked her car.

I will not suffocate her. She needs time to mull things over. But she has to know things between us won't get better if we don't discuss them. She needs to hear the whole story.

When she reaches her car, her hands dive in her purse and shove stuff left to right as she searches for her keys. She pulls out the fob and unlocks her car as I jog up to her.

"Baby, please don't leave. Let's go back up to my room and talk about this." We need to talk, that is the only way to resolve this.

"No, Gavin. As much as I want this, as much as I want us to be together, it feels like the world is against us. And I can't do it. I can't fight anymore. I fought for so many years. Cried a million tears until my eyes couldn't do it anymore. And it's happening all over again. My heart fell in love with you all over again and I let it. *Stupid, stupid girl.* As soon as I allowed myself to be vulnerable, I got crushed. I feel like the earth is swallowing me whole, like it's clawing at my insides and eating me alive. And I can't deal with it. Can't deal with you. Not now."

Her words paralyze me. Make my limbs numb and my heart hollow. Pain spills out of her and infiltrates me like liquid poison. Slithers in my veins and takes up residence. And it doesn't just hurt. It kills.

The first time we were separated, it was against what I wanted. Against what either of us wanted. But I had no say or power to stop my parents from moving us across the country for my mom's promotion. Although I was older, I was still just a child.

Now, I may no longer be a child, but I inflict her with the same heartache and torture. Except this time around, our emotional state has evolved. We understand love and hope and pain and anguish. We grasp fear and hopelessness and sorrow and dejection. And in the blink of an hour, I have given all of them to her.

I have never hated myself as much as I do right now.

I step into her, a tear slipping down my cheek as she steps back and bumps into her car. But I ignore her retreat and reach up, framing her face in my hands. This will not be the last time I see her; I won't let it be. This is not how our story ends.

"I fucked up, and I'm so sorry. So, so sorry. But I will fix this. I swear to you, I will fix this. And when I do, I'm coming back for you. You can count on it. Because, Cora" —I pause, pinching my eyes shut— "you and I belong together. No matter what obstacles come at us, we belong together. I love you. And I will always love you. Until my last breath. Until my dying day."

I lean down, press my lips to hers and kiss her softly. Our tears blend at our joined lips and I don't know which are hers and which are mine. When I break the kiss, I lick our tears from my lips and step away. She stares at me a second as hundreds of thoughts invade her mind. Then she rushes to get in her car, starts the engine and drives away.

Away from me. Away from us.

I will give her time, but I won't go down without a fight. Not this time. Never again.

CORA

I can't breathe. Literally.

A block from Gavin's hotel, I turn onto a small side street and shift my car into park. The engine idles quietly as I rest my forehead against the steering wheel. Tears flood my eyes and blur the world around me. Violent sobs wrack my body as I lose all sense of composure. With every breath I try to inhale, the emotional boulder in my throat grows larger and heavier.

He said it isn't real. That this supposed engagement is a farce. A fallacy. Said *she* is only a friend. Just a friend. Nothing more. But if all of what he said is true, why do I feel like this? Empty. Broken. Shattered. Desolate.

Why do I feel as if I have just lost the one person who makes me whole? The one person who soothes the ache. Makes me smile. Mends the wounds once created from his loss. A loss he had zero control over.

I replay snippets of the conversation in my head, trying to find truth in Gavin's words. Trying to *listen* to what he said. Really listen. Because the moment she announced their supposed relationship, the world spun off its axis. I wobbled. Stumbled backward in time. Back to a time when vows were made. To the day he left and promised to return, but abandoned me for more than a decade.

He swears he and this other woman are not in a relationship. That he and this other woman are not betrothed. That they are just friends. Only friends. But why would Gavin's friend say such things? Cruel words meant to inflict pain. To make me suffer.

As is, my memory is one huge blob of confusion right now. It mixes in words and visuals from various conversations. Mingles them like partygoers. And I hate it. Hate that I don't know what is real and what is artifice. I have no way of knowing what memory is fact or fable.

So how can I decipher what to believe and what to disregard? And how the hell will I handle what happens next? I just don't know. Can't think past what just happened or the laceration in my heart.

The one thing I do know with absolute certainty is I cannot sit on this beach another minute, crying my eyes out. Sooner or later, a cop will tell me to move along. Tell me I cannot be parked here because I don't have a permit. Who cares if I cry so hard I risk an accident. Who cares if I have a meltdown and can't feel my limbs.

And with that, another round of sobs takes hold. I let it out, fishing a napkin from my glove compartment to blow my nose and dry some of the tears. When my cries slightly settle and I can breathe a little, I decide going home isn't the best option.

I grab my purse from the passenger seat and dig out my cell phone. With shaky hands, I unlock the phone and call

Shelly. The ringing blares in my ear while I attempt to stop crying altogether. On the third ring, Shelly answers.

"Hey, girl. How's it going?" Shelly cajoles.

I don't answer right away as I still work to control my tears and breathing. But it is no use and I start blubbering like a baby. The semi-composed state I was in moments ago vanishes.

"Cora?" she beckons, panic edging her voice. "Cora, are you okay? What's wrong?"

"I... I'm... Shelly..." I fumble, my words a mess of inconsistency. Just like my head. Just like my heart. "Shelly, can I... can I come over?" I manage to frame the question around my sobs.

"Oh my god! Are you okay, Cora? What's happening?"

She still hasn't answered my question. *Please just tell me to come over. Just tell me it is okay.* Not that I really need an invitation to her house, but I don't want to intrude if she has plans.

"Shelly, please. Please can I come over?" I plead through my incessant tears and sobs. I wish the blubbering would just stop. It hurts. Every muscle and bone and organ just hurts.

"Yes, of course you can. Are you okay to drive? I can pick you up."

As tempting as her offer is, if I leave my car on the beach it will get impounded. And that is a whole separate nightmare I don't need. Bad enough my heart is in shambles, I don't need to have automobile and financial issues too. Shelly lives in a small one-bedroom in Largo, and I should be able to make it there in twenty minutes. If I collect myself mentally, driving to her house shouldn't be an issue. It won't take long. Then I can let it all go again.

"You don't need to come and get me. I'm leaving Clear-water Beach. Should be there in twenty to thirty, depending on the traffic."

"Cora, you've got me worried. Did something happen? Are you okay? Is Gavin okay?"

Just hearing his name brings about a new bout of tears. My chest caves in on itself as my heart shrivels and lungs forget how to function. *Breathe Cora.*

"I'll tell you when I get to your house. See you soon."

And before she can say or ask anything else, I disconnect the call. If I plan to make it to her house in one piece, I need to clear my head as much as possible. Her infinite questions won't help matters. She can ask them all when I get to her place.

I sit unmoving in the car another couple minutes, taking deep breaths and attempting to refocus on physical objects.

A man walks his dog on the sidewalk. The neon signs across the street promote beer and pizza and a live band. A child swings wildly between her parents as they head into a seafood restaurant. *Breathe in. Breathe out. Just remember to breathe, Cora.* The flash of the pedestrian crossing sign lights up. An older woman rides by on a tricycle with colorful lights.

Once calm enough to drive, I turn the car around, drive off the beach and head in the direction of Shelly's place.

A couple blocks down, I crank up the radio and play loud, upbeat music. Then I roll down the windows and let the wind pelt my skin and whip my hair. Minutes later, I no longer smell the salty beach air and am hit with the occasional scent of fast food or well water. But right now, I would rather smell the foul odor of greasy meat and sulfur than the beach.

Because no matter how much time passes, the sight, smell

and feel of the beach will always remind me of Gavin. Always.

After weaving down a couple streets, I park my car in front of Shelly's apartment building. As I get out of the car, I spot Shelly running down the stairs and heading in my direction. She slams into me and wraps her arms around me, squeezing me with boa constrictor strength. And I don't pry her off me. I simply cry into her shoulder. Soaking her hair and shirt. Couldn't tell you if anyone passed by us. I honestly don't give a damn.

We stand like this for a while before she breaks the hug. "Come on, let's go inside."

I don't say a word, stumbling beside her with my arm hooked in hers. She guides us inside, takes my keys and purse and sets them on the coffee table. We plop down on the couch and she hugs me close again, stroking my hair. She lets me cry and sob until my body can no longer do either anymore. Shelly knows exactly what I need and doesn't bother trying to ask more questions. Not yet, anyway.

When my sobs recede, Shelly assumes I have reached the max quota for tears in one day. She leans away from me and ducks her head to look me in the eyes. "You want to talk about it?"

And for the first time since I arrived, our eyes finally meet and hold. Her expression a heaping pile of concern as she regards me. My eyes feel ten times bigger than normal and sting from crying for the last hour straight. No doubt they are bloodshot and lifeless.

Lifeless. Exactly how I feel right now.

"It's Gavin," I say as I stare at my fumbling hands in my lap. If I look back up and see sadness in Shelly's eyes, I will lose it again. And I am so tired of crying. So very tired. It hurts too fucking much.

Shelly rubs my back with gentle, endearing strokes. "What about Gavin?"

I swallow, not wanting to speak about the fiasco that happened tonight, but knowing full well I need to get it off my chest. To tell someone. To get insight from someone I trust.

Gavin told me none of it was true. That they were only friends. But if they were only friends and not actually engaged, why would he hide all of it from me? He never mentioned her as being one of his friends. Or a fellow model. Actually, he hasn't mentioned anyone he knows in California aside from his mom. And something about that doesn't sit well with me.

Does he not want me to know about his life the last thirteen years? Does he have something to hide?

Inhaling deeply, I prepare to recant the evening before I called. *Deep breaths, Cora. You need to let it all out.*

"Gavin and I went back to his hotel after spending the day together. He invited me up to his room and I obliged. Everything was good. Perfect, actually. We cuddled on the couch and started watching Netflix. Halfway through the show, someone knocked on the door. We were both confused by it, but Gavin said it was probably someone at the wrong room and he'd send them away."

I stop talking. Stare at my fumbling fingers in my lap. Pick at a loose thread along the hem of my shirt. Bite the inside of my cheek and try my best not to start crying. Again.

If what Gavin said was true, why is this so hard to say? Why is it so hard for me to believe? To believe he is telling me nothing except the truth. Once upon a time, I never doubted a single word Gavin spoke. So, why do I doubt him now?

And although the answer lingers at the edge of my thoughts, I don't dare voice it. Not now. Not yet.

"Take your time, Cora. Do you want some water?"

I nod as I wring my shirt between my hands. She returns seconds later and hands me a glass. I drink the water and thank her. After I place the glass on the table, I rip the bandage from the wound in my chest and continue.

"When Gavin didn't come right back to the couch, I wondered who was at the door and what was taking so long. I headed for the door and heard him arguing with a woman. At first, I couldn't make out what they were saying, but could tell they knew each other. For a moment, I thought maybe it was his agent. When I was close enough to hear them talking, I heard Gavin tell the woman he was planning to move back to Florida. At that point, I knew it wasn't his agent because they'd already discussed him moving back. The woman seemed pissed and asked what was so great about being here. Just as she asked him, she caught sight of me."

Shelly gasps and slaps a hand over her mouth as her eyes widen. And suddenly, it seems I don't need to tell her what happens next, because she already knows. She may not know the pertinent details, but she has a vague idea. And I plan to tell her everything. To get it all off my chest. I need to. Because bottling this up will kill me.

"The second her eyes landed on me; an evil smile lit up her face. Like she knew who I was. Like what would happen next would hurt me and Gavin, but she didn't give a shit. Anyway, after she saw me, she became sweet and formal. She introduced herself—"

"What's her name?" Shelly interrupts.

"Layla."

For a minute, Shelly lifts her eyes to the ceiling and studies the popcorn as if it is art. She searches her memory bank for anyone with the name Layla. But her search will yield no results. Because if Gavin didn't mention her to me, I am positive he didn't mention her to anyone else. Not even Micah. Why would he?

"Don't know her," Shelly confirms.

"Me either. She's one of his California friends. After she introduced herself, she asked who I was. Seconds after, Gavin tried to make her leave. More than once. But she was insistent on staying and butting in. After no one spoke for a moment, she smiled big again and tells me she's Gavin's fiancée."

Shelly's jaw drops to the floor as she stares at me. As her mouth closes, she narrows her eyes. "I'm sorry, what? I must have misheard you. Did you just say this bitch is his fiancée?"

I nod as a fresh round of tears escapes and spills down my cheeks. "But he swears it's not true. He wanted to *explain* it to me, but I bolted. And after he chased me down the hall and through the lobby and to my car, I didn't want to hear any of it. Because even if what he says is true, why didn't he tell me? We've talked so much over the last week. So why not explain it to me then? Why hide something like this if it means nothing?"

And that is the biggest question of them all. If what Gavin told me is correct—that he and Layla are not together—why not tell me about her from the get-go? If there is nothing to hide, he should have been forthcoming. Not let me find out later or in some roundabout way.

Shelly nods as she sits immobile. Her eyes fog over as her brain works double time. I stare at her as she sorts through all the details and tries to devise possible reasons why Gavin left this one piece of information out. Layla isn't some minor tidbit. Not equivalent to admitting you have a dog that may not get along with my cat. No, Layla is a huge bomb to leave unattended. A bomb that blew up in both our faces.

As it stands right now, my heart feels like it has been run over by a semitruck. Then it backed up and squashed me a second time for good measure. My head hurts—from the endless tears I keep crying and the thought that Gavin lied to me. Yes, it was a lie of omission. But he could have just told me and purposely chose not to.

And that hurts more than anything.

With his line of thinking, I have no doubt he planned to fly back to California and cut ties with whatever "fake engagement" he and this Layla woman have. Then, I would be none the wiser. Right? But I am a firm believer in the old adage "everything happens for a reason." There is a reason Gavin never brought her up. Perhaps he thought it would be pointless. Maybe he thought the two of us would never meet and didn't see why it was pertinent to disclose that part of his past. Or maybe he couldn't figure out a way to tell me without hurting me. I have no clue. The only question rolling around in my head now is why did I need to know? What do I gain from this?

Do I only want to know because it is a piece of Gavin? A part of his past that doesn't include me. A gap filled by another person. Another woman. A woman who he claims is just a friend after she flaunted their familiarity.

Is this me punishing myself? Pushing him away so he doesn't break my heart again? Although, fragments are chipping from the edges and falling to my feet.

"I don't want you driving home tonight," Shelly says as

she sweeps a few stray hairs from my face and tucks them behind my ear.

And the last thing I want tonight is to be alone. Shelly probably knows this—twenty-plus years of friendship teaches you these things. Plus, going home would entail me stripping the sheets from my bed. Sheets that smell of Gavin and me and the two of us tangled together this morning. Sheets full of memories of his lips on mine, his hands on my skin, his body fit perfectly against mine.

"You're okay with me staying?"

"As if you have to ask." She leans forward and wraps her arms around me. "You are always welcome in my home. No matter what."

I hug her as if it was our last. Shelly is a great friend. The best a girl could ask for. And I am thankful every day I have her in my life. To have her big heart and warm hugs.

After the couch transitions to my makeshift bed for the night, Shelly gives me one last hug before going to her room. I turn off the tall floor lamp across the room and slip under the blanket. The moment my eyes close, flashes of Gavin spill from my memory.

Memories of us as teenagers—at school, under our tree, walking the beach at sunset, our first kiss—and memories of the last week—his cocksure smile, how easily we slipped back into old habits, the way he *looked* at me, how he held me, kissed me, promised me the future.

And I am crippled by the pain that spins a vicious web throughout my body. It twists and spirals and weaves itself around my organs and engulfs me with an unfamiliar force. The gravity of it all crushes my heart ten times more aggressively than it did thirteen years ago. Knocks the breath from my lungs. Blinds me.

I draw my knees to my chest and wrap my arms around them as another wave of tears bleeds from my eyes. As my body tremors more violent than the earth ever could.

How could I let this happen again? How could I get in this deep? Let myself fall in love with Gavin Hunt a second time?

The answer is simple. Always has been. I belong to Gavin. But does he belong to me?

three

GAVIN

Thirteen years ago

The plane jolts forward as the wheels touch down. A shriek from the brakes echoes in my ears and I wince. I stare out the window and take in the landscape surrounding the airport as we taxi to our gate. I haven't stepped off the plane yet and I already hate this place. Hate everything it represents. Hate everything it stole from me.

I reach around to my back pocket and grab my phone. After switching off airplane mode, I open the text screen and type out a message to Cora.

> Just landed. It's only been hours, but I miss you already. So much.

My phone jingles and pings with notifications as it catches up from being offline the last six hours. Seconds later, Cora responds. Her notification the only one I check.

> I miss you too. Text or call when you get to your new house.

House is the operative word in her message. Because where my parents are moving us to is a house. Not a home. There is only one place I will ever call home. Wherever Cora is. She will always be my home.

> I will. Hopefully we'll get there soon.

"Let's go, Gavin." Dad nudges me and tilts his head toward the plane's exit.

I swipe my backpack from under the seat in front of me and shuffle out of the cramped seating. Once we deplane, I hang ten feet back from my parents. Let the throng of people separate us on occasion. Although my mom's promotion is a good thing for her career and our family, I am beyond irritated with this whole situation. The only way to express my anger and frustration is to ignore them.

Is my logic juvenile? Yes. Do I give a fuck? No.

As we walk through the airport, Mom and Dad take turns peering over their shoulder every other minute. They have concerns, I get it. But where the hell am I going to go? Not like I can jump on a plane and leave. I have no clue where I am. Nor do I know anyone here. All my friends live in Florida. Every part of my life exists on the opposite side of the country. The one person that matters most, the one I left my heart with, is thousands of miles from here.

I grind my teeth so hard my jaw aches. The thought of making new friends sends a fresh wave of irritation through my veins. Feels as if I am entering kindergarten all over again. The new kid. In the middle of high school. Just before the school year ends.

Complete and utter bullshit.

We reach the baggage claim and wait like fish for bait.

The metal carousel circles around a continuous loop. I lean against a far wall and watch as my parents patiently wait for our two pieces of luggage. Normally, I would wait beside them. Offer to help. But seeing as I hate this whole situation, I choose to stand here and go through my notifications.

Micah sent a text while we were in the air.

> Let me know when you land bro. Can't believe your gone. Who am I going to do stupid shit with now?

I type out a quick reply to him and tap send.

> Right? At least you know other people there. I'm a loner here. Fucking hate it.

My parents step up to me, but I keep my eyes on my phone as if unaware. How long can I avoid eye contact with them? At this rate, weeks seem probable. If I piss them off enough, would they let me go back to Florida? Maybe, but I highly doubt it. Micah's parents would probably let me stay with them if we asked nice enough.

"Gavin, we're leaving. Put your phone away. You can text your friends later," Mom snaps.

Is she pissed at me? Good. Maybe a dose of her own medicine will do her some good. Because pissed is all I have felt since she told me we were moving to this shithole. Since the moment she told me I didn't have a choice—or voice—in the matter. She didn't even give me a chance to protest. Her word was the final say.

Fucking bullshit.

I follow in my parents' wake as we exit the airport and my Dad hails a cab. After our luggage is crammed into the trunk, I slide in front beside the driver rather than sit with one of my parents. I have no animosity with Dad, but it seems only fair I treat them equally. After all, they are a team. And they made this decision together. Without me. Without taking any part of my life into account.

We drive away from the airport and I lean against the window, staring at nothing. I don't care if this place holds good qualities. Mountains or celebrities or monuments. None of it matters. Because I don't want to be here. An hour later, the cabbie parks in "our driveway." He helps Dad get the luggage from the trunk before driving away a minute later.

I stay rooted at the end of the driveway and stare at the house I will never call home. A desert-colored Spanish-style house with vines growing up one side of the exterior. Large, grassy plants rest along the front edges of the structure; red rocks fill in the plant bed. The grass mowed with perfect precision. Sporadic large windows fill the walls with the occasional extended half-round window. A small iron gate encloses the driveway from the house to the set-back garage.

Nothing about this house resembles the home we left behind in Florida. This place feels like something to flaunt. A dollar sign. A pretentious badge of honor. Nothing about it could ever be homey. The core of it too frigid and formal. Too "look at me and the salary increase I just earned."

My stomach roils at the idea of my family becoming snotty or ostentatious. Of throwing black-tie parties and drinking with our pinkies out and tilting our noses higher.

When did my parents become these people?

Several minutes pass before I decide to go inside. My parents nowhere in sight when I enter. No doubt they are wandering the property and making sure there is no damage. I scan the bare interior, the moving truck not arriving until the day after tomorrow. *Fucking bullshit.* We have to sleep on the damn floor until our shit arrives. Could we not even get air mattresses?

I walk down a hall and find the room Mom said would be mine. Once inside, I shut the door and lay on the tan carpet. No matter how many photos or posters I add to the walls, this room will never be mine. At most, I will only live here the next two years and then fly back to Florida. Back to Cora and Micah and everything I love.

I crawl over to the suitcase deposited in my room—probably by Dad. Unzipping the case, I riffle through the contents until I locate what I search for. Tucked between my jeans is a small wooden box. I trace my fingertips over the lightly stained grain, a tear slipping from my eye as I stare at my most prized possession. My favorite birthday present from my favorite person.

The box is about the size of a novel, but deeper. Cora used a wood burning tool and inscribed our names on the top surface as well as the date when we became official. Then she got artsy and added a beach sunset.

I brush my fingers over our names and the tears spill heavier. Not even a full day has passed and I can't breathe. The constant warmth I once felt beneath my sternum is now cold and sunken and empty. Without Cora nearby, the world wobbles off-kilter. Revolves slower. Shifts to an endless night.

Flipping the small latch, I open the box and stare at the contents. Lose focus as the one person who means more to me than anyone else is just a memory in a fucking box. One by one, I pull each item from the box. One by one, I cry a little more. So many photos. Of us together—laughing, kissing, watching television. Of Cora by herself—some posed, some candid. Goofy faces, serious faces, expressions she reserved only for me.

Drawings she did on napkins, scrap pieces of paper and other random types of paper. Some folded, some small enough to sit open in the box. Most she doesn't even know I possess. Small tokens of her I kept since the day we met.

Pieces of her. Pieces of *us*.

I set the drawings on the fluffy carpet and spread them out so I have an unobstructed view of them all at the same time. Once I have them all spread, I go back to the box and take out the next items. Photos.

Polaroids and regular four-by-six printed images. Cora almost always had a camera with her everywhere we went. She kept it stashed in her purse or backpack, taking it out whenever an opportunity presented itself. Most of the photos on her camera—an older, thirty-five-millimeter film Nikon— were of places, things or other people. Every once in a while, I would snatch her camera and shoot pictures of her. And every once in a while, we were able to get someone else to take a photo of us together.

Sifting through the photos, I land on one of my two favorites. The photo is just of Cora. We were wandering along the trail in Walsingham Park and I had been holding her camera for a bit after she stopped to use the restroom. At the time, I had been walking ten feet behind her. Her eyes drifted up to the trees, searching for birds or squirrels. Or maybe she was simply admiring the trees—she did that sometimes, got lost staring at the trees. I lifted the camera to my eye and snapped the shutter, capturing her profile with the sunbeams haloing around her. She looked like a peaceful angel. My peaceful angel.

When she printed the black and whites, she teased me and asked why I took the picture. My response to her was "you just looked so peaceful and in your element. I wanted to capture the moment." All she did was nod and smile.

My second favorite photo was of the two of us. More like our silhouettes. In the photo, we stood side by side with an arm around each other. A friendly guy on the beach snapped the photo as the sun set behind us. It wasn't noticeable to most people who glanced at the photo, but we were both smiling like idiots. Giddy after dating each other for six months. Just looking at the photo now makes me smile like a fool. A fool madly in love with his soul mate.

I set the two photos beside each other and stare at them a while. Go back to the time they were taken. Remember how I felt those days. How the sight of her made my heart swell and breath vanish. Tears drip from my chin and splatter on the photos. I trace my finger over Cora in each of the pictures.

Fuck. Two years away from Cora will feel like an eternity.

"Gavin?" Mom bellows from somewhere outside the four walls that will now be my room.

I ignore her call a minute as I continue going through the box. Get lost in the drawings and photos as tears continue to fall. But the moment doesn't last long.

Knock, knock, knock.

"Gavin, didn't you hear me calling you?" Mom asks. In my periphery, she stands in the doorway with her hands on her hips, staring at my profile and the scattered images.

After a moment, I lift my tear-stained eyes to hers. *Yeah, I heard you. But I don't fucking care.* That is what I want to say to her. But I don't. Instead, I lie.

"Nope."

I don't elaborate. Don't give her anything to expand on. Because I don't want to look at her. Don't want to speak to her. And a second later, I go back to staring at the items in front of me. But she interrupts me again and I groan.

"Well, Dad and I were thinking we should go out and grab something to eat. Maybe see what's near here too. Sound good?"

She is doing her best in a shitty situation she is aware upsets me. And I guess I should reciprocate and try not to be too much of a dick. I mean, is it really such a bad thing that she is good at what she does? That her boss deemed her better than others in her field. A good son would be happy for his mom. A good son would be proud. But every time I try to be happy for her, all I think about is how I drew the short end of the stick in this whole situation. How I had no say or alternative.

I may be sixteen, but shouldn't my voice count in matters like this? Shouldn't I have a say?

"Yeah, Mom. Can you give me a few minutes? I want to call Cora before it's too late for her."

Something new to deal with. Fucking time zone differences. Bad enough I don't get to see her or speak to her regularly. Now I have to fight with the fact that our lives exist with a three-hour time disruption.

"Sure thing. Ten minutes. And then we'll go."

"Thanks, Mom."

She gives me a sad smile then closes my door and walks off. Once she has been gone a few seconds, I call Cora.

She answers on the first ring. The moment I hear her voice, every live wire inside of me calms. Almost three thousand miles away and Cora still holds the balm to my heart. We talk nonstop for ten minutes—her more than me. She talks about Shelly hanging out with her and staying over at her house. How they have been watching *Lord of the Rings* on repeat and Shelly wants to kill her. This makes me laugh for the first time in weeks.

And then Cora becomes quiet. So quiet I wonder if she fell asleep. I close my eyes for a minute and picture her sleeping with me curled up behind her. Our bodies flush and my arms wrapped around her waist. Before I ask if she is still awake, she whispers into the phone.

"It hasn't even been a whole day and I already miss you so much." Her voice trembles over the line and I know she is holding back tears. I won't tell her, but I saw her collapse outside my house as we drove away. She may have thought we were far enough away, but we weren't. And the sight of her on the ground crying crushed me. The fact I couldn't turn the car around and go to her, scoop her up in my arms and rock her to soothe the pain, kills me.

"Me too, baby."

"I'm getting a job soon. Save up money so I can fly out to see you. Maybe by our anniversary."

Hope filters through her words and spreads from her phone to mine. With it, I sense her warmth and a hint of gladness. Maybe that's what I should do too. Find a job and save money. Teens don't make much money, but earning something is better than nothing at all. Maybe I will call it my Cora fund. Both of us can save up to fly back and forth.

"That's a good idea. I'll do that too."

Just as Cora starts talking again, Dad walks into the room and signals it is time to go. I nod and hold up a finger. He taps his watch and walks out, leaving the door open. Door open equals time is up.

"Gavin?"

"I'm still here, baby. Mom and Dad said I need to get off the phone. We're going out to dinner."

"Okay." Her voice drops so low I barely hear her. And I wouldn't be surprised if the second we hang up, she starts crying all over again. I will too. Because this situation is annoying and heartbreaking and fucked up. And I hate that I can't hold her right now. Can't press her against my chest and rub a hand up and down her back. Can't promise her everything will be alright. Although, the prospect of getting a job and saving to see her again lights a fire inside me.

"I wish I didn't have to."

"I know. I love you."

"I love you, too. I'll call you in the morning."

Seconds later, and with much reluctance, the call ends. As sad and frustrated as I am with being stuck in a situation I can't reverse, hope flares anew for us. And we both hold on to that hope with every breath we take. Because hope is all we have.

But little do we know, things don't always go according to plan. And life has a way of throwing curveballs. Curveballs that batter and bruise hearts.

four
GAVIN

Present

Something jabs me in the ribs as I roll from my side onto my back. I swipe my hand behind me in an attempt to remove said object. I pat and swipe and wave my arm. Whatever it is, it's still there. What the hell? I dig near my ribs and after no success locating the source, I flop over, land on my back and groan. Not only am I being stabbed by some invisible foreign object, but my body is on fire.

I open my eyes and squint, feeling disoriented for a moment.

Never-ending blue, puffy white clouds and the morning sun brighten the sky directly above. In my left periphery is a tall oak tree, the limbs hang overhead while the leaves flutter in the slight breeze. To my right is a row of bushy grass plants. The smell of grass and earth and something floral hits my nose. Birds chirp all around. Squirrels scamper past me. And I swear I hear ducks quacking nearby.

When I roll to sit up, every muscle in my body reacts. My

back stiff, neck throbbing, shoulders sore, eyes swollen. Like I partied all night and missed all the good parts.

Once I reorient myself and attempt to work the pain from my muscles, I squint at my surroundings. Adjust to the brightness and focus on what is in front of me. Gray siding, black trim and window treatments, and bushy shrubs.

Cora's house. More accurate—Cora's back patio.

I glance over to the driveway and notice her car is still missing. And the fact that she hasn't been at home all night worries me in more ways than one. She was so upset when she left my side last night. She tried to fight it, but I could tell the dam was about to burst the second she left. I only hope wherever she is, she arrived safe.

If anything happened to her, if she got into a car wreck, I would never forgive myself. Wouldn't be able to live with myself.

"Fuck…" I mutter as I stretch my neck and back.

I walk over to the stoop by her back door and make myself comfortable. There is no way I am leaving until I know she is home and she is safe. Even if that means I sit here for hours. She may not want to talk to me right now, which I completely understand, but I won't let her run away from this. From us.

Not when I just got her back. Not after all the strides we have made. The rekindling we have done. The love I saw in her eyes when she looked into mine. I refuse to lose her.

No matter what it takes, I will fight for her. For me. For us. No chance in hell I am letting this slip through the cracks. And although it took me far too long to come back to her— and under the wrong circumstances—I won't throw in the towel now. Not happening. I won't let her give up so easily either. Our lives may be in different places now, but one fact remains one-hundred-percent unchanged.

We love each other. Plain and simple.

And nothing or no one will steal the love we share from us. Never again.

⁓

I pull my phone from my pocket—again—and check the time. Ten thirty-five. Not only have I been awake and sitting by Cora's back door for over two hours, I have been at her house for close to twelve hours. And she hasn't.

Luna is probably freaking out inside looking for her Mom and her breakfast.

Slowly but surely, I start to freak out a bit too. By now, I thought she would be home. The fact that she isn't, has me worrying more—about where she is and why she hasn't come home. Elbows resting on my knees, I drop my head in my hands and groan. *Please let her be okay.* Not in some hospital getting treated for injuries because she couldn't focus enough to drive.

But another thought crosses my mind. A thought that boils my blood and chills me to the bone simultaneously.

Who is she with? After our argument last night, would she go running into another man's arms? And not just any man, but a man she trusts. A man she is comfortable with and confides in. *Jonas.*

Would she go to him to be consoled? Would she use her friendship with him to punish me? God, I hope not. The Cora I know doesn't seem the type to do such petty or callous things. But the Cora I know isn't the Cora that exists today. And that scrap of knowledge stings more than anything.

Even if Cora refuses to see it, it is more than obvious Jonas likes her. Hell, any man who looks at a woman the way he looks at Cora doesn't just want to be friends. He may even love her.

At the thought, my skin prickles. He could be soothing her right now. Wiping her tears away. Holding her in his arms. Shushing her cries over another man. A man who claims to love her, but supposedly has a fiancée. A fake fiancée.

And suddenly it feels as if I just handed over the love of my life to another man. "What the fuck was I thinking?"

I wasn't thinking. That much is now obvious. My reaction to a friend's unfortunate situation was simple. Or so I thought at the time. My friend needed help and I offered up my solution. To make people believe we were engaged. An easy, straightforward way to improve her life. No big deal, right?

Wrong. Evidently.

But it isn't real. And Layla damn well knows nothing about our engagement is tangible. There will never be a wedding or vows or permanency. No flowers or additional jewelry or change of name.

So why the show? Why the hell did she act like a catty bitch last night? I saw the wicked gleam in her eye, the vicious curl of her lip. Why did she intentionally try to hurt the one person who matters most to me? I don't get it. Don't understand her motive. What does Layla stand to gain by ruining what Cora and I have? If Layla really was my friend, if she really cared about me as a person, she would have cheered me on. Not shattered my dreams.

So many questions need answering, but they will have to wait until later. Right now, I need to focus on fixing my relationship with Cora. It will take time to mend our relationship, but she needs to know the truth. From my lips. A truth I should have told her from the get-go.

Once I fly back to California, circumstances will change. Life will change. And unfortunately for those in my line of fire, the people stepping on my toes with stiletto heels, they will wish they never fucked me over.

It is one thing to fuck with me, individually. But it is a whole new ball game when you involve people I love.

My internal tirade gets disrupted when I hear a car pull into Cora's driveway. When I lift my head from my hands, I catch her profile behind the tint. But she is so focused on parking the car, I don't think she has spotted me yet. Not like most people survey their house the second they get home.

So, I choose to stay seated on the stoop and let her see me when she is ready.

My eyes remain glued on her as she opens the car door and steps out. As she swipes her fingers under her eyes and sniffles. As she steps around the front of her car and starts for her back door. Her eyes swollen and red. Cheeks blotchy and wet. Hair windblown. Clothes the same she wore last night. Posture defeated. And the second she notices me on her back stoop, I catch the break in her stride as she stumbles a little and takes a step back.

"Gavin?" she asks as if it is impossible for me to be here. Her voice gruff and scratchy and parched. "What are you doing here?"

I rise, roll my neck and shoulders, and take a few tentative steps toward her. But when I do, she steps back again and keeps the distance between us. There may be ten feet between us, but it feels like ten miles. And she wants this distance because I hurt her. Again.

"Hey, baby. I was worried about you after you left last

night. You were so upset. A little after you left, I got a ride here to make sure you were okay. When I saw your car wasn't here, I worried. So I stayed, wanting to be here when you got home. I needed to know you were safe and knew you wouldn't answer if I called or texted. And at some point, I must've fallen asleep."

We stand there and stare at each other. She doesn't say a word while I study her more in-depth. Her eyes are bloodshot, her green irises more opaque. Dark half-moons paint the pale skin below her dark lashes. Lines crease her forehead and the small space just above her nose pinches her brows together. She bites the inside of her cheek as she looks everywhere but at me. The blotchy patches on her cheeks spread down her neck and onto her chest.

It has only been one night and she already looks like she hasn't slept for weeks. And I am the sole reason. If she looks like this now—after just one night—how will she look for the several days I am gone? How did she look for the *years* I was gone?

A red hot poker scalds my heart at the pain I have caused her. The pain evident in her eyes and her posture and the way she reacts to me. How she purposely backs away when I try to get close. When I try to repair the shifting fault lines in her heart.

But I refuse to let everything we have gained get thrown aside like last week's leftovers. Our relationship isn't garbage and neither is how we feel about each other. Last night's debacle with Layla was just another rift. But we will get past this. We will flourish. Together.

"Gavin, I think you need to leave."

"Baby, please—"

"No," she yells. "You don't get to call me that anymore.

You don't get to be smooth and sweet and all *baby* this or *baby* that. Not after what just happened. It's time for you to leave. I'm exhausted and Luna is probably crying for me. So, please. Just. Go."

"If you'd just let me explain—"

"No, Gavin. The time for explanations has passed. You should've told me about her a week ago when we were catching each other up on life. I haven't withheld anything pertinent from you. And I'd thought you'd done the same. But I guess that's what I get for thinking." She stops for a moment, chest heaving and fists clenched at her sides. When she speaks again, her voice drops and I have to fight to hear what she says. "So, *please*, I beg of you. Please leave."

I don't want to stand out here and argue with her. Cause a scene and have her neighbors come check to see if she is okay. If anything, I want to walk her inside and wrap her in my arms and tell her everything will be okay. That I will fix the problem I created. That I will right my wrongs. And that I will return to her again.

But actions speak louder than words. And right now, she needs actions. Actions that tell her I won't break my promises. Not again. Actions that prove Layla is what I say she is. That she is a friend I did a favor for and nothing else.

I take a step toward her, and this time she doesn't back away. Her frame wilts like a sad flower, I know it's due to hurt and sleep deprivation. When I stand an arm's length from her, I reach for her hand. She doesn't stop me, but closes her eyes and hangs her head in defeat. She is tired and hurt and needs time to think. But I need her to not give up. Not on me and not on us.

Taking advantage of her non-retreat, I hold her hand for a beat. "Baby," I whisper. "I know you're upset with me. I would be, too. But I promise you, I will make this right. You and me—I am not giving up. It's not my style. Never has been. My initial reason for returning may have been for work, but once I laid eyes on you again… it was as if I could finally breathe for the first time in thirteen years. As if I became whole again. I screwed up. Big. I own this mistake. Am punishing myself for it. But when I fly back to Cali tomorrow, they won't know what hit them." With my other hand, I lift her chin so her swollen eyes meet mine. "Once I've fixed my mistakes there, I will be back. And then, I will fix what I've messed up here."

Her chin trembles in my grip. She tucks her lips between her teeth to keep from breaking down in front of me. Tears pool in her eyes as they dart between mine. She wants to believe me—I see a tinge of hope just beneath the surface—but doesn't know if she can. When all is said and done, I will be the man she deserves. The man she can believe and count on. No matter what.

"I love you, baby," I choke out as a tear rolls down my cheek. Because I won't leave here without her knowing how I feel. We may have only reconnected a week ago, but I have loved Cora half of my life. No use in denying it. "And I will be home soon. Before my birthday."

And before I can stop myself, I lean forward and place a tender kiss on her lips. Our lips may touch for less than two breaths, but those two breaths are equivalent to forever. And as difficult as it is, I back away and drop my hands from her. I grant her the space she needs.

Without another word, I step around her and walk toward the park across from her house. But just before I get out of earshot, I overhear her wails as they bounce off the trees and wisp away in the wind. Her cries for us. And for herself. And the love that binds us together like nothing else. A love that brought us together, shredded us, and will unite us again.

The second my feet touch the grassy park property, tears stream down my face. I stare back at the house briefly, and although I cannot see her, I *feel* her. Feel her anguish. And I vow to never be the reason she cries like that again. Vow to wipe away all her pain.

five
CORA

Once I make it inside, I throw my purse to the floor and go feed Luna. From the back door to her food bowl, she weaves between my legs and meows her love for me. At least I have someone who will give me her undying love. All she wants in return is the occasional scoop of food, water, a clean litterbox and my affection.

If only human relationships were so simple.

I scoop Luna some food and pet her a few times while she eats and purrs simultaneously. Once she is sated, I head to the bathroom and do my business. A moment later, I swap out my clothes for a tank top and undies then crawl into my bed. Since I left the door cracked for Luna, I fetch my eye mask from my nightstand and block out any semblance of daylight.

Even if it's just a few hours, I need some sleep. Because no matter how much I tried to fall asleep on Shelly's comfy couch, it never happened. My mind ran vicious circles in the dark. And the muffled tears never let up.

One moment, my mind was trying to rationalize the reasons he would be in a fake relationship with someone. Why he would let the world think they were engaged. What would Gavin gain from a setup like that? Especially if he professes to love me the way he does. But instead of coming up with viable answers, all I did was cry more. And I prayed that Shelly couldn't hear me sobbing into the pillow.

A few minutes later, Luna jumps onto the bed and curls up beside me. Her purrs soothe in a way nothing else does. As if she senses my forlorn demeanor, she inches her way up to my shoulder and nestles in the crook of my neck, purring stronger. I tug the sheet higher and get hit with Gavin's smell on the cotton. Upset as I am, his beachy-pine scent soothes me. Settles my soul. And within minutes, I fall asleep.

I jolt awake to the sound of my phone ringing. As badly as I want to ignore it, I can't. It could be someone other than Gavin calling me. When you work for yourself, you never get a day off.

Rolling over, I slap my hand over the surface of my bedside table until I come into contact with my phone. Not removing my eye cover, I manage to answer the call. "Hello?" My voice is raspier than a grizzly bear.

"Cora, it's Mom. Did I wake you, sweetie?"

I push the mask up to my forehead and hold the phone away from my ear a second, checking the time. *Holy shit.* It's just after three in the afternoon. I am more than thankful for the sleep, but most of the day has withered away. But it's not as if I had plans, so whatever.

"Yeah, but it's okay Mom. Is everything alright?"

A second later, a knock raps at my back door. I bolt upright and hold my breath as my heart hammers a vicious rhythm in my chest. *Shit.* Did Gavin come back? Please, please, please don't let that be him. I don't think I can deal with him—or us—right now. I just need more time to process everything.

I shove the covers from my legs and plant my feet on the floor, reluctant to move. The knock comes again as I pad down the small hall to the back door. Unfortunately for me, the back door is solid and I'm unable to see who stands on the other side—unlike my front door. I really should invest in a peephole or one of those video doorbells for the back.

As I stand at the door, hand on the knob, reluctant to turn it, my mom speaks up. "Cora, it's me. I'm the one knocking on your door."

Relief hits and I remember how to breathe again when I discover Gavin isn't the person outside my house. In the last two minutes, I somehow forgot I'd been holding the phone to my ear and my mom was on the other end. Probably because the moment there was a knock at the door, Mom stopped speaking. If she would have just told me it was her outside, I wouldn't be tiptoeing through my own house and she'd be inside already.

I twist the knob and swing the door open. I shield my eyes as the bright afternoon sun temporarily blinds me.

Stepping off to the side, I let Mom pass and then shut the door. I follow her into the kitchen and notice she's putting food in my fridge. "What's all that?" I ask.

"I stopped at the Patch and picked up a few things for you. Figured you wouldn't be in the mood to go anywhere." Her tone casual and body language easygoing. As if today is just another day.

She pulls out a couple pans and pots and starts chopping vegetables on the cutting board. Then she fills a pot with water and turns on a burner. I follow her movements for a few minutes while she busies herself in my kitchen. She moves as if she has cooked here hundreds of times, when it is quite the opposite. Of the countless times Mom has been in my home, never once has she cooked here. So watching her right now is peculiar. It isn't an anomaly to see my mom in the kitchen. But to see her in *my* kitchen, bustling around like she cooks here every day, is weird.

"Mom?"

Lifting her eyes from the cutting board, she peeks up at me. "Yeah, sweetie."

"What made you think I might not be in the mood to go anywhere?"

I have a sneaking suspicion what the answer is, but I need to know for certain before making assumptions. Before opening my mouth and spilling all the juicy details of my wretched love life.

"When Shelly came into the shop this morning, she looked a bit rough. I asked her why and she said you were at her apartment last night. She said you were upset, but didn't tell me why."

And thankfully Mom isn't one to pry, but I have no doubt she wants to know why her twenty-nine-year-old daughter spent the night at her friend's house. Pretty sure she also wants to know the source behind why I was so upset. Because why would a grown woman, who owns her own home and lives alone, go to her friend's place and spend the night? Adult friends don't generally have sleepovers on purpose.

Does Mom know Gavin is in town? Mom was friends with Gavin's mother, but I have no idea if they have kept in touch. Does she know that he was the model I photographed all week? It wouldn't be surprising if Shelly told her everything, but maybe my best friend kept this news to herself. Shelly picks and chooses what to share with Mom. She doesn't want to be the gossip mill, but she also wants to look out for me.

"Yeah, it was a rough night," I say.

Mom nods then throws noodles in the boiling water before heating up the other pan. Once the pan is hot, she adds the chopped veggies to the pan and tosses them. And right now, I love Mom more than ever.

Shelly may not have told her the reason why I am upset, but she must have indicated it was pretty bad. And what did my mom do? She left work early and went to the store, buying me groceries and comfort foods. And now, she stands in my kitchen and cooks me stir-fry. She may not know the extent of what has me upset, but she knows I need her comfort more than anything.

When the pasta finishes, she scoops it out of the water and adds it to the veggies. Then she pours in a sweetened soy sauce from my fridge. After it all comes together, she portions us both out a plateful and we go to the couch.

A few bites into the delicious meal, Mom speaks up. "So, you want to talk about it?"

She doesn't make it uncomfortable. And when I glance up from my plate, she's digging around in her plate with her chopsticks. Mom has always had a finesse with conversations. Something I never had. Not with anyone except Gavin. And even that was questionable over the last week.

Conversations with Mom have never been awkward—not even the period and sex talks when I was younger. She always has this gentleness about her. One which could console the most anxious soul. And right now, her tranquility is the exact balm I need.

Thinking back, the past week had been great. Or so I thought. Until *she* showed up last night. Until some "fake" relationship they had was used as a weapon against me. The smile she threw after she spotted me in the room, that was nothing short of malicious. She knew her words would hurt me. Hurt us. And she tossed them like landmines and waited for the fallout.

Without further ado, the tears start back up and I immediately hate my stupid emotions and bodily functions. Can I not cry for a few non-sleeping hours? Is that too much to ask?

After I get my tear ducts under control, I peek up at my mom. "How much do you know about this past week? Besides me telling you I had a photo shoot on the beach."

She sets her plate on the table, half her food forgotten. "Shelly said Gavin was your model for the shoot."

I nod. "Did she say anything else?"

"Only that she was worried about you. But she gave me no specifics."

I set my plate beside hers, mine hardly touched. Eating is the last thing I want to do, but I appreciate that Mom isn't pushing the topic. For a moment, I stare at the fireplace as flashes of the past week flicker through my mind. Next thing, I cover my face with my hands and start crying. If Gavin leaving thirteen years ago is any indication of what is to come, I may as well just throw in the towel. Trying to be "okay" is getting old. And I am so tired of pretending to be something I am not.

Normal. Happy. Thrilled with my life.

"I let him in again, Mom. I let him wiggle his way into my heart and he broke it all over again." I stop, unable to contain the torrent spilling from my eyes.

Mom leans into me and wraps her arms around me. She shushes me while she strokes my hair and murmurs unheard words into my ear. Her hand runs slow circuits up and down my back, soothing me like only a mother can. The occasional kiss to my crown as she squeezes me closer. The extra squeeze in her hug every once in a while.

"I've got you, sweetie. No matter what, I've got you."

I sniffle between sobs. "Thanks, Mom. I love you so much."

"I love you, too. And if you want to talk about it more, I'm here. Okay?"

I squeeze her tighter and nod into her neck. "Maybe another day. I just need a day without tears."

When I told Mom I needed a day without tears, I didn't mean today. I had already cried thousands of tears today and was okay shedding more.

But shortly after Mom left, Shelly called. As if the two of them were playing telephone tag and I was the name they passed back and forth. Shelly told me she was bringing Erin and Jonas over tonight. That we would watch movies and eat junk food and just hang out together.

The first thing I wanted to tell her was not to come over. That I wanted more alone time. Honestly, the only thing I want to do is sleep. Sleep for days or weeks or months. Sleep an eternity and erase all the bad memories. I just want everything that happened to fade away. Out of my mind. Out of my heart. Gavin. Layla. The whole thing. I want it all gone. Forgotten.

But there is no chance in hell Shelly will ever let that happen. She is determined to keep me from drowning. To keep my head above water as I gasp for breath. For life.

And that would be why my living room resembles something from our preteen years—blankets and pillows and snacks strewn across the floor. The television plays some movie from Netflix. To be honest, I have no clue what we are watching. Since the movie started, my eyes have been glazed over. My mind in a fog.

All four of us lay on the floor. Shelly on my left, Erin on her other side, and Jonas on my right. The only source of light spills from the screen. Occasionally, the room goes dark. I relish those scenes the most. The ones that give me a semblance of solitude. A breath of privacy.

Currently, Shelly's fingers play with my hair as her eyes remain glued to the television. Erin is out of my line of sight, but I assume she's focused on the movie. And although my eyes aren't absorbing a single minute of the movie, I am fully aware that Jonas has been staring at me for the last five minutes.

And I don't know how that makes me feel.

I glance over at him—to confirm—and catch him before he can look away. His eyes crinkle at the corners and his sadness for me weighs heavier than I can bear. When he turns back to the movie, he scoots down and lays flatter. And something inside me flips. Begs for his comfort.

Shelly and Erin bring me solace, but it isn't the same. Women experience emotion different than men. They also console in other ways.

I roll onto my side and snuggle against Jonas's frame. Without hesitation, he wraps his arm around me and draws me closer. His heat warming my cool skin. But the second he places a kiss on the crown of my head, I lose it. The flood gates open once again and I cry into his shirt. Soak the cotton. With each round of tears, he holds me tighter, strokes my hair softer, shushes my cries more, and I clench his shirt in my fists harder.

We lay like this for hours—me curled into his side and him cradling me. The first movie ends and a new movie starts right after. I have no idea what plays, nor do I care. I just want to lay here and cry my eyes out. Cry until I have no more tears. Cry until I pass out.

After my tears subside a while, I sit up and notice Erin and Shelly fell asleep at some point. I envy how peaceful they both look. And I pray to whatever power resides over me, *please let me sleep tonight.* I need a deep, dreamless sleep. Just one solid night.

Jonas sits up and tenderly tucks my hair behind my ears. I don't doubt I look a hot mess right now. Hair a rat's nest. Pajamas still on from earlier when Mom was here. Eyes puffy and bloodshot. Lips cracked. But the way Jonas stares at me right now, I feel the exact opposite. His swirly blue-hazels are gentle as he searches my face.

"You want to go lay down? Maybe try to get some sleep? I'll tuck you in."

God, I hate myself and the fact I was never able to be anything but friends with Jonas. He is such a good man. A family man. Is someone I depend on. Someone I trust. Someone I care about. He likes me on a much deeper level than friendship. In the back of my mind, I think I have always been privy to this. I just shoved it away. Smothered it. Because my stupid brain has never been able to let go of Gavin.

But after everything that has happened, maybe I should let myself try again. Let myself find love with someone else. Someone who won't abandon me. Someone who will do anything for me.

"Yeah, okay," I say.

Jonas stands and extends his hand out to me. I take it and

rise from the floor. He walks me toward my bedroom with his arm around my shoulders. A sudden nervousness hits me when we walk into my bedroom. It's like nothing I have experienced with Jonas. Like a hurricane swirls beneath my ribcage.

I slip under my covers and he slides them up to my chin before sitting beside me on the bed. He gazes at me with an expression very un-Jonas. His forehead bunches and straightens and bunches again. When he reaches forward and brushes his knuckles across my cheek, the gentle touch trips a live wire inside me. I lean into his touch and close my eyes momentarily. The pent-up emotions I have ignored with Jonas detonate with ferocity.

I study his blue-rimmed hazels as they hone in on my lips. His eyes perplexed and loaded with indecision. Then his tongue darts out and wets his lips. Adam's apple bobs in his throat. But after a second, I catch a slight shake of his head. The indiscernible gesture probably wasn't meant to be seen, but I am the body language detector and pick up on the smallest of signals.

"How are you?" Jonas asks, voice soft and endearing. And something tells me that wasn't what he wanted to say. But I shove the thought aside.

When most people ask me this question, I tell them I am fine. That everything is okay, although I silently scream in my head. Although I am slowly shattering inside. But there are a select few people I am straightforward with, Jonas being one of them. Shelly, Erin, and my mom being the others. I talk with Dad, but we discuss different stuff—less of the emotional, more of the rest.

"I don't know. Feels like I'm falling apart. Like someone took a chisel and hammer to my heart and started chipping it away all over again. It took so long to somewhat heal from the first time. Jonas, I don't think I'll survive this time." As the final words slip from my lips, tears roll down the sides of my face and spill to the pillow.

Jonas scoots closer, gently plants his hands on either side of my face, and leans over me. He hovers there a moment, inches from my face. From my lips. "You will get through this, Cora. I won't let it be any other way." He lifts one hand from the bed, brushes my hair from my face, and wipes away my tears. His calloused fingers so tender on my temples. "This time will not be the same," he says, huskily.

"How can you be so sure?" I ask, needing some form of reassurance.

"Because you have me and Shelly and Erin and so many others. We're all here for you. On your team. And no matter what happens, we'll be here for you."

I nod, not knowing how else to respond. But the truth in his words erases some of the chill in my bones.

"Try to get some sleep. If you need me, I'll be on the couch. And we'll all be here when you wake up in the morning."

Jonas leans in and I hold my breath as he presses his lips to my forehead. His lips are soft and warm. I close my eyes and allow myself to feel something other than sadness for a brief moment in time. To envision what life could be like if I gave Jonas a chance. If I set my heart free from the cage it has been in for far too long. Because life with Jonas would be good. Filled with smiles and laughter and warmth and love. I don't have to experience it to know it.

When he slowly lifts his lips from my skin, I shift below him and move my lips closer to his. And for a split second, our lips touch. The air crackles and steals my breath. But as quickly as our lips make contact, he breaks away.

"No, Cora." He rears back and scoots farther away from me, his eyes closed and head shaking.

Rejection hits me with incomparable force. Tears sting the backs of my eyes as I press a hand to my lips.

He doesn't want me? How could I be so stupid? What the hell was I thinking?

"I'm sorry. I just thought…" I stumble over my own words as I fight crying in front of him.

When he opens his eyes, glassy hazels stare back at me. "Please don't apologize. Believe me, I have wanted this—us—for so long. But after seeing you around Gavin this past week, it's quite clear where your heart lies. He hurt you, but you wouldn't be this devastated if you didn't still love him."

"I don't love—"

Jonas holds up his hand to stop me. "You're upset right now, and I understand why you're saying that. But you can't run from the truth, Cora. And as much as I care about you, I don't want to be the runner-up. For a long time, I thought I had a chance. But after seeing you two together, and seeing how devastated you are right now… you never fell out of love with him. And that's okay. If us just being friends is the only way I get to have you in my life, so be it. At least I get to have you."

Jonas said he cares about me. That he would be with me, if I could give him my whole heart. Although he didn't outright say he loves me, part of me deep down knows he does. But our love isn't the type to stop time. The type that consumes every breath and thought and cell. And that's okay. Because at least I still have him. Even if it isn't the way he wants. And that speaks volumes to the type of man he is.

I nod. "Okay. Thank you."

His brow knits in the middle as he tilts his head. "Why are you thanking me?"

"Because I'm so lucky to have you in my life. Lucky I met you. Our friendship is like none I've had." I swallow past the emotional lump in my throat and blink back tears. "I wouldn't get through this without you. Wouldn't make it out of this whole without you. You will always have a special place in my heart. Always."

"I know." He leans forward and kisses my cheek, his lips lingering a little longer than friendship warrants before he sits back up. "Ditto. Try to get some sleep. And in the morning, we'll all go out to breakfast."

And before I respond, Jonas gets up and walks out of my bedroom, closing the door behind him. I don't know what I did to deserve a man like Jonas in my life, but I am indebted to whatever power brought us together. Maybe the universe knew I needed someone as tenderhearted as Jonas to help heal my heart. Not completely, but enough to live in the world.

I roll over and hug the other pillow to my chest, catching Gavin's scent. I inhale deeply and, for the first time in twenty-four hours, allow myself to purposely think about Gavin. Flutters echo in the chambers of my heart and I hug the pillow tighter. I imagine my arms wrapped around him as his scent fills each alveolus in my lungs.

Within minutes, my eyes grow heavy and drift shut as I dream about beaches and sunsets and giant evergreen trees.

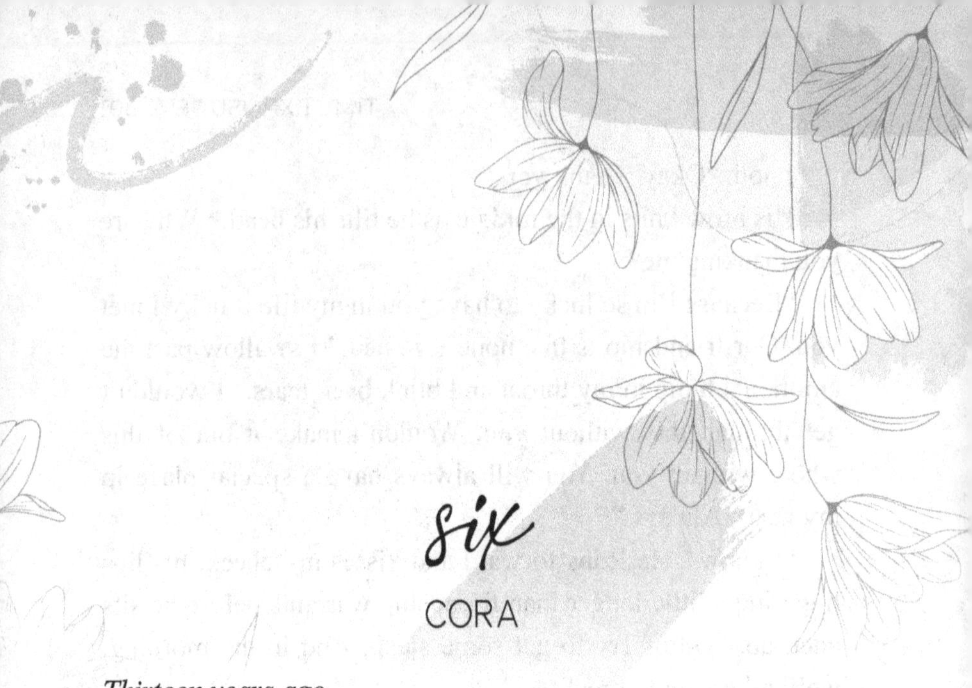

six

CORA

Thirteen years ago

Summer was once my favorite time of year. Now it officially sucks.

It has been two weeks since Gavin left and all I feel is hollow. A mere shell of the girl I was weeks ago.

Talking with him on the phone every day relieves some of the anguish in my heart. But it never fully dissipates. The strangest part of it all… Before Gavin, I was this loner girl. Someone who never cared for the company of others—with the exception of Shelly. Before Gavin, it had never been challenging to sit beneath a tree by myself and get lost in a book. To hang out in my room alone and listen to music. To walk in the park and listen to the leaves rustle and the birds chirp.

Now, I don't want to even imagine sitting beneath *our* tree when school starts again. It is bad enough Gavin won't be there, but I also don't have Shelly to hang with since she goes to another school. Listening to music hasn't been the same and I have no desire to step foot outside unless absolutely necessary.

I reach for my sketch pad and pencils and drag them closer. For the next two hours, I get lost in art. At least with art, I create whatever I feel. Art doesn't have to be rainbows or cheeriness or the sunny side of life. It can be anything at any given time. Emotion spilled on paper or canvas and up for interpretation.

When I finish, I dust off the page and take in my drawing. The graphite dons the page in sharp lines and subtle smudges. The scent of pencil shavings pricks my nose. A layer of shiny carbon coats the edges of my palms and several fingertips.

On the page, I drew a beach sunset with a silhouette couple walking hand in hand by the water. In the bottom right corner, I scribble the signature I add to all my art pieces. Before I fold it into thirds, a tear slips from my eye and lands on the page.

I don't wipe it away. I let it stay and bleed through the paper, knowing Gavin will see it when I mail it to him.

On a piece of notebook paper, I start writing a letter to Gavin. Although we talk on the phone regularly, there is something different about sending him drawings or pictures and letters. Like I am sending a physical piece of myself to him. Something for him to hold in his hands when he can't hold me. Something he can look at in the future when he needs me with him. A form of solace in our time apart.

Gavin,

I miss you so much. Sunsets aren't the same without you by my side.

And I'm so tired of everyone asking me if I'm okay. Why would they think I'm okay? My boyfriend, the love of my life, just got shipped off to California. I mean... would they be alright if it happened to them?

I seriously doubt it.

Have you gotten your room situated yet? I know it'll never be like your room here, but maybe you can make it as close as possible.

Thanks for sending me the picture of the California sunset. It's definitely a different view than anywhere here. I hope we can share the sunsets there together sometime. More to add to our memories.

Have I mentioned how Shelly has been following me around all summer like a lost puppy? It's annoying as fuck.

I know she means well, but is it wrong for me to not want to be around anyone else right now?

Whatever. I don't really care what anyone else thinks. All I know is this sucks.

It's like I'm hyperventilating all the time. I'm never able to catch my breath. And it's like my heart is literally missing. If I thumped on my chest, I wouldn't be surprised if it sounded like tapping on a watermelon.

Anyway. The point of these letters isn't to depress you. You miss me as much as I miss you. I just wish I could hug you. You give the best hugs. Did I ever tell you that? No other hug on earth compares to yours. It's warmth and peace and home all wrapped up in the perfect package.

Fuck! I'm crying again. I am sick and tired of crying. My eyes hurt. They're always red and puffy and I have to hide them behind big sunglasses everywhere I go.

This really fucking sucks!

I really hope you're able to come home sometime during the summer. Even if it's just for a long weekend. I'm not picky and will take whatever I get.

Okay, I'll wrap this up. In a few hours, you'll call me and we'll talk until we're forced to hang up. But I never want to hang up. Ever.

I love you so much!

Cora

I trifold the letter and stuff it in an envelope, along with the drawing. After I address it, I ask Mom for a stamp and then walk it out to the mailbox. I place it in the mailbox like it's my most prized possession. And for good measure, I press my palm over the envelope and send a piece of myself with the envelope to Gavin.

When I walk back inside, Mom tries to lure me into the kitchen. "Want to make cookies with me?"

Do I look like I'm five and I want to lick the dough from the mixer blades? But I don't say that because I know she is only trying to lift my spirits. She has been trying since Gavin told me they were moving. And more so since the day his parents put him on the plane. I am grateful to have her as my mom, but her love will never be the same as what I give and receive from Gavin.

She means well, and I love her greatly for that, but I just don't see how making cookies will make up for losing someone.

"No thanks, Mom."

I walk back to my bedroom, lay on my bed and curl into a fetal position. I hug my phone to my chest and close my eyes. It won't be long before Gavin calls, but until then I just want to sleep. Sleep away all the minutes and hours and days between when I get to talk with him again. Sleep away every tick of the clock until

I get to see him again. And hopefully that day arrives soon.

Present

Is this what dying feels like?

All the years spent apart from Cora and I never felt as horrible as I do now. Did I miss her every goddamn day? Hell yes, I did. Seconds felt like years and years felt like centuries. Did I want to kick myself in the balls for the choices I made? More often than not. Do I regret my idiocy? More than ever.

But the past cannot be changed. It is what it is. No use dwelling on what has come to pass. The future… now that is something I have more control over. Or at least I hope I do.

My stomach churns as I picture her on the ground crying. I stop breathing. Clutch my chest because it feels like I am having a fucking heart attack. Fear rips through me and shreds my insides. And I let the feeling consume me. Let it slither through my veins and take me over. Let the pain settle in my bones. Because seeing Cora in that state was like having someone throw mace-coated sand in your eyes. And I deserve to suffer for not sharing everything with her.

I will accept my punishment. Will let it weigh me down

temporarily. Because our relationship can only go up from here.

Since leaving her house yesterday, I have made a new best friend. The porcelain throne in my suite and I have spent quite a bit of time together. I keep telling her I want to see other people, but she is a persistent bitch. As is my stomach, which has kept nothing down.

I press a loose fist to my mouth as I stand beside the bed. I close my eyes and take a deep breath. For the love of all that is holy, please do not let me throw up again. One—I don't like it. I loathe it with a passion. Two—my body cannot handle much more of this. My head hurts from all the dry heaving. Lips are dry as fuck and starting to crack. Throat feels as if a carpenter scraped a layer of tissue off with sandpaper.

I take a few more deep, methodical breaths and am thankful when my stomach finally calms.

I resume packing my suitcase, but the whole act is robotic. Pull from hanger. Fold clothing into a shape other than a ball. Put in suitcase. Repeat. Shoes set inside. Brush. Toothpaste. Toothbrush. Razor. Hygiene products zipped in a bag.

After everything from the closet, dresser, and bathroom are packed up, I walk around the remainder of the room and do a small search. Inspect the kitchen area and small living space. When I get to the couch and table, I lift the cushions like I usually do when I travel. All it takes is one time losing something to develop weird habits like this. And when I hold the seat cushion up, something shiny catches my attention.

I reach for it and discover the shiny object is a hair clip. One that had been in Cora's hair earlier and she took out when we got to my hotel room. She must have slipped it in her pocket and it fell out when we were watching television.

I turn the small clip over in my hand again and again,

studying the intricate design. It's nothing girly. Just a simple metal clip with a simple purpose. But it belongs to her.

Cora has never been a girly-girl. But she has never been a complete tomboy either. She resides somewhere in the middle and is absolutely perfect. A girl... A woman not afraid to sweat or get her hands dirty or belch around her friends. A woman who gives as good as she gets and isn't afraid to speak her mind and sees the world as a piece of art. A stunning woman that still puts on a dash of makeup and occasionally wears dresses and fixes her hair with hair clips.

I stare at the clip—a mix of girly and punk rock and hard rock. One-hundred-percent Cora.

I tuck the clip in the pocket of my jeans in the suitcase. When I get home, I will add it to our box. A box that isn't as full as it would have been if we had kept in contact over the years. If *I* had kept in contact with her.

Once my temporary life in Clearwater is packed up, I roll my suitcase to the elevator and press the down button. I step into the car and head for the ground floor. I walk past the front desk and give a courtesy wave on my way to the exit. This is it. After I walk out this door, I am headed back to California.

But not for long.

"Did you already schedule a ride, sir?" the valet asks.

"Yeah. They should be here soon."

"Very well, sir. Have a safe trip home." My body recoils a little at the word *home*.

"Thanks," I tell him, not wanting to be impolite.

When I return to Cora, I will be home. We will be home once I fix my mess and we are together again. Because Cora is home. Always has been. Always will be. Nothing can change that.

The Uber driver picks me up and heads for the Tampa

airport. He shoots the shit with me during the entire ride. More than once, I want to tell him I would prefer a quiet drive. But I don't. It's not this guy's fault I am in a foul mood. It's not his fault I left out important details of a favor I did for a friend. And it's not his fault that my so-called friend took said favor and used it as a weapon, attempting to kill the best thing in my life for her own selfish reasons.

Unforgettable. Unforgivable.

When he pulls over at the airport drop-off, I thank the driver after he hands me my suitcase. The doors whoosh open and a wall of cool air hits me as I enter the airport. Weaving through the sea of bodies, I head to the baggage check area. Once I finish checking my luggage, I head upstairs to the gates and TSA checkpoint.

Thirty minutes later, I slip my shoes back on and walk toward the gate. I stop at one of the restaurants and order something small to eat. While I wait, I open the text history between me and Cora. Does this make me a glutton for punishment? Probably, but I don't fucking care.

I have messaged her several times since she got in her car and drove away from me on the beach two nights ago. Most of them say the same thing. *I'm sorry. How are you? I miss you. I love you.*

But she never responds to a single one of them. Not that I really expect her to. If our roles were reversed, I wouldn't do anything different.

Regardless of her lack of response, I type out another text to her. And I will type out many more between now and when I return. Because I will return.

My food arrives and I eat it, not really tasting it. But I repeatedly tell my stomach to keep it down. At least until I land in Los Angeles.

Minutes later, the airport announcement over the intercom says my plane has started boarding. I file into the boarding line and shuffle onto the plane. Once in my seat, I put my earbuds in and shut my eyes. My stomach twists and my palms break out in sweat, but for very different reasons than when I left Los Angeles. This time, the panic forms out of fear.

Fear that I won't be able to fix my mistakes when I land in California. Fear that I won't be able to return to Cora like I desperately want to. And worst of all, fear that she won't take me back when I do return to Florida. Because no matter what happens, I am coming back. Even if it means I have nothing.

The moment I deplane in California, I am a man on a mission. After I text Cora and let her know I landed safely, I bolt from the terminal and head for the baggage claim. As per usual, the airport is a madhouse.

When people bump me along the way, I am more vocal about my irritation than usual. "Fucking asshole" leaves my lips far more often than not. People need to learn some damn etiquette—like moving aside if you plan to text or check apps on your phone. *For the love of God, show some fucking respect.*

And the second I step foot outside the airport, for the first time in years, Los Angeles feels nothing like home. Like the very first time I arrived. If anything, now it feels like a cesspool of hungry and desperate people. A façade disguising itself as reality. And I have no desire to be a part of it.

I was brought here out of obligation, but why did I stay so long? This question has cycled through my head countless times over the last week. Haunted me every waking minute.

Why?

I have been financially secure for years. So why didn't I leave then? Why didn't I pack up everything I own and move back to Florida when I could have? Moving would have been easy. Too easy.

But I hadn't moved for several reasons.

Until a week and a half ago, I hadn't spoken with Cora in years. It wasn't to intentionally hurt her. More like I thought I was doing the right thing when I couldn't see me making it back to her. So, I was doing right by her. At least that is what I told myself. I was letting her go. Letting her move on and find love again.

Only I didn't share that with her. I made the decision all on my own. Because I figured a clean break was the best way. For obvious reasons, I am an idiot. Live and learn, I suppose.

When I get in the Uber, I tell the driver I would like some quiet. I need time to think, to strategize. And I can't do that while a bored driver shoots the shit with me. Thankfully, he respects my request.

After battling late-day traffic, the driver pulls into Mom's driveway on the outskirts of Burbank. I thank the driver, grab my luggage and walk up to the house. Mom's house looks much the same as it did thirteen years ago when we moved to California. The only difference is the paint has faded slightly, the plants have been swapped for more colorful versions, and the tree in the front yard is a little taller and bushier.

Although I have adjusted to Mom living here, this house has still never felt like home. Just a layover until my path realigned.

Maybe I should have messaged Mom before just showing up on her doorstep. She will probably think me crazy. Question me endlessly. Popping up here is nowhere near my norm. Whatever. Perhaps I am going crazy. But if being crazy equals being happy, consider me certifiable.

I punch my code into the door lock and step inside. The moment I pass the threshold, the scent of curry and bell peppers and grilled chicken attacks my nose. A second later, my stomach growls in response. Obviously, the airport food didn't hold me over long.

"Mom?" I call out.

"Gavin, is that you?"

Every time she asks that, it makes me laugh. Does she have other children I am unaware of? Better yet, is there another guy in her life that could be walking through the door? The latter never crossed my mind until now. I wouldn't expect my mom to remain celibate after Dad passed, but she still wears her wedding jewelry. Wonder if I need to give her the okay to move on? If I need to tell her it is okay to find love again. That I am okay with her loving someone besides Dad.

Maybe another time.

"Yeah, Mom. Are you in the kitchen?" I ask as I walk in that direction. I figure I will ask a stupid question in return. With all the deliciousness floating through the air, she is either cooking or just sitting down to eat.

The second I round the corner and the kitchen comes into

view, the grilled peppers and spices hit me full force. My stomach bellows out and constricts, and I pat my abdomen. *Calm down, we will eat soon.*

"Hey, honey. What are you doing here?" She smiles, wraps me in her embrace, and I squeeze her a little harder than usual. "Is everything okay?" Concern laces her voice since I have yet to let her go.

I give her one last squeeze, take a deep breath, then let her go. She steps back to the stove, but has her eyes on me. "No, everything's not okay. I just flew back from Clearwater."

In front of me, Mom freezes with the spoon mid-air above the pan. Her eyes search mine, looking for clues as to what I am thinking, before pinching tightly with sadness. "Oh, Gavin. Was that where your shoot was?"

"Yeah. I didn't think I'd see her. But I was so far off base. Mom… she was the photographer for my shoot."

Mom sets the spoon on the rest and comes to stand beside me. She rubs my back, trying to soothe away my pain. She remembers, all too well, my rebellious days after we moved to California. The torment I endured and inflicted on everyone around me.

"What can I do?"

I turn to her and hug her again. When I release her, I relay my plan to her. And I tell her what happened in Clearwater with Alyson and Layla. How both of them behaved as if their needs and desires supersede mine—even with me in the epicenter.

The fire in Mom's eyes is like nothing I have seen before. Even with all the shit I put her through, she never showed this side. At least not to me. Her cheeks burn bright red as she balls her fingers into tight fists at her side. Right now, Mom is as livid as I am. If not more.

"I'm moving back, Mom. But I have a lot of work ahead of me."

The fire leaves her eyes and is replaced with a gentle smile. "Please tell me what I can do to help. Of course, I'll miss you, but I understand. Your heart never left Florida, honey. Not once."

Since Dad passed away two years ago, Mom and I have grown much closer. For a little while, I let go of the anger and resentment I held toward her. Once I understood she had no choice—take the promotion or possibly lose her job—my forgiveness was easier to dole out.

"True. But I messed up, Mom. I don't know if she'll forgive me."

Mom walks over to the stove and turns off the burner. She grabs two bowls from the cabinet and portions us both some food. We walk over to the small, four-seater dining table and sit. She sets a bowl in front of me before speaking.

When her eyes meet mine, they are serious and determined. "Gavin… Don't stay away and wonder what if this or what if that. If there is one thing losing your father taught me, it's that life is much shorter than we give it credit for. You have to do things now, while you still can. There are so many things your father and I didn't get to do together. Things I will never get to do with him. And I'm fully aware he'd want me to keep living my life. To find someone else who brings me happiness. But I'm not ready for that. It's too soon. Maybe one day…"

I reach across the table and take her hand. "When you're ready, Mom. It's okay if that doesn't happen for many years to come. Or if it happens sooner than you expect. Anyone who says otherwise is an asshole."

"Gavin," Mom scolds. I shrug her off. "Anyway. You and

Cora are young. You have what looks like a lifetime ahead of you. But I thought the same with your father. So, I chose to work hard and save for us to do everything after retirement. But we can't predict the future. I never thought I'd be spending my retirement without your father. It's a hard pill to swallow. And it's not something I want for you. To live in regret. So whatever I can do to help you, let me know. Because your happiness matters more than anything else in my world."

I give her hand a gentle squeeze. "Thanks, Mom. You always say what I need to hear. And after I sort out all the details tomorrow, I'll let you know."

Silence rings around us a moment, but soon Mom and I fall into easy conversation. She talks about work and some new software they are developing to detect specific heart defects in the womb. Some new, experimental noninvasive technology. I listen to every word she says, but a lot of what she tells me is gibberish. A strange blend of medical termi-nology and techie talk. But it's my mom, so I pay attention to every detail. I smile at her excitement.

When she finishes her story, I tell her about the shoot in Clearwater for Global Beach Magazine. How the magazine will reach major cities across the world. I also let her know I have no doubts about finding a new agent, especially after this shoot. Then I share the last shoot I plan to do here. That it involves Layla. Alyson hasn't told me what the shoot is for yet, but I can only assume it's something to do with couples. If that happens to be the case, I will be speaking with that photographer the moment I arrive on set.

After we finish eating, Mom drives me to my house. We exchange hugs and promises to keep in contact throughout the week. I unlock the front door and wave at Mom as she backs out of the driveway. I stand in the darkness a moment and breathe in the stale air and vacancy around me. When I flip the light on, I scan the empty and soulless house I have lived in for the last eight years.

Then I drop to my knees and cry. "I'm finally going home."

eight

CORA

The sun burns fiery as it collides with the horizon.

Over the last week, I have visited the beach every evening. Sat in the same exact spot and nestled my feet in the warm sand. Watched the sun plummet into the water and fizzle into darkness. Smelled the mustiness of the dampened earth. Felt the salty breeze brush against my skin and whip my hair across my face.

Every night is different. The way the sun glows, how the sky changes colors, the scents in the air and on my skin, the sounds of the waves crashing or people chatting, how the breeze fluctuates. All of it. One night, I sat here in the rain. Actually, it was a downpour. But I refused to leave. If anything, I compared the changes in the atmosphere to the temperance of my mood. Like Mother Earth was going through mood swings and taking me on the journey. And I plan to embrace every leg of said journey.

A half hour after the sun is no longer visible, I rise from the sand and walk back toward my car. The drive home is forgotten, and at times I am surprised I make it home in one piece. I recall getting in my car and parking in the driveway, but nothing in between. Every day is the same.

I unlock the back door and flip on the lights. The scent of daily flower deliveries dying on my kitchen counter permeates the air. For the last five days, a new bouquet of flowers has arrived on my front doorstep. Red roses. White roses. Yellow roses. A mixed variety of roses. And a mixed variety of non-roses.

Each bouquet from my mom and Shelly's florist shop. Each bouquet sent with a small note. And I read each one of them. Absorb all the words. Unlike the text messages I continue to get from Gavin.

The notes sweet and short.

I miss you, baby.

Sunsets are never the same without you.

Tu es les étoiles de ma lune.

Can we watch Lord of the Rings on repeat for a week straight?

Soon, baby. Soon.

Surely, my mom and Shelly are enjoying Gavin's whole charade a little more than most people. And as bad as my house started smelling yesterday, I can't throw any of the flowers away. I just can't. Maybe I should dry them. Drying them would at least eliminate the funk in the air.

Luna weaves figure eights between my legs, purring and mewling as we head toward her bowl. After I give her a scoop of food and a few pets, I head to my room to change clothes. I love the scent of the beach—it conjures up so many wonderful memories—but I don't enjoy the constant sand on my skin. Beach sand is nature's equivalent to glitter.

A few days ago, Shelly stated we were going out. There was no asking and I wasn't allowed to refuse. Everyone was going and we were visiting the nightclub Micah works at in Tampa. Although I didn't want to go, I had no energy to fight Shelly. So I caved. It wasn't worth the argument.

I riffle through my closet and grab a pair of black skinny jeans and an equally black short-sleeve top. On a normal night, I would brush my hair and make myself look presentable. But since I currently give no fucks… I drag my hair up, combing it with my fingers, and securing it with an elastic band. It's sloppy and tired looking and I don't give a shit. If Shelly wants to force me to go out, she will suffer the consequences of my appearance.

Undoubtedly, Shelly will give me a ration of shit, but whatever. She can suck it up like I am.

Minutes later, a knock raps at the door. "It's open," I scream, louder than necessary.

The door opens and three pairs of feet trample across my wood floor. I remain on the couch, staring at the unlit fireplace. Visually tracing the rough grain of the chopped raw wood in the firebox. Pondering if I will ever get to light a fire and snuggle close to Gavin. I briefly close my eyes and take a deep breath. Nowadays, no breaths seem deep enough.

"Why the hell is your back door unlocked?" Shelly asks in her best motherly tone.

And I don't want to listen to her lecture me, just because it is all I have heard for days. If she felt an inkling of what I do, she wouldn't bother with such frivolity. "Because I've only been home for fifteen minutes and knew you guys would be here soon."

Shelly walks over to me and points her finger in my face, her other hand on her hip. "That's no excuse. Lock your freaking door."

I shake my head at her. "Yeah, sure thing *Mom*."

Erin and Jonas walk over and stand beside Shelly. I scan them head to toe. Everyone looks great. Hair, attire, overall presence. Me? Looks like I rolled out of bed five seconds ago. But I am not out to impress anyone, so who cares. If people stare, let them.

"You ready to go?" Jonas asks, voice soft with a hint of concern.

"Yeah, let me *lock up* and we can go." I smirk at Shelly and rise from the couch. I give Luna a couple pets and kisses, then we head out.

The drive to Tampa is a blur. Traffic is busy as usual, but I just stare at the lights along the highway. Shelly, Erin, and Jonas try to include me in more than one conversation, but I wiggle my way out of each one. Nothing I have to say matters right now, so it is better just to stay silent and stare out the window.

After we find a place to park, we walk down the sidewalk to the club. Music shakes the walls of the surrounding buildings. Car exhaust floats in the air. Bright headlights blind us as we head to the club's entrance. And I am numb to it all.

Once inside, we find a tall tabletop with stools near the bar. Jonas goes to the bar and buys us all a round. When he returns with our drinks, I practically chug the entire beer. Tonight will be a long night. One of many, unfortunately.

Forty-five minutes and three more beers later, I am somewhere between tipsy and drunk. And for the first time since we arrived, I listen to the music playing. Some electronic dance music I haven't heard before. The beat holds my attention while the bass resonates in my bones. If I wasn't in loner mode, I would head out to the dance floor and give everyone the show of their life. But thankfully, some microscopic piece of logic still resides inside me.

Micah comes over to the table and shoots the shit with Jonas for a few minutes. Moments later, Jonas, Shelly, and Erin get up and go out to the dance floor. Leaving me alone with Micah. Who has hated me since Shelly and I became friends in the third grade. But the way he regards me right now is different. A sort of sympathy residing in the lines of his face. Sympathy he has never directed at me a day in his life.

"How are you?" Micah leans over and asks.

I bring the bottle to my mouth and finish off my beer. "Tired of people asking me how I am. You?"

"I've been better." I catch him glancing over at a woman behind the bar. She's pretty—simple makeup, darker blonde hair piled high on top of her head, a smile that would light up the night sky.

"Who is she?" I openly point at the woman behind the bar.

"Could you please stop pointing?" A few seconds after I comply, he continues. "That's Peyton. She's the new bartender."

"And how long have you been in love with her?"

If Micah had a drink, he would have spit it across the room. Did I hit the nail on the head or what?

"I'm sorry, what? She's only been working here for a couple weeks."

"The length of time she's worked here and how you feel about her are irrelevant. How long have you been in love with her?"

He stares at me like I have two heads. "You're right, it's irrelevant. But you know what isn't? You and Gavin."

I roll my eyes. Nice change of subject. One I cannot ignore or evade. "Ugh, can you please not join the *Save Cora and Gavin* party? If someone isn't talking to me about it every day, the daily flower deliveries are. Isn't it okay for me to just want to go bury myself in blankets and darkness?"

"Seems you are," he states, lifting his chin toward my hair. "Your hair looks like it hasn't seen a brush in weeks. And I know you love rocking the black, but not every day is a funeral."

"You don't get to judge me," I say, pointing my finger in his face. "Black is life. And maybe I feel like death every day. Why do you fucking care?"

He sighs and slumps forward. "Normally, I wouldn't care. But since I talk to Gavin every single goddamn day now, it seems caring is my new middle name." He cocks his head and plasters on a pissy smile.

Gavin and Micah are speaking to each other every day. What the hell are they talking about? Me? Us? There is no us. There hasn't been an "us" in thirteen years. And especially when he decided to stop returning my calls or responding to my letters shortly after he moved away. No matter how much time has passed, those memories still sting. Burn. Char.

"You guys talk that often?" I mumble, staring down at my beer bottle.

"Yeah. He's got a lot happening all at once. Cora…" I

glance up at Micah when he says my name. His expression shifts to something more sullen. "He hurt you, I get it. Believe me. But you two need to talk. Really talk. If you don't want to speak to him on the phone, at least respond to one of the million texts he's sent you. Of all people, I figured you'd be the first person to listen. You don't need to explain anything to me, but don't shut him out. Not when he's doing everything within his power to make things right. Not when he's doing everything to come back to you."

Over and over, Gavin told me he would fix this. Told me he would come back to me. But I had heard those words before. Granted, we were kids and didn't have the means to follow through. But like I told Gavin before, actions were what I needed. Lies are made up of words just like truths. And other than flowers, love notes, and his constant reaching out to me, I haven't actually *seen* his actions.

"I'll think about it. But I make no guarantees. I've been dealing with a lot on my end too."

"Like I said, I get it. I've been burned in the past."

And that is the most personal thing Micah has ever shared with me. This whole conversation is surreal. Maybe whoever burned Micah made him realize that being a dick wasn't all it is cracked up to be. Hallelujah!

Shelly, Erin, and Jonas return to the table. They laugh about something, sweat shining on their skin under the multicolored lights. Seconds after their return, Micah slips away. Goes back behind the bar and wistfully side-eyes the new bartender.

I repeat Micah's words in my head. Gavin is fixing things. Gavin is doing everything to come back.

To Florida.

To me.

And the light that snuffed out in my heart a week and a half ago, it flickers for a second. A blip. But sometimes, a blip is all it takes. Sometimes, a blip is what turns darkness into light.

nine

GAVIN

Thirteen years ago

"I'm sorry, Gavin. We just don't have the money to let you fly back to Florida right now," Mom says with a sad smile.

Although she is trying to empathize with me, she has no idea how I feel. And I don't know what upsets me more—the fact I can't fly back to see Cora or that Mom plays the *I understand* card. "But you promised, Mom," I yell across the room, nails biting my palms.

"Don't you take that tone with me. And I never *promised* you'd be able to fly back this summer. I said we would see. And it's not possible right now. I'm sorry."

I storm off to my bedroom, slam the door behind me and lock the handle. "I hate you!" I scream at the walls as I fist my hands in my hair.

"Gavin! Come back out here and apologize to your mother! Now!" Dad stands on the other side of the door, banging.

"Fuck you! Both of you!"

I pick up my desk chair and throw it across the room. One

of the legs shatters on impact and I stare at the rubble. A moment later, I punch a hole in the wall beside my bed. Then I collapse on the bed and cry into the comforter.

I lay on my side and draw my legs to my chest. Hours pass and all I can do is lie here and cry. Cry until my eyes burn and my throat numbs. This is utter bullshit. They promised me I would be able to fly back to Florida during the summer. They promised I would be able to see Cora soon after we settled.

But their promises are lies.

It has been a fucking month. We are pretty fucking settled. Although, I don't think I will ever settle here. Everything about this place feels like a death sentence. A prison cell keeping me away from the one person I want more than anything. And why did they make a promise they never had any intention of fulfilling? Just to pacify me? If that's the case, I am more pissed.

Grabbing my phone from my back pocket, I call Cora. Hearing her will settle the anger inside me. Cora has always held the elixir to my soul.

"Hey, Gavin." Her voice perky and happy when she answers. This is exactly what I need right now. Just her.

"Hey, baby. I miss you."

"I miss you, too. Did you talk to your parents? Are you flying back soon?"

The hope in her voice echoes through the line. And I hate that I am about to destroy it. Well, my parents are destroying it. But I am the bearer of the bad news, and I hate it more than anything. Hate that I can't give her—us—better news.

"Yeah, I talked to them."

"And?"

"And they said we don't have the money right now. That there's no way I can fly back this summer."

"Oh," she whispers. And the disappointment is evident in that single word. "Oh. Well, that sucks."

"That's putting it nicely. I told them I fucking hate them."

We stay on the phone—silent—for a moment. She tries to muffle the sound, but I hear her crying. And my heart shatters further because there is not a goddamn thing I can do to make this better. I hate that I can't be there with her. I hate how helpless I feel. That I have no way to console her. To hug her close and kiss her hair. Rub a hand up and down her back, over the back of her head as I press her to my chest. This whole situation is such fucking bullshit.

"Gavin?"

"Yeah, baby?"

"Please don't hate your parents. It's your mom's job that did this, not her specifically. Your Mom would never intentionally hurt you or us." She chokes out the words and I hate that she is fighting her tears to say nice things about my parents.

But she is right and I know it. Though, I don't know who else to blame for us moving so far away. I am drowning and no one is jumping in to save me. No one tosses me a life preserver.

"I don't really hate them. It's this whole situation that I hate. But I have no other way to express how it's making me feel."

Silence steals the air between us again. But the silence is not uncomfortable. Never has been with Cora. If anything, it calms me. Settles my soul. Gives a peace only she provides.

"Can we talk about something else? Anything else? I

don't care what it is," she says. "Have you been to the beach out there yet?"

I love how she knows my favorite place on earth. How she knows it is the one place where I feel solace, other than with her. How she understands my love for the water, the sand, the comfort.

"We went to the beach for the first time a few days ago. It's not the same as the beaches at home."

"How so?"

"The sand grains are bigger. And the water is fucking cold, even in the middle of summer. I didn't get in past my knees. And even that only lasted a few minutes."

"Did you get to stay and watch the sunset?"

God, I love her. Love how she knows me, inside and out. Love how she soothes me so easily. Sunsets are the best, but they will never be the same without her. If I never saw another sunset, but was able to see her again, I would be one-hundred-percent okay with that. Without her, a sunset is just a ball of fire disappearing from sight. Sunsets hold no magic without Cora at my side.

"No, baby. My parents didn't want to stay that late. But maybe we'll get to watch a California sunset together one day."

"We *will* get to watch one together. More than one." The optimism in her voice spreads warmth from the center of my chest to the tips of my fingers and toes.

"One day. Until that day comes though, you watch the sunsets there for me. And I'll watch them here. But I'd rather wait until you're with me."

"Me too."

For the next hour, we talk about random things. Places we went together. Things that made us laugh. And it's not until I hear her yawn that I realize it is past midnight in Florida. Another shitty side effect of this move—the three-hour time zone difference. I would stay up all night and talk with her. But we are both tired, more mentally and emotionally than physically.

"I should let you go to bed, baby."

"As sweet as that is, it doesn't matter much. I only sleep a couple hours a night now. But I guess you're right."

I don't want to hang up the phone. Even if we sit here and say nothing for hours on end, just hearing her breathe on the other end makes me feel at home.

As if she can read my mind, even with several states and thousands of miles between us, she says, "Maybe we can just lay down and set our phones on our pillows. We can pretend that we're side by side."

"That sounds like the best idea I've heard in days," I tell her as I fight the tears stinging the backs of my eyes.

And for the next two hours, I listen to her sleep. Listen to her soft breaths and occasional sleep-spoken words. Words like *love* and *soon* and *forever*.

ten

GAVIN

Present

This shoot with Layla is exactly what I thought it would be. A shit show to flaunt our "relationship." Well I hope she is prepared for said relationship—as well as our friendship—to end. Because the line has been drawn and this is definitely over. Hope she enjoyed riding in my wake while it lasted.

The photographer directs us here and there and I follow through as if nothing has changed. But everything has changed. And in about fifteen minutes, Layla and Alyson are about to find out exactly how much it has changed. In less than a minute, everything in their world will tip on its axis. As it did mine.

They shouldn't have pushed me here. They should have let me pursue my relationship with Cora. Live my life how I want. But neither of them seemed capable of handling life when I wasn't improving theirs. Now… now there is no other option. They did this and now they will pay the consequences.

A few more clicks of the camera and the photographer

announces the shoot is a wrap. As soon as those words are spoken, I distance myself from Layla. And she notices immediately.

"You okay?" Layla asks as she approaches me.

I slip a hoodie over my head before chugging my water dry. During the whole process, Layla stands a foot away and regards my lack of speech and eye contact. Good. I hope it makes her sweat. Hope it makes her question why I have been so standoffish. Hope it unsettles and worries her. It should.

But she won't have to question much of anything in a moment. Shit... meet fan.

Out of the corner of my eye, I spy Alyson walking toward us. I drag in a deep breath and prepare for what will happen next. If I know these two women well enough, one will go into hysterics while the other throws a rage fit. Not that I care, but let's see how right I am.

"Gavin. Layla. Great job out there today," Alyson chirps. Her whole demeanor is as it was before we ever went to Florida. Chipper and smiley and completely artificial. Since she has been my agent, I always sensed her artifice. But I passed it off as being out in Los Angeles, and that is how most of the population is. Now, I see things differently. Now, I see she only cares about me for one reason. My signature on her paycheck.

Alyson starts scrolling through her phone and ignoring Layla and me. As she has done a thousand times prior. So, I steel myself and start the inevitable.

"Alyson. Layla. We need to talk."

Layla stares at me, her amber resin eyes asking me question after question. But I ignore her and stare at Alyson, who has yet to look up from her phone. With each passing second, the fact that she continues to ignore me pisses me off further. So to grab her attention, I opt to snap my fingers in her face.

When she finally looks up from her still lit-up phone screen, irritation rests on her face. Irritation for me disrupting her. But I don't give a fuck.

Welcome to the club of pissed-off people, my name is Gavin.

"Gavin, I was just reading an email for another shoot. If you would've waited another—" Alyson attempts to hold the floor, but I cut her off.

"Stop," I shout. My voice bounces around the small studio. The eyes of crew members still in the room look our way. But I don't give a shit. I am over this. More than over it. "As I said a moment ago, we need to talk. The three of us."

"I heard you, Gavin. Can it not wait? I have other appointments I need to get to." As she says the words, she flicks her wrist and glances down at the gold and diamond watch on her arm. This irritates me more.

"No, Alyson. It cannot wait," I seethe.

She locks her phone and rests her hands on her hips. She purses her lips and regards me as if I am behaving like a stubborn child. Obviously, she has forgotten her place in this world. Has forgotten the fact that she only has a paycheck because I grant her such a privilege. Sure, she has other clients, but none of them are as big as I am or as fruitful to her bank account. If anything, she should be vying for my attention. Doing whatever makes me happy.

"Well, spit it out. As I said, I have other appointments to get to."

Beside me, Layla starts biting her fingernails. It is such a disgusting habit. One I tried to help her curb time after time. By the time I finish, she probably won't have any nails left.

My eyes dart between the two of them—one worried, the other annoyed. "You're fired," I state firmly, not an ounce of regret in my voice.

Alyson blinks a few times before taking a step back. Confusion mars her face for a beat as she lifts a hand to her chest. "Sorry, I think I may have misheard you. What did you just say?"

I want to laugh and shake my head, but bite my lip and resist the urge. She heard me loud and clear. Just doesn't want to believe it. "You heard me just fine. But if it needs repeating... You. Are. Fired." She jerks her head away as if I slapped her. But before she says another word, I face Layla next. "And you... I don't ever want to see you again. We're done. No more fake engagement. No more friendship. I hope you enjoyed the ride because it's time to exit."

Layla goes wide-eyed and stands speechless. She stares at me slack-jawed as her eyes glaze over. A million thoughts and questions flit across her face, but she remains stoic. After a moment, she finally locates her voice. "This is because of *her*, isn't it?"

I don't owe either of them an explanation after the shit they have put me through, but I answer her anyway. "If I'm being honest, it's not just because of Cora. But yes, Layla, she is the shift that has made this happen. It was a long time coming, and she gave me the push I'd been missing for years."

"You can't do this!" Alyson yells, not caring who heard her outburst. She points her French-manicured nail in my face. "We have a contract." Her eyes light up, hoping she caught me in some loophole I forgot about.

But I didn't forget about our contract. She must have me pegged as an idiot. Joke is on her.

"Actually, I can do this. We *did* have a contract. A contract I had my attorney look over when I told him I wanted to seek a new agent. After some light reading—" I smirk "—it was determined that our contract period ended almost two years ago. But seeing as we had been doing so well together, neither of us paid much attention to that fact. Too bad for you."

Alyson is a deer in the headlights. She has no comeback for the truth I just laid on the table. No rebuttal for the fact that we carried on for an additional two years without signing a new contract. This hiccup is a win for me, and a major loss for her. If she would have continued looking out for my best interests, our business relationship may have continued. But greed took hold. And greed loses in the long run.

While Alyson marinates in the loss of being my agent, I turn and speak to Layla. "You know, we had a great friendship. One I never questioned. We were always there for each other. Had each other's back. But your ego surpassed your morality not too long ago. And the stunt you pulled in Florida… it's unforgivable."

A lone tear rolls down her cheek, her perfect stage makeup not smearing or running. Sadness hits when I question if I should believe this tear or not. As a model, Layla is an actor. She knows how to put on a show for the camera and crowd. Knows how to make people believe what she is selling. So how can I believe this lone tear is real? That it comes from somewhere genuine.

The answer is simple—I can't.

"Gavin," she chokes out and sniffles. "I'm sorry. It's just… Alyson called me and told me what was going on. That you planned to move back to Florida. And I just reacted. I freaked."

I shake my head. "You *just reacted*? You *freaked*?" I laugh at her, incredulous. "No. What you did was behave like a child who didn't get her way. Because if I moved away from you, you wouldn't get to ride my coattails anymore. But instead of talking with me, you chose a different tactic. Chose to be bitter and selfish and vindictive. Too bad it didn't work in your favor."

Her tears flow a little more steadily now. Maybe they are real, but no chance in hell am I letting my guard down enough to question their validity. If my guard goes down, she will push her guilt on me to appease herself.

"Gavin, please," Layla begs. "If our years of friendship mean anything to you—"

"No," I shout. "You don't get to pull the friendship card to manipulate me. After the stunt you pulled, knowing full well what it would do, there is no friendship card anymore. It expired the moment you used me as a pawn in some game to keep me. You know what she means to me, and you used that knowledge as a weapon. Friends don't do shit like that, Layla. Friends congratulate each other when good things happen."

In my periphery, Alyson unlocks her phone and begins to frantically go from screen to screen. I told my attorney I planned to speak with Alyson and Layla after the shoot ended, and gave him an estimated time as to when that would be. By now, he has emailed the termination paperwork to Alyson. A few seconds later, my thoughts are validated when Alyson slaps her hand to her mouth and gasps. As if she did not believe me.

My work here is done. And I have other obligations to attend to. So, without another word, I turn my back on them and walk away. Both women try to garner my attention as I head for the exit, but I ignore them as I push through the door.

Already, a major weight lifts from my chest and I breathe a little easier.

~

Studio lights blind me as a man attaches a small microphone to my shirt. "Mr. Hunt, could you please say a few words so we can test the mic?"

I have the sudden urge to behave like a child with a toy microphone. I tap the mic clipped to my shirt a few times. "Testing. Testing. One, two, three. Can you hear me?"

A woman behind a soundboard with headphones over her ears gives a thumbs up. The man beside me returns the gesture then fidgets with the mic a little more, trying to disguise it behind my shirt. A moment later, he walks off and leaves me to sit on the studio stage alone.

Before I have too much time to ponder how long I will sit here alone, Janet Maverick sits in the plush armchair beside me. Janet Maverick—one of Hollywood's top reporters. When she talks to a crowd, people listen. And that is the exact reason I came to her. So my story will be heard by the masses.

"Hey, Gavin. How are you today?" Janet asks, genuinely interested.

"Oh, you know. Things aren't so hot. But I'm hoping this interview will be the fresh start to things getting better."

She nods. "I'm sure everything will work out. Just stay positive."

A moment later, the stage crew crowd around us. We are asked to get in position on set. Janet and I are asked to say a few last things for a final check of our mics. Then a woman behind one of several cameras begins counting down with her fingers before pointing at Janet.

"Good evening, Los Angeles. If this is your first time tuning in, I'm Janet Maverick. And you're watching The Heart of Hollywood. Tonight, I am honored to have Gavin Hunt on stage with me." Janet faces me and gives a warm smile. "Welcome, Gavin."

I have been in front of a camera hundreds of times, but in this moment an overwhelming sense of stage fright consumes me. "Thank you, Janet. It's great to be here," I stumble then cough. A stagehand points to a bottle of water beside me, signaling me to drink. Glad someone is looking out for me.

Janet carries on as if there is no reason to panic. As if millions of people aren't flipping on their televisions to watch this very moment. Right now, I envy her this.

"For those of you who aren't familiar with the man beside me… First of all, shame on you," she jokes. "Seriously. Mister Gavin Hunt is a model. You may have seen his work in a magazine or twenty. He has also appeared on the cover of several romance novels. Ladies, check those book covers."

Someone behind the soundboard presses a button and some previously recorded laughter echoes around us.

"But let's get down to the nitty-gritty," Janet says. "Gavin, you just returned from a photo shoot in Florida. How did it go?"

I hold Janet's gaze, doing my best to ignore the cameras and crew focused on us. After a quick inhale, I answer. "The photo shoot was phenomenal. It was nice to return to Florida after being away for so many years."

Janet perks up at this. "Return to Florida? Is that where you're originally from, Gavin?"

"It is. I moved out to California when I was sixteen after my mom received a promotion. This past trip was the first time I'd been back."

She nods, her face studious over my response. "So, what can we look forward to seeing after this shoot?"

"I was doing a shoot for Beach Global Magazine. There will be several images with a new line I'm helping them promote. Casual wear for the beach and city. As well as swimwear and undergarments," I say, waggling my brows.

Janet lays her hand over her heart before fanning herself. "Gavin, you can't just say things like that. Now I'm blushing on national television." She swats me with a small pad of paper.

"The magazine is set to release at the beginning of summer. Make sure you get your copy. I guarantee you won't be disappointed." I wink at her.

"Ladies, you heard it here. Keep your eye on the magazine stands." Janet takes a sip of water, then switches tactics. "Other than work, Gavin, how is life treating you?"

This is why I came here. To expose my life to the masses. Tell my story—the truth as well as the web of lies. I need the façade of what Layla and I had to be uncovered. For all the stories of our perfect "engagement" to be brought out in the light and diminished.

"Well, Janet, things are a bit rough right now," I say.

"Aw, I'm sorry to hear this. What's going on?"

"My trip to Florida ended up becoming more than just a work trip. For the first time in thirteen years, I ran into the love of my life."

Janet gasps and slaps a hand over her mouth, eyes awestruck. "Oh my, Gavin. I don't know what to say. Why has it been so long since you've seen this woman? And wait… what about your engagement?"

The perfect segue into clearing the air. Thank you very much. "That's part of the reason I'm here tonight, Janet. I want to clear the air about a few things. The first thing being my engagement to Layla Hendricks. After running into my high school sweetheart, many things were put into perspective. One of those things being said engagement. An engagement that was done purely for business reasons."

"Well, you are just full of surprises tonight," Janet states.

I nod. "Indeed. Layla and I have been friends since I moved to California. But that's all. My heart has always been in Florida. As my career took off, Layla struggled. Our agent got her shoots with several well-known photographers, but nothing boosted her career. After a year, our agent suggested we pretend to get engaged. That my soaring career would lift hers. So, I agreed. Layla was my friend, and I wanted to help her. But while I was in Florida, that favor and my friendship was taken advantage of. As of today, I have cut all business ties with my agent and Layla. And have also severed my friendship with Ms. Hendricks."

Janet and I sit in silence for several long seconds. Now that I have said my part—gotten the falsehoods of my engagement to Layla off my chest and told the world I am in love with someone else—relief rushes through my veins. A weight that has anchored me in place for years instantly lightens. With such a simple action, I feel a hundred pounds lighter. Now, I need to repair things between me and Cora. And with my level of determination, I will fix us.

"Wow, Gavin. I'm not even sure where to begin. If you don't mind sharing with us, what happened in Florida that sparked this dramatic change? Other than seeing this mystery woman."

I hadn't been given permission to mention Cora's name, so keeping her anonymity is vital. Although, Hollywood will figure out who she is eventually. But until that day arrives, my lips remain sealed.

"Janet, there aren't adequate words to explain what seeing this woman did to me. It's as if my heart started beating again." At my words, Janet and a few of the female crewmembers swoon. The visual adds a smile to my face. "When I was younger, I didn't have a say in my family moving to California. But now, I make all my decisions. And that's why I have chosen to move back to Florida."

Saying the words aloud, announcing them to millions of viewers, sets my pulse to a wild gallop beneath my sternum. But after seeing Cora, after being in the same space as her for a week, there is no possible chance of me staying away. Not anymore. Cora is everything I always wanted. A breath of fresh air. The only person to soothe and satiate my soul. Moving back to Florida is something I should have done years ago. For too long, the flashing lights and starry eyes distracted me. But I have no doubts this is the right choice. Cora has always been the right choice.

"Well, Gavin. I'm not sure I know what else to say. California will miss you. I will miss you," she says, smiling wide.

"You haven't seen the last of me, Janet. I'm not leaving the industry. Just making some personal changes. But you'll still get to glance at my pretty face," I tease.

"Whew. That's good news. I'm not sure how my life would continue if I didn't see you around the city." She pauses, reaching across the space between us and resting her hand on mine. "Thank you for sitting with me today. It was wonderful to see you. Keep us posted on how things go with this mystery woman."

"Will do, Janet. Thank you for having me."

As Janet says her parting words into the camera, I review all the things I need to do in my mental checklist.

Fire Alyson. Check.

Give Layla the boot. Check.

Review my new agent's contract. Still need to do.

Call Micah. Still need to do.

Deal with the house. Work in progress.

As I walk off the stage, my phone dings in my pocket. When I retrieve it, there is a message from the realtor I contacted yesterday. Her timing couldn't be more perfect. And I take it as a sign everything will work out as planned. At least that is what I hope.

"Of course, you can stay with me, man. I'd never leave you on the streets. When do you think you'll get here?" Micah asks.

Not sure why I was worried, but I am so relieved he said yes to me staying at his place until I buy a new house. Micah and I have known each other almost twenty years, but I had my doubts about him agreeing to let me stay. He may be my best and longtime friend, but how he acted around Cora while I was in Florida had me antsy to hear his response. The fact he said yes alleviates another concern.

"Maybe in the next few days or so. The house is under contract and I'll know more tomorrow or the next day. Is it cool if I ship some boxes and my car to your place?"

"Sure thing. Whatever you need. Mi casa es su casa. Just let me know when they'll be here, so I'm home when they arrive."

The sale of my California house is moving much quicker

than anticipated. And I took it as yet another sign. The cosmos are rooting for me—for me and Cora. The stars aligning invigorates me, has me doing things at maximum speed. If the forward momentum continues at this pace, I will be back in Florida within a week. Hopefully sooner. Fixing things with Cora can't happen fast enough. Being with her again, especially.

"Thanks, bro. I'll shoot you a text with the shipping info. For now, I'm only sending clothes and necessities. When I find a place, I'll have everything else shipped."

Micah and I talk for a few more minutes, catching up on other things. After we hang up, I go into beast mode. By the end of the day, ninety percent of my house is packed into boxes. Lucky for me, I have never been a packrat. By no means am I a minimalist, but over the years I had no desire to fill my house with endless knickknacks. I suppose I always knew I would pack things up.

I call the shipping company and set up a time to have the boxes and my car picked up. After, I set up for the remaining boxes and furniture to be shipped to my mom's house. When I told her how quick things were progressing with the sale of my house, she offered her unused two-car garage as storage space.

Everything came together with ease. How can I not believe in fate? Everything continues to line up for us to be together again. If it isn't divinity, I don't know what it is.

But as I lay awake in bed, I question how I will fix things with Cora. As smooth as things are going, a twinge of doubt lingers in the back of my mind. It taunts me and has uncertainty creeping in my veins.

What if she rejects me? Although the chemistry between us is more than obvious, I hurt her. More than once. Hurt like that doesn't just vanish. What if she doesn't forgive me? The possibility lingers in my thoughts and gnaws at my heart. Because as much as I have done to prove my promise to Cora, the possibility of her not letting me back in still stands. Which begs the question…

What if all this is for nothing?

eleven

CORA

News travels fast in the photography and modeling circuit.

Only two days have passed since I sent over the finalized photos from Gavin's shoot to the magazine. Riffling through thousands of images of Gavin wasn't easy by any stretch of the imagination, but eventually I selected my top three from each look the magazine wanted. Most of the images I sent aren't my personal favorites—those I kept all for myself—but they are notable and sales-worthy photographs.

As I sip on a cup of hot caffeine, I read the fifth email from a local company seeking my photography skills. And I am in complete awe. Doing this photo shoot with Gavin has already opened multiple doors for me. Some doors I wish would have remained closed. The doors trapping my heart and memories in the dark corners of my mind.

I keep thinking of Gavin's promise to return to me. His promise to fix past mistakes and explain all the things I didn't understand. But as each day passes, I wonder if he will follow through with his promises. If the perfume from days' worth of flower deliveries was any indication, he plans to return. The only thought constantly rolling around in my head is how we move forward.

So much of our lives has changed. Adulthood changes people. But so much of what we once had remains untouched.

At one point in our lives, Gavin and I shared everything with each other. There were no secrets between us—intentional or by accidental omission. With the latest revelation—his supposed fake engagement to *her*—I wasn't sure I could give Gavin my trust. I want to believe it is possible for us to get back to where we were years ago. The place where I knew every facet of his life and vice versa.

Because the end of us couldn't be *this*—an ugly, painful, heart-wrenching reality.

The way things are now, they are so different from when we were younger. What I thought was pain at age sixteen is nothing compared to this vacant space beneath my breast bone. At least, back then, I experienced sensation where my heart resided in my chest. Now, my heart feels numb and hollow. The organ still beats, still pumps blood through my veins, but it only does so to keep me in existence. There is no life behind the rhythm. No real purpose. Just a machine doing its job.

My phone pings with an incoming text. Reluctantly, I glance at the screen. Although I haven't responded, Gavin continues to text me updates. Last I heard, he fired his agent and broke off his friendship and fake engagement with *her*. That text brought an actual smile to my face. But we still have a long way to go.

You, me, Jonas. Bar. Tonight.

Shelly has always known how to make me smile and

laugh. Her simple text does exactly that. Her message short, sweet, and to the point.

As much as I want to be a hermit and hide in my shell of a house, Shelly has the right remedy. A night out with my friends is exactly what I need to boost my mood. To sit amongst the crowd, sip on a beer and listen to people belt out karaoke. The solution to every bad day in history is awkward karaoke.

> Sounds good. What time?

> Six. We need to grab a good table before the crowd arrives.

> See you at six.

I read through the emails again and decide to accept two of the offers. Respectfully declining the others, I tell them to reach out in the future and check my availability. The two I accept are in the Bay Area. One is for the city of St. Petersburg, who has requested for me to do a cityscape with some patrons. The city is looking to update images for tourism since the city has changed so much in the last five years. They want to show off city life and all the wonderful things the area has to offer. The other offer is for boudoir photos of a couple in Tampa. Details are vague, but enough for me to be comfortable and accept.

After I respond to the emails, I make the mistake of opening the file on my laptop titled "DO NOT OPEN." Because, for some reason, I am a glutton for punishment.

For the next hour, I scroll through photo after photo of Gavin. From the photo shoot, and times when he wasn't paying attention. Frame after frame after frame. Years ago, I had photos of us from high school digitized. Those same images were now parked in this folder. And I cannot force myself to look away.

Click. Click. Click.

Cue the tears. And the burn in my nose. Followed by the clog in my throat.

As each image from our younger years passes over the screen, I cry uglier and harder. I tremble from head to toe as my vision blurs and a tight pinch pierces between my lungs. The onslaught of memories set off the full emotional spectrum and it is pure misery. And I welcome every ounce of it.

At least anguish is better than numbness. At least it reminds me I am still alive. Because some days, I wonder if this is one huge nightmare. Some sick, twisted version of hell. Some days, life is hell.

~

I wake up on the couch, the blanket cocooning me and Luna purring on my chest. The light of day dims, but the sun is still up. I give Luna a few pets before cuddling her in my arms. After a moment, I bolt upright and Luna hisses at me before scampering off.

"Sorry, Luna."

Shit. What time is it? I told Shelly I would meet her and Jonas at the bar.

I glance at the clock on the kitchen wall, noting it's five-twenty. Flying off the couch, I head for my room and riffle through my closet. Thank goodness the bar is a short drive from the house, otherwise I would be screwed. After picking out a top and a pair of jeans, I jump in the shower and wash away the pool of sorrow I have been swimming in all day.

Once out and dressed, I feed Luna and grab my keys and

wallet. I dash out the door and drive to the bar. Seven minutes later, I park in the lot and step through the bar doors.

I spot Shelly and Jonas at our usual table and walk over to them.

"Hey, you look like shit," Shelly says, not sugarcoating my wayward appearance.

"You really know how to flatter a girl. *Thanks*. I haven't been sleeping much. You're lucky I got a nap in before tonight, otherwise I'd look so much better."

I flip her the middle finger. But she knows I'm teasing her.

"Sorry. You know I call it as I see it," she apologizes with a shrug.

"True. Can we please talk about something else?" I didn't come out to talk about how depressing my life is. Tonight is about having fun and feeling better. If that isn't going to happen, I will just go home and wallow alone.

"Yeah, sorry," Shelly says.

The waitress approaches the table and sets down three beers. Mine is at my lips within a second, half of it down my throat. At this rate, I will be drunk in no time. We order another round and some appetizers.

By the time karaoke starts an hour later, I am somewhere between tipsy and drunk. And it is a nice place to be. In this state, not much of anything matters. Life has no issues. No drama. No life-altering decisions need to be made. It's all rainbows and unicorns and horrible singers on small stages.

As some overly primped woman sings the words to Bon Jovi's "You Give Love a Bad Name", I lean on Jonas. His arm wraps around my shoulder and keeps me from teetering off my stool.

Jonas really is a great guy. I hope he happens upon the right woman one day. As much as we went back and forth, part of me always knew nothing more would evolve between us. Jonas has a big heart and will be perfect for a very lucky lady one day. But that lady won't be me. And I hope he knows Shelly and I will need to approve whoever this future mystery woman will be. She will have a lot to live up to.

Jonas presses a kiss to the top of my head. "Are you okay?" he whisper-asks just loud enough for me to hear.

For a second, I nod. But the nod slowly transitions, and soon I shake my head before turning my face into his shoulder.

God, I am sick and tired of crying. My bloodshot eyes ache and feel as if they are swollen to twice their size. My throat scratches every time I speak and throbs with each breath I take. And honestly, I don't know how much more of this I can handle.

Jonas delicately rubs a hand up and down my back. Says soothing words only I hear. Shushes me and tells me everything will be alright. And his kindness has me on the cusp of crying harder, but I resist. There is only so much my body can handle.

Two lackluster karaoke songs later, we all agree to call it a night. We pay our tab before I stumble out the door. Jonas drives me home in my car and Shelly follows us so she can take Jonas back to his Jeep. The drive is short and filled with low-volume rock music from the radio. Jonas doesn't speak up while I lean against the window with my eyes closed. Minutes later, we park in my driveway and shuffle out. Shelly and Jonas walk me inside, hug me goodnight and disappear out the door.

Once alone, I kick off my shoes and peel off my jeans, crawl into bed and curl into a ball. Luna jumps up on the bed and nudges her head against mine. For a beat, I pet her soft fur and a sense of comfort washes over me as she purrs loudly and professes her unconditional love.

"At least you'll stay by my side, pretty girl," I whisper.

As if she understands me, Luna meows in response. I snuggle her into my chest and fall asleep, waking on and off through the night. Throughout the night, dreams of photos and drawings, hand holding and kisses, goodbyes and love letters haunt me every hour. As they do every night. And probably will for the rest of my life.

twelve

CORA

Twelve and a half years ago

Today is the most important day of my life. But it doesn't matter. Not anymore.

On this day two years ago, Gavin and I officially started dating. Before he moved to California, we celebrated every possible relationship milestone. One month. Three months. Six months. One year. But today, on our two-year anniversary, I haven't heard a word from him.

His lack of reaching out to me can easily be blamed on time zone differences. The hour is still early in California, and he is probably sleeping. But a sinking suspicion in my gut tells me it has nothing to do with the time zones. This nerve-laden ache has been getting bigger each day we are apart.

Six months has passed since Gavin left Florida. Six very long, dark months. The last four… I haven't heard from Gavin at all. No return phone calls or texts. No response to the numerous letters I have mailed him. As if he vanished from the earth. Poof. At one point, I called and asked Mrs. Hunt if

Gavin was still alive. She apologized profusely and told me Gavin was not doing well with the transition.

Neither was I, for that matter.

Since Gavin left, life has been complete and utter shit. My mom is lucky if I get out of bed each day. After weeks of tears and depression, Mom and Dad took me to see a therapist. We talked, she prescribed me anti-depressants and that was all she wrote. But pills will never replace my heart. Pills will never make this ache vanish. Only Gavin can do that. And he is gone.

Poof.

As with Gavin, everything I ever loved disappeared. My love for art has been almost nonexistent. School is going down the drain at a rapid pace. The only thing that kept me attending each day was the opportunity to sit under our tree. To trace my fingertips over the carved wood where our initials reside, along with his words only for me. Under that tree was our spot. Will always be our spot. The only physical piece of him I have a connection to every day.

I call Gavin's house and the phone rings twice before Mr. Hunt answers. "Hello?"

I waited as late as possible, so it isn't too early on the west coast. Currently eight in the morning in California. "Hi, Mr. Hunt. It's Cora. Sorry to call so early. Is Gavin awake?" I pick at the hem of my jeans as I wait, nervous.

"Good morning, sweetheart. It's not too early. But I'm sorry, Gavin isn't home. He stayed over at a friend's house last night."

"Oh," I say, disappointment evident in my tone. "Okay, thank you. I'll try calling his cell phone."

Before I hang up, Mr. Hunt speaks. "Cora? I'm so sorry about everything. I know neither of you is handling this well."

I bite my tongue to avoid crying in the phone. I wonder if he knows how distant Gavin and I have become. Miles and states aren't the only things that separate us now, it is also our lack of connection. Our lack of communication.

Is this what happens when soul mates are ripped apart? They drift and fade and become shells of themselves.

"Thank you, Mr. Hunt," I manage. "Please let Gavin know I called."

"I will, sweetheart. If we don't talk again before, have a happy Thanksgiving," he says.

And I almost lose it on the phone. "You all too." Then I hang up.

I wait a few minutes, gathering my thoughts and emotions. The last thing I want is to call Gavin and cry during our conversation. Although, nowadays I cry more often than not.

Opening Gavin's contact on my phone, I tap the little phone image before bringing the phone to my ear. *First ring.* God, I have missed hearing his voice. *Second ring.* But not more than I have missed his touch. *Third ring.* Or the feel of his lips pressed against mine. *Fourth ring.* And the way he held me close any chance he got. *Voicemail.*

"This is Gavin. Leave me a message. Or don't. I really don't give a shit either way."

Why isn't he answering? By now, it seems as if he purposely avoids me. And I don't know why. Because he won't fucking talk to me.

Beep.

"Hey, Gavin. It's me. Your girlfriend. Although that seems questionable since you haven't spoken to me in four months. Not once. I really miss you. And of all days to not respond to me... guess I should've known you'd find someone else to love. Thanks for having the balls to tell me. Whatever. You probably won't even listen to this. But if you do... Happy anniversary. Hope you have a *great* day."

I hang up and throw my phone across the room, screaming at the top of my lungs. And it's no surprise, no one comes to my room and asks what is wrong. Because Mom and Dad both know. They know what day today is. They know that I have only gotten worse with each passing day. Mom also knows I haven't spoken to Gavin in months. The longer I don't hear from Gavin—let alone see him—the more bitter I become. The more withdrawn I become. Whatever his reason for cutting me off, it would have been nice if he made me privy. As it is, I feel like I have been played.

After screaming a few more times, I rummage through my closet. When I locate my art supplies, I yank them down and cast them across my bedroom floor. For the next few hours, I submerge myself in charcoals and my art pad. My fingertips are coated in black coal, and I am certain my face has streaks from where I scratched my face a couple times.

But it doesn't matter. Nothing fucking matters.

I draw and shade and accentuate. When I finish the first image, I tear it from the pad and start a new piece. This process happens on repeat for hours. By the time I stop, the sun has begun setting. Three finished drawings lay in front of me, another still attached to the pad and left unfinished. I stare at the three images as a tear drips from my chin and splatters on the charcoal.

The first is a replica of the first day I met Gavin. Both of us sitting under our tree, before it was blemished by his pocket knife. Before it was *our* tree. I recall that day and how eager he was to make conversation with me. Continually ignoring him, I read my book and secretly memorized the lines of his face out of the corner of my eye. I listened to his breathing pattern and tried to match mine to it. I glanced down at his hands and watched them fumble as he sat nervously beside me.

The second image is a flashback to two years ago. Of Gavin and me at the beach, in the water, kissing for the first time. That day was pure magic. No other day compares to how I felt when his lips grazed mine for the first time. Like an incinerator ignited low in my belly, heat spreading throughout my body in the cool Gulf. And no matter who was looking, we stayed like that for hours in the water. Tangled limbs and hungry kisses. On that day, he became mine, and I became his. Forever.

And the third image makes me blush. In this piece, we are topless. Lips locked. Bodies crushed together. Hands in the other's hair and groping body parts. This was us. Exposed and vulnerable and losing ourselves in one another. And the night we lost our virginity. A night that will be forever engraved in my memory. Not just the physicality, but also the way his eyes softened and his breath caught and my name rolled off his tongue.

The more I stare at the drawings, the harder the tears fall. Before too many hit the pages, I swipe them away and fold up the pages. The unfinished page stays attached to the pad—a picture of me now. More like a silhouette. Because all I feel is darkness. Nothingness.

Grabbing one of my school notebooks, I open it to a blank page and write a letter to Gavin. One I hope he reads.

Gavin,

Today is our two-year anniversary. And all I want to do is talk to you. But we haven't talked in so long. Now, I am just empty inside. Lifeless. Moving to California wasn't your fault. You hate it. I hate it. And there is nothing we can do about it.

I called your house earlier and your Dad told me you stayed over at a friend's house. I'm happy you've made new friends out there. And I'm happy you seem to be moving on without me.

I won't bore you with my life. Because it's one big shit show on my end. Maybe I'll start my meds again, so at least I experience some form of happiness. Even if it is fake. Fake is better than nothing at all. Right?

Inside this envelope are three drawings of happier times. After this, I may just burn all my art supplies. Because anything worth capturing doesn't exist anymore. Not since you left. Not since you stopped talking with me.

Why? Why have you stopped talking with and writing me? Did you find someone else already? Was I that easy to forget? Am I not even worth friendship?

I hate myself. I hate my life. Hate that I have given you my heart and you've stomped on it until it turned to dust.

Does your heart feel like a black hole? Because mine does. It feels like this dark, hollow place that sucks all the happiness from the world and demolishes it.

It doesn't matter anymore. None of it does. You. Me. Us. Who were we to think we would see each other again? We're fools. Or at least I'm a fool. Because I believed we would. Believed this separation was a temporary blip in our relationship. Something easily fixed after a little patience.

But it seems I was wrong.

Because it feels like you have moved on without me. Left me to rot with the garbage.

And I'm done. Done spending every second of every day wondering what you're doing. If you care or think about me still. It's pretty obvious what the answer is, especially if you never speak to me. This situation sucks, but I never imagined you'd do this to me. Ghost me.

So, goodbye Gavin. It was my privilege to love you. And maybe one day in the future, I will get the chance again. God, I hope so. Because I will never love anyone the way I love you. If I'm honest, I don't ever want to love anyone else. I'd rather die alone, miserable and frail.

I hope you read this and it makes your heart hurt the same as mine. I hope it makes you shed as many tears as I have. And I hope you find it in your heart to come back to me one day.

Because I will always love you. Forever.

Tu es les étoiles de ma lune.

Cora

I fold the paper into thirds and set it with the drawings as I search the house for a large envelope. When I locate one, I shove the drawings and letter inside, addressing it to Gavin and slapping on too many stamps. A minute later, I walk to the mailbox and place the envelope inside, raising the red flag.

As I walk away from the envelope, I settle into my new reality. A reality where Gavin and Cora don't exist. A reality where love dies and hearts shatter into millions of little fragments. And a reality where nothing matters, because what is the point. What. Is. The. Point?

thirteen

GAVIN

Present

I stare off in the distance as my Range Rover is loaded into a freight box with a few boxes of my clothes inside the car. The car should arrive at Micah's house tomorrow evening. My SUV being loaded and shipped has reality setting in. And my nerves zapping like live wires.

This is really happening. I am going home.

Car with three boxes inside should be at your place tomorrow night.

MICAH

Cool. I'll let you know when it arrives. What time is your flight tomorrow?

10am, with a stop in Houston. Should be in Tampa between 7-7:30pm.

If your shit arrives before you land, want me to pick you up?

Nah. I'll just grab an Uber.

> See you tomorrow. Tell your mom I said hi.
> Fly safe.

After my car is driven off, I go back in the house that no longer belongs to me and breathe deeply. In Los Angeles, houses sell faster than imaginable. At least that is what my realtor said. Regardless of the reason, I am happy to have things coming together. Call it divine intervention or luck of the draw—I don't care—but thank god I was able to check every item off my to-do list.

Scanning the empty house, I sigh. The day I put my house on the market, I also asked every person I knew if they wanted to purchase any of my furniture. A few hours ago, the last piece—my bed—was picked up. With not much furniture in the first place, it wasn't challenging to sell a bed with two nightstands, a couch, loveseat, coffee table, and a dining set. I had buyers lined up on the first day. In less than half a day, each piece was claimed.

Everything kept falling into place. And after each domino fell, I thanked the higher power watching over me. Because obviously someone out there wanted me to repair our broken relationship.

My phone buzzes in my palm, Mom's name and picture flashing on the screen.

"Hey, Mom."

"You ready, honey?"

"Yeah, I just have a couple more boxes for your garage." Yesterday, I took over the majority of what I planned to keep. All I had left was my carry-on for the plane and two small boxes.

"Okay. I'm leaving the house now. We can grab something to eat after I pick you up. See you soon."

"See you soon."

~

Mom and I sit in silence at the dining room table with two open pizza boxes between us. Of all the things to have for dinner on my last night here, Mom suggested our favorite pizza place. Honestly, it didn't matter what we ate. As long as we spent this time together, I was happy. And as much as I dislike California, I will miss Mom terribly.

"I wish you would come back to Florida with me," I tell her.

She sighs before taking a bite of pizza. After she finishes chewing, she says, "Gavin, maybe I will return in the future. But for now, my place is here. Maybe I'll feel different once you're gone, but I won't know until that happens."

I nod, accepting her answer. "Just hate that you'll be out here alone. If Dad was still alive, I'd feel different."

"I'm not alone, Gavin. Believe it or not, I have friends. Lots of them. And we spend time with one another." Mom points her slice of pizza at me and laughs. "Just because I'm a mother and older, doesn't mean I forgot how to enjoy life."

"Ha ha. Fine, I guess I believe you'll make it without me here. But if anything changes…"

"I promise you'll be the first to know."

We finish eating and put the extra pizza in the fridge. Plopping down on the couch, we spend the next two hours laughing at old episodes of *The Simpsons*. The night is the perfect end to my time in Los Angeles. Next to my mom, laughing and spending time together.

And right then, I send a wish to the universe that Mom will want to move back to Florida soon. Because I need her just as much as I do Cora. The only women in my life that matter. The only women who keep me whole and in check. My secret request is selfish, but I don't care. There are some things in life worth being selfish over. Like love.

We rise from the couch around ten thirty, give each other a hug, and head to our respective rooms. I kick off my shoes and tug my shirt over my head before landing on the bed. I stare at the ceiling for a while, counting the plastic, glow-in-the-dark stars I stuck to the ceiling when we first moved here. The stars were a constant reminder of Cora and the French sentiment I once told her. She truly is the stars to my moon. And she illuminates everything important in the world. Everything important to me.

And soon, very soon, I will be near her again. See her again. Breathe her in again. Touch her again. Because we haven't reached the end of our road. Not by a long shot. Anyone who tells me otherwise is a fool.

Shortly after I turn off the lamp, I fall asleep under the same stars I did almost thirteen years ago. Stars that spark my mind to dream of the most beautiful woman. The woman I love. The woman I have to win back. No matter what it takes.

When I wake in the morning, Mom is in the kitchen cooking us breakfast. As I sit at the breakfast bar, she slides a plate of eggs, sausage, and toast in front of me. The last woman to make me breakfast was Cora. And I laugh, remembering my first taste of meatless sausage.

"What's so funny?" Mom asks.

I share my story with her and she laughs too. So many things have changed over the years, yet one thing remains the same and true. My love for Cora. And no matter how much has changed for either of us, I will love her regardless.

Mom and I finish breakfast, then talk about my new agent

and how I plan to stay with Micah until I buy a new house. I help her with the dishes and then we prepare to leave. The drive to the airport goes faster than usual. Before realization sets in, Mom and I hug at the departure drop-off. After someone honks their horn, we break apart.

"Call me when you land, please."

"I will, Mom. I love you."

"I love you too, honey." For a moment, I stand rooted in place and stare as her car exits the airport drop-off.

This is it. The day I have been waiting for. Today, I am going home.

One of the hardest things I have ever done is sit on my ass and do nothing. Literally, nothing. Especially when I could be out there, trying to win back the love of my life.

But somehow, Micah has convinced me to sit in his house and be patient. To bide my time. The only thing keeping me sane is searching the internet for houses. Several nice houses have sparked my attention, but none of them give me a sense of fulfillment. And I think the reason is Cora.

If I buy a new home, I want Cora to be a part of the process. To hear her opinions on the appearance—inside and out. Get her input on which kitchen she likes better. If the house gets enough light or has the right number of trees. Or maybe which house she pictures us growing old in together. Which house she imagines us raising children and grandchildren in, their little feet trampling through a large back yard and playing on swings.

I slap my laptop shut and stop staring at houses. No matter what I do to occupy my time, every piece of my life always circles back to Cora. She is literally in every thought I own—awake and asleep.

Turning on the television, I search for something to watch. When I scroll through the guide and see *Lord of the Rings*, I laugh. If the cosmos aren't trying to tell me something, I don't understand what the hell is happening. One sign after another pops up. From the second I decided to mend my mistakes and our past, fortune has been on my side. And after seeing this, I vow to not spend another day sitting on this couch, bored out of my skull, doing nothing.

Just as I start watching the movie, Micah bursts through the front door. "Guess what?" he asks, a little out of breath.

"Whatever you're dying to tell me must be good if you're out of breath."

Micah flips me off. "Well, I was about to give you the best news since your return yesterday, but now I think I'll wait." He cocks his head and smirks.

Fucker.

"Don't be a dick. I'm sorry if I hurt your feelings." I frown at him for a half second, but the sarcasm doesn't go unnoticed. "What were you going to say?"

He stares at me a minute, tapping a finger against his lips. "A little birdie told me a specific photographer will be out and about tomorrow, taking photos."

At his words, I fly off the couch and grab his face. Practically throttling his skull off his spine. "Where? Tell me where." My voice frantic while my body sings.

"Ah, ah, ah. Not so fast. Tit for tat, my friend." Micah waggles his finger in front of my face.

I drop my hands from his face. "What could I possibly do for you?" At this point, I would do just about anything to see Cora again. Sitting in this house is making me nutty.

"How about you just owe me one in the future? Deal?" Micah asks.

Definitely a deal I can't pass up. "Deal," I say. Micah extends his hand and we shake on it.

A minute later, Micah shares with me all the details Shelly told him about Cora's shoot tomorrow. Shelly knows I have been back in town since yesterday, but Micah asked her to not make Cora aware. But by Shelly knowing I returned home, she and Micah have been secret go-betweens for me. Their sibling bond has never been better and I love how much they are team Gavin-and-Cora-together-again.

Later, when I try to fall asleep on the couch, I spend an hour planning how I will surprise Cora. I have it all mapped out in my head. But the hidden weight in my wallet makes me second-guess what might go down.

My only hope is she doesn't run the opposite direction.

fourteen

CORA

I park my car along Central Avenue, near Fifth Street. After I feed the parking meter, I walk into the nearest coffee shop and order a coconut milk latte.

After I'm slightly caffeinated, I wander for a few blocks. I take in all the sights, categorizing what would be great to photograph. Murals on select buildings. Downtown life. Restaurants and museums and shops to visit. The Sundial. The historical Vinoy hotel. Tampa Bay, from the St. Petersburg side. And that's only downtown. I have dates scheduled to shoot other parts of the city.

Once I make it back to my car, I have over ten different sections of downtown St. Petersburg I plan to photograph. I grab my cameras from the back of my car and head toward the farthest location. As I stroll through the morning crowd, I glance over my shoulder a time or two. Every other storefront, I get this odd feeling someone is following me. Like my intuition is having a light bulb moment. But each time I check, I spot no familiar faces in the crowd.

Starting at First Street, I snap photo after photo. A restaurant here, another there. One storefront after another. Downtown has so many unique shops, it is difficult to choose what to photograph. So, I snap as many as possible. Once I go through the editing process, I will siphon out what stays and what goes.

The closer I get to my car, the more it feels as if someone is following me again. So instead of being obvious and staring up and down the street, I step inside a cafe and order a drink.

Once the young girl behind the counter hands me the drink, I sit one table away from the window and stare outside. Girlfriends flock into shops together, smiling and laughing. A man with a little girl on his shoulders walks by. Minutes pass and I recognize no one on the sidewalk, but the twinge in my gut remains.

Five steps from opening the door, I spot him. Gavin.

He stands across the street, in front of a clothing store, watching me. How long has he been there? Why wasn't I checking across the street too? Clad in a pair of dark gray and black checkered shorts, a form-fitting black T-shirt, and dark sunglasses shielding his eyes.

I don't need to see his eyes to know he has missed just as much sleep as me. Has been in just as much pain as I have been.

We stand staring at one another for a moment. And it isn't until someone else leaves the cafe that I move from where I have been locked in place. As my feet shuffle toward the exit, he raises his hand and waves.

When I step onto the sidewalk, I shift to the side and move out of pedestrian foot traffic. The moment I lock eyes with Gavin again, he starts crossing the street and walking in my direction. When he crosses the double line in the center of the street, I run. And I hear him yelling and running after me.

"Cora!" Gavin screams. "Cora, wait!"

With my arms pinning the cameras to my chest, my run morphs into an awkward jog. I weave in and out of the growing crowd, spotting my car in the spaces one block away.

I will make it before he catches me.

Repeating the mantra with my eyes focused on the driver's side door of my car, I almost jog in front of a moving car. Almost. But Gavin yanks on my bicep just in time to pull me out of the street.

"Oh my god, Cora! Are you okay?" Gavin holds me at arm's length and inspects me head to toe. Once he determines I am unscathed and his breathing settles enough, he speaks up. "You didn't have to run into traffic to get away from me."

Stunned, I stare back at him. Is he really here? Is he back? For good? I shake my head, not wanting to get ahead of myself. One step at a time, Cora. No sense in getting your hopes up when you don't have all the facts.

"I wasn't purposely running into traffic. Just wasn't paying attention. Sorry I scared you," I say. Because it's true. I would never do anything to that extreme.

Gavin bends at the waist, places his hands on his knees and breathes heavily. After a moment, his breathing regulates and he stands up straight. "Why were you running from me?" He studies the lines of my face as his bunch just above the bridge of his nose.

"Don't know. Guess I thought it'd be better than confronting you and losing my shit. The last few weeks have been a clusterfuck. Not sure how much more I can handle," I admit.

He nods and purses his lips before relaxing them again. "I deserve that. Can we please go somewhere and talk? There's a lot I need to tell you. And even more wrongs I need to make right." He shoves his hands in his pockets and teeters back on his heels as he regards me.

We silently stand on the sidewalk for a couple awkward moments while I weigh my options. If I don't grant him time to get everything out in the open, he will continue to pursue me tomorrow and every day thereafter. Plus, I need to know where everything stands with his agent and *her*. And where we stand. But where we stand will depend on what he tells me.

I would like to believe I am capable of forgiving him for the lies. Because deep down, he didn't do it with the intention of hurting me. He simply thought it was something he could resolve without issue.

Only time will tell.

"Yes. Let's find somewhere to get lunch. Then you can tell me whatever it is you need to. But I make no promises about how I'll feel afterward."

He nods. "I accept that. If I were you, I'd feel the same."

Gavin and I walk to my car and I stow my cameras. A few minutes later, we stroll into the Cider Press Cafe and get seated near the window. I peek at him over my menu, waiting to see his expression as he reads the food options. As soon as his gray irises thin and pupils dilate, I laugh. At least eating here will lighten the mood as we discuss some heavy stuff. Because right now, I need a good laugh more than anything.

Eleven years ago

I stand in a sea of suffocating black polyester. Bodies bump against me every five seconds, and the lack of personal space pisses me off. Who the hell organized this damn function? Whoever the fucker is, they should be fired. Because this is nothing short of chaos.

After a few minutes, we are all corralled through a doorway and led out to a spread of plastic folding chairs facing a stage. On the stage is a podium, a table, and several more folding chairs. The principal and other school staff sit on the stage chairs, their robes puffy and sashes colorful. A person stands in the aisle along the student seating, directing us to which row we're to sit in. Not like it matters, we all have our names written on a card that we hand to someone to read.

Once we are all seated, various teachers stand at the podium and share positive words for the future. I choose to ignore their words. The only reason I agreed to do this whole ceremony bullshit is the end result I hope to receive. A trip home to Florida.

The ceremony passes with nothing monumental occurring. When it ends, I walk into a room where we get our actual diploma. The second it is in my hands, elation courses through me. This small rectangle of paper is my ticket back to Cora. My ticket home.

Although we haven't spoken in close to two years, I hope she will forgive me. When I stopped answering her letters, calls and texts, my intention was to do what was best for her, since I had no way to see her. To let her go.

But after that letter and those drawings she sent me, I am nervous as hell about how she will react to seeing me again. I went about things a shitty way, but what else was I supposed to do? We were in a fucked-up situation and I thought what I was doing would mend it all somehow.

But I was wrong. Dead wrong.

I walk out of the back and go in search of my parents. They stand outside, waiting for me with giant smiles plastered on their faces. After a handful of photos are taken, we head to the car and drive to a restaurant for my graduation dinner. In the car, they reminisce over the ceremony and how nice it was. I stare out the window and pray it won't be much longer before I don't see this skyline again.

Once we order food and my parents express their unwavering excitement, I mentally prepare to ask the question I have been waiting to ask for the past two years. Asking is going to burst the joy bubble they are trapped in, but I don't care. My bubble hasn't held joy since I was forced to leave Florida and step foot in this state.

"Mom? Dad? Can we talk about me moving back to Florida?" Straight forward and to the point. No need to beat around the bush. A man on a mission.

Mom tips her head to the side as a frown takes residence

on her lips. Dad doesn't move, his expression stoic. Their lack of communication says more than any words ever will. The silence tells me the trip I have longed to make won't be happening. But I refuse to believe it until I hear the actual words. Until they tell me I cannot go.

"Gavin—" Mom starts, but pauses to look at Dad for silent support "—I would love nothing more than for you to be where you want to be. But things have been really tight for us financially. And right now, we just don't have the money to fly you to Florida."

I fucking knew this would happen. Knew it. As soon as we got here, I should have gone to every store and restaurant and applied for a job. Bagboy, stocker, cashier, busboy. Anything. If I had, maybe I would have more than enough money by now to leave. But I was so wrapped up in throwing a pity party for myself, I didn't do shit.

Fuck my life.

"So there's nothing we can do? Didn't you have some college fund for me? If so, cash it in. I have zero plans to go to college, especially here."

"Son, I wish it were that simple," Dad chimes in. "We did have a college fund for you, but we had to cash it in shortly after we moved here. Things have been a little tougher than we suspected. I'm sorry."

You have got to be fucking kidding me. Not only can I not go back to Florida, but college isn't even an option. I may not have wanted to attend college, but they banked on my not mentioning it. Score one for the parentals. Zero for the child. Fucking bullshit.

"Wow. I don't know how to respond to any of this. You both knew my plans after graduation. How could you not say anything to me? You could've suggested I go out and get a job. If only for three or four months. At least I'd have money to fly home."

"This is home, Gavin," Mom says.

"This has never been home, Mom. You know it just as much as I do," I snap.

"Don't speak that way to your mother," Dad states, his voice sharp and stern. "We have had to make tough decisions for our family and I wouldn't change a single one. You may not have liked our choices. You may not like your life here. But you *will* respect us."

Wow. Just wow. So does respect only go one way? The parents *deserve* it, but their children don't? What sort of asinine bullshit is that? Yes, I was underage when we moved and didn't have a say in the matter. I accept it. But to purposely hide this... I am done.

"Sorry, Mom. Sorry, Dad," I seethe. "I respect you. This just fucking sucks! And I can't help but wonder why neither of you said a damn word to me sooner. Oh, I know," I say, holding up a finger and firmly pressing my lips together. "Because you knew this would be my reaction, that's why. Fucking bullshit."

"Watch your mouth, Gavin," Dad snaps.

I shake my head. "It's a little late for that, Dad. You forget, I'm an adult. Like you never swore when you were younger."

Mom and Dad go silent on the opposite side of the table, shutting down the conversation. Our server delivers the food a minute later, but I don't eat a bite. Instead, I open up the photos on my phone and scroll through the folder marked "C+G." With each swipe, my throat swells and the back of my eyes sting.

Fuck.

There is one singular thing I have wanted for the last two

years. One thing that provided purpose and gave me hope. To go home to Cora. To see her beautiful face cupped between my hands again. Listen to her laughter as I tickle her in that spot under her ribs only I know about. Wrap my arms around her waist and draw her close to my body as we lay on the couch and watch *Lord of the Rings* for the hundredth time.

But now it seems that won't be happening. Not unless I figure out how to get there on my own. And it looks as though that is my only option. But I will make it happen.

My fourth job interview ends like the previous three. With a *"we'll get back to you soon."* Which equals we have no intention of hiring you. Why is it so fucking hard to get a job? Working retail isn't rocket science.

I walk out of the preppy clothing store with my head hung low. *Where the hell will I get a job?* At this point, I am not above selling shit on the streets to get the money I need. Whatever it takes to get me back to Cora. And although I haven't spoken with her in far too long, in my mind's eye, I picture her face lighting up the moment we reconnect. As if we scoured the earth to find each other and succeeded.

There is one more interview on my list today. One more opportunity. And I hope like hell it won't end like the last four. This interview is a long shot, but I have to try. At this point, what do I have to lose?

Two hours later, I walk through the front door of Elite Models. My stomach twists in a knot and a bead of sweat rolls down the back of my neck. When I approach the reception desk, a woman ten years my senior gawks at me head to toe.

Her perusal isn't distasteful, but makes me want to curl inward.

"Can I help you?"

I step closer to the counter. "Yes. I have an interview with Sharon and Gus."

The woman peels her eyes away from me and scans her computer screen. A few scrolls and clicks later, she locates whatever she had been looking for and smiles. Her fingers tap the keyboard before she picks up the phone and dials.

"Your next candidate is here," she says. Her eyes pop back to my body and visually rip away my clothes. The act is a total violation and I wonder if this is what girls feel like when men ogle them in public. If so, it is awful and makes me want to cover myself with my arms.

She sets the handset back down, but keeps her eyes trained on me. I want to look away, escape the unease of her gaze, but choose not to. Because who knows how she will visually obsess over me when I turn away.

God, this is awkward.

A set of smoky glass doors open and a man walks out. He could be Dad's age, maybe older, but is layered in makeup and trendy clothes that shave years off his appearance. His hair is styled like a magazine ad—not a single strand out of place. For a moment, inferiority swamps me. *I can't do this.* But I have to do this. Every other option has been tossed away.

"Gavin Hunt?" the trendy man asks and I nod. "Hello, Gavin. Gus." He extends a hand and I shake it. "It's nice to meet you. If you'll follow me, we'll get started."

I follow him through the smoky doors. With each step, I ask myself if doing this is the right thing. If getting sucked into the limelight is how I get back to Cora. The hall we walk down is littered with countless photos. Women, men, people my age, people my parents' age. The images range from luxurious to hobo and everything in between. Each face is beautifully sculpted and emotionally connecting with the onlooker.

How the hell do they do that? How the hell would *I* do that?

There is no way I can do this.

Two hours later, I shake Sharon and Gus's hands. They don't throw me the infamous line I have heard at every other interview. Instead, they tell me what time to return on Monday. Relief courses through my veins.

Finally, an opportunity.

Not only did I land a job. I landed the opportunity of a lifetime. Modeling will not only flood my pockets, it will have me back in Cora's arms sooner than expected. Today ends on a high note and I wish I could share the news with the one person who matters.

Soon. After I get a couple photo shoots under my belt, I will call Cora and let her know the good news. That I will return home.

~

Why is this shit so goddamn difficult?

Every photo I have studied makes modeling seem effortless. Smiles and smirks and deadpan expressions. All in my repertoire. Stand in front of the camera, plaster your face with whatever emotion the photographer seeks and pose. Boom. Photo acquired.

Wrong.

After several failed attempts to appear smoldering, I am asked to put my shirt back on and report to Karen on the third floor. What the fuck is smoldering anyway? If I didn't fear the repercussions of having my phone out, I would search the term online.

Instead, now I sit in a room with five other people. Our chairs in a small circle facing each other. Feels like I am at a group therapy session. My knee bounces and I gnaw on my thumbnail.

A fifty-something woman glides into the room. Yes, glides. For a moment, I wonder if she wears special shoes under her floor-length, flowy dress. She owns the room in one breath. Everyone in the circle equally mesmerized by her appearance. Her finesse. Her ability to instantly garner everyone's attention.

"Good afternoon. I'm Karen, your modeling coach."

Modeling coach? Damnit. Obviously, my modeling skills were zero on a scale of a million. Because this sounds like school. And school hasn't been something I excelled in since moving.

The girl beside me leans in close. "Is it just me? Does this lady make you feel as inadequate as she does me?"

I lean an inch away and glance at her a moment. "Uh, I guess." I shrug. Inadequate wasn't quite the word I would choose. Maybe intimidated.

The girl smiles big at me. Her smile makes me more uncomfortable than Karen's entrance and presence. Not able to pinpoint my discomfort, I opt for niceties and extend my hand to her.

"Hi, I'm Gavin."

She stares at my hand a moment, a few emotions flit across her face but don't linger. Then she takes my hand and shakes it. "Layla." Her eyes ping to mine and she keeps our hands connected. I want to yank it back. Her touch scalds my skin. Not in the way Cora's touch heats every molecule inside me. Rather, Layla's skin on mine is invasive. Parasitic. Wrong.

When she doesn't remove her hand from mine after an uncomfortable five breaths, I slip mine away. The second she looks away from me, I wipe my hand on my jeans. Something about this girl makes me uneasy. The only person I read easily was Cora. So, it confounds me to not figure out why this girl makes me uneasy.

Maybe she is just as upset about being in this class as I am. Maybe she is only trying to be friendly.

I lean back in my chair and listen to Karen prattle on about why we are all here. Honestly, if this class makes me better at modeling, I am all for it. It gets me one more step closer to Cora. The main reason I'm doing this in the first place.

For her. For us. And our future.

Hours later, the class ends. All of us numb from the lessons on facial expressions and how to achieve them. According to Karen, we will be seeing her five days a week for the foreseeable future. Once she determines we are worthy of "graduating," she will pass such information to the appropriate people.

In other words, it may be weeks or months before I model. Weeks or months before I take a decent photo. Weeks or months before I earn a penny.

On the upside, the modeling agency pays for the classes. Only because we are "assets." Calling me an asset is objectifying, but I suck it up. Modeling is just temporary. A stepping stone to get me where I need to be.

As I leave for the day, Layla stops me. "Hey, Gavin. You

want to grab something to eat? I could eat a cow after today." She laughs and it sounds forced. Awkward. Exaggerated.

All I want is to go home and crash. But it would be nice to know someone else in this boat. Someone I can talk to when I have a rough day. A friend. "Yeah, sure."

The moment I agree, a rock plummets in my gut. It sinks and settles deep. Nausea threatens and I shove it down. Layla is a nice person—at least that is what I continually tell myself. Our relationship will only consist of friendship. Nothing more.

No one will ever take Cora's place. No one.

Present

The server walks away and I wonder what the hell I just ordered. Some mock version of pulled "pork." Except this place serves no meat. Cora assures me it was a good choice, but I will be the judge.

Cora picks up her water and sips it while staring out the window. Her fingers twist and roll the paper straw while her eyes narrow slightly then go back to their normal shape. Occasionally, she bites the inside of her cheek. Beneath the table, her leg bounces and ghosts against mine every other breath.

Does she feel it each time her skin grazes mine? She is so lost in her thoughts, I doubt it. But I do. Every. Single. Time.

"Cora."

Her eyes dart from the window to mine as she snaps out of her fog. "Huh?"

"Why are you so nervous?"

She rolls her eyes and it is fucking adorable. "Don't be silly, Gavin. I'm not nervous." Her leg bounces faster.

I tilt my head and study her a minute. "You know you can't fool me. So why try?"

Cora huffs and sets her water down. A second later, she tucks her hands under her thighs. We sit in silence a moment, staring at each other. Holding her gaze has never been uncomfortable, whether for five seconds or five minutes.

And then I remember the reason why we are sitting together right now. The reason she's giving me a chance. Because she is waiting to hear my truth. A truth I swore to tell her. That I plan to tell her. I only hope she listens. Truly listens and digests what I say.

"I'm sorry," I say. An apology is the best place to start. Unfortunately, I have far too much to apologize for.

Her leg finally stops bouncing. "Sorry? And what exactly are you sorry for?" Her question slaps me in the face. A slap I more than deserve. A slap I will take like a man.

I reach under the table and rest a hand on her knee. The simple and innocent touch soothes my nervousness and helps me focus. "Where do I begin?" I pause a moment to gather my thoughts. She needs to know everything, but I don't want to bounce from one end to the other and back again.

My question was meant to be rhetorical, but she answers. "How about the beginning. I find that to always be the best place."

Cora's snappy demeanor has me on the cusp of smiling. On the verge of teasing and light sarcasm. But the last thing I need is to piss her off more, so I resist the urge and trudge forward.

"I'm sorry I stopped answering your calls and texts. Sorry I didn't return a single one of them. My parents had thrown every hope I had of getting back to you out the window. So, I thought I was doing the right thing by letting you go. By giving you a chance to move on without me. To have a life and smile and maybe find love again."

A glutton for punishment, I refuse to look away from her. Refuse to not see every emotion she feels as my words set in. As I share the reason why I abandoned her years ago. Even as her eyes brim red and well in the corners. Even as her brow furrows and lips purse. She breaks eye contact and shifts her gaze to the street, not looking at anything specific. She just has difficulty looking at me. A tear rolls down her cheek and she swipes it away with the back of her hand. Her chin quivers as she clamps her lips between her teeth.

I walked into this knowing sour memories would be rehashed. That me spilling my truth, telling her where my head was at, would be hard to hear. But fuck, it hurts to watch her break down in front of me. To see her fighting off emotions as we sit in public and talk about the most painful parts of our past.

After a minute, I give her knee a squeeze. Her soft green bloodshot eyes come back to mine and the emotion in them is raw. It claws at my heart and shreds it in a million pieces. As painful as this is, I did this to her. And I deserve every gut-wrenching second of the pain I feel. Her pain.

"Why didn't you tell me?" she croaks out. "Why didn't you call or text or write and tell me what was happening? We shared everything with each other. Everything." She shakes her head. "But you up and decided to make this monumental decision without me." She sucks in a breath and speaks on the exhale. "Gavin, I shut down. Detached from the world and crawled into a hole. All I wanted was to talk with you. My best friend. My everything. And you shut me out."

A fist wraps around my heart and constricts the organ like a squeaky toy. Over and over and over.

How could I have been such a dick? How could I have been so selfish? Everything I did was in the hopes of Cora not being in pain. At least that's what I kept telling myself. I thought letting her go was the best option. What other option was there? I had no way to get to her, and my parents did nothing to help. So, in my eyes, letting her live life without restriction seemed like the better option. I didn't want her to feel obligated—to me or the possibility of me.

Obviously, I am a fucking idiot.

"No matter what I say, it'll never make up for what I did. But I'd like to try now. Try to fix what I've done. Will you let me try? Please."

I reach for my wallet and she follows my every move. Behind my license, I retrieve a folded piece of yellowing paper with tattered edges. After a deep breath, I set it on the table and slide it to her.

Cora's red-rimmed eyes study my face. Her eyes dart between mine. Her lips press in a firm line and wobble side to side. And her chin continues to tremor as she reaches for the paper. Fixing this is not enough. I need to make it up to her every day of forever. And I will. I swear I will.

She sniffles and nods. "You know I will. But you have to tell me everything. No more secrets." She holds up the paper. "What's this?"

Before I answer, the server delivers our food to the table and cuts off our conversation. Cora tucks the paper in her pocket and I know she will read it when she is alone. Read the last letter she sent me, smudged with her tears and mine.

I stare down at the basket. I have no clue what I am about to eat, but I pick it up and bite down. An odd texture licks my tongue, but tastes weirdly like pulled pork. I shrug and continue eating while Cora giggles across from me. At least my eating brings a smile to her face. A smile is a smile, and I will call it a step in the right direction.

A few minutes pass before I wipe my hands clean and lean back in my chair. "I sold my house in California. Currently, I'm sleeping on Micah's couch until I find my own place."

Cora sits quietly across from me. Questions flit over her face, but she doesn't ask a single one. Her mouth opens and closes. This happens a few times before she finally speaks. "Oh. What about your mom?"

I love how she worries about my mom, now that I moved away. "She'll be okay. I think she was surprised it took me so long to move back. We argued so much the first two years out there. She expected me to run away and hitchhike back to Florida." The idea was given serious merit, but was ignored after the reality of how far I *wouldn't* get settled.

Cora nods and I continue. "When I got back to California, I sat down with Mom and discussed my plan to move back. Told her about the photo shoot with you. Also told her my time out west should have ended years ago. She was more than understanding and offered to help me in any way possible."

"I miss your mom," Cora says.

I lean forward and lay my hand on her knee under the table again. "She misses you, too. I wouldn't be surprised if she visits soon, now that I've moved away. She'll probably wait until I have a place." I sip my water, allowing a few breaths to pass before I speak again. "Alyson and Layla have been dealt with also."

I don't miss the way Cora flinches when I say Layla's name. The way her lips curl for a split second. But she collects herself and responds as if she had no reaction. "Uh, I'm not sure what to say."

"There's nothing to say. I'm only sorry you were on the receiving end of their jealousy. The moment I got back to California, I reviewed my contracts and sought out a new agent. After I finished my final shoot with Layla, I fired Alyson and told Layla I never wanted to see or hear from her again. It went about as smooth as expected."

"Gavin, you didn't have to do that. Not for me."

Although her words tell me I didn't need to make such a drastic change in my life, I don't miss the way her body sags in relief. The small shift in her demeanor speaks a thousand words her lips won't. Ease slips into her expression and I know what I did was the first step in the right direction.

"Yes, I did. But not just for you, I did it for myself also. Too many nights have passed since I set out to come back to you. When I started modeling, it was to earn as much money as possible so I could fly back to Florida. To you. I hadn't spoken to you in over a year, but not a day went by where my goal changed. Being with you has always been my endgame."

She scoots back in her seat and her knee shifts out of my reach. Her elbows rest on the table as she lays her forearms toward me. Palms up, her hands rest as an open invitation for mine. As eager as I am to lay my hands on hers, to feel her warmth, to connect with her intimately, I don't rush this. I slowly withdraw my hands from under the table and place them in hers. Beneath my palms, her fingers trace steady lines along my skin.

I close my eyes and surrender to my senses. How her soft skin faintly brushes my palms as she trails her fingertips there. Subtle hints of her frankincense and gardenia scent wisp in the air and flutter in my nose. A small hitch in her breathing as she continues to reconnect a bond once severed. The shiver down my spine and fast-growing bloom of heat in my chest as it all swirls together.

God, I want to kiss her. More than anything.

When my eyes reopen, Cora sits across from me slack-jawed. So fucking beautiful.

No matter how much time has passed, she is still the only woman I see. The only woman I want beside me. Today and every day that follows. Cora is it for me. And I assume the same holds true for her. Because she has never moved on from us either. Not fully.

"Gavin, how did *she* go from being your friend to your fiancée?" I don't miss the way Cora says *she* with distaste on her tongue. But I don't blame her. No doubt I would feel equally as disgusted if the situation were reversed.

"Layla wasn't getting as many callbacks or opportunities for shoots. My career, on the other hand, was booming. Alyson sat down with the two of us and threw out the idea of us "being engaged." Of course, it would be strictly for publicity reasons, but I still wasn't keen. Alyson said we would cut it short after Layla was seen enough times with me. But every time I brought it up, Alyson told me to wait another month. That some brand was on the fence of signing Layla. And I obviously bought the lie every time. From the get-go, something didn't sit right with me when it came to Layla, but I ignored it. I'll never be so naïve again."

I curl my fingers into hers and stare at our hands a moment. The reality of my naïveté is a punch to the gut. How much time was stolen from me because of it? Countless months and years. All because I had tunnel vision—Cora standing in the light at the end. Alyson and Layla—both who knew about the woman in Florida, but not who she was—took advantage of me. Of my eagerness to return to her. They played me. And I had been the damn fool falling for every line and promise.

"After my last shoot, I had an interview scheduled with The Heart of Hollywood. Millions of eyes would see or hear my interview. I blasted the truth to everyone. About Alyson and Layla. How my engagement was a ruse to garner attention for Layla and her lackluster modeling career. And then I told millions of people about you. About us. How I ran into the love of my life and instantly decided I was moving home."

Across from me, Cora gasps. For a completely different reason, her eyes pool, soften. Her lips tremble. And I can't take it anymore. No longer able to stay on the opposite side of the table, I rise and slide into the seat beside her. She watches my every move as she bites her lower lip.

"Gavin," she whispers.

I frame her face with my hands and brush away a fallen tear. Leaning into her, my lips a breath from hers, I tell Cora the words only meant for her.

"I love you. Only you. Always."

And as badly as I want to kiss her, I resist the urge. With all the shit I have put Cora through, I won't fuck this up. I want her to want to kiss me. Want her to initiate. Need her to be the one who moves us forward. No matter what, my heart is hers. Always has been. Always will be. But I crushed her heart all those years ago. And I will wait however long it takes for her to be ready for us. For me.

Cora wraps her hands around my forearms and grips them like it's her last breath. Her gaze unwavering as her watery green eyes stare up at me. "I love you, too." She pinches her eyes shut and wetness slips between her lashes to my fingertips. I wipe them away, then lift my lips to her lids and kiss them each with reverence.

"I know it will take time, but I vow to make us whole again. Whatever I need to do to fix us, I will. Without you, nothing else matters."

She attempts to nod, but my hands keep her face hostage. We both laugh a moment, and I am certain we look like lunatics. But as long as Cora is with me, I don't give a damn what people think of me. With her by my side, I can be anyone.

After I drop my hands, I switch to a more serious tone. "Go out with me. On a date. Please?"

Cora reaches up and cups my cheeks, scratching my jawline before her hands fall to my chest and rest over my heart. "What if we go out with everyone? Obviously, you know Micah and Shelly, but I would love for you to get to know Jonas and Erin better. They've been there for me when I needed them. They're family. And I really want you to be comfortable with them."

Hanging out with everyone else isn't exactly what I had in mind for a date with Cora, but I will take every moment she grants me. If this is important to her—Jonas and I being friendly—I will set aside my jealousy. Jealousy over the fact that this guy has spent more years with her than I have. Although their relationship is strictly platonic, I am not blind to the way he looks at her. Maybe time with him is the perfect idea. For both of us.

"Okay, let's go out with everyone. When? Where?"

She claps and fidgets in her seat. "Yay! I'll talk to Shelly and we'll figure everything out. Then you'll be the next to know."

Her happiness is infectious. It lures me in and holds me captive. And I stay willingly, a prisoner of her heart. Whatever it takes to make my girl happy, I plan to do it. Because seeing her smile brightens the darkest skies.

After I pay the bill, we walk back to her car hand in hand. Our stride is leisure. Our voices absent. And it is absolute perfection. When we reach her car, I spin her around and wrap my arms around her. I rest my chin on the crown of her head and gently rock side to side, shutting my eyes and relishing the weight of her body pressed to mine. Her arms snake around my back and squeeze me tight. I don't want to let her go. Not now. Not ever.

I kiss her hair, release my hold on her and run my hands down her biceps. "Call me when you get everything sorted out with Shelly."

She tips her head back and meets my sunglass-covered eyes. "I will. Promise."

I step back and play with a strand of her hair. "I love you. See you soon."

God, I don't want to walk away, but know I need to. Cora needs to have control over what happens with us. What happens next. Unbeknownst to her, I have put my life and the future of us in her hands. My fitful heart and restless soul sit nestled inside her. This time around, she makes all the decisions and I make none.

"I love you, too."

As soon as she says the words, I pivot and walk away. Her eyes singe me as I amble down the sidewalk, away from her and into the unknown. But there is no other place I would rather be.

seventeen

CORA

It feels as if I am in grade school again as I stand outside the entrance of Dave and Busters. Bright orange and yellow paint coat the brick exterior. A large, angular metal awning hangs over the entrance. The automatic doors whoosh open then glide shut. The action mesmerizes me briefly until Shelly comes up behind me, bouncing like an adolescent.

What is it about an arcade that makes you feel twenty years younger? Who knows, but whatever it is, I love it.

Shelly unlocks her phone and scrolls through her text history. A moment later, she assures me everyone should be here in the next ten minutes.

We loiter near the entrance, steering clear of patrons coming or going, and get lost in our cell phones. Shelly zones out in social media land while I check my email. A few minutes later, Erin and Jonas walk up.

We are catching up when I spot Micah and Gavin getting out of an all-black Range Rover. Black paint, pitch-black tint, blacked-out logos. All. Black. Although I only see Micah on occasion, I know this car isn't his. This must be Gavin's car.

And the idea of him owning an all-black custom vehicle has me smiling like an idiot.

When they approach us, Micah rolls his eyes at me and I laugh. Micah and I will never share best friend status, but we will always be family. Not only because of my friendship with Shelly, but also because of Gavin. Micah will just have to learn to live with me being around. He is the grumpy big brother I never had and I am the annoying little sister he wished he didn't have.

Gavin steps up and encircles me with his arms, kissing the top of my head. A charm of hummingbirds takes flight in my chest, wings fluttering rapidly and stealing my breath. The more Gavin inserts himself back into my life, the less I want to resist him. Part of me recalls the last time we were in this place—inseparable— and what life was like when he left. That part of me keeps the barrier I have built around my heart upright. Solid. Impenetrable.

Or so I keep telling myself.

When I got home from St. Pete and emptied my pockets, the worn paper mocked me for hours. Until I unfolded the creased edges and saw what he gave me. What he had stashed in his wallet. *My letter*. The last letter I wrote him. On our anniversary, six months after he left.

Seeing that letter again stirred up more than a decade's worth of emotions. But the fact he kept it, tucked it in his wallet, said more than words ever would.

He promises to repair every cut and scrape and rift between us. And I believe him. But I need evidence. And until I see the proof with my own eyes, I still can't expose myself fully. Not yet. Not until I have absolute reassurance he will stay.

After we load up our gaming cards and purchase drinks,

we wander through the arcade and scope out all the games. Micah heads over to the virtual reality area while Shelly, Erin, and Jonas go toward the classic arcade games. As soon as Shelly decided we were coming here, my first thought was Skee-Ball. Not only was it my favorite arcade game to play. It also happens to be Gavin's favorite.

"Skee-Ball?" Gavin asks. He cocks a brow up in challenge.

"As if you need to ask."

One of our many rendezvous years ago was to a local arcade. We would play Skee-Ball for hours. Not for tickets, but for bragging rights. Gavin won more times than I did. But when I did win, I rubbed it in his face for weeks. Whatever tickets we won, we handed over to children nearby.

Tonight would be no different. Minus the tickets.

I have been here with Shelly and Jonas several times over the years. And I have broken some high score records. Not that I plan to give this statistical information to Gavin. But my Skee-Ball game is strong. So strong, I am willing to bet money he hasn't played since the last time we played together and can add another Skee-Ball trophy to the shelf. Which works great for me.

We step up to the lanes and swipe our cards. I glance over at him and feel a little cocky. "You ready to get your ass handed to you?"

He throws his head back and laughs, his entire frame shaking. "Who's handing it to me? You?"

"Not sure how good your game is, but I've been practicing." I pop an eyebrow and give a snide smile.

"Have you now?" The balls roll down the chute and clunk together. "What makes you think I haven't been practicing?"

I pick up a ball and shrug. "Call it a hunch." Then I face

the lane, swing my arm back and release the wooden ball. It rolls up the lane with perfect precision and flies into the 100-point hole. With pride lighting up my face, I face Gavin again and shrug again. "Whatcha got, Hunt?"

"Oh, it's on, baby." Gavin smirks and lines up to shoot the ball. But I zone out. Molecule by molecule, my body comes alive. Warmth blossoms in my chest, spreading its petals open like the roses Gavin sent me. I get lost in the intimacy of this moment. Of his term of endearment for me. In the banter and ease with which we slip into it like second nature. How being beside him feels right on so many levels.

As much as I want to ease into a life with Gavin, it won't happen. Because that is not how things have ever been between us.

From the first day we met, under our tree, we were destined for more. We slipped into friendship easier than anyone else. Our friendship morphing into best friends was inevitable. We loved spending time together and laughed without effort. Everyone said they knew we would start dating. It was only us who didn't see it happening. Not until that day at the beach over Thanksgiving break.

Our first kiss. The most amazing and memorable kiss of my life. The kiss that started it all.

From that moment forward, I never wanted to kiss another person in my life. My body sang for Gavin. Hummed with hunger and lust and love. No one else has lit my soul on fire like Gavin. And no one else ever will. When one person holds the key to your heart, no other key will ever unlock it. Gavin has always been my key.

Watching Gavin beside me, my heart swells like a hot air balloon—hot and combustible. All the old feelings I buried for thirteen years assault me in the middle of the arcade. Hit me like a hammer to the chest and leave me breathless. I want to yell and cry, cheer and sing, throw myself at him and crush him in my arms. He tosses another ball up the lane, oblivious to my never-ending stare down, and scores another forty points. He glances up at my score and notices it hasn't changed since my first roll.

Gavin rotates his head and drops his gaze to mine. "You okay, baby?" There it is again. The familiar endearment I love rolling off his tongue. And the flutters that come along with it.

Fuck. They're coming. The back of my eyes sting as I nod. I swallow down the expanding boulder in my throat and work to answer him. "Yeah, I'm good."

He sets his ball down and steps up to me, running his fingers through my loose strands. "What's wrong?" Bending his knees, he comes eye level with me. "Talk to me."

I swallow again and tip my head back, batting my lashes. *No crying, Cora. No more tears. Not even happy tears.*

"Just remembering us. This." I gesture to the lanes. "How things were before. How comfortable and easy it is to be with you."

He stands tall and peers down at me, his thumb dusting over my bottom lip. "We've always had this effortless connection. Do you know why that is, baby?"

I fear opening my mouth, fear speaking. Afraid my words will be unintelligible. Garbled. So, I swallow and shake my head.

Gavin presses his palm against my breastbone and locks his steely eyes on mine. "Because I'm here." Then he reaches out, takes my hand, and places it over his heart. Beneath my palm, his heart beats a vicious rhythm. "And you are here. Before we met, we held a piece of each other hostage. It wasn't until we found each other that those pieces reconnected. As if they'd known each other in another lifetime."

I will not fucking cry.

"Cora, you're it for me. No matter how hard I tried to forget about you, no matter what I did over the last thirteen years, you always danced in my dreams and called out to my heart. I may have ignored it for stupid reasons, but it was there nonetheless."

Goddamnit.

He is going to make me cry. He rests his cheek against mine as his lips hover near my ear. My chest rises and falls as I gasp for breath. I pinch my eyes shut. Swallow hard. Curl and uncurl my fingers.

"I love you, Cora. More than anything or anyone in this world. And fuck if I don't want to kiss you in the middle of this arcade, in front of all these people."

My breath comes faster, but I don't say a word. Will he kiss me? I want to kiss him, but still hesitate. Kissing Gavin again will end any chance I have at resistance. We need time. Time to relearn each other. Time to adjust to a newer version of us. A little more time.

Or am I being absurd?

We have spent so much time apart. Days and months and years disconnected. Broken. Hurt. Do I really want to waste more time? Do I really want to keep him at arm's length? No, I don't. And keeping us divided when he has done everything in his power to bring us back together is asinine.

I lean back from Gavin just enough to see his eyes. If I shift an inch to the side, we would kiss. His eyes lock on mine and read every thought passing through them. And I know he knows what I think. He doesn't flinch or veer from his position. A second later, his eyes close and he draws in a labored breath.

This is it. The moment we have been leading up to. The inevitable.

I line my lips up with his, leaving only a shadow between us. Just as I lean in, just as I'm about to give myself over to him, someone brushes my arm and I retreat.

"Hey, man. Sorry to interrupt. Can I talk with you a minute?"

I open my eyes and spot Jonas beside us. His gaze fixed on Gavin, who is staring at me. Gavin's eyes burn with familiar longing. Something I saw every time he looked at me years ago. Something primal and potent and only ours. It resonates in my marrow. Keeps the chambers of my heart beating. Jonas may be inches from us, but we only see each other. Only *feel* each other.

Gavin's eyes still connected with mine, he answers Jonas. "Sure, man. What's up?"

Jonas shifts foot to foot. "Maybe over there." Jonas points to a table ten feet from us.

"Yeah, no problem." Gavin kisses my forehead. "I'll be back in a minute, baby. Finish my game and yours."

I nod and watch as Gavin and Jonas walk over to the empty table and sit down. They sit so neither of them faces me, but I see both their profiles. Jonas starts talking and Gavin listens intently. Seeing as I can't read lips, staring at them will get me nowhere.

So, I go back to the game, tossing ball after ball up my lane and Gavin's. When his game ends, I finish the round on my lane. Occasionally, I peek over my shoulder at them. They don't shift in position. Neither of them appears to be angry or ready to throw down—which is a good sign. Two more rounds pass before Gavin walks back over to me. His expression neutral.

"Hey. What did Jonas want to talk to you about?" I ask.

He wraps his arms around me and squeezes me close. "I'll tell you in a little bit. Are you hungry?" He kisses my forehead then leans back to peer down at me.

I don't argue with him. If Gavin says he will tell me later, he will. "Yeah. Let's find everyone else and grab dinner."

Micah seems a bit perturbed when we disrupt his virtual reality simulation, but agrees to meet us at a table. A moment later, we locate Shelly and Erin playing Dance Dance Revolution—Jonas teasing their dance skills.

We all converge at a table and order drinks and food. Light chatter fills the space between us. The dynamic between Gavin and Jonas has shifted into something unfamiliar. They sit opposite one another, but don't look or speak to each other. I find it very peculiar. I want to ask Gavin what they talked about, but remind myself he will share with me later. So, I ask Shelly and Erin who is winning their DDR showdown.

I never got into DDR. Classic games have always been my thing. Pinball, Skee-Ball, Pac-Man. But I love Shelly and Erin's enthusiasm for DDR. So, like the amazing best friend that I am, I listen as they regale us with colorful accounts of their competitions. And to be honest, they are pretty hardcore. Intimidating. Kind of makes me glad I never got into it.

Micah and Gavin talk quietly beside me. Micah mentions Peyton and I stop listening. It isn't my place to interrupt two guys chatting about a girl. Especially one I don't know. Who knows how much Micah has told Gavin. But if Micah is bringing her up again, one thing is certain. Micah has a major interest in her. Hopefully Gavin can reassure him that it is okay to move on from his ex. She was a real piece of work and it sucks he still harbors feelings for her.

I peer at Jonas and note his eyes glued to me. How long has he been staring? I wiggle in my seat and Gavin places a hand on my thigh. Ease passes through him to me and I relax into his side.

Jonas mouths *you okay?* His eyes pinch at the corners and his lips form a tight line. I smile and nod at him. *Yeah. Perfect.* I mouth back as I rest a hand over Gavin's. Everything is exactly as it should be in this moment. How it should have been for years.

When we finish eating, Jonas, Shelly, and Erin leave. When hugs are exchanged, Jonas whispers in my ear. "Good to see you happy. It suits you."

"Thank you," I whisper back, hugging him a little harder.

Micah tells us he will be back after another game and then be ready to leave. After Micah walks off, I ask Gavin what he and Jonas talked about earlier.

"Jonas was quite forthcoming." Gavin takes my hand and weaves his fingers with mine. "He told me he's been in love with you for years. We spent most of the conversation getting to know more about each other. And now, I know he's a good guy. I also know he won't be more than your friend because he doesn't want to hurt or lose you." Gavin pauses a moment and chuckles. "He also told me if I ever hurt you again, he'd cut my dick off."

"Oh my god," I say, slapping a hand over my mouth.

"Yeah. At least I know he'll protect you if I'm unable to." Gavin lifts my hand to his lips and presses a few soft kisses to my knuckles. Warmth spreads up my limb, weaves its way through my chest and strikes my heart like lightning. "He also wished us luck. Said this, minus the last couple of weeks, is the happiest he's ever seen you. And that's all he wants."

I swear the guys in my life are out to make me cry. There will always be something I love about Jonas. My love for him is more familial, but love nonetheless. How the hell did I get so lucky? How did I end up with so many wonderful people in my life? Family and friends and people I don't want to live a day without.

"Well it sounds like you two had a great talk." And it sounds like they built a bridge and are trying to meet in the middle for me. I hope one day Gavin and Jonas will be good friends. After time passes, I picture them laughing over beers together.

When Micah finishes his game, we decide to leave. We wander through the parking lot and over to my car. Gavin hands his keys to Micah. "I'll be there in a minute." Micah nods and leaves us. We stare after him as he walks to the Range Rover masked in the shadows.

Once Micah slips into the SUV, Gavin takes a strand of my hair between his fingers and plays with it. "Go on a date with me, baby. Just the two of us."

Every muscle in my body screams at me to say yes. But the wall around my heart stands firmly in place and says we need a little more time before it is just the two of us.

Earlier, I almost annihilated that wall by kissing him, but life intervened. And that little disruption made me wonder if it was a sign I was moving forward too fast. Can't be sure. If Gavin loves me, he won't mind if I tell him to have a little more patience. After all, he had the patience of a saint while we were together.

"Don't hate me," I say as I squint. "Is it okay if we hang with everyone again tomorrow night?"

Please be good with this. Please, please, please.

He strokes my hair, grazes his thumb along my jawline, then kisses the tip of my nose. "If that's what you want, baby. As long as I get to spend time with you, I'm happy."

I sag into his touch. "Thank you."

He kisses the crown of my head then hugs me as if he never will again. "For you, anything. I'll see you tomorrow, baby. Drive safe. I love you."

"I love you, too. See you tomorrow."

Gavin breaks our hug and starts toward his car, fingers still in mine until distance separates us. As he gets in his car, I get in mine. He and Micah talk a moment until he puts the car in gear.

I idle in the parking lot a moment, waving to Gavin as he and Micah drive off. He hasn't mentioned it, but tomorrow is Gavin's birthday and I want to surprise him. I want to host a game night. Ask everyone to bring food and drinks and laughter. Maybe decorate the house and have a cake. Make it one of his best birthdays yet.

Gavin and I may have been apart more than a decade, but some dates will be forever engraved in my heart. Including the day Gavin was brought into the world. And Gavin is definitely worth celebrating.

Eight years ago

Today is the happiest and saddest day of my life.

November twenty-first.

Mine and Cora's anniversary. If we were still together, today would be our seventh anniversary. If it were a wedding anniversary, I would buy her something made of wool or copper. We would be corny like that, buying gifts according to outdated anniversary traditions. Finding unique ways to celebrate our time together.

But we haven't celebrated an anniversary together in over five years now. Not that I plan to celebrate this date as anything except ours. This day, until the day I die, will be ours.

Fuck.

I want to call her. Am desperate to hear her voice.

Would she still sound the same? Is she happy? Does she miss me like I fucking miss her? Some days, I don't have it in me to breathe, let alone exist in the world. Every time I talk with Micah, I ask vague questions about Shelly in the hopes he will give me a hint of something regarding Cora. But he gives nothing away. And it fucking sucks. He knows I won't come right out and ask, so he dances around my inadvertent questions.

Rather than hunt for a gift I will never give Cora, I opt for something else. Something permanent that will add a piece of her to me. A lifelong reminder—not as if I need one, but somehow this enhances our bond. With things booming in my career, I have gone back and forth for weeks about this. But it is my fucking body and I will do with it what I please.

I walk into the tattoo shop and walk up to the reception area. A young woman with fluorescent green hair peeks up from her magazine. She swivels the lollipop in her mouth from left to right a few times. "What can I do for you?" She pops the lollipop from her lips, licks them, then puts the lollipop back in her mouth. Don't know why, but it annoys the shit out of me.

"I have an appointment with Talon," I say.

She scans the screen before clicking the mouse. "I need a copy of your ID and for you to fill out this paper." She hands me a clipboard. While she makes a copy of my license, I read over, fill out, and sign the form. She hands me back my license. "He'll be with you in a minute. You can have a seat." She points to a leather couch off to the side and goes back to her magazine as if I never walked in.

"Thanks," I mumble.

A few minutes later, a burly man greets me and introduces himself as Talon. His arms are sleeved with a mishmash of tattoos. Muscles twice the size of mine. A bald head with full facial hair. And he towers over me by at least five inches, which is saying something considering I am six-two. Intimidating is definitely an adjective I would associate with this guy.

Talon leads me to a small cubicle with a black leather seat. He tugs a lever and flattens the table. "Have a seat, man. Here's the image you sent me." He slides a paper toward me. "This is what you want, right?"

"Yeah, between my shoulder blades," I reply.

Talon nods. "Is the size good? Or you want it bigger?"

I study the image a moment. Go big or go home, right? "Let's go a little bigger. Whatever you think will look best with the space."

He walks away and I stare around the booth. The short walls are littered with photos of other tattoos Talon has done. They range from intricate to minimal. Symbols and portraits and watercolor and quotes. Some with tons of color, others done with thin lines of black ink. Seeing all these photos—a portfolio of sorts—is reassurance this guy has done enough tattoos to not fuck mine up.

When he walks back into the booth, he shows me the new, larger version of the tattoo. "Look good?"

"Perfect. Thanks, man."

Talon directs me to take off my shirt, lay on the table, and find a comfortable position for my arms. He tells me how long he thinks the tattoo will take and that we will take occasional breaks, if needed. After everything is prepped and ready, he dips the tattoo gun in the ink and presses a peddle. When the buzz erupts next to me, I startle.

"You have any other tattoos, man?" Talon prompts.

"Nope. This is the first."

"Virgin skin," he says with a wicked gleam in his eye and wide grin on his lips. "My favorite."

The buzz cracks again and a sting pricks my skin. I close

my eyes and take a deep breath. Sweat breaks out across my skin as adrenaline floods my veins. As he moves the needle over my skin, a blend of pain and thrill courses through me. Each line of ink he impregnates my skin with, I grow one step closer to Cora. She is the only reason I would mar my skin with something so permanent.

An hour into the tattoo, Talon asks me why I am getting a *Lord of the Rings* tattoo.

Not many people in California know Cora's and my history. I have mentioned things about her to Alyson and Layla, but never her name and never too much detail. Cora is my heart. Something I have no intention on spreading like free samples. Even though we have been apart for years, I hug her essence close to my chest and protect it with every breath.

"My soul mate." It's all I say.

But that isn't enough for Talon. He wants more. "You're getting a tattoo for a girl? Shouldn't that be hearts or butterflies? Maybe initials or a date?"

He teases me, knowing I will tell him more. And he is right. "Nah, she's not a hearts and butterflies kind of girl. She is, on the other hand, addicted to *Lord of the Rings*. So, this is fitting and perfect."

Talon teases me further. "Aren't you a sweetheart. Does she have a tattoo for you?"

His question is innocent, but it gets under my skin and stabs at the throbbing organ beneath my sternum. "No, she hasn't gotten any ink yet." At least not that I am aware of. I haven't seen her in years, but I couldn't imagine her getting a tattoo without purpose. Talon doesn't need such information, though.

A few hours pass before the tattoo gun goes silent. He sprays something on a paper towel and swipes it over my newly tattooed skin. Although my skin is slightly numb, the wiping stings. A minute later, he helps me up and hands me a hand mirror. "Use that to check it out on the wall mirror." He points to a floor-length mirror opposite his booth.

I walk over and turn my back to the wall mirror and hold up the one in my hand. Twisting to see from different angles, I glance over the black ink on my back. Absolutely perfect.

"What's it say?" Talon asks as I stare at the mirror. "Elvish, right?"

"Yeah. Above the stars it says *love*. At the roots, it says *forever*. *Lord of the Rings* fan?"

"Only seen them once, but remembered the tree. So, I assumed the writing. Your girl will love it, man. The nipple piercings, too."

"Thanks."

One day, I hope she gets to see it.

Present

The stereo blares in the living room. Queen's "Another One Bites The Dust" at a volume way too loud for this early in the morning.

Micah comes up and taps my shoulder. "Get up, brother. Happy motherfucking birthday."

You have got to be fucking kidding me. I groan, roll to face the back of the couch, and smother myself with the pillow over my face. "Go away. It's too fucking early for this bullshit."

"Nope." He yanks the pillow from my hands. "I haven't celebrated a damn birthday with you in years. We're rectifying that right now. Up you go." He tugs the blanket off me and walks away, whistling like a cocky bastard.

"Asshole," I grumble as I sit up. "What time is it?"

Micah walks back into the room, pillow and blanket gone, and tosses a shirt at me. "Almost ten. For us normal folks, early was three hours ago. Uppity up." He steps up beside the couch and waves his hands as if to push me off.

"Since when do you get up early. Don't you mainly work at night? Like late?"

He doesn't respond.

After a minute, I get up and stumble to the bathroom. I crank the shower to scalding and step in. The water slowly washes the sleep off me, and soon I step out.

Once dressed, Micah suggests we go out for breakfast. I agree, but tell him he has to go with me to an appointment after. He directs us to a mom-and-pop restaurant where the line for a table is ten deep. After we get seated, we order breakfast and talk about everyone hanging out later tonight. He tells me he didn't hang around everyone else while I was in California because it felt weird. Supposedly, he has no idea what tonight entails, but I believe he knows more than he lets on.

Micah changes the topic and asks why Jonas pulled me aside last night. Says he checked on us from his spot in the arcade a few times. I smile and relay the conversation. Good to know Micah always has my back, even when I don't know it.

"That's pretty ballsy of him," Micah states. "No lie, he's spent a lot of time with Cora. I'm shocked they've only remained friends all this time."

"Yeah, we touched on that when he admitted he was in love with her."

"And what did he say?"

I chuckle. "He said he's actually tried a couple of times to push for more, but she stopped him. The only time she didn't was when I left, and she was pissed and drunk. She leaned in to kiss him and he cut her off. Told her he didn't want to be a backup option. She told him how sad she was and that she just wanted to feel something again."

When Jonas told me that last tidbit, I cringed. I did that to her. Made her so desperate for affection she was willing to fall into the arms of someone she didn't love. Not romantically, anyway. Hearing the truth was a hundred punches to the gut. I never want her heart to feel such depravity again. Never want her to be desperate for love because she feels she has none.

"Dude, that's some crazy shit. All in all, he's a good guy. He's never done anything horrible to Cora, Shelly, or Erin. Their relationship is odd, but they all have a good time together. I hate to say it, but he helped her smile again."

"Fuck."

"Don't beat yourself up over it. For years, there was nothing you could do about it. And you can't change the past. It's done. So now, you just move forward. She loves you, bro. Always has, always will. He just kept her afloat while you were gone. Be thankful for that. Some of the shit Shelly told me painted a pretty ugly picture. She didn't leave her house for months after you left. Almost flunked school. A lot of people were worried about her."

Although Cora and I stopped talking after a couple months, she was always front and center in my mind. The times we did talk after I moved to California, she never portrayed what Micah tells me now. She masked her pain, and she did it well. Either that or I relieved it when we talked. I can only imagine how it all went to shit when I stopped talking with her altogether. Every time I hear a new snippet about our time apart, the fault line in my heart opens wider.

But I deserve the pain. Deserve to let it tear me apart inside. Every horrible memory. All the sleepless nights and days of depression. Because her pain is my pain. And I pledge to never let her experience such pain again.

Micah and I eat breakfast in silence. Once we finish, we

pay and head to my appointment. I crank the radio while we drive, silencing any further conversation. I need to clear my head and music is my favorite form of therapy.

When we pull into the parking lot, Micah laughs loud enough I hear him over the music. After I cut the engine, Micah asks, "So what irreversible decision are you making today?"

"Shut the fuck up." I get out of the car and walk into the tattoo shop, Micah following in my wake.

I go through the normal spiel with the lady at the front counter, filling out the form and providing identification, then sit and wait to be called back. She twirls her pink hair and pops her bubblegum loudly.

Ten minutes later, I sit in a chair with my shirt off. The artist prints the tattoo and Micah is staring at me with a gleam in his eyes.

"Speak your mind," I tell him.

"You're really going to do this?" Micah asks.

"Isn't it rather obvious I'm doing this?"

"You can still back out."

"Backing out is not an option." I shake my head at him.

"But this is different than the other one, bro. And it doesn't get more permanent."

I cock my brow at him. "Actually, other permanent things have also crossed my mind."

Just as Micah is about to give me a ration of shit, the tattoo artist walks back in. He verifies I want the tattoo on my left pec and presses the layout to my skin. A couple minutes later, the tattoo gun is piercing my skin and a new form of euphoria filters through my bloodstream. This is different from the last tattoo. More. Everlasting. And I wouldn't change it for anything.

"So, who's Cora?" the artist asks.

"Girlfriend," I say. Micah makes a face that indicates otherwise. "Although, I'm hoping she'll be more one day." At this, Micah shakes his head.

"Don't we all, man. My old lady and I have been together for years. Can't imagine life without her. Just haven't bucked up the courage to ask her yet. You?"

"Soon."

"Really?" Micah asks in disbelief. "You have got to be shitting me."

I drill holes in his head with my death stare. "Yeah. Why would you think otherwise? She's it for me, bro. Always has been. Just because you turned into a manwhore…"

"Let's not talk about me right now. We'll be here all day. Maybe we should be talking about the fact that you plan to marry Cora. Have you asked her?"

The artist laughs at our banter. "Not yet. But I'm not waiting. When the time comes, it's happening."

"You're ridiculous," Micah says.

"Why? Because I love her? Because I refuse to fuck this shit up again? Nothing will keep me from her now or in the future."

Before Micah chimes in with something snarky, the artist speaks up. "You two whine like a pair of bitches." He laughs, then goes back to the tattoo.

I tip my head back and close my eyes, shutting Micah out and dropping our conversation. He is such a pain in my ass sometimes. When the tattoo is done, I check it in a mirror and pay the artist.

When we get back in the car, Micah speaks up for the first time in an hour. "What's the French line?"

I tell him the line I memorized a lifetime ago. "Tu es les

étoiles de ma lune. It translates to *you are the stars to my moon.*"

"You really are lost," he says before laughing and cranking the music.

"In the best way. One more stop to make, okay?"

He nods. "Yeah, sure. Where to now?" I don't answer him as we pull onto the street and head south. He shakes his head and shrugs. "Whatever, bro. It's your day."

Damn right it is.

We arrive at Cora's house just before six. In her driveway is her Subaru, a motorcycle and a Beetle. I park behind her car and glance over to the window by the back patio. Through a crack in the curtains, I spot people running around like rapid fire. I squint and shift my head to the side to get a better view, but don't see anything else.

What the hell are they doing in there?

"Don't be upset," Micah says. When I shift to look at him with narrowed eyes, he shrugs. "She wanted to do something for your birthday."

For the first time in years, my birthday isn't an upsetting day. In fact, this is the best birthday I have had since my teens. Heat spreads through me like warm honey. She intentionally planned a gathering for my birthday. Not just so she and I could spend time together, but also so others could celebrate too. God, I missed celebrating birthdays and holidays and monumental occasions with her. They were never elaborate, but she added flare to the day.

"I'm not upset," I say. "Far from it. Best birthday I've had in a while."

We step out of the car and take our time walking to the back door. No doubt Micah texted Shelly as we got closer, so it should be no surprise when we knock. Just as I bring my hand up to knock, the door flies open and Cora stands on the other side. She is all smiles and slightly out of breath.

My girl. *My. Girl.*

"I was beginning to wonder how long you were going to sit in the driveway," she says.

"You knew we were out here?" I ask.

"Yeah. Shelly saw you turn onto the street. Come in, come in." She waves us in and her excitement is infectious.

Micah steps past her and wanders into the house. But I step up to her, my mouth an inch from hers. "Thank you. This is perfect." I wrap my arms around her and kiss her forehead.

"You're welcome. Glad you like it."

"I love it. I love you."

She squeezes me tighter. "I love you, too. Come on, everyone is waiting."

We step into her small house. Once in the open space, I scan the rooms. Added to her normal decor are shiny happy birthday banners and cheesy kid's decor. On one wall is a plastic version of pin the tail on the donkey. The moment I see it, I burst out laughing. She loops her arm in mine and keeps us going forward.

On the kitchen countertop is a small round cake, *Happy Birthday* piped in white over the black icing. Next to the cake is an array of finger foods and alcohol. When I glance over at the dining table, which has a couple chairs added to the ends, I spot a small pile of gifts next to a stack of board and card games.

"I vote food first," I say.

"Second that," Micah chimes in.

And just like that, we all clamber into a line and grab platefuls of finger foods. We clear the games and gifts from the table and gather around to eat. When our plates are almost empty, Shelly pipes up and suggests I choose the first game. I riffle through the choices and go with the adult version of Watch Your Mouth.

For the next thirty minutes, each of us slobbers over semi-dirty phrases that sound absolutely filthy. Cora tries for a solid two minutes to say something no one can translate. While this happens, I pull out my phone and record a video of the whole show. I will definitely be watching that over and over. After we have all laughed our asses off, we opt to take a game break and dish out cake.

Cora and Shelly make a show out of adding twenty-nine candles to the cake and lighting them. The lights go out and everyone sings happy birthday to me as Cora holds the cake between us. The entire time everyone sings, I stare at her. Watch the mini-candle flames flicker on her skin. Take in her smile, remembering how long it has been since I saw her smile like this. Genuine and wide and happily. When the song finishes, I silently wish to spend every day of the rest of my life with Cora, then blow out all twenty-nine candles in one breath.

Cora smiles, then takes the cake in the kitchen. She hands me a big enough piece of cake for two and I take it back to the table while she finishes cutting it.

With a forkful of chocolate cake in my mouth, Shelly shoves the stack of gifts toward me. "Happy Birthday, Gavin."

I thank her after I swallow. "You didn't have to buy me anything." After I shove another bite in my mouth, I unwrap the small box. As soon as I see the package, I spit cake out of my mouth. "What the hell, Shelly?" Thank fuck Cora is still in the kitchen messing with cake. Not sure if she would be embarrassed or giggly or shocked.

I stare down at the one-hundred-count box of condoms and shake my head. When I peek up at Shelly, she shrugs in the same manner Micah does. "Not like you won't use them. Especially if you guys are back together. Plus, they were on sale at Costco."

As discreetly as possible, I wrap the paper around the box again and push it aside. The other two gifts are simple and normal. A gift card and a card with cash. Somehow, I will use the cash and card to buy them all something in return. I don't need gifts as long as I have Cora. She is the greatest gift of all.

For the next two hours, we play cards and shoot the shit with each other. Tonight is the most enjoyable evening and birthday I have had in a long time and I bask in the sentiment. My mom or parents always did nice things for me over the years, but it was never the same as when I was with Cora. Now that she is back in my life, I will never let anything break us apart again.

Erin yawns and it starts a ripple effect throughout the room. Within ten minutes, Erin, Shelly, and Micah pile into Shelly's car, and Jonas hops on his motorcycle. In the blink of an eye, only me and Cora stand in her house. And the solitude is heaven.

I help her clean up a few things that need to be put away now. After, we sit on the couch and simply hold each other. Only with her is silence comforting. I close my eyes and enjoy the warmth radiating off her and soothing me. Reminisce in the affection and warmth we once shared as I dream about what the future holds.

"Do you want to watch a movie?" she whispers into the dim-lit living room.

"Only if you want to. I'm content like this."

She turns into me more and presses her hand over my heart. I suck in a breath when her weight covers a portion of my new tattoo. Her eyes widen at my expression. "Are you okay? What's the matter?"

I sit up a little and kiss her forehead. "Yeah, baby. I'm okay. Just got a new tattoo today."

Cora perks up next to me. "You got a new tattoo? Can I see it?"

Eventually, I knew Cora would see my new tattoo. I just had no idea it would be tonight. Not that I fear her seeing it. Only curious how she will react.

I scoot forward a few inches and tug my shirt over my head, tossing it aside. The moment she sees it, all air leaves the room. "Gavin," she gasps. "I… I don't know what to say."

As I sit back against the cushion, she shifts closer to me. Her fascination with the ink is cute. By the way she studies it, I know she wants to run her fingers over it. "It'll heal over the next week," I inform her.

Her eyes well as she peeks up at me. "You know that's forever, right?"

"You are my forever, Cora. No other name will brand my skin. No other woman will have my heart. It has belonged to you since the first day of high school. The day I joined you under that tree and you drew me beside you on a sketch pad."

Tears spill from her eyes. "You're my forever, too. I tried to move on for so many years. Tried to care for another person. God, how I tried. But it never happened. Even when I tried to force it. Because I could never imagine life with someone other than you. So, I tucked you away for safe-keeping in the hopes you would return."

I pinch the ends of her hair and play with it between my

fingers. Fuck, I want to kiss her. But I promised I wouldn't kiss her until she initiated the kiss. And fuck if that isn't the most difficult vow to keep right now. Because everything about this day, this moment, cries out for me to lean forward and press my lips to hers.

She brings a hand to my other pec and skims over the flesh. Electricity shoots through every atom, cell, and molecule in my body. I swear to god, if she doesn't kiss me soon, I will break my promise. Because as patient as I am, this is pure torture.

Just as I am ready to cave on my desires, she leans forward and presses her lips to my left pec, an inch above the tattoo. "I love you," she says, breath hot on my skin.

And a switch flips inside me. Fire heats my blood, scorches my skin, has me panting for breath. I become a starved man and Cora is what my body needs to survive.

twenty

CORA

The moment I kiss Gavin's chest, a ticking time bomb detonates beneath my lips. As if my lips on his skin is the invitation he has been waiting for. The key to solve a riddle.

Before I grasp what is happening, Gavin scoops me up in his arms and walks toward my bedroom. A moment later, he tosses me on the bed and crawls over me. His lips brand my navel as he shoves my shirt up my torso and over my head. Every press of his lips is kindling added to a raging inferno inside me. An inferno that has always been there, but faded with his absence.

He peppers kisses across my collar bone and up my neck, nipping and sucking. His forearms press into the mattress on either side of me and cage me in. I knead the sides of his ribcage and around his backside, digging my nails into his bare flesh.

"Oh god, Gavin," I gasp, tipping my head back.

His lips graze my jawline and finally land on my mouth. Liquid heat swipes across my lower lip and begs me to open up for him. The second his tongue brushes against mine, I lose all coherent thought. Gavin is everywhere. The saltiness of his lips on my skin mingles with my taste buds. His fevered skin heats up every inch of my skin. The piney-beach scent only Gavin has seeps into my senses. Fuck, it's too much.

He hovers above me a second. "I want you, baby. To be inside you."

"God, yes."

As soon as I grant him permission, Gavin's hands travel to my waist and unfasten my jeans. He jostles them down my hips and yanks them to my ankles before depositing them on the floor. The pads of his fingers graze the tips of my toes and slowly descend over the tops of my feet. "Do you know how long I've waited for this?" Heat dances over my ankles and ascends my shin. "How long I've waited to see you?" Tingles play over my knee and tease the distal end of my thigh. "To touch you." Sparks ignite in my quads and I squirm beneath him. "To love you."

His hands reach my hips and I am ready to explode from anticipation. But he remains idle, his fingers toying with the bands of my panties. I pant and wriggle beneath him. "So, what are you waiting for now?" I tease, egging him on.

A smirk tugs at the side of his mouth. "Baby, I'm just reveling in the moment. I won't take you or us or our lives for granted. Never again."

"Gavin…" I whisper into the darkness.

He lowers himself and presses a sweet, earnest kiss to my lips. Packed with intensity and longing and hope. "I love you, Cora. I have loved you for as long as I can remember. And I will love you for the rest of my days." We kiss as if the past thirteen years never happened, as if time was never stolen from us, and the world rights itself again. Stars burn brighter. Planets align. And everything goes back in its rightful place.

As our lungs gasp for air, Gavin breaks the kiss and his

lips trace my ear and down my neck. He massages the sides of my torso as he lavishes kisses down my sternum, between my breasts, and stops at my navel. Fingers skirt around my backside and unhook my bra. Heated breaths paint my navel for three unshakable beats before his hands glide out and slip the black barrier from my breasts.

Neither of us moves for a moment. Instead, we lay impossibly still and absorb everything about this experience. The last time Gavin saw this much of my body, I was a sixteen-year-old girl. Although my body hasn't changed drastically over the last thirteen years, I am not the same. And neither is he. Not just our bodies, but also who we are as people. Yes, I am still that girl under the tree in the courtyard who fell desperately in love with Gavin Hunt. A boy who only wanted to share the shady tree with me.

But now, I am the woman who has fallen in love all over again. The woman who is brave enough to give myself over to him, wholeheartedly. As heartbroken and devastated as I was over the last thirteen years, I forgive him for the things he could not control. Things neither of us could control. For all the moments he wanted to come back to me and was unable to. As much as I tried to deny it, Gavin was always here. Tucked away in my heart. Rooted deep in my bones. Flowing through my veins. Hiding in the corners of my mind. Holding me captive. Telling me to be patient and wait for him. I see this now. All these reasons are why I was never able to truly let anyone else into my heart. Because Gavin had it. *Has* it.

And he always will.

"I love you, Gavin," I whisper as I comb my fingers through his hair.

He shudders above me before he feathers a kiss to my navel. The pads of his fingers imprint my back, my sides, my hips. They knead and paw and bruise in the most delicious way. His kisses transition from sweet to hungry and ravenous. I curl my fingers into fists and tug his hair as my back arches off the bed and I gasp at his touch. Gavin nips along the hemline of my underwear until he reaches my hip. He sucks and sucks and sucks, and it is not until a moment later that I realize he is marking me. Claiming me. As his. The notion of his lips and tongue bruising my skin sets me on fire and I moan.

After he is satisfied with his work, he raises enough to peer up at me. "Fuck. The way your soul coos for me, baby. You're my own personal heaven and I never want to leave."

"Never."

"Never," he repeats.

Gavin slips his fingers beneath the band of my panties, grazes the skin below one, two, three times, then hooks the cotton in his grip and peels it away from my body. After he tosses them to the floor, he stands at the foot of the bed and ogles every inch of me. His steely eyes sear my flesh as he takes in every inch of me.

Normally, I would be shy under such scrutiny. But with Gavin, I crave his appraisal. Long for his eyes to drink in every fragment of my wanton body. Beg for his undeniable *need* for me.

Over the years, I never allowed this with the few people I'd been with. Never let them that close to me. Hell, I never removed my clothes. I was good with celibacy.

But with Gavin... I willingly bared every aspect of myself to him. Heart. Soul. The good, bad and ugly. He is the missing piece. My forever. The be-all and end-all. And there will never be anything that stands between us.

My eyes lock on his for three panting breaths before he

breaks the connection. His drift down the lines and curves of my body, and mine do the same. Down his neck, across his collar bones, the hollow spot at the base of his throat. When I get to his pecs, I groan as I read my name permanently imprinted on his skin. Who knew something so simple could be the hottest display of affection. My heart is a fierce monster beneath my breast bone—pound, pound, pounding to be set free.

In my periphery, Gavin unbuttons and lowers his shorts. Black boxer briefs barely contain his erection, and I unabashedly stare at his groin. *Was he always that big?* I swallow and know he hears it.

He palms his erection through the cotton. "See something you like, baby?" A hint of sarcasm laces his question.

"You have no idea," I say, brazen.

My eyes pop back to his as he shoves his underwear to the floor. A second later, he presses a knee into the mattress and crawls back up my body. No barriers. No secrets. Just me and Gavin.

He kisses up my stomach, my breast, my neck, and stops when we are eye to eye. "I want nothing between us, Cora. Ever." He inhales deeply and shuts his eyes a second. "I've always used condoms. It's been a while since the last... and I got tested after."

I reach up and lace my fingers behind his neck, draw him down to me and press my lips to his. He doesn't want either of us to admit that we have been with other people since each other. Doesn't want to tell me the ways he filled the void. And neither do I. But this is us. Open. No holds barred. No skeletons.

"Thank you." I kiss him again. "I've been tested, too. And I'm on the pill."

His whole body relaxes. A second later, his lips are on mine as he grinds his length against the apex of my thighs. I lift my hips and add more pressure. And god is it amazing. His pecs squash my breasts as his abdomen slides against my belly. Strong hands frame my face and Gavin worships my mouth with his. I caress his biceps, the sides of his torso and slip my hands around to his lower back. Time has made Gavin's body a work of art. A sculpture. A god-like effigy worthy of worship and devotion.

I grab hold of his ass and paw at the muscular flesh in my palms. His hips rock into mine as his erection coasts up and down my entrance. A moment later, his palm grazes down my side and slips between us. With a lift of his hips, he slips his hand between my thighs and runs a finger over my slit.

"Fuck, baby," he growls. "You are so damn wet."

As his finger toys with my lower lips, I pivot my hips at the perfect time and his digit sinks inside me. It may be only one finger, but it consumes me. A second later, I rock forward again. Back and forth. Faster, faster. Gavin inserts another finger and I moan. His hand pistons as my hips plunge and we form the perfect rhythm.

As I fuck his fingers, he reveres my mouth, my neck, my breasts. He is everywhere. Every molecule. Every fiber. Every beat of my heart and breath in my lungs. Too much and not enough at the same time. Breath and heat and sweat. Friction and passion. While one hand pistons inside me, his other slides into my hair and clutches at the crown. He locks me in place with his grip and his lips and his fingers.

Fire blazes hot in my epicenter. Building faster, hotter. Gavin nips along my jaw and stops at my ear. "So fucking hot, baby," he whisper-growls. Then sucks at the spot just behind my ear. The one only he knows about. The spot that tips me over the edge.

White hot heat detonates low in my belly and ricochets through every muscle. I pinch my eyes shut and stars glow on the backs of my lids. I bow into his body as mine clutches his fingers with every ounce of strength. High pitch gasps for air whine from my lungs and Gavin crashes his mouth to mine. Dizziness warps my vision as I ride the wave of my high.

For a moment, we lay motionless—Gavin hovering above me. Panting as the scent of sex floats in the air. I haven't had an orgasm like that in years. Too many years. And I want more. So much more.

"Gavin?"

"Yeah, baby?" His breaths as labored as my own.

I kiss along his jaw and graze the flesh with my teeth before reaching his lips. Pressing one, two, three kisses to the soft lips I could lose myself in for days on end. When I break the kiss, I frame his face with my hands and lock eyes with him. Then kiss him one last time. "Please, I need you inside me," I whimper.

A growl reverberates low in his diaphragm and ripples into me like a tidal wave. He scoops one arm around the back of my shoulders and the other around my hips. Before I realize what is happening, he flips us over and straddles me over his thighs. All the times we had been together years ago, I never sat atop him. Never had control when we had sex. And now, I feel like a goddess. Like the master of our world. Of Gavin.

"Ride me, baby," he purrs.

His request is gasoline to the fire blazing in my belly, I press my palms flat on his chest, lift myself and position my entrance over his cock. Inhaling deeply, I lower myself onto him slowly. Inch by inch, I take him to the hilt and audibly gasp once I am seated.

Gavin sets his hands on my hips and locks me in place. And for a moment, neither of us moves. We relish in being connected like this once again. Skin to skin. Completely vulnerable. Absolute exposure.

His breathing spikes and I lean down and take his mouth with mine. The kiss starts slow. Sweet, gentle pecks. Then I paint his lower lip with my tongue and he invites me in. Our tongues taste and devour one another for a beat. And then I rock my hips back and slam them forward.

He breaks our kiss, my mouth an inch above his, and hisses. "Fuuuuck…"

I do it again, sinking my nails into the flesh just beneath his pecs. When I roll my hips again, Gavin thrusts up and hits a spot deep inside me, a place only he reaches, and I cry out. One thrust, then another, until we find a rhythmic dance only two lovers know. His hands roam my abdomen and my breasts before he sits up. One, two, three more rocks of my hips and I orgasm a second time.

A second passes and before I catch my breath, Gavin flips us back over and hovers above me. "Wrap your legs around me, baby."

I do as he says, locking my ankles together, and he thrusts hard and fast into me. Gone are the moments of sweet caresses and gentle strokes. Now, the inferno blazing between us is set to atomic levels. And if this burn doesn't get satiated, both of us will implode.

Gavin buries his face in the crook of my neck, lips and tongue sucking my skin. One arm braces my shoulder while the other clutches my hip. He pumps in and out of me—faster, harder, hungrier. His mouth, his cock, his heart, it is almost too much to bear. Almost.

Sweat pulses from our pores and slicks us from head to toe. His breath hot on my neck as his teeth clamp down on the tender skin. Our cries of pleasure mingle in the air and bounce off the walls. And I climb, climb, climb back up the peak once again. "Oh god, Gavin. Don't. Fucking. Stop," I pant out.

His grip on me tightens as his hips buck harder. He grunts into my skin, and I know he resists his own need to come. Resisting so we can prolong this reunion. And that fact sets me off again. Has my walls constricting and my vision fading.

My body a limp noodle as I come down from my orgasm. Gavin brings his lips back to mine, kisses them tenderly, and whispers, "One more, baby." I nod and he pulls out of me, flips me on my belly, and hikes my ass in the air.

With my profile against the sheets, I stretch my arms above my head and clutch the pillows in my fists. He lines himself up with my entrance, but doesn't push inside. Not yet. He leans over me and whispers in my ear. "I love you to the ends of the earth, Cora. Forever." When he lifts off of me, his fingertips dance over my neck before tracing down the length of my spine to the base of my tailbone. It is more than just a touch. It is devotion. Awe. Adulation. Reverence. Intimacy. Worship.

With both hands squeezing my hips, he eases inside of me. Each inch forward is a step closer to heaven. Closer to where Gavin and I will be for all eternity. Together. Connected. Unbreakable. Inseparable.

When he is fully seated inside me, I mewl into the sheets and tighten my fists. He relaxes his hands for a split second before clamping down harder. Tomorrow, my body will artfully display the evidence of our reunion. And I plan to revel in every single line and stroke and strawberry on my skin. Cherish them and create new ones before they fade. Memorize the feel of them and how they came to be.

Gavin doesn't move for a minute and I peer over my shoulder at him. His eyes closed and brow furrowed. Before I open my mouth to ask if everything is okay, a tear rolls down his cheek. I push up so I'm on my hands and knees, ready to spin around and soothe whatever sadness has taken hold. Just as I straighten, he presses a palm flat between my shoulder blades and presses me down to the bed.

"Gavin, are you okay?" I ask, genuinely worried.

His hand rests between my scapulae a beat before gliding back to my hip. "Never better, baby," he chokes out.

"Then why are you crying?"

My eyes still trained on his as he stares down at me. "Because I haven't been this happy in a really long time."

"Happy tears?" I ask because I have to be certain.

"Yes, baby. Happy tears." And then he rocks his hips back and drives forward.

He fills me so fully, I forget how to breathe. How to speak. My eyes roll back and I groan. "Oh fuck…"

In. Out. Stroke after stroke, he brings us both closer to nirvana. His hips slap my ass, balls whack my clit, head of his cock rubs the nerve endings inside my walls. Building. Climbing. Taller. Higher. His tempo increases and I know he is trying to get me there before he lets go. As if confirmation of my thoughts, his hand snakes around my waist and his finger circles my clit. His hips piston faster as our moans consume every lick of empty space in the room.

"Gavin…" I wring the sheets in my fists. "So close. Don't stop."

He adds more pressure to my clit and circles faster as his

hips thrust like a well-oiled machine. I clamp my eyes shut as my breath comes in short, staggered whimpers. On the next stroke, the head of his cock strokes perfectly over the nerve cluster in my walls and I detonate. A grunting scream rips from my throat as he continues to slam into me. My vision blanks as I convulse and milk his cock.

My orgasm feels like a never-ending stream of consciousness as Gavin releases inside me. Only when his hips slow and he collapses over top of me, does my body calm down.

"Holy shit," he breathes into my hair.

Gavin rests his head beside mine, arms clutching my breasts and belly, and heaves. No intimacy compares to what Gavin and I share. It isn't just the sex—although sex with Gavin is literal euphoria.

Intimacy with Gavin is so much more. Friendship and love. Sunsets and strolls in the park. Shared whispers and tender kisses. Side glances and subtle smiles. Speaking without words. Acceptance. An incomparable bond. A life force all its own. The promise of forever.

My hips drop to the mattress and I relax more than I have in thirteen years. Gavin lays beside me and I roll to face him. He drags me closer to him, weaves our legs together, and plays with the ends of my hair. Tenderness bleeds from his pores into mine. So pure and true. He leans in and kisses my lips, the tip of my nose, then my forehead.

When our breathing regulates, he traces my cheekbones with his finger, then my lips—his eyes fixed on the movement. One, two, three heartbeats later, his gray eyes lock on mine. Gets lost in them. We lay like this for minutes or hours, entranced with each other. No words are spoken—not that they need to be. We simply breathe each other in. Realign our souls. Remember the feeling of us.

For the next several hours, we memorize every inch of the other's body. Learn all the new lines and curves and dips and scars. And get lost in paradise time and time again.

~

I peek over Gavin's shoulder at the clock and check the time. Five twenty-one. For the last seven-plus hours, we have worshiped one another. And although I would love nothing more than to pass out wrapped in his arms right now, a different idea pops in my head.

I bolt up and fumble through the darkness. "Cora, what are you doing?" His mumble is sweet and inquisitive as he props himself up on his elbows.

"Get dressed. I want to go somewhere."

Gavin glances at the clock, then flops on his back. "Come back to the bed and cuddle with me. We can go later." As adorable as he is in this very moment, I resist the temptation of falling back into the sheets with him.

After stepping into a fresh pair of lacy boy short panties, I slip on a pair of black jeans. "Can't wait. It's time sensitive."

Gavin sits up and stares at me as I yank a shirt from a hanger. In the dark, I have no idea what shirt it is, nor do I care. I tug it over my head then walk over to the bed and grab his hand. He gives in and stands up, pulling me to his chest and kissing me. "Okay, baby. Where are we going?" he asks as he locates his clothes and dresses.

"It's a surprise. But you'll love it. Promise."

While Gavin finishes dressing, I head out to the kitchen, feed and love on Luna, and make us both a large to-go mug of coffee. When he emerges from the bedroom, I hand him a steaming mug and place a kiss on his cheek. We're quiet as we walk out the back door and get into my car. After a little maneuvering around Gavin's car, we get on the road as I speed toward our destination.

Less than thirty minutes later, we land on Central Avenue in downtown St. Petersburg and head toward the water. The streets are still dark, but slowly waking up in the early morning hours. Soon, I park the car, feed a meter on Beach Drive and grab a blanket from the back of the car—one I kept back there to protect my camera equipment when I cart it onto the beach during shoots.

Gavin slips his hand around mine and I guide us near the waterfront. Near the new pier is a small man-made beach. We open up the blanket and spread it out on the sand. Gavin sits with knees up and legs spread, and I sit down between them. He wraps his arms around me and pins me close to his body.

"This is perfect, baby," he whispers, his chin resting on my shoulder as we stare out at the Bay.

I relax into him more. "It's time for a sunrise. Our lives have been filled with countless sunsets. Time to start fresh with new traditions. I want just as many sunrises as sunsets."

Sunrises are the start of something new and invigorating. Although Gavin and I have known each other for what feels like a lifetime, we hit a snafu. A fault we couldn't scale until the time was right. During that time, we grew. Into ourselves and into adulthood. We had the chance to discover who we are without each other. And fate still found a way to reconnect us. Make us whole again. Give us a chance to start anew.

A sunrise after the darkest sunset.

The sky pinks near the horizon and Gavin squeezes me tighter. "I'm sorry it took me so long to get back to you. Believe me when I say, if I had known it'd be this long, I would have done things differently."

I shake my head. "No, Gavin. Everything is how it's meant to be. Was our time apart the most gut-wrenching experience of my life? Yes. There has been no pain worse than losing you. Never will be. But would I change any of it? I don't think I would. It sounds wrong, but I think the years have taught us so much. Taught us how to love. Showed us what we'd miss without one another. Many couples stay together for years and grow unhappy with their relationship. A rift divides them and they fall out of love." I pause, take a deep breath, and collect myself. "If that would've happened between us… as hurt as I was when we lost touch, I never stopped loving you. I suppressed it. Smothered it. Buried it deep in the corners of my heart and packed it tight with dirt. But it has always been there."

Gavin inhales deeply and drags me impossibly closer to him. "I could never not love you, Cora Davies." Everything about his statement is permanent, carved in stone, and I fall inconceivably harder for him.

The light pink sky blooms into a hot pink-orange as the sun edges closer to the horizon. Darkness fades from the sky as a faint blue comes into view. Another couple walks onto the sand and sits fifty feet from us, phone out and snapping images of the glowing scenery.

I lean my head against Gavin and marvel in his warmth behind me. His arms holding me close. His fingers drawing soft patterns on my forearms. I sigh and feel the pain of the last thirteen years lift away. Beautiful colors paint the sky. A few clouds linger and add touches of lavender and gray. Feeling like I can finally breathe for the first time in over a decade, I whisper, "Life is perfect."

Gavin shakes his head beside me, and I turn to glimpse his expression. A smile stretches his face from ear to ear and displays his perfect white teeth. "There's only one thing that could make life perfect."

His steely-gray irises swirl with love and passion and admiration. I get lost in his eyes. Eyes I missed every day. Eyes no camera captured the way my memories did. Momentarily, I forget what he said and shake my head to snap myself out of the temporary fog.

"And what's that?" I ask, matching his smile.

He lifts an arm from my waist, cups my cheek, and brushes his thumb in small circles. I lean into his touch and sigh. His other arm holds me unimaginably closer. Eyes hold mine as he breathes slow and steady. Quiet for a beat, his expression turns intense. Fierce. One-hundred-percent serious. His lips part and I drop my gaze just as he licks them. "If you were my wife."

All air gets sucked from my lungs.

twenty-one

CORA

Three years ago

Women swarm the room, buzzing around like worker bees eager to aid the queen. The queen—actually, the bride—sits on a tall chair, labeled "Bride" in silver letters on the back, and breathes heavily while another woman does her makeup. Her thick, black locks are pinned back partially and curled. Eyelids brushed a soft blush. Lips coated in a neutral gloss. A subtle shimmer added to her skin.

Most brides are so nervous on their wedding day and never remember all the little moments. Like this one in the dressing room of the church. Which is why I am here. To capture the bride with her bridesmaids tending to her. Her mother keeping the bridesmaids—as well as people not in the room—in check. Novelty items such as jewelry and robes and hangers.

I bring the camera to my eye and snap a handful of images. Before anyone stepped foot in here, I walked around the grounds and took several photos of the church, flowers and various displays. The wedding is nowhere near luxurious.

Sherrie—the bride—was adamant about keeping the ceremony clean and simple and pristine. Not an overabundance of flowers or decor. Whites and creams and a hint of blush-pink. Very subtle, but utterly breathtaking. The photos of her gown on the hanger will be coveted for years to come.

"Twenty minutes, ladies," a woman shouts from the door before disappearing.

As if that is the cue they have all been waiting for, everyone's pace triples. Bridesmaids zip each other up in their blush-colored gowns before removing the bride's dress from the hanger. Once the makeup artist steps away, the bridesmaids step front and center. I bring the camera back to my eye and snap continuously as they help her into her dress.

When the dress is in place, her maid of honor hands her the bouquet and everyone steps back a moment, allowing me to take some individual photos of her before she leaves the room. After I finish, hair and makeup step back up and double-check to make certain everything is perfect.

She makes such a beautiful bride. Something I will never be.

I shake off the errant thoughts and leave the bridal suite. A moment later, I knock on the door for the groom's suite. A guy with dark hair, gauge-pierced ears, and a wicked smile answers the door. For a moment, I flashback to another guy who had similar features, a guy I once cared about, but push it aside and slip on my professional mask.

I lift my camera and waggle it. "Is everyone decent? I'd like to get some photos of the groom's suite before the ceremony begins."

He peeks over his shoulder then steps aside and gestures me to enter. "Sure, we're dressed. Can't speak for decent," he snickers.

I ignore his insinuation and walk into the room. Snapping a few pictures, I tell the guys to do whatever it is they were doing before I came in. The guys relax and start joking with each other, slapping backs and teasing the groom about how he will only have one piece of ass for the rest of his life. But the groom lights up at the idea and I capture every little tweak in his lips. Every crinkled uptick near his eyes. Every ounce of joy he exudes.

Love is a funny thing. When you see it with your own eyes, it is unbelievable. Unparalleled. Simple touches—the way he tucks your hair behind your ear or toys with the ends of the strands or draws art on your skin with his fingers or holds you close every chance possible. A small upturn of the lips—just enough to let you know he is thinking of you. A slight lean of the body—because he can never be too close or get enough of you. Love sneaks up on you, slithers itself around your heart like vines, blankets you in warmth and security and joy, and blossoms like a field of wildflowers. It is incredible and incomparable and incomprehensible.

And I hope to never feel it again.

I take a few more photos of the groom and groomsmen, excuse myself, and head for the main area of the church. Once there, I walk in and photograph the crowd in the pews. Candid images of family and friends, old and young. People carry on conversations about how the bride and groom met and fell in love instantaneously. They recant how inseparable they are and how they never imagine them apart. After several more clicks of the shutter, I head back to where the bridal party will enter. And thankfully, away from all the puppy-love conversations.

It isn't as if I don't believe in love. Love is real and

magical and undeniable. But love is also a rusty, jagged hunting knife in my chest. Twisting and depressing.

The music shifts and I take a deep breath. Ten seconds later, the groomsmen walk through the large wooden doors. I snap photo after photo. The guy who answered the door to the groom's suite passes me and winks. I continue taking photos and don't acknowledge the gesture. If I were any other woman, I would melt into a puddle at his feet. Swoon at the prospect of him asking me to dance later or grab a drink or exchange phone numbers. He is definitely gorgeous, but unfortunately for me, I am far from interested. In anyone. Ever.

I purse my lips, bring the camera to my eye, and continue photographing the wedding. After all the groomsmen pass, the music changes again. The wedding march—a standard, but elegant choice. Once upon a time, this song popped into my head. Impregnated visions of white gowns and black suits and promises of forever. But I was young and naïve then. I am neither of those things anymore. And after my dreams were obliterated, I am quite content becoming an old cat lady. At least as a cat lady, I will receive nothing but unconditional love.

The wedding passes and a million photos are taken. But it is not until the reception when I lose my shit.

Upbeat music fades from the sound system and the deejay speaks up. "This is for all the lovebirds in the room. Grab your guy or lady and head out to the dance floor."

A new song crackles through the speakers. A song I haven't heard in years. One that cracks my heart and cripples me on the spot. The twangy guitar intro to "Better Together" by Jack Johnson floods every available space in the room and drowns me instantly. Tears prick my eyes and, within seconds, roll down my cheeks. An emotional ball the size of a softball lodges in my throat.

I can't breathe.

Fuck. I can't be here. I can't be here.

The groomsman hottie approaches me, a smile plastered on his face until he notices my state. "Hey, you okay?"

I shake my head. It is too much. All of it. The bride, the groom, the promises, the happiness, the music. One big ball of happily ever after. Something I thought I would have. Until my heart got ripped from my chest and annihilated.

"I need to leave," I tell him. "Now."

"Do you need a ride? I can drive you."

As great as the idea sounds, I decline his offer. The last thing I need is to lose my shit with a guy that resembles the reason *why* I am crying. All that would lead to is another hot mess.

After I pack up my camera equipment, I find the bride and groom and apologize for my early departure. Thankfully, all the necessary photos for the wedding have been captured. Now it is just flat out party time. They hug and thank me and then I bolt out the door. Away from the reminder of broken promises.

When I reach my car, I set everything in the back then get in the car and lock the doors. I sit there, alone in the lot, for over thirty minutes, crying in my hands. Sobbing as if I am sixteen all over again.

Over the last decade, I have lost so much in my life. All of that loss wraps around one person.

Gavin Hunt.

Losing Gavin was like cutting out my heart with a spoon and tossing it in the darkest, deepest parts of the ocean. Without him, I had no reason to love. No desire to love.

Nothing has changed. Over the years, brick by brick, I slowly built a towering wall around the space where my heart once sat. Reinforced it with steel beams and barbed wire. Hardened myself to everyone. Family. Friends. I would never allow someone to do to me what Gavin Hunt did—crush my heart and run away with my soul.

Right here, in the parking lot of the reception hall, where two lovers celebrate their joyous union, I make a vow to myself. A vow that will never be broken, because I hold the key. I am the gatekeeper of this truth.

"I will never open my heart to anyone ever again. I will never love another person ever again. And I most definitely will never marry anyone."

Present

"Life is perfect," Cora whispers as we stare toward the rising sun.

Now that things are finally back as they should be, now that the stars have realigned and I can breathe, life is pretty great. But I wouldn't say life is perfect. Pretty close, but not quite.

I shake my head and Cora peers over at me. My smile stretches so tight my cheeks hurt. I can't help it. This is what she does to me—shines a light on every shadow, lifts me up, makes me feel alive and whole and worthy. When I am with her, life is worth living. A life with her is worth living.

"There's only one thing that could make life perfect," I tell her. For some reason, I feel as if I should be nervous. Should have sweaty palms or be biting my lip or fidgeting. But I don't have a nervous bone in my body. If anything, I have never felt calmer a day in my life.

Cora studies me intently, her vibrant green eyes glowing in sunrise. She scans my eyes and forehead before dropping to my lips. She is absolutely stunning right now and I make a mental note to see a million more sunrises with her at my side.

As if coming out of a daze, Cora shakes her head and asks, "And what's that?" A hint of teasing lingers on her tongue.

But I am dead serious. More serious than ever. More than any other time in my life. Nothing in my life or this world matters if Cora isn't beside me. And I want her beside me through it all. The good days and bad. Our young days and old. With children and grandchildren. I want it all, and only with her.

I peel one arm away from her waist, frame her cheek in my palm, and swipe my thumb over the soft skin below her cheekbone. As soon as I do, she leans her face into my palm and I scoot closer to her. I stare into her magnificent green irises—a perfect blend of the trees and the sea.

Cora is everything I want in my life. Beauty and charisma and spunk and passion. She holds the key to my heart and is the guardian of my soul. In the last thirteen years, she has never left me—in spirit, anyway. Every woman I looked at was compared to her. And there was no contest. Hands down, Cora is it for me. There is not a single person walking this earth I want more than her. She gives me breath and life and purpose and love. Without her, I wander the earth with no destination.

"If you were my wife," I announce.

Cora gasps and freezes in my arms. For three of my breaths, she doesn't breathe once. And then she inhales deeply. Deeper than I have ever heard another person breathe. "Gavin…" She says my name as if it is her dying breath.

"Cora, I have spent far too much time away from you. Without you, I am a shell of a man. Every second we were apart, I merely existed. It wasn't until I saw you again that I remembered how to breathe. That my heart remembered it had another purpose other than beating. I dreamt of this day, but feared it would never happen. No more. Life is too short to not spend it with the person who matters most." I spin around to face her and prop myself up on one knee. "Cora, I know what life is like without you in it. I never wish to experience pain or darkness like that again. Nor do I want you to. The day my plane touched down here, I somehow knew life would be better. I didn't have the answers, but I felt it in my bones. And I wasn't wrong. How could it not be kismet bringing us back together? I belong to you, Cora. And I would be honored to be your husband. Will you marry me?"

Behind Cora, the other couple on the beach have their camera turned toward us. No doubt they're recording this. Another win in my favor.

Please let her say yes.

When she doesn't say anything for a moment, I remember the box is still in my pocket. Maybe if she sees the ring I bought, she will realize just how serious I am. I fish the soft, black box from my pocket and lift the lid. Nestled inside the box is a two-carat, square-cut black diamond in a tall setting. Along each edge of the black diamond are three smaller white diamonds. Several white diamond chips burrow in the titanium band from top to bottom. Hugging the engagement band is a matching wedding band with larger white diamonds.

Her hands fly to cover her mouth as she gasps. A second later, she lowers them to her chin. "Gavin…" she whispers. "Oh my god." Her glazed green eyes dart to mine and tears spill out, sliding down to her illustrious smile. "Yes. A million times yes." Cora crawls up on her hands and knees and launches herself at me. We fall to the sand and laugh.

I wrap my arms around her body and squeeze her with every ounce of strength I possess. "Fuck, baby. I love you so goddamn much."

After a minute, I sit us up and kiss the hell out of her. She tastes like salt and passion and forever. The best fucking taste in the world. And I am the luckiest man alive because she just said I get to keep her forever.

When the kiss breaks, I scoot back an inch and take the ring out of the box. She juts her left hand toward me and I slip the link to forever on her ring finger. The second it rests in place; the sun brightens the world more. I slam my mouth back on hers and kiss her as if she has already slipped a ring on my finger. The sooner, the better.

Forever will never be long enough with Cora. No matter how many lives we live, we will always find each other. Eternally.

After we dial down our public display, the couple from down the beach walks over and congratulates us. They offer to send us the video they recorded plus a few still pictures and I instantly jump on their offer, thanking them. We talk with them a few minutes before we shake out the blanket, fold it, and walk back to the car.

The second we get in the car, Cora's stomach grumbles and we decide to grab breakfast. As we head back toward Clearwater, I stare at the engagement ring on her finger. She isn't left-handed, but now she proudly drives with her left hand on the wheel. Every time the sun catches her ring just right, a halo flashes on the interior roof of the car.

Like an angel. My angel. My future wife.

After all these years, I wasn't sure if we would find our way back to each other. But we did. And I wasn't sure if I would see this day. This exact day. The day when Cora and I were back together and she wore my ring on her finger.

And now that the day is here, an odd flutter ripples beneath my ribcage. The sensation light and exhilarating and eternal. Does she feel this fluttering right now? The exultation of finally living the life you were destined to live.

We pull into a parking lot and hop out of the car. Although we are both dog tired, there is enough adrenaline coursing through our veins to keep us both up all day. I sidle up to her left and slip my hand in hers, loving the way it feels when the ring grazes my palm. Until it comes to fruition, I imagine no other moment or emotion or experience topping this.

After we eat breakfast, Cora starts driving us back toward her house. As much as I want to lay in bed with her curled in my arms, there is something else I want to do. "Do you mind if we make another stop?" I ask.

She glances over at me a second, then faces the increasing traffic. The wind whips her hair across her profile as I inhale a hint of her frankincense-gardenia scent. "Yeah, sure. Where to?"

"I'll give you directions," I tell her.

I guide her through traffic for four or five miles before telling her to pull into a parking lot. When we park, she peers up at the sign, shakes her head, and laughs. "Really? Again?"

Laughing right alongside her, I shrug. "What can I say? There's just something I need to do before we go home."

Cora cocks a brow at me and I know it is due to my casual reference to *home*. But she won't argue with me. For us, home has never consisted of four walls, a floor and a roof. Home has always been when we are together. "Alright."

We get out of the car and walk up to the storefront. I open the door and Cora's eyes scan every inch of the tattoo shop.

Luckily, this shop is open more hours than most due to the number of artists. I walk up to the counter and the woman that looks up at me shakes her head. She is the same woman from yesterday. Hot pink hair, the front half rolled up and pinned close to her scalp, the back half left loose to her shoulders. She blows a bubble from her gum and lets it pop like it's second nature.

"Everything okay?" she asks. No hello or how are you. She must assume something is wrong with the tattoo I got yesterday.

"Everything is fantastic," I say and she rolls her eyes. "I'd like to get another tat."

"Oh," she perks up. "Well, the same artist who worked on you yesterday isn't here right now. You cool with that?"

"That's fine. It's nothing extravagant."

After a few minutes, I fill out the same form again and give her my ID. Once the formalities are out of the way, a woman comes out of the back. Her right arm is decked out in a full sleeve of ink. From what I can tell, it appears to reach her back as well. Her hair is a rich, dark brown and she has it pinned in a messy bun with a folded bandana tied at the top. She has this whole 1950s pinup girl/rockabilly vibe going on.

"Hi, I'm Autumn," she introduces herself and shakes my hand. "Looking for something specific today?"

"Gavin. Nice to meet you. Yeah, I want to get a wedding band tattooed on my ring finger."

Beside me, Cora sucks in a sharp breath. No doubt she wasn't expecting that. "Gavin, you don't need to do that," she says.

"I know, baby," I tell her. "But I want the world to know I belong to you. And no one else. Always."

Cora nods and doesn't utter a sound. The tattoo artist,

Autumn, guides us back to her booth and has me sit in the chair. Currently, Cora and I are the only patrons in the building. Not having people coming and going right now is nice and odd at the same time. When the gun sparks, Cora startles next to me. I reach out and she takes my hand.

Twenty minutes later, I stare down at the thick black band at the proximal end of my fourth finger. Tears sting the backs of my eyes as a thick boulder of emotion lodges in my throat.

"What do you think?" Autumn asks.

I clear my throat and croak out, "It's perfect."

Cora stares at me in awe and sheer amazement. Then her eyes flick to Autumn. "Have time for me?" she asks.

"Yeah, sure. Just fill out the paperwork and give me a moment to sanitize the station."

Cora hops up and goes to the woman at the front. I amble behind her. "You don't need to get ink unless you want to, baby."

"I know. And I want to."

I nod and watch as she fills out the consent form and provides her license. Ten minutes later, we are back in the booth and Cora is sitting in the chair. Her shirt is hiked up and rests on her bra. Thankfully, the only skin exposed is what anyone would see if she were in a bathing suit. Otherwise, I might have hovered over her worse than a parent of a teenager.

"You ready?" Autumn asks Cora.

She nods and takes my hand. When Autumn presses the pedal and the gun starts buzzing, Cora jumps a little. I draw circles with my thumb over her hand and try to soothe her nervousness. "It only hurts for a minute. Then it numbs a little from the vibration."

The gun draws black lines on her skin just below her left

breast. I sit mesmerized as Cora gets her first tattoo. It isn't just the fact that this is her first tattoo, but what she decided to imprint her skin with. Autumn dips the gun in the ink then comes back to Cora's ribcage.

When Autumn swipes some of the excess ink off, I squeeze Cora's hand a little tighter. Cora peeks up at me, her smile brighter than the sunrise this morning.

"You okay?" she asks.

"I didn't think this day could get any better. But I was definitely wrong."

"Wait until you see what I do next." Cora giggles.

Wait, what? Is she getting another tattoo? Maybe she means something completely unrelated. Something when we leave here.

Another ten minutes pass before the tattoo gun is set down and Autumn is cleaning the tattoo and covering it up. Just beneath Cora's left breast rests my name in a feminine font. I am completely awestruck. It was one thing for me to get her name permanently etched into my skin, but I never expected her to reciprocate.

As I stand dazed, Cora asks me to go to the waiting area. For a moment, I am confused and ask her why.

"It's a surprise. Please," she pleads.

I nod and walk out to the waiting area, plop down onto the couch and grab a magazine. Every time I hear Autumn's tattoo gun spark to life, I peer toward the back of the studio. All I see is Autumn's head hunched over Cora.

What is she getting now?

Forever passes and I haven't heard the tattoo gun spark up in minutes. I toss the magazine to the table and rise from the couch. After I wear a new pattern into the linoleum floor, Cora walks back out to the waiting area. I pay and we walk out the door. The walk to the car is silent and I am dying more than ever to know what else she had done.

Once we are in the car, I ask, "So, what else did you get?" For whatever reason, I am more antsy now than I was when I asked Cora to marry me.

Cora faces me and juts her left hand toward me. On her ring finger, where her engagement ring sat less than twenty minutes ago, is a black band of ink that matches mine. It is slightly thinner, but otherwise mirrors mine. "Baby…" I whisper. "You didn't need to do that. I got you rings."

She nods and smiles. "I know, but I want the world to know I belong to you. No one else. Always." Cora throws my sentiment from earlier back at me. It steals my breath and kick-starts my pulse. Thank god we are in the confines of her car, otherwise I may have hit the ground. When I glance down at her right hand, I notice she has moved her engagement ring to that side. She takes stock of where my eyes focus and answers before I ask. "I'm only wearing it on my right while it heals. Promise."

The fact that she worries if it bothers me her engagement ring sits on her right hand is adorable. Honestly, which hand her ring is on is the furthest thing from my mind. Right now, I want to take her home and make love to her until our bodies give out. Celebrate that we are finally getting the happily ever after we deserve after so many years apart.

Today, Cora permanently gave herself to me as I have her. With each passing second, the day gets better and better.

I nod. "Let's go home, baby. I'm dying to make love to my fiancée."

November 21 - Seven months later

"Come on, Cora. You do *not* want to be late today," Shelly yells from the living room.

"I'll be out in a second," I yell back at her. I scan the room, checking every surface to make sure I haven't forgotten anything. Satisfied, I grab the two bags on my bed then turn and walk out of the bedroom.

When I enter the living room, I glimpse my best friend who is currently trying to wear a new pattern into the wood floor with her heels. She mumbles under her breath, but stops when she spots me.

"Did you feed Luna?" I ask.

"Yes. Everything is done. You ready to go?"

I glance down and inventory the bags in my hands. "Ready," I answer. "Erin picked up the other totes and food already?"

"Yeah, she left a few minutes ago."

I nod. Shelly and I grab our purses, I give Luna one last

pat and kiss, then we head out the door. We deposit the bags in her back seat and jump in the front. Seconds later, we are on the road and driving toward Sand Key park.

I stare out the window, take in the blue skies, fluffy white clouds, and sparkling sunlight, then thank the weather gods for keeping everything perfect today.

The weather has turned cool, but it isn't cold yet. Thanksgiving is right around the corner and this year I am thankful more than any year prior. For destiny and Gavin and the best circle of friends a person could ask for. Too often, we take life and the people we see daily for granted. After losing Gavin and getting him back, I take nothing for granted. Each day, I thank my lucky stars life brought us back together.

Over the last seven months, the emotional scale of our friends was all over the place. One day they loved us. The next, they freaked out. Shelly questioned me for hours once I flaunted my engagement ring. She had seen all my tears. All of them. She experienced my pain. Both times. And she wanted to be sure I wasn't acting on a whim. That I hadn't said yes because I felt pressured by the question or situation.

Everyone thought the engagement and us getting married was too soon. Irrational and foolish. That we should wait. Give it a year or so. Especially after rekindling what we once lost. Spend more time learning the adult versions of each other.

"You can't rely on your feelings from the past, Cora." Shelly had said. And I don't.

What I felt for Gavin in our early teen years is nothing compared to what I feel for him now. Circumstances ripped us apart. Tested our strength and ability to love. Time had been our enemy, but also our saving grace. Without time apart,

Gavin and I may have become complacent in our relationship. Grown apart. But time hardened us. Made us see the world and life and love in a different light.

When we each hit a point in our lives of numbness, of not caring about anything aside from daily monotony, fate brought us back together. Showed us how life could be if we gave us another chance. The short road was rocky, but our hearts knew from day one.

Hints of skepticism floated in the air from our friends, but every time they saw us attached at the hip with rosy eyes, their doubts were squandered.

Now when I look at my friends, all I see was happiness. For me. For Gavin. And for what we have together.

In no time, we drive into the park and weave around the outskirts. Shelly drives to the designated location, not far from the beach parking, and parks the car.

Soon, we have all the bags out of the car and in the makeshift dressing room. Shelly attacks me with makeup brushes as soon as my butt hits the chair. I close my eyes and let her do her magic while I go to my happy place—Gavin. As Shelly swipes a soft-bristled brush over my cheek, Erin walks into the tent.

"Hey, ladies. How's it going in here?"

Erin is dressed in a knee-length bloodred lacy dress with a nude underlay. Her curly red locks are pinned up in a loose chignon while a few long strands frame her face. Her makeup is subtle and accentuates her freckled skin. Shelly has her hair pinned in the same fashion. And soon, Shelly will don the same dress when she finishes my makeup. Seeing my best friends like this is surreal. For the longest time, I never thought a day like today would be in my future.

"We are on schedule. How's everything else?" Shelly asks Erin.

Erin gives two thumbs up. "All according to plan." Before I can ask what *according to plan* entails, Erin sneaks out of the tent and leaves.

Shelly continues the task at hand. I follow her hands with my eyes and wish there was a mirror nearby for me to catch a glimpse. Considering I barely wear makeup in the first place, it seems as if she put every product from Ulta on my face. As if she reads my mind, she meets my gaze and smiles.

"You don't need to worry about anything. Today will be perfect. Take a deep breath and let everything happen how it's meant to."

I nod, close my eyes again, and let her work her magic.

One breath in. One breath out.

GAVIN

Standing on the semi-warm sand, I wriggle my toes through the soft grains as I peer over my shoulder at the closed-off tent.

Shelly's car is parked just outside the tent, so I know my girl is inside. What are they doing inside that small tent? Can't be much based on the size. And how much longer will I have to wait to see her? I check my watch. Thirty minutes. Only thirty more minutes and she will stand beside me.

I stroll farther down the beach and out of the view of the tent. Popping my earbuds in, I crank up my music and stare out at the water. Feels like it has taken us a century to reach this exact moment, but the day has finally arrived. Finally.

Fifteen years ago today, my best friend became something

greater than I could fathom at the time. Something bigger than my fourteen-year-old brain could comprehend or imagine. She became the love of my life. Honestly, she had been since day one, but I wasn't equipped to understand such things.

If we had been together the whole time, no doubt married before now, we would celebrate our fifteenth anniversary today. But rather than celebrate this day as boyfriend and girl-friend—an antiquated term—today, we will officially become husband and wife.

Cora will be my wife. Mine. Forever.

The second everyone found out we were engaged, the first question that popped up was "Have you set a date?" We hadn't discussed dates, but, funny enough, we both blurted out November 21 at the same time. It was our day. Always will be. Until death do us part, and beyond.

Someone taps my shoulder and I turn to see Mom as I take an earbud out. "Hey, sweetie. You should probably get in position. Things will start soon."

I nod. "Thanks, Mom. Love you." I kiss her cheek.

She kisses the air next to my cheek, careful to not smear her lipstick on me. "Love you, too." After a quick hug, she walks off and joins everyone else not in the tent.

I wander toward the makeshift aisle, arch, and chairs. Cora and I are far from traditional. But our style resonates in every flower arrangement, decor piece, and article of clothing we all wear today. We kept the number of attendees to a minimum—twenty people, including Cora's maid of honor and my best man. On the aisle side of each row of chairs is a small bundle of black calla lilies and red roses—identical flowers to Cora's bouquet and the boutonnière flowers. Although Erin isn't in the wedding party, we got her an identical dress to Shelly since she is taking photos for and with us.

The arch at the end of the aisle is decorated in black and red sheer fabrics and flowers. Cora's mother and Shelly did an awesome job with the floral arrangements. They truly scream us and our style. As does our ensemble for the day. Although I have yet to see her dress, Cora and I are both in black. While Shelly and Micah are in red.

I slip my earbuds in their case and set them, and my phone, with my other clothes.

Before I grasp the gravity of it all, I walk down the aisle, bare feet crunching in the sand and heart jackhammering in my chest. When I reach the arch, I spin and stand in my place. Hands clasped at the front of my waist.

Micah walks up and stands beside me and pats my shoulder. "You nervous, bro?"

I stare down the aisle and shake my head. "I've been waiting for this day my entire life. Just can't wait to call her my wife." Those words hold so much truth.

As soon as the words leave my lips, the music starts. "Back In Black" by AC/DC blares from the setup speakers and echoes off the water. This song has nothing to do with weddings or love, but is one-hundred-percent us.

Gavin and Cora.

And the best fucking song to replace the traditional wedding march.

My breath comes in sharp bursts as I fumble with my fingers, eager to see her. One, two, three heartbeats later, Cora steps around a sand dune and I stop breathing. Dress black as night, several layers of tulle ghost the sand as she grips her father's elbow and walks toward me. The V-line bust of her dress is vintage lace that comes to a point at her solar plexus and also decorates the length of her arms. And just below the hollow of her throat is the locket her mother gave her years ago. A locket that now holds pictures of us.

"Fuck, she is gorgeous," I mutter and a couple people laugh. But I give no fucks. Cora is absolutely stunning and I refuse to take my eyes off her.

That is my wife. Mrs. Cora Elizabeth Hunt. My best friend. My lover. My life.

CORA

I round the sand dune with Dad on my arm, catch sight of Gavin near the arch, and suck in a breath.

Goddamn. I am one lucky-ass woman.

Gavin stands clad in a long-sleeve black button-down, the top two buttons undone, and black dress slacks. His red rose and black calla lily boutonnière rests above his left breast pocket. A thin layer of stubble accentuates his jawline as his hair kicks up with the occasional breeze. And the second he sees me, he bounces a little in place.

At the end of the aisle, Dad clings to my arm and gives me a quick squeeze. "Ready, pumpkin?"

I peek up at him for a split second, then revert my eyes back to my husband—*husband*—twenty feet away. Am I ready? I have been ready for this moment for as long as I can remember. "Yeah, Daddy. I've been ready."

We both take a deep breath, then Dad slowly guides me down the aisle and closer to Gavin. The love of my life. The man I don't ever wish to live a day without. The other half of my soul.

When we reach Gavin, Dad gives me a kiss on the cheek, unhooks his arm from mine, and goes to sit next to Mom.

Gavin and I lock eyes and the world around us disappears. The only other person in our bubble is the ordained minister. He begins speaking the preplanned speech, but neither of us hears a word of it. We are both well aware we don't have lines to speak for at least another minute. Until then, we drink each other in. Bask in the love we share.

I love you, Gavin mouths.

I love you too, I mouth back.

"Gavin and Cora have prepared their own vows and will read them to each other now. Gavin…" the minister says.

Gavin takes a deep, shuddering breath and keeps his gaze locked on mine. "Cora… We have overcome so many obstacles to get to where we are right now. And I'm so glad we did. All that aside, I remember the first day I fell in love with you. The first day of freshman year. Yeah, we were barely friends that day, but one look at you and I knew you were the one. Under that shady oak tree, our tree, everything changed. And afterward, in art, when I caught you drawing me into a self-portrait, I fell even harder."

The backs of my eyes burn. Tears threatening to break free. My throat closes in on itself as emotion chokes me. My fingers wring the stems of the bouquet as I hold his gaze.

"Months later, on this very day, we became more than friends. We became each other's everything. Every single damn day, I am thankful for you. For the love you give me. To have you at my side. To have you in my life. More than anything, I am thankful you gave me your heart and love in return. I've already experienced life without you, and know that will never happen again. Cora Elizabeth Davies, I give you me. All of me. The good, the bad and all the parts in between. I want to experience every day, for the rest of our lives, with you by my side. Forever."

He plucks the matching wedding band for my engagement ring from his pocket and slips it on my finger, resting it atop the tattoo that matches his own, then slides my engagement band on after. I stare down at our hands and breathe easier than I ever have. Everything about this moment, about Gavin and I joining our lives in every possible way, feels more right than anything.

Feels more at home than ever before.

Gavin finishes his vows and I swap my bouquet with Shelly for a tissue. I dab my eyes and take a deep breath. "Cora..." the minister says.

GAVIN

Cora slips her hands into mine and her fingers tremble beneath mine. Her eyes stained red from the happy tears she cried while I said my vows and slipped her wedding band on her finger. She peeks skyward and bats her lashes a few times before bringing her eyes back to mine. Then she smiles and my heart gallops in my chest.

"Gavin..." My name is a prayer on her lips. "You have brought so much into my life. Laughter and love, strength and beauty. Together, we have been through so much. Time may have been stolen from us, but you can't shake destiny. And that's what you are—my fate. My destiny. Fifteen years ago, you became something greater than my best friend. You became my everything. My first boyfriend. My first real kiss. And some things we won't discuss in front of company."

I burst out in laughter and our audience mimics.

"From that fateful first day during freshman year, the one where you sat beside me and ate the nasty school casserole, I knew we would never only be friends. But friends was the perfect place for us to start. Because through our friendship, we fell madly and deeply in love with each other. Gavin, I never want to experience another day of our lives apart. How can I not believe in kismet when it brought you to me more than once? Gavin Eli Hunt—see, even our parents knew we were two halves of a whole and gave us similar middle names. Life without you isn't one worth living and I am eager to see what the future holds for us. I love you beyond comprehension. Will love you until we both take our last breath. Always."

Cora takes my black titanium band in her nimble fingers and slides it up my ring finger. Nothing has felt as amazing as this moment right here. The moment we seal our lives together and become one. A unit.

My life is her life. And hers is mine. My fucking wife.

Fuck.

The tears are coming and I am about to cry like a bitch. But I don't give a shit. This woman is in my blood. My heart. My every breath. And fuck if I don't want to kiss the hell out of her right now.

The minister starts talking and I work hard to listen. Needless to say, it is a challenge. "Cora, do you take Gavin to be your lawfully wedded husband? Through good times and bad, sickness and health, until death do you part?"

Cora's smile brightens the setting sun. "Hell yes."

"That's my girl." I laugh.

"Gavin, do you take Cora to be your lawfully wedded wife? Through good times and bad, sickness and health, until death do you part?"

"Fuck yeah. And we're never dying, baby."

The crowd roars in laughter as the minister pronounces us

husband and wife, and finally gives us permission to kiss. I wrap my *wife* in my arms and kiss the fuck out of her. In front of everyone, I kiss her like no one else exists.

Because no one does. And never will. It is just me and my girl. Forever. Always.

Five years later

"You alright, baby?" I ask Cora as we hit the three-mile marker of a five-mile trail in the redwood forest.

"I need a water break."

We stop on the trail and drink water for a minute. We have been hiking a little more than an hour, but we are more than halfway. Cora has been a trooper during this trip. Nonstop adventure. But we plan to only be in California for a couple weeks and I want to show her all the wonderful parts. The places I knew she would fall in love with.

California is definitely different than Florida with all its monster-sized trees and mountains. The scent of the air and saltiness of the water is different too. As much as I miss the landscape and long list of adventures here, I love our little slice of Florida more.

For our five-year anniversary, Cora suggested we come out to California and visit Mom, but also share some adventures of our own. The redwoods, Yosemite, and some of the obvious tourist spots. Our trip so far has been incredible.

Currently, Mom is watching Clara, our three-year-old daughter. Us visiting California is more than a treat for Mom. Not only does she get to spend time with me and Cora, but she also gets to spoil Clara rotten.

Clara is the most amazing gift Cora has given me, aside from her heart. Until the day Cora told me we were pregnant, I never pictured myself as a father. Not that I didn't want to have children with Cora. More like I was so wrapped up in our bubble, I didn't envision beyond it.

But becoming a parent is one of the most awe-inspiring experiences. From learning we would soon be three instead of two to watching my gorgeous wife's belly grow to seeing my daughter enter the world. As a man, I saw the world one way. As a husband, I saw it another. Now, as a father, I see so much more. More love. More possibility. Just more.

"Ready to finish the back half of the trail?" I ask Cora.

"Ready as I'll ever be."

We continue along the rest of the trail, hand in hand. On occasion, we stop and admire something we see. Plants and trees, animals and streams. Nature and wildlife in California are the polar opposite of Florida, and Cora is in seventh heaven. Being in the middle of the forest is one of her favorite things and, every opportunity we can, we adventure somewhere with forestry.

After we reach the end of the trail, we call Mom's house and talk with both her and Clara. Since we are in northern California, we won't be at Mom's tonight to tuck Clara in. Cora and I are staying at a bed-and-breakfast just outside of San Francisco and enjoying a couple days of our anniversary alone.

"Night, night, Daddy," Clara says. Her voice is the cutest thing I have ever heard in my life. The melody is a sweeter, younger extension of Cora. Part of me wonders if Cora sounded the same when she was Clara's age. Either way, it melts my heart and makes me goo in her little hands.

"Night, pumpkin," I say and make a kissing sound into the phone. "Be good for Nana. I love you and we'll see you tomorrow."

"Love you, Daddy."

"Here's Mommy."

I hand the phone to Cora and she and Clara have an in-depth conversation about which is better—chocolate chip cookies or brownies. Cora tells Clara her favorite is the brookie we buy at the vegan bakery near home. Cora yanks the phone away from her ear as Clara starts yelling "brookie" over and over. Clara and Cora exchange goodnights and I love yous before disconnecting the call.

"I really hope Mom isn't feeding her cookies and brownies. We'll never be able to curb her cravings once we leave," I say and wince.

"Yeah, I hope not either."

I drive us back to the bed-and-breakfast and we get ready to go out for our anniversary date. As Cora puts on her jeans and sweater, I notice the way she stares at her outfit with extra scrutiny.

"Everything okay, baby?" I ask as I pull her into a hug.

She snakes her arms around my waist and squeezes me tight. "Everything's fine. Just wondering if I brought warm enough clothes. The weather here is so much different than home."

"You look beautiful," I admit. "And if you get cold, just say the word and I'll keep you warm." I kiss the top of her head.

Once dressed and ready, we head to the restaurant in the

city. Since Cora loves everything Asian, I thought she would love tasting how amazing food is out here. We arrive at the restaurant and are seated right away. After we order drinks, I notice Cora didn't get a glass of wine—her typical choice when we go out and don't have to worry about Clara.

Cora plays with her napkin and then places it in her lap. She stares at her lap a minute before locking her gaze with mine. Teeth capture her bottom lip and worry it.

"Baby, you sure everything is okay? You're worrying me."

She releases her lip. A smile brightens her face as she holds my gaze. "We're pregnant." And just like that, her confession steals my breath.

CORA

"Gavin? Did I break you?"

A minute ago, I told Gavin we were pregnant. Again. I expected his response to be like last time. Screams and cheers and swinging me in the air. Instead, he just sits across from me, frozen. A few minutes ago, he said he was worried. Now it seems to be my turn to worry.

Does he not want more children now?

It's not as if we have done much in the prevention department. We have actually been pretty up-front about children and our future. Especially after we learned I was pregnant with Clara. Since I don't have much time left to safely carry a baby, we thought trying now for a second baby was better than waiting.

But now, his current state has me not so sure.

Finally, his face relaxes. "You took a test?"

"Yeah, a couple days ago, after a trip to the store with your mom. She doesn't know, though."

"Why didn't you tell me you thought you were pregnant? I hate that you were wondering alone."

I didn't have a logical explanation as to why I hadn't told him yet. Guess I just wanted to give it another day or two before I took a test. Plus, we were going on our trip.

"Sorry I didn't let you know I suspected it. I'll blame it on foggy, pregnancy brain. You're not upset, are you?"

Gavin shakes his head. "No, baby, I'm not upset. The opposite actually. I just wish I could've waited for the positive result next to you. I know it's way too early to know, but I hope Clara gets a little brother."

I roll my eyes and he laughs. "I'm sure Clara will love him or her, no matter what gender they are. You sure you're okay, daddy?" Heat pierces Gavin's eyes and I swallow. The same heat that pops up every time I call him daddy… in my seductress voice.

"You don't need to worry about daddy, baby," he growls across the table. "But let's take the rest of the trip easy. Had I known before today, I wouldn't have taken us on a five-mile hike in the mountains."

"I'm not that fragile, Gavin. Besides, I need to maintain my girlish figure for as long as possible. Soon enough, I'll look like a whale."

Gavin shakes his head. "No, baby. You'll be the most beautiful woman in the world, still. There is nothing sexier than the love of my life carrying my unborn child inside her belly. If anything, you get sexier with each stretch mark."

Heat rises to my cheeks. "Gavin…" I whisper.

Dinner goes by much quicker after the *we're pregnant* conversation. Chinese food in San Francisco is phenomenal.

Anytime we eat Asian in Florida now, I will undoubtedly whine and complain. Plus, I think pregnancy makes it taste even better.

We arrive back at the bed-and-breakfast and head to our room. Three breaths after the door closes, Gavin and I frantically rip each other's clothes off. In the last five years, a few things have changed in our relationship.

The addition of Clara.

Our need to kiss and grope and be completely consumed by each other.

How much we love each other.

The last two have multiplied to levels I never knew existed. With each passing day, I don't think I can possibly desire or love Gavin more than I already do. But each day I wake up next to him, his warm skin and beachy-pine wrapped around me, I learn a new truth.

Our love is boundless.

Gavin yanks my shirt over my head and tosses it to the floor before bruising my lips with his. The rest of our clothes hit the floor seconds before we land on the mattress. Everything about us—our life, our love—grows hotter with each passing day. As Gavin kisses down my body, he stops and hovers above my abdomen a moment.

"Hey, little man. Yeah, Daddy is predicting you'll be a boy. Don't let me down, okay? Us guys got to stick together." I laugh and Gavin continues. "Anyway, I can't wait to meet you. And for you to meet me and Mommy and Clara, your big sister." Gavin presses his lips to my belly and kisses me tenderly.

Gavin Hunt. My best friend. My lover. The best husband. And an even better father.

"I love you, Gavin," I whisper.

He crawls up my body and kisses me reverently. "I love you, too, baby. Forever."

"Always."

Want more Gavin and Cora? Get their bonus story on my website!

Ready for the next story in the Bay Area Duet Series? Single parent, cinnamon roll hero, tattoo artist heroine, second chance at love... Jonas and Autumn's love story will make you swoon in the Inked Duet.

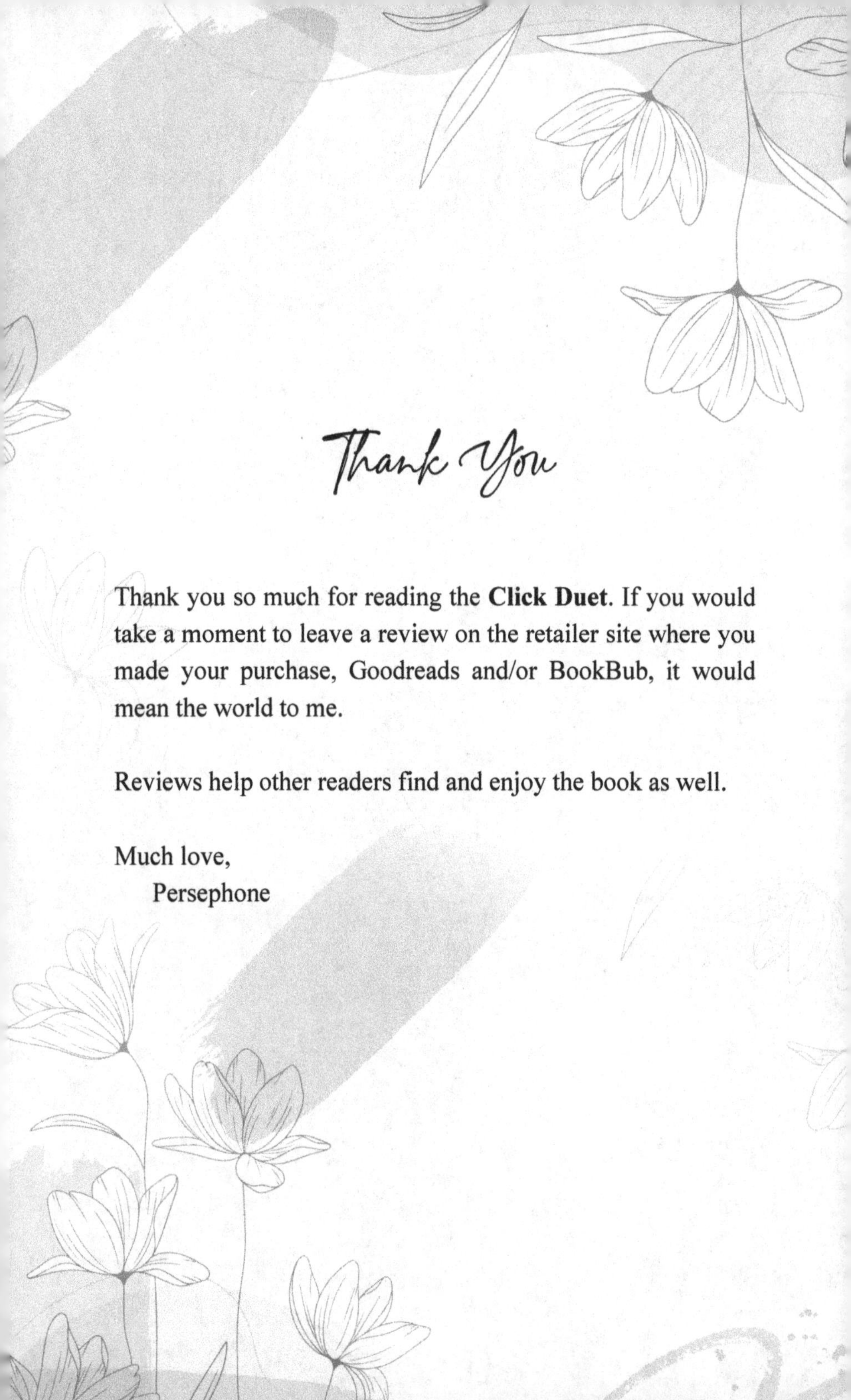

Thank You

Thank you so much for reading the **Click Duet**. If you would take a moment to leave a review on the retailer site where you made your purchase, Goodreads and/or BookBub, it would mean the world to me.

Reviews help other readers find and enjoy the book as well.

Much love,
    Persephone

The Inked Duet

A man with a broken heart and a woman scared to put herself out there. Love is never easy. Sometimes love rips you apart. Fine Line (Inked Duet #1) and Love Buzz (Inked Duet #2) is a second chance at love, single parent romance with a pinch of angst and dash of suspense.

The Insomniac Duet

He was her high school bully. She was the outcast that secretly crushed on him. More than ten years later, he's her boss, completely oblivious to their shared past, and wants no one but her. More importantly, he doesn't understand her animosity toward him.

The Artist Duet

A tortured hero with the biggest heart and a charismatic heroine with the patience of a saint. Previous heartache has him fighting his desire to be more than friends with her. But she is everywhere, and he can't help but give in. The Artist Duet is an angsty, friends to lovers slow burn.

Transcendental

A musician in search of his muse and a woman grieving the loss of her husband. Two weeks at an exclusive retreat and their connection rivals all others. Until she leaves early without notice. But he refuses to give up until he finds her again.

<u>Depths Awakened</u>

A small town romance which captivates you from the start.
Two broken souls have sworn off love. Vowed to never lose
anyone else. But their undeniable attraction brings them
together and refuses to let go.

<u>One Night Forsaken</u>

One night. No names. No romance. Just fun. Nothing more–at
least, that's what she tells herself. Until he appears in her
coffee shop months later with that addictive smile. She swore
off commitment. He vows to never love again. But the more
they fight it, the more life brings them together.

<u>Every Thought Taken</u>

As young children, an unshakable friendship brought them
together. As teens, they discovered an undeniable love. Then
life pulled them in different directions–into darkness and
light–and slowly ripped them apart. Years later, he returns
home in the hopes of a second chance with his first love and
to conquer the demons of his past.

Click Duet Playlist

Here are some of the songs from the **Click Duet** playlist. You can listen to the entire playlist on Spotify!

I Still Wait For You - XYLØ
Malibu Nights - LANY
i love you - Billie Eilish
High School Sweethearts - Melanie Martinez
The Beach - The Neighbourhood
Falling - Harry Styles
Out Of Love - Alessia Cara
BLUE - Troye Sivan, Alex Hope

Acknowledgments

First up… my family!

Thank you for always cheering me on. For standing in my corner and supporting this journey in my life.

To my wife… for always being one of my biggest fans. For reading my books (when you get a break in your work schedule) and helping me brainstorm ideas. Also, you pimp me hardcore. Ask everyone you meet if they read books and then market like I pay you. Love you!

To my daughter… when I hit it big, you *will* be my social media guru. You're also one of my biggest fans 🖤 I wouldn't be as inspired if you hadn't entered my life. I am so proud to be your mom. Love you bunches!

To my dad… thank you for supporting my endeavors, boosting me when I need it, and being the best dad a woman could have. I wouldn't be the woman I am today without you. Love you more than words!

To Ellie and Rosa at My Brother's Editor… thank you for always correcting my commas, em dashes, words that I think should be one, words that should be one but I think are two, polishing my manuscript, hinting more detail, letting me know I used the same word a million times, and giving the best feedback. You ladies work so hard and I am proud to have you on my team. All the love to you both! xoxo

To Kat Savage… I love your face! Thank you for always making my books beautiful. And thank you for your wisdom and expertise when I ask or suggest really stupid shit. That's why I don't do graphic design. Thank you for enduring my random emails and texts. Thanks for putting up with my annoying ass when I can't decide on what I want 😂 Thanks for all you do. You constantly inspire me to be better.

To all the kick ass peeps in Persephone's Playground… no words will ever be enough to express my gratitude. The fact that you love my words enough to join the reader's group… I am eternally grateful and humbled every day. I love you all!

To my incredible author friends… you know as much as I do that no set of words strung together will ever express the gratitude we have for the help we give each other. Thank you to the moon and back for being a part of this journey, reading my words, lending an ear (or screen), and sharing my cover reveals and releases. Having you in my world is the best gift. I love you all and am thankful to have you in my life!

To every person you picked up this book and read it… thank you from the bottom of my heart. Having someone choose to read your words is an author dream come true. And I wouldn't be where I am without readers. I am beyond humble that anyone wants to read the stories in my head. Thank you will never be enough. So much gratitude and love for each and every one of you! xoxo

Connect with Persephone

<u>Connect with Persephone</u>
www.persephoneautumn.com

<u>Subscribe to Persephone's newsletter</u>
www.persephoneautumn.com/newsletter

<u>Join Persephone's reader's group</u>
Persephone's Playground

<u>Follow Persephone online</u>

instagram.com/persephoneautumn

facebook.com/persephoneautumnwrites

tiktok.com/@persephoneautumn

bookbub.com/authors/persephone-autumn

goodreads.com/persephoneautumn

amazon.com/author/persephoneautumn

pinterest.com/persephoneautumn

About the Author

USA Today Bestselling Author Persephone Autumn lives in Florida with her wife and psycho cat. A proud mom with a cuckoo grandpup. An ethnic food enthusiast who has fun discovering ways to vegan-ize her favorite non-vegan foods. Most days, you'll find her with a tea latte or fruity concoction in her hand. If given the opportunity, she would intentionally get lost in nature.

For years, Persephone did some form of writing; mostly journaling or poetry. After pairing her poetry with images and posting them online, she began the journey of writing her first novel.

She mainly writes romance and poetry, but on occasion dips her toes in other works. Look for her non-romance publications under P. Autumn.